unarmed

in

paradise

THE MACMILLAN COMPANY
NEW YORK · CHICAGO
DALLAS · ATLANTA · SAN FRANCISCO
LONDON · MANILA

In Canada
BRETT-MACMILLAN LTD.
GALT, ONTARIO

ELLEN MARSH

unarmed

in

paradise

THE MACMILLAN COMPANY · NEW YORK
1959

to my father

Fred T. Marsh

bridges

1   On a night in May of 1950, he swung around the corner, big and blond and insolent in overalls that seemed to have been made for a bear. A girl was sitting outside the Tabac with an Arab half-caste and an American. He stopped because the Algerian called to him and because the American had the look on his face of wanting to buy a drink. He ambled over.

"*Tosca*," he remarked, leaning heavily on the little round marble-topped table. "Tonight makes twenty-three times I have done *Tosca*, and I decided to get drunk. Hallo."

Marcel performed vague introductions, with his passive and untrustworthy North African smile. He seemed to think his friend needed explaining:

"A good fellow, you know, when he's sober. He works in theater décor. Once he got me a job."

"I don't remember," the big one said rudely.

"Why, yes! As a carpenter, *mon vieux*."

"Is that so? I am very glad." He straightened up with the clear intention of going on his way.

The girl thought of him roaring around the corner. In the blue light from the café she said suddenly: "I need a job. Can you get me a job, Monsieur?"

"That is a question for your embassy, Mademoiselle."

She smiled and bent her head. There was a long pause in which there was some meaningless conversation among the others, and the two started moving in an odd kind of harmony: She moved her chair subtly, and he, openly defying his own snub, took the chair next to hers, abruptly, and they exchanged hardly another glance until, some time later, the American went home; the Arab disappeared.

It was strange, once he had sat down, like a conspiracy in which they were not quite alone.

He said, as if he had always known her: "What do you want to do now?"

"To drink a beer."

He agreed as if it were a brilliant and utterly new idea.

"Was it true about *Tosca?*"

"Oh, yes, quite true. I hate *Tosca*. It's the worst opera ever written. It makes me suffer more each time I hear it, and then I have to go out and get purged. However," he added cavalierly, "nearly everyone has a professional hazard."

"You are a workman?"

"Yes."

"Don't you remember getting Marcel a job?"

"I don't recall ever meeting him. Why do you ask me all these questions?"

"Well, they're the only things I know about you."

"I know nothing about you. How old are you?"

"Twenty-five."

"Good," he said enigmatically.

The waiter was piling up chairs and tables under the awning. They moved inside and sat in a booth in the brassy glare of mirrors,

2

in the acrid smell of stale smoke and the litter of cigarette butts and dirty glasses. She got up and went to the W.C. and when she came back, hands in her coat pockets and waiting for him to move over, he looked at her for a second time. She stood simply looking down at him, politely.

She was rather a long slim girl with a lot of dark hair smelling of soap. Her hair was the unruly kind with which ordinary vision fights a losing battle, but it was shining and pretty. She looked out from under it with something between hope and loss, as if she half expected to find again whatever it had been. . . . He did not care to know what. It was a look he knew, and she had beautiful mad-dog eyes to go with it. Her coat hid everything else but narrow feet in low-heeled American shoes.

When she sat down he gave her a comradely pat on the thigh, laughing at her jump and surprise, along with his own. I will ask her if she likes Beethoven, he thought.

He had a bold profile with a straight nose slightly turned up at the end, making him look like a small boy with a slingshot in his back pocket.

"Do you like Beethoven?"

It had the desired calming effect. Her face lighted up. "Oh, yes." She drank half her beer in her enthusiasm.

"I prefer Mozart."

"There is no question of preference. . . ."

"Yes. Yes, there is in the end."

"Are you really French? You do not seem French."

"From the North," he replied, evasive. "Near Normandy."

He was a liar, all right, but such a bad one that he probably made even the truth unbelievable. There was nothing French in his looks, but something familiar, racially. Flemish? Oh, well, it didn't matter. She felt very warm toward him.

"You're a curious one." He laughed. "What were you before you became an American?"

"On my father's side I have been American for three hundred years," she said with dignity. "I was born in Germany."

He broke into a fluent but comical species of German. It seemed that he had been shipped there during the war. The Tabac was closing, and they crossed the boulevard Saint-Germain in the mild May air.

3

"An idiot quarter," he stated, waving his arm, returning to his slangy French. "For the pigeons—bohemians—American tourists. I never come here except to get drunk. I live in a suburb to the south."

On the other side of the boulevard, he continued: "I have a house there. I am married, but I don't love her. It's the boy I love. He is eight years old."

Struggling to digest this information, she said stupidly, "Eight?"

"I had him when I was only a boy myself. I decided to have a boy so we could go out and have fun together while I was still young."

She sighed. It was reasonable, in his way.

"You're not married?"

She shook her head.

"I could see that. You're not running from anyone in particular. You're tormented and bored," he described her sympathetically, looking down at her untutored hair and round chin. "I used to have a motorcycle, but I sold it because my wife was afraid of accidents. Now—"

Suddenly in the rue de l'Echaudé, he seemed almost to collapse with shyness, averting his face, shrugging his big shoulders in an odd, feline manner. She did not understand him. In the street light his face was not that of the large boy in the booth who had patted her thigh, nor of the blue-eyed one who had snubbed her at the sidewalk table. There was a flatness and broadness of the cheeks, a certain Mongol slant of eye—and that peculiar twist of the shoulder—that filled her with dread.

"Now," he concluded in a sudden burst—"I don't know how to get home. The métro stops running at twelve."

She nearly laughed, half in relief, half in bitterness. This at least was normality. She asked coldly, "What do you usually do?"

"I flop somewhere. I stay with a pal."

"Well, you can do it now."

"Not tonight. I'll sleep under the bridge."

Ahead stretched a street that led to the Seine. They could smell the river and almost see it.

In front of her little hotel, under the light, they looked at each other. She had seen something that frightened her, and something else. There it was again, the appeal; the monstrousness had gone. He was—strangely, strangely—her brother.

"It's nineteen kilometers," he said. "But there is the bridge."

4

If he went now it would be for ever. She gave herself a push. "Come," she told him. "But be quiet."

She went up the old-carpeted stairs ahead of him, the fear of discovery pounding in her throat, he amused at all her caution over a cynical concierge and about—she feared—to thump and roar on the first small impulse of malice, perversity, humor. But he was quiet. Inside the dingy brown room with the bed, the sink, closet, and window, he moved to lock the door. She said sharply: "No, no! Go to bed and to sleep. I am giving you shelter. Sleep now and let me alone!"

"I am a dog." He grinned and, after he had pulled off his shoes and overalls, climbed into bed against the wall, carefully covering his blond legs with mock humility.

She got into her pajamas behind the curtain that screened the sink and that hideous symbol, the bidet. Then she joined him in bed, meticulously preserving the space between them, raising a long (he thought) delightful arm to plunge them in darkness, falling into sleep like an exhausted child. When she awoke, horribly pinned down and struggling for breath, it was all she had dreamed and dreaded under the street lamp—horror, treachery, deceit—the light gray in the window and a maniac in her bed. She would be raped and murdered. They would read about it in *France-Soir*.

Immediately, it was the weight that she could not stand. Her muscles swelled and she threw him violently against the wall. Black rage . . . She was up and had torn open the door. "Get out!" she screamed. "*Allez-vous-en!*"

He smiled at the extent of her terror and the comparatively polite language it evoked. "*Dieu*," he declared with true admiration, "you are strong as a horse."

He had two faces, the good and the evil. She reached for an empty wine bottle in the corner.

"Come!" he said. "Come now!" and came after her, and suddenly everything in the room was flying.

She hurled his clothes, his shoes, her shoulder bag, in his face. She made no noise, and no one came. He ducked back into bed under the blankets, and she heard his muffled laughter. "Stop, stop," he choked under the sheet. "I give up!"

She stopped. She closed the half-open door and locked it. She

5

made him get up so that she could brush away the tobacco that littered the bed, from a tin and pipe that she had thrown at him. Then she went back to bed, staring at the ceiling, silent. The room looked like hell.

The dawn broke over Paris. He began to talk to her.

"I am not French," he said. "I'm Russian."

She drew a long, deep breath. "So that's it." For a while she slept quietly. She was very tired. He did not bother to turn off the light. It mingled horribly with the gray of dawn.

It was the longest night she had ever spent; it seemed absolutely endless. She could not have slept more than a couple of hours when she awakened to his telling her that he was a baron, his arms crossed negligently under his head. "*Je suis baron,*" he repeated, for the pleasure of seeing the sleepy scorn in her eyes.

"You look more like a peasant. I saw you all over Vienna in uniform—that's where I saw you."

"Yes," he admitted cheerfully, "I am a common type. They say I am more the New Type than the Old. But I have very fine wrists and ankles." He showed her his ankle.

"That is unnecessary in a man."

"They used to polish my boots, the others."

"I am American and a democrat."

"You are peasants."

"So are the Russian nobility."

"All right," he conceded generously, "we are both peasants. That's why we are strong. You're a fine strong girl. A type for a Russian." He felt her arm judiciously.

She snatched it away. He complained: "You were very bad to me this morning. You hurt my head."

"And you?"

"Yes. I am very bad. Forgive me."

"I thought you were a maniac."

"Of course, we do not know each other. It's a handicap. Are you a Communist?"

"No!"

"Good. I can't bear women Communists. You are a *besprizornye.*"

6

"A what?"

"A lawless child. A self-made outlaw."

"Perhaps you thought I was a girl . . ."

"No," he rebuked her, offended. "We do not think like that."

We? She was getting wider and wider awake. It all seemed intolerably unreal and silly. She blinked her eyes.

"No girl ever put so much trust in me," he said, "as you did this morning. It touched me deeply."

"Thank you."

Lying flat, they turned their heads and regarded each other, eye to eye. That impasse was skirted when he reached up to a shelf and brought down a book. It was a thin book with her picture on the back of the cover. "So that is your name—Carmian Wills. Are you sure it is not a misprint?"

"No. What is yours?"

"Dmitri Mikhailovitch Koubyankov."

She laughed ironically. "Why didn't you tell me you were a Russian?"

"I thought you would send me away."

"It's the only reason I didn't. If you were anything else you would be absolutely crazy."

"But you're an American."

"I am a free citizen. Are you White or Red?"

He scowled with the first sign of temper. "I hate the band of them, corrupt and rotten. I am a Russian, neither Red nor White. Black, if you like. But I fought with the Red Army. They liberated me from a death camp in Poland, and I rode along with them on a tank to Berlin with a machine gun in my hands. I fought the Battle of Berlin. The Americans loved us in those days."

She patted him shyly. He seized her hand and kissed it and lay back staring at the ceiling.

"This room is sordid. My God, how sordid it is!"

"As a Parisian you ought to be used to that," she replied, stung.

"Before the war it was very good here."

"That's what they say everywhere—in Austria and Germany."

"*C'est l'époque.*" After a pause he said, "I don't know how to talk to women. I am shy." In French it was *sauvage,* and she reflected that he was both.

7

"I'm not women."

"But I want you to love me," he muttered, moodily, kicking at the bedclothes.

"I do," she said, just as sullen. "I think I do."

Confusion vanished in the coming together of tender flesh, so surprisingly sweet and inflammable. You are mine, he told her; you are me. It was unavoidable.

Of course, it changed everything.

". . . We kicked down the door and shot them all." He took a machine-gunning position, his eyes light and wild and joyful in the sunlight from the window, his hair gold and falling over his eyes. "There was one young German who looked straight at me. He looked so surprised. Then he was dead. You understand, dead. They had arrested me in Paris, beaten me at Dachau and sent me to Poland to get rid of me. I was a Russian, an *Untermensch* not worth the grub he ate. But this kid looked—"

"Surprised."

"Yes. Death was so quick."

"I see how he looked," she said, looking at him.

"Listen. Do you speak German better than you speak French?"

"Yes, I lived there sometimes."

"Then we shall speak German." He switched without effort into his Franco-Russian parody of that language. "I must go to work now, but I will be back at noon. Stay in bed and sleep."

He sprang out the door, still talking, blew her a kiss and was gone like a genie.

She went to the window and looked out. One ought to go out with such happiness inside, not sleep it away. She leaned at the window dreaming, while people messed around with garbage cans and stirred overhead. Gutter cats prowled and perched on roofs. Out of sight but close by, the boulevard came to life. She smiled to herself over some sententious remarks he had made about biological selection; his drollery was sublime. When weariness overcame her she went to bed. Back at noon. She *knew* he was coming back.

2 The week that followed was phantasmagoric, as if all surrounding reason had exploded through some violent chemistry of their partnership. United, they seemed to be unbearable.

The first day he came at noon, bringing with him a bottle of Vichy water as though it were champagne, and returned to work.

At six o'clock Jean-Philippe appeared.

She was lying across the bed when he knocked. He hopped in with a briefcase under his arm, a withered little man—or boy—with a domed forehead growing bald at the temples, wild frizzy hair on top, a sharp nose, no chin, and rodent eyes. He was very gay. "Madame," he announced with flourishes, "I come on an ambassadorial mission."

She gazed at him blankly.

"M. de Koubyankov has sent me to escort you to the Mabillon where he awaits you. Voilà!"

She dressed behind the curtain with misgivings, for he looked odd, perhaps even slightly criminal. But when they arrived, her Russian was sitting there, on the terrace of the café, looking tranquil and dreamy. His eyes had changed to pale blue, and he was wearing clean dungarees and a clean shirt. An habitual nonobserver of clothes, she noticed this only because he had been so spectacularly unkempt.

He rose to push up a chair. "You've met my secretary? Jean-Philippe . . . Madame."

"Of course we've met," she said impatiently.

The air was charged with the Parisian spring. Am I mad? she thought. Are they cretin and criminal—am I still dreaming? The Fates were nudging her, making cabalistic signs; they were generous when the stakes were high and danger at hand. They offered her escape, knowing she would not take it.

She brushed back her hair in a house-cleaning gesture. "Have you known him long?"

"Oh, a long time!" said Jean-Philippe, who had not been asked.

9

The Russian said: "Today. I found him at noon. The gods sent him to me, for I needed a secretary. I don't like that sort of work myself, and he has the nose to be one."

They looked at Jean-Philippe's nose. He laughed loudly. *"Oh, ce Dimá!"*

"Once I had a cook, but he drank too much. Since that was his wages I couldn't afford him."

"What are *his* wages?"

"Nothing!" crowed Jean-Philippe, with an indulgent swimming smile.

"A good secretary ought to find money," said Dima. "He will bring us some. You'll see."

"You understand German," she commented to the secretary. Apparently it had become everyone's language today.

"He was in the S.S."

"Heil Hitler!" Jean-Philippe barked, shooting out his arm, and collapsed with laughter.

Even Dima was embarrassed. "Sh-h," he said gently.

The gentleness touched her and she looked at J.-P. with interest, beginning to sense desolation. At the same time she grew aware of a very young girl sitting at the next table, sullen and indrawn among noisy students. It was a girl she had met in the quarter, recently arrived from Palestine. She had been in the Nazi camps during her childhood and seemed to spend all her money, what she had of it, on chocolate bars, darting into the bakeries with an air of frenzy. The girl had heard Jean-Philippe and turned her head to look at him indolently, for a second, without surprise. He was not her enemy. She knew her brothers at one glance. She despised them.

"I was the youngest S.S. officer in existence," said J.-P. "Fourteen!"

"They drafted you to shine their boots."

"I was on vacation in the Alsace when they rounded us up. They thought I was Alsatian."

"What a mistake. It's a wonder they didn't put you in the *Volkssturm*."

Jean-Philippe burst out laughing. "Heil Hitler!" he shouted.

Dima shook his head. "He is going to give us trouble, this secretary. He does not carry his liquor well."

Faced with the imminency of being fired, Jean-Philippe pulled himself together. He addressed himself to Carmian. "I understand that you have published a book of poetry. Perhaps I can help you; I am in the publishing business."

"Not poetry," said Carmian. "And I don't think it would be good translated."

"We will go to Gallimard." He went on to tell them a spicy but mixed-up tale of his publishing father and his father's mistress, while they all had another Pernod.

Dima broke up the party; Carmian paid the bill since he had no money; the secretary was dismissed: "You will come to the hotel tomorrow afternoon. It's a foul hole and we have to get her out of there. Bring some money with you."

"*Jawohl!*" Jean-Philippe agreed merrily.

He staggered off. "Will he really come?" she asked, incredulous.

"Oh, yes. He is Destiny. I found him today."

He looked down at her in the rue de Seine and asked her: "Are you unhappy?"

"I don't know."

He swooped down and hugged her. "Forgive me if I did something wrong. I don't know people. I'm not used to thinking about people. I'm only good at working. I am very stupid in life."

"I'll help you if you like."

He looked at her, silent. It was a look of pride, of proprietorship and promise, that the sculptor gives his clay before he begins.

In the morning he turned his pockets inside out and searched the floor. "I sometimes throw money away when I'm drunk," he explained.

"Really? Why?"

"Well, on purpose in a way. Then when I am broke I look in corners and under the bed. Just a habit."

"Never mind; I have money."

"All I have is at home."

She made coffee on the spirit lamp. They drank, and smoked the last bent cigarette together; it was acrid and most of the tobacco fell out. He wore a hard gray look she had never seen before. The boy, both kind and cruel, had given way to a worried man. She would have exchanged him for even the sly Tartar face, under the street light of the rue de Seine, that had been hers.

11

"I must go soon."

Yes, yes. She did what was expected of her. She said: "If you want to go, you must go."

On the bed, his head against the wall, he threw her a glare of passionate hatred, watching her suddenly straighten up and turn her back on him.

Her back, as she looked out the window, seemed about to break. He heard himself asking, "Will you come with me?"

She turned about, she smiled—he would never forget the shock of it—and said: "Really, I don't want you to lose everything and become unhappy through me. Perhaps we could stay together for a while. Just a little while."

"Hah! No risks, no harm done—a good compromise!" He laughed and spat on the floor. "That's an American arrangement."

Triumph invaded her like a flood, for having won his contempt, his desertion. "It seems to me," she said calmly, "the only way."

But he had bounded from the bed and was bent retching over the sink.

She stood frozen, frightened.

"Dima!"

He pushed her away, white and gasping, and flung himself on the bed, turning his face to the wall. She refused to be pushed and laid her arms in a circle round his head and kissed his hair. "I love you." Then louder, as to a deaf person, "I love you."

His furious breathing slowed. He looked at her with pain-gray eyes, encountering her desolation. "What have they done to you?" he asked.

"To me?"

"I knew it when I found you."

"Oh, nothing—not like you."

"The lower part of your face is childish. Not the eyes, though. They are a hundred years old, as if you were staring down corridors of time."

She sank down on his chest; he tightened his arm around her. After a time he declared: "I don't like your name. What shall I call you?"

"I was named after a grandmother whose name was Karla Maria Anna. But they used to call me Cammie."

12

"Cammie. . . ."

They slept, exhausted, until there was a pounding on the door. It might have been the firing squad.

In a way it was. When she had tied the belt of her bathrobe and opened the door, there stood two young Americans.

"Jerry," she commented hopelessly.

He was a strained-looking boy with a cowlick and that innocence with which Americans look out of their eyes when in Europe. He shouldered his way in, the other following, and stared at the long sprawled figure on the bed. He was pale and kept one hand pointedly in the pocket of a superfluous raincoat, the weather being fine.

"Come on, get dressed," he told her, keeping his eye on Dima. "You're getting out of here."

She had the sensation of nightmare. "I am not."

The Russian glowered savagely at the boy, more narrowly at the hand in the pocket. He pulled a clasp knife from somewhere, snapped it open, and ran his thumb melodramatically along the blade.

"Come on, Cam," Jerry ordered. The other boy edged up to protect him. They conferred in an undertone.

"You have no right!" Carmian said. "Now go."

"He's a madman," said Jerry.

Dima sneered. He understood English when this was convenient, although he did not speak it. The other boy shrugged: "You heard what she said."

"She doesn't know what she's doing."

Dima growled aside to her, "He must take me for an idiot, pretending he has a gun in his pocket. It's ridiculous."

"Jerry, I asked you to stop making a fuss and leave us alone."

He responded by sitting down on the only chair, and straddled it with the air of one about to reveal an unhappy truth to the now pacing but more philosophical Dima. Knife and hand-in-pocket had been discarded. The other young man avoided the glance of the girl, gazing doggedly at cracks in the wall, whistling soundlessly.

Jerry bent toward the Russian; he tapped his own forehead with great care.

"*Madame est malade*," he said.

Dima's long slim broad-cheeked face crinkled into a demonic

smile. Ceremoniously, he poked a forefinger at his own temple, twisting it. "Get out of here before I break your head," he advised gently.

But he was beginning to like him, his pluck—as he liked all Americans—she could see, and smiled inwardly. "He's my friend!" she protested.

"You are my wife," he returned, "or are you not?"

"*Ja, ich bin deine Frau.*"

The other two were stupefied by the discovery that they communicated in German. Jerry rallied: "Your romance can't be doing you an awful lot of good, Cam. You look like hell."

"Oh, you know how I drink," she said cheerily.

"Yes," he conceded, reminiscent.

"How did you find me?"

"I know"—Dima was scowling—"the type who was with you at the Tabac with the African."

He gave her a specific glare which she did not mind. She was happy that there was to be no violence.

The other boy asked, "Are you in love with him, Cam?"

It was a silly question, she reflected, but she was sympathetic—he had just lost a lover with great pain. She nodded, and he embraced her and shook Dima's hand. Then he walked to the door and said, "Come on, Jerry," and walked out.

Jerry threatened: "I could go to the embassy. If there's any trouble, I will."

"You're welcome," said Dima, lying down. "I'll be there."

Jerry left. After a while his footsteps went down.

She sat with one slender hand over her face. Even collapsed, her posture caught at his heart, like the boy's grief.

"Is he another lover?"

"I have no lovers but you."

She sat beside him on the bed, and he took her cold hands. "Do you want to marry me?"

"Yes."

"It will be hard. But you must have patience."

"I will."

"*Bon,*" he exulted in relief, "*c'est fait.* I shall go into action. *Zoum!* Nothing can stop me when I want to do something!"

She lifted her head to look at him with real interest. He was

14

telling the truth. He was like a crushing machine. "When did you first want to marry me—just now?"

"When you took me up here. And you?"

"The moment I saw you. Later, you remember?—you patted me on the leg as if we had known each other since we were born."

"We have," he said. "Now it's a matter of my divorce. Also, I am probably fired."

"Why?"

"I should have gone to work before the arrival of your American gangsters."

"My friends."

"All right, your friends. What am I?"

"You are my man."

His breath caught. There was a little catching, shutting sound in his throat. "When you said that about staying together—for just a little while—"

"No, no—"

"I thought you were a delusion and worthless. I thought I had lost all that was lyrical in the world and that my heart would burst."

"I didn't mean to make you sick. I thought I was helping you."

"No, no," he said.

"If you had agreed, it was I who would have been sick."

"We must go *together*," said Dima. "Forward together."

3

Jean-Philippe appeared in the evening with his briefcase and three hundred francs. *Trois cent balles*. It's all I could find."

"It won't go very far," Dima said gloomily.

"I have money," Carmian repeated. It came from an inheritance in Germany, marks that she had smuggled out, changed at a loss in legitimate French banks, and kept in her suitcase. There was a wad she could hardly hold in one hand, all folded and neat.

"No!" said Dima. "Are you making reparations? Leave that to the governments. I have an idea—wait here." He bounded out the door.

Jean-Philippe settled himself calmly in the chair, where he unpacked his ragged briefcase and proceeded to write fluently, without preliminary thought or hesitation, on his knees.

From the sink where she was washing her underwear, she threw him shy and envious looks. He wrote steadily and evenly, as if it were an exercise in handwriting.

"What are you doing?"

"It's my book," he said, the pen flowing, without raising his eyes. "I've been working on it for a year."

"What's it about?"

"Oh . . . everything. Everything!" he said, and laughed.

"You have a good pen."

"Yes."

Dima came back in an hour. He was very excited. "I found my old friend—Boris! He is waiting for us in the Rhumerie. He is just back from England. Come, I want you to see him."

"But I thought . . ."

"Dima does not operate on logic," J.-P. remarked with complacency.

"He has money!" said Dima of Boris.

He swooped down to embrace and kiss her knees. "Come, *dushka*, we'll have something to eat there. He is my best friend. We did the Resistance together. We drank up all the German officers' wine! I haven't seen him in two years."

She laughed, and Jean-Philippe came along, diplomatically unobtrusive, as was his rôle.

Boris was a bear with a big bass voice and a big black beard, and when he roared, which was his way of speaking, one received a fine shower of spittle if one did not take the precaution of standing back. She was appalled at the cold and ruthless penetration of his little black eyes buried in fat, and Dima's subjugation. Dima pranced and glowed, holding her up for his approval. Boris alone drowned out every other sound in the place; the Heil Hitlers that Jean-Philippe might have been prompted to utter went unheard. J.-P. drank too much and too quickly at the sight of Boris' fistful of thousand-franc notes and he began to droop like a tired bird upon the bar stool.

Boris was a rabbi's son, a poet said to be fifty years ahead of his time, and unpublishable, but it was also known that one day he would become great. He ignored human beings and all live things, except as shadowy figures in the landscape, and wrote about stones and streets and telegraph wires and steel structures. His poetry took the form of prose and had the rhythm of the Old Testament, and it was harsh, inexorable. He had no home but traveled to all countries that interested him at the moment for reasons perhaps vague to others but specific to him, going well dressed with money in his pocket, returning tattered and broke. In England he had spent most of his time on the docks at Liverpool watching the sea gulls. They were the most interesting thing there, he said. The British authorities had asked him to leave. They had even paid his passage. His next trip would be to Germany, for he wanted very much to see the ruins: there were so many stones and meaningless configurations.

He lived on pensions, a war pension (*d'ancien militaire*), a *pension de juif*, and a *pension de fou* since they had found he was schizophrenic. On these he managed to satisfy his own peculiar and sporadic appetites, with the additional help of a room in the Kouby-ankovs' suburban house to which he returned to write after excursions abroad. He had almost no need of women. An occasional prostitute was all he required.

He was thirty-five and looked fifty. He made Dima look like the mildest man in the world. He was a machine for destruction, and smelt of death.

Boris roared that she was a fine girl and even went so far as to lower his voice while he said tender things about her in soft, throaty Russian. He asked her about her writing. Dima glowed like the sun. "Oh, it's good!" he answered for her. "I can see by the look of the page that it's good!"

Jean-Philippe sagged off the red leather bar stool. They deposited him in a corner and went on talking. "I don't want any tiffs in here," the *patron* sputtered, wagging his hands. Their Russian unnerved him. They all looked at Jean-Philippe, and Boris and Dima got up and carried him outside and laid him on the sidewalk.

Carmian ran out and knelt beside J.-P. She felt his forehead and held his limp hands. "You can't do that," she objected, coming back to the bar. "He's already quite cold!"

17

"Call the ambulance then," said Boris. "Maybe he's dead."

They laughed uproariously. But Dima called the ambulance. I came and carried off Jean-Philippe in it.

That was her first encounter with Boris.

Her second was on the next day. J.-P. showed up toward noon refreshed and cheery. He had spent a good night in the hospital and repeated some of his verbal sallies with the doctors in which, clearly he had been victorious. He also mentioned that Boris was still in the quarter and would be waiting for them this evening around the corner.

"Russians are like that," Dima said with pride. "Once they start something, they finish it."

"Well, it rather depends on what you want to finish."

"Everything," he told her. He was on his feet—he could never sit still very long—and took a backward step as if to gather momentum, and swung himself forward with both arms raised high Zoum! It was the push to Berlin. "Poetry—a binge—a war—a love What does it matter? It's the pace that counts. Keep the pace, and it will carry you."

That night, Boris being broke and still in high gear, she spent two thousand francs. Dima tried hard to hide his chagrin; but he stuck to his guns. Jean-Philippe told her some more about his publishing father . . . divorced . . . an invalid. He commenced to droop again and this time they took him home, Dima and she, since no one knew where he lived, and put him to sleep on the floor of her room, giving him the blanket. Dima took her in his arms. He told her a story in which he and Boris, Henry Miller, and Louis Armstrong were strangely merged; it seemed they had all met together in prewar days. He talked about Boris and the war—when everyone had been marvelously happy fighting the Germans—and went suddenly to sleep. He pouted like a child when he slept.

In the morning the *flics* came.

There was the sharp rapping on the door: "Police."

Carmian bolted upright, clutching the covers. She saw Dima go gray, and his mouth whiten. She prodded the sleeping Jean-Philippe with her foot. "Open up."

J.-P. stared at them, rumple-haired, eyes wide with fright. Then he got off the floor and let the cops in. There were two of them in

18

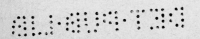

civilian clothes. They glanced at the bed without surprise, and back at J.-P.

"What are you doing here?"

"I—er—spent the night." He giggled unprepossessingly.

"The boy had no place to go last night," Dima protested. "We put him up." Carmian could feel him quivering. He was in mortal terror.

"Vos *papiers, Madame.*"

Numbly she handed them her passport, which she extracted from her pocketbook on the night table. They looked hostile, examining it, one page after the other."

"You have no French visa."

"No, I crossed the border before the three months were up. You will see the exit and entry dates."

"That is correct. You will need a French visa and a *carte d'identité* in two weeks if you wish to continue your residence in France."

The second one returned her passport with a small bow.

Extending a naked arm, she accepted it and nodded. "Monsieur."

Dima now gave them his red card—the lowest in the hierarchy of foreign classification—marked *réfugié russe.*

They were startled, and glanced at Carmian.

There was an all-around exchange of stares.

"It's in order," the first one said, returning it.

The other shook his head ambiguously: "*Une américaine et un russe,*" he remarked. "*C'est du propre.*"

Jean-Philippe's papers, it transpired, were not in order.

"You are coming with us."

"I am a French citizen, Messieurs!"

"*Viens.*"

They ushered him out in a fury of protest.

"How mean," said Carmian, breathing heavily and close to tears.

"Well, he has the mug for it. No cop could like him."

"But it's not right!"

"He'll be back tonight; don't worry."

"What do you suppose they meant by *c'est du propre?*"

"Clean. If any two people are in that ridiculous position it must be clean, *dyevutchka.* Do you see?"

19

"No, I don't think so," she said. "I believe they meant: 'This is really the end.' "

"You would. Looking for irony where there is none."

Suddenly restless, he got up, walked up and down on his long strong legs, and began to dress. "We spend our days in bed," he fretted.

"We get interviewed there, at any rate."

"It is time for action. Besides, I'm hungry."

"Why were you afraid of them?" she asked angrily. "On account of Jerry and my embassy?"

"A routine raid? Stupid! They need fines from the foreigners to fill the coffers."

He said with sudden hatred: "You wouldn't understand, you and your passport. They're whores for the Americans, that's why. I'm a second-class citizen and police bait. During the war when I distributed false ration cards to confuse the Germans, they caught me and beat me up. It didn't matter that the English told us to sabotage in every possible way. The French police beat me up in jail, and then the Germans carted me off to Dachau. I hated the French worse than the Germans! I was helping the poor to get food and helping France at the same time. Did the BBC help? Not me, certainly. I still have a police record, five years after the Liberation, and I have to report to the Préfecture once a month as an ex-criminal."

She stared at him through her dark eyes.

He threw an arm around her, abruptly cheered, and said: "You are on the side of the underdog, *mon petit*, like all Americans. Let's go eat. I'll have money tomorrow."

They had an early, plebeian lunch, steak and red wine on a checkered tablecloth in some lost little hole they never managed to find again. She did not share his contempt for Saint-Germain-des-Prés; it seemed to foster lovers, even old Diderot thinking on his pedestal in the middle of the sidewalk across from the Tabac. The streets were gray and sad and full of love.

"I am sorry," he said. "You don't understand because you were never in prison."

"Oh, yes I was," she said with her shy-curling smile.

"You?"

"Oh, yes." She turned her head. Even the girls in their tight

20

black pants were saddening and amusing here and, like the Israeli girl, full of a sweet desperation.

He looked bitter to the point of wildness, which made her explain calmly: "Driving an automobile while intoxicated. Resisting a police officer," as if reciting a school lesson.

"That is piggishness."

"Yes, but you see . . . That was a week before my mother drowned in the Atlantic. They let me out quite soon. It was in a little town in New England where they did not know me, and I hurt no one." She looked at him steadily.

"Before your mother—?"

"Yes, a week before."

The significance of that settled on him slowly as a cloud, but surely, for that was his way. "And your father?"

She laughed lightheartedly. "Oh, they've always been divorced."

"*Amerika!*" he murmured.

"But we were not normal. Didn't you mention a motorcycle?"

"Did I? I suppose I did. We are strangers, you and I." Smoke drifted beautifully across his squinting, slanted eyes. "How did you get into such trouble? Here we don't look for it."

"I had just published my book. It was a success. I felt better in jail."

"You are ferocious. Boris said so."

She was cold and silent. He went to pay the waitress, and there was a terrible pain in her heart.

Returning, he said, "Come," gently, and took her arm.

He went to the Opéra at two o'clock, returning with his pay envelope and the news that he had been fired. He had already known it, but his face was ashen. He threw the envelope on the night table after extracting a hundred-franc note, and went out again.

She sat down on the bed and folded her hands, gazing at the wall. Paris was a cat looking skyward and black nights dreaming of rains. Behind it was her mother, dead in the long gray swells of the Atlantic. A memory came to her of the night in the Rhumerie, where a young girl had been crying earnestly into the public telephone: "*Non, ce n'était pas du sang, c'était du vin qu'il s'est versé sur la figure!*" Not blood but wine that he had poured on his face. It had seemed mysterious beyond words.

She raised stunned eyes when he came back to the room, with a bottle of *rosé* foresightedly uncorked.

He jumped up and strode around the little room with a tumbler ful, tossing it down. "We must get out of here. Tonight."

Her common sense returned; the cloud that had settled and lifted became less fearful. "You mean," she asked, "because of the police?"

"That's one reason. But what is the matter with you—that you can stay here in this . . ." He waved a wild arm.

"I don't believe they'll come back."

"I am sensitive to ugliness; it crushes me! That's why I'm good in my work. I'm a *metteur-en-scène*, and just beginning. Have you no aesthetic sense?"

"Of course," she said, "I was merely thinking of other things."

"I have a home in Châtenay—my pictures, my books, my clothes! Everything I own is there. My son. How long do you think I can go on like this?"

"Then you must go home."

He moved his jaw, staring at her bitterly.

"You should not have stayed with me this long," she said.

"You picked me up!"

A wave of pain crashed through her. She seized her glass and threw it at him. He was splattered with wine, but the glass missed him and went out the open window. They heard it smash on the street. She lay down on the bed and turned her face to the wall.

There was a long silence. Then she felt his hand on her shoulder. "Look at me."

She did, through burning tears.

"Do you want to stay with me forever?"

"Yes."

"Then come, pack up; we'll go together."

The concierge, a sour, careworn young man, inquired: "Was it from your window that a glass was thrown?"

"Yes," said Dima nonchalantly. "Excuse us, it was an accident. We are giving up the room and will settle the bill tonight. Meanwhile will you be good enough to keep the luggage?"

He nodded curtly.

They came back in an hour accompanied by a big bearish man with a black beard, and the shifty small type who had been escorted out this morning by the police. The young Russian, much to his surprise, paid the bill.

He was glad to see them go. "Au revoir, Messieurs; au revoir, Mademoiselle."

"Madame," Dima corrected him in a grave and courteous voice, bowing slightly.

"Good luck," the concierge replied ironically.

Carmian went quickly out. For ever after, that remark seemed like an evil omen.

4 It was daylight on the boulevard, by a happy coincidence apéritif time. Boris carried one large suitcase, Dima another, and J.-P. a typewriter, clamping his briefcase under his elbow. They parked everything around a table of the Mabillon café and ordered four Pernods.

"Now that we are bailed out, where do we go?" J.-P. asked cheerfully.

He was regarded with disfavor.

"To your house," Dima proposed.

He laughed heartily, his Adam's apple bobbing. "Mais non, mon vieux! Where I'm staying there are not enough beds as it is."

"You should have stayed at the police station."

"They wouldn't let me."

"I don't blame them," said Boris.

"Oh, come now," said Carmian.

They drank despondently. "I'm broke," Dima said. "I paid the hotel and a few debts at the Opéra. My pay's gone."

Three pairs of eyes focused slowly on Boris. He was staying in Châtenay at Dima's house. He appeared to be thinking hard, darting little glances at all of them with his beady eyes cushioned in flesh. He was subject to a nervous rash which inflamed his cheeks and ears, creating crusty little sores. Dima had assured Carmian that it was not communicable. She shrank from him and was ashamed—after

23

all it was harmless and not his fault. Chez Gallimard he was known as a great poet: that was the main thing.

"Why can't we go to Olga's?" Dima suggested.

"Who is Olga?" said Carmian, lost and anxious, looking at her battered luggage.

"The sister of Boris," said Dima.

"No," Boris rumbled, "we might get shot," and added a few sentences in Russian. Jean-Philippe laughed stupidly. They were pensive, finishing their drinks, until Dima had another idea:

"Lala!" he cried. "We will go chez Lala!"

Boris and he broke into uproarious laughter, rich in mutual agreement. Dima paid the bill; they collected her baggage and hailed a taxi; the suitcases went on the roof, they squeezed inside, and Dima named the street and the quarter, directing him to a section between Alésia and Montparnasse. The driver had never heard of it.

On the way, Carmian asked, "Who is Lala?"

"Darling," Dima said, pressing her hand. "I forgot you didn't know. It is my mother."

"You haven't lived," said J.-P.

At the rue Maison-Dieu they descended. J.-P. now paid the driver, since no one else seemed inclined to. They went through ancient wood portals into a courtyard, where a chicken was scratching aimlessly, up some very narrow unlighted stairs on to a landing which was in pitch darkness. Dima said, "Wait here," and knocked on what sounded like a very far door. They lurked uneasily, unseeing. A female voice was heard dimly; the door was unlatched. There were exclamations of surprise, perhaps of reproach and even rage, in Russian.

Dima came back, groping for her and drawing her inside, the others following at a discreeter pace with the luggage.

The room was small, oblong and dark, pierced with a falling ray of sun. There were a couch, a table and chairs, an impression of brownness and clutter; faded oil paintings, icons, and photographs hung everywhere. Only the sunlight through the iron grillwork outside the window was beautiful. A woman was arranging some flowers in a vase, posing there. To pose so falsely, after the preliminary explosion, seemed to Carmian a bit of artistry in the old grand manner that merited respect. She wore a blue velvet suit and hat, and swiveled her neck to look over her flowers with a catlike smile. "Bo-

24

our!" she sang in a heavy accent. Her voice was extraordinarily sweet
and high, like a girl's.

"Come in!"

Lala's eyes were a light gray-green set in wrinkles. They seemed
as kind as such eyes can ever be, perhaps with the acquired kindliness
of age. Carmian saw them widen with shock and utter amazement, then narrow, focusing over her shoulder.

Jean-Philippe had come in dragging a suitcase.

"Maman," Dima began. . . .

J.-P. went back for the typewriter. It was not he, apparently, to
whom she had lost her gracious airs. She pointed a finger at Boris,
lurking in the background.

"Not that one!" she screamed to her son. "Not in this house!"

Whereupon she unloosed a torrent of tears and curses hardly
flattering to the futuristic lion of NRF. It was quite lovely, shrill but
with falling cadences: Russian—one might say, if that were not
redundant—in the extreme. Also, it sounded a bit like chocolate in
the mouth.

Boris, unmoved, sat down in the best chair. There was not a
large choice.

In the middle of a great wail, Lala wiped away her tears and
went to make tea. Dima and Carmian sat side by side on the couch.
J.-P. squatted on what appeared to be a sea chest. Presently her voice
called something lilting and sweet from behind the curtain that hid
the kitchen.

They rolled eyes and made signs at each other, rather uncomplimentary to Lala but expressing relief.

She fussed and bustled with a magpie chatter, covering the
table with a cloth, putting down cups and saucers. There was a
samovar, but she did not use it. She ignored J.-P. rudely, both as
a non-Russian and as a member of an inferior class, although there
was no truth in this. Her attitude toward Boris combined familiarity
with contempt. Her son she petted absently. To Carmian she was
winning and kind: Americans had taken the place of the former
Russian gentry in the world. They, now, were the aristocrats.

Seated on the old hand-painted chest, teacup in hand, she made
conversation, in French: "I have just come from Châtenay—see the
pretty flowers I brought! Denise is worried about you," she said to
her son.

He tensed himself and stared her hard in the eye.

She smiled lovingly, undeterred. "Denise said you had been missing for a week—"

"Four days—"

"You should have telephoned her. What shall I tell her when I go back?"

"You will tell her nothing," Dima growled, clenching his teeth. "I do not love that woman. I never have."

Carmian began to move about as if the couch were hot. J.-P. stared at his knees, Boris at nothing.

"After all, she is your wife," Lala continued, with growing enjoyment. "She puts up with Boris. And the boy—"

He took off his shoe and threw it at her. Lala shrieked. Carmian jumped up, horrified and revolted.

"Sit down, darling," Dima begged; "you don't understand. She always does it! That's what she wants, don't you see?"

Boris stroked his beard, black eyes snapping with interest.

J.-P. felt obliged to disapprove. "*Voyons, Dimá!*"

But the strangest reaction was that of Madame de Koubyanko herself. She closed her eyes for a moment, fingering her temple, and opened them again on Carmian, wearily. "You see what I have to bear, Mademoiselle? He is a savage, that boy. Well—" She shrugged. "I must go to my sister Shura's now. After all, I have a living to make." She disappeared into another room, closing the door firmly.

Carmian sat down. It was growing dark, and Dima turned the switch that flooded the place improbably with light. It came from a homemade chandelier, a kind of wooden wheel suspended directly overhead.

"Where shall we sleep tonight?" she asked.

"Here," he said.

"And Mamotchka?"

"She won't be here."

"But it's her house!"

"Listen—she doesn't care. She doesn't think. She plots. She loves the idea of you. It provides excitement and intrigue and that's what she lives for. She might have been angry if you had not been pretty or . . . I don't know. But she likes you."

26

"*Merde, alors,*" said Boris. "You talk about Lala as if you didn't now hell. There is nothing to drink here."

"Oh, I'll go get some!" offered J.-P. accommodating as ever.

"Make it red, thirteen per cent."

Lala flounced out of the adjoining room with some lumpy bundles. She had smeared Vaseline on her eyelids and rouged her mouth. he complained: "You turn on the light too soon."

Boris yawned. "We haven't our prayer beads with us, Madame."

She ignored him, drawing herself up. "Dimitchka, put the tea hings away." However, she changed her mind for some reason, parked er bundles on the floor and swept everything off herself; she patted he tablecloth smooth and stood back to survey glory. They watched er in silence. She did not leave. She sat down on the painted chest.

"I thought you were going," Dima said.

"I'm tired!" she wailed instantly. "May I not stay in my own partment as long as I want?"

"It's not an apartment—it's a dump. *Un taudis.*"

For the first time her odd green eyes glinted in anger, but she omposed herself rapidly. Perched like a girl on the chest, she turned er neck in that reptilian movement to gaze upon Carmian with an xalted smile.

"*Vous êtes amér-ricaine, Mademoiselle?* How did you meet my on?"

"Through friends," Dima said quickly, glaring.

J.-P. misplaced one of his nervous giggles.

"You met him in a café? He is always in the cafés. How is it hat you have no fixed living quarters? Have you been with him all hese days?"

Dima shook his fist at her. "Witch! Shut up!"

Her smile grew winsome. "It merely astonished me because the oung woman is American. She is lovely, but perhaps she is not an merican of the upper classes. They are so puritanical."

Carmian swayed with rage in her chair, before standing up. For second they all gazed upon her rage and her distress. Dima pulled er back by her arms. "Be calm, she is a child. She does not mean it. he is like a parrot who wants to see if it can torment you."

"Your mother!"

"Listen, my dear; I have had her all my life."

27

But she was deafened by the drumming in her blood. "Madame," she said trembling, "I am very much afraid that I can no longer stay here."

"She has a bad temper, the little one," Boris remarked approvingly.

"Quiet, Boris! No, stay, stay, Mademoiselle. I must go now and leave you alone." Lala averted her face, collecting her bundles in one arm. With her free hand she deftly opened a tin box on the sideboard, withdrew something swiftly that she held out to Carmian and smiled. It was a lemon-flavored lollipop.

"Take, take," she urged, smiling.

"*Merci, Madame.*"

Ill-suppressed laughter burbled out of J.-P.

Sparkling, smirking once more, Lala flitted out, shaking her finger at Boris. "When I come back you will be gone, do you hear? I shall be back at ten. Dima—no drinking here! You will make spots."

And she was gone.

After a while, Dima said, "J.-P., get us a bottle of wine."

"Old man, I have no money—after the taxi, you understand."

They sat in disgruntled silence. "I'll pay for it," said Carmian and went to her suitcase. Boris brightened, favoring it with sentimental glance.

But he complained: "I'll probably have to return to Châtenay tonight. Your mother will throw me out." Now that solace and festivities were in the offing, or at least not completely unobtainable, it seemed a bitter fate.

"You're a generous girl," said Dima, and to Boris: "Don't be an ass, she has no sense of time. She will very likely miss the last métro and stay overnight at Shura's. They hate each other so much they adore each other's company."

"*Mais elle est magnifique,*" J.-P. declaimed in accents of the Comédie Française.

On hearing this phase of the secretary's voice, a more practical thought was awakened in Dima. "Darling, give him some money for food—two, three hundred francs."

"What'll I buy?" asked J.-P., receiving crumpled bills from Carmian, quite dazed, his hair standing up like a coxcomb. It was a good thing he had so much hair, for the shape of his head was disturbing.

"Bread, sausage, pâté, cheese . . ." Dima recited patiently.

"Herring," said Boris.

"Well, I don't know if I can procure all that—but ha, ha! *On verra!*" He bounded out and down the lightless stairs.

"He's batty," said Boris, "that one."

"J.-P. is all right," said Carmian.

Dima interpreted. "She is tolerant. It is very American to be tolerant."

"I like him. Such a funny little boy."

"It's the poet in her."

"What sort of American are you?" Boris demanded, hooding his eyes.

"English, German, French . . . Indian."

Boris was delighted. "Indian!"

"A little."

He said to Dima: "I shall call her Tamawak."

"Only a little."

"Yes. She is fierce sometimes," Dima said.

"I am not talking about that. She walks like an Indian."

"Tama—what? Oh—*Tomahawk!* It is merely the American manner of walking," Carmian explained.

"Tamawak!" sang Boris, intoxicated by the idea. "You grip the ground with your toes and take long strides."

"She is a poet," Dima elaborated raptly, "in her very body."

By now this aspect of herself caused Boris considerably less pleasure than her exotic ancestry. He changed the subject. They started to gossip about the Nouvelle Revue Française, which they referred to as NRF or Gallimard, explaining to her that it was a great publishing house in France. They mentioned Denise, who was literary, in this connection, and Carmian sank into a silent uproar. It seemed no one could refrain from mentioning Dima's wife for ten minutes.

Dima stroked her hair. Not only did he observe her inner revolutions and depressions, he seemed to feel them with his skin. Dima's compassion was more moving than that of most people, it sat so ill on him. He laughed a little, even, "No, no," shaking his head.

"No, what?" asked Boris, suspiciously.

"Denise. Never mind. She is only a girl a bit older than Carmian, pretty and charming. Also, she's an intellectual—and a dictator. Authoritarian. She wouldn't let me listen to music when she wanted to read. She would sit across the room, amused, watching me drink. She had lovers. She told me that I was uneducated and knew nothing. A dictator, eh, Boris?"

"She's not my wife," said that one. "Lock her in a closet, ha-ha. That's what she wants." Having said his piece, he shifted restlessly. "Where is that pixie?"

J.-P. came at last, breathless. It was always astonishing, in fact breath-taking, to see again how little chin he had, adorned with the wisps of a beard. Ravenously, they fell over the food, and the wine was gone almost as soon as they had begun. J.-P. was dispatched for another bottle, while Boris lay back to tell them a little more about his trips abroad. These had been remarkably disastrous to everyone concerned but himself; he usually managed to get back in fairly good form for writing. Even Africa had thrown him out—Algeria, for living in the Casbah disguised as a native. He had been bitten by a camel, riding across the desert. As for people, he made no secret of not liking them at all.

Boris drank most of the wine, becoming almost articulate in the process, for his stammering had stopped. He demanded another bottle, but J.-P. demurring bravely, he shuffled out to get it himself.

During the lull Carmian studied an assortment of family photographs on the wall. There was Lala—unrecognizable in a ball dress and tiara, a young girl with a nineteenth century neck, beautiful shoulders, and an oval purity of face; vacant-eyed, with no hint of the wrinkled ruse to come. There was a Russian man—Dima's half brother, ten years older than he. There were aunts and uncles. Six little girls in fur hats with muffs stood in the snow, their governess smiling in the middle, a very dark church with onion turrets looming up behind. They were all pretty and laughing, and one imagined the steam of their breath escaping on the winter air. These were the sisters Rajenska a long time ago in Moscow. Lala, the eldest and tallest, was amazingly there with the rest of them in the snow.

Dima explained the pictures to her. There was also his son, a husky blond eight-year-old. And another snub-nosed boy in a faded picture. She looked long at him. He had a rebellious mouth and straight hair almost obscuring his eyes, sheepdog-like, and he clutched a puppy to his chest, shielding it and fighting the world plainly at bay. Pride, temperament, and arrogance were written on him; he was full of passions. She was sorry for this little boy and

30

looked up at him beside her to see what had really become of him. The high sloping forehead, high cheekbones, fleeing planes, upturned nose were the same. Slavs looked like that. But could he not be happier than in the picture? Or was that puppy still there, assailed?

Dima dashed into the next room and came back with a framed photograph of a dark, nearly bald man with handsome features and large brilliant eyes, tortured eyes. "That was my father—a gentle man."

"Did he die?"

"When I was twelve. He was a chemical exporter—he—"

They heard Boris coming back. He replaced the picture hastily in that inner, mysterious recess—the other room—that the Kubyankovs did not want her to see. J.-P. had been dozing but woke up and held out his glass with complete equanimity. Boris swore, pouring, and spilled some on Lala's tablecloth. Dima bunched it up and stuck it on the top shelf of the old Breton buffet, where it kept company with the painting of a fish, a bread basket, and innumerable empty jars.

They talked about the days of the Occupations. There had been all kinds. They elaborated on the German one. J.-P. woke up and tried to join in but was utterly drowned out by the wild deep voices. They reminisced on the chicanery of the German officers' wine. Dima and Boris together had been hired by the German army at a military post north of Paris, where Boris had found himself splendidly in charge of hardware at the PX. The fact that Boris, the rabbi's son with beard, had been thus exalted convulsed everyone else—but the Germans remained ignorant of their error. "It took us two weeks to drink up the officers' wine in barrels," Dima mused. "One night Boris drew the last drop. 'It's time to go,' he told me. The same night we"—he hit his wrist nervously with the side of his hand—"made off."

One time in Paris Dima had come into possession of a German supply officer's uniform. He had the looks for it. With friends outside in a car with a Wehrmacht license, he had come out with a permit for fifty kilos of coffee. They were loaded aboard by German privates. It was a great success, and they gave the coffee away.

The laughter died down a little. "If only we had it now," Boris said sadly, eyeing Carmian's suitcase.

"No," Dima said sharply in Russian. Then he smiled. "If it's coffee you want, Lala has pounds in her bedroom."

"Does she sleep with it?"

"No, on top. It's under the bed. She keeps everything there. Once she accused me of stealing her ancestral pearls. For two weeks she drove me crazy with tears, with cries. Finally she found them under the bed between boxes."

"I thought there was damn little of anything in there," said Boris, gazing dismally at rows of empty jars in the buffet.

"How are you, darling?" Dima asked intramurally and, leaving Boris to his sorrow, patting and kissing her. "Are you happy?"

"Don't be afraid of Lala," J.-P. advised her rather dreamily. He was a strange boy. She had never thought to observe tenderness in those undistinguished brown eyes. Why, he was fond of her!

"Lala, Lala . . ." said Dima. "When the Americans were just outside Paris and the Liberation was all over the place—gangs of marauders with firearms mostly, hunting down 'collaborators' for sport and loot—some idiots came here for Lala when she was alone. I was in Germany. Maybe they had heard about my brother's wife —he was in Germany, too, in the labor draft."

"What about her?" she asked, sensing a sudden depression in him.

"Well, the girl slept with the Germans. Besides, these louts claimed to be Communist, and Lala was White Russian. She was snippy to them when they came to the door. So they told her they were going to shoot her, and she went mad." He laughed, fluttering his fingers and eyelashes in a bald imitation of his mother. " 'Please, Messieurs!' she said, *je vous en prr-rie*—outdoors! I have just mopped the floor and you will make a mess of it,' and out she marched into the hall. They were so scared they ran away."

"Do you think she knew—"

"*Elle n'en sait rien,*" Boris said drunkenly.

"The kind, then, who is good in wars."

"We need another bottle," Boris said.

"No," said Dima. "Enough."

Boris lumbered to his feet and tugged at Carmian's suitcase. She was shocked. Dima tried to conceal his shame; he pushed his friend into a chair. "Tomorrow."

"Boris—*mon dieu!*" J.-P. chirped unnecessarily.

It was almost with relief that they heard a key turning in the lock.

"I should have known," said Dima. "*Bon soir, Madame la Baronne!*"

"Good evening," replied Lala, aware in a sweep of her reptilian glance of the state of the apartment. She carried a heavy roll of some sort of paper about three feet wide which she rushed into her bedroom, complaining furiously, meanwhile, through the closed door.

By the time she came out again Dima had cleaned off the table, and her rage was modified to irritation. "You," she commanded J.-P., "go home while there is still the métro. You should be asleep in bed, a child like you."

He rose meekly, gathering up his briefcase. "Where shall I find you?" he asked Dima in a professional tone.

"I don't know, but I'm not worried. You will find us."

Lala said unexpectedly: "Do you want a job? I have a job for you."

J.-P. shrugged, trying to hide his lack of confidence or desire behind a rather ashen grin. "That depends. What kind of job?"

"Pasting up posters. Come to see me tomorrow—no, the day after."

"At your service." He bowed. "Good night."

"He has manners, even so," she remarked when he had gone.

"He's crazy," Dima said.

"I wish yours were as good. It's not always the education."

"His father is a rich man."

"Rich?" She tinkled laughter. "In our house we had a family of fourteen and twice as many servants."

"What a waste."

"Shut up! You have no respect. Shura complains that you do not see her."

"I detest her."

This did not seem to displease Lala intensely; she changed the subject. "Where is the tablecloth? . . . Ah, you have ruined and hidden it. I see it now on top of the buffet. For shame! You, Boris— I thought you were staying in Châtenay."

"He can stay here," said Dima.

"*Where?*" she shrieked. After that there was talk back and forth in growling and spitting Russian, and it was an hour before they were all finally bedded down, Dima and Carmian on the couch. Lala herself tucked them in and handed them each a towel for the morning. After some hesitation she unearthed another for Boris and threw it at him. Then she turned out the light and went muttering into her room.

33

Boris slept under the table, flat on his back, his beard rising and falling with his snores. The other two shook with stifled laughter, hugging each other deliciously like children in the dark.

5   In the morning she was off to some job or rendezvous before any of them could lift a head. "Get *him* out of here," she ordered Dima, departing. "*She* may stay."

Carmian was bewildered.

"She likes you." The door slammed. "Didn't I tell you? Lala loves a secret. Now she can lord it over Denise."

Carmian had begun to discover the common characteristics of mother and son. This blind rushing, for instance—Russians rushing into the wind, destination unknown. It was action more than aim or purpose that appealed to them. They would rather run halfway across town than make a telephone call. There was none of the famed Russian languor about them. They were of the other type, and their metabolic rate was awesome.

Her own was the opposite. She had always avoided physical effort, preferring to use her brains. After the publication of her book —hailed as a tour-de-force for such a young woman—even her brain had grown tired. The flush of victory was all gone, and she had since been surprised to note that there were times when she was full of hatred—she did not know for what.

Her father had been an army man, and later, when her mother already seemed destined to ruin his career, he had gone into the consular service and they had lived in Europe. Then her mother, who was left to her as a curious memory of longing mixed with fear, had taken her away to Germany . . . and then again all over Europe to sleep in hotels and sit in cafés endlessly while she—Cammie dreamed of what she was going to do. The urge to create had been irrepressible in her at all ages. She had danced until she was six; at seven she had been briefly a passionate carpenter and had begun to paint, and at eight to write novels. At twelve she had composed music with only the faintest idea of how to do it, but here she bogged down in technical difficulties. No matter where the flood was dammed up, it burst forth in some other place.

Her mother was like Lala in that she lived for excitement, but

34

of a different kind. It had been hard to be the child of a child, harder still when her mother drowned by accident one day in the long gray swells of the North Atlantic. Endowed with the pathos of the dead, she was loved even more; she was Death and Mother both, robbing death of its power. Carmian had ceased to be afraid of it.

Her father was a humorous, dark-spirited man who now lived in New York. Ages, aeons ago, she had known him very well and they had all been happy. Since then, and since the time when she had come into life full of everything that one needed, there had been mostly loss.

Now she felt again a glow, a haze, a heart-shaken expectancy. She let Dima sweep her along in his buoyant stride and forgot to look back. It no longer seemed necessary.

"*Les Mohicans*," Boris mumbled after he had extricated himself from the table legs. "*Le Dernier des Mohicans*. Have you read it?"

"Of course. I am one, so to speak."

Dima laughed approvingly from behind the little screen where, clattering and banging, he was creating a Portuguese omelet. The sun illuminated the little room, the brownness and dust, not to be compared with the sadder dust of the rooms of hotels. It was undeniably pleasant here. The best thing, she reflected, was the iron grillwork just outside the window—a delicate design. Across the street a splotchy white wall bore a burden of tattered political posters, screaming for readers.

Carmian said, "I should like to wash."

For a moment Dima, coming from the kitchen, looked startled. "Yes, of course," he said, "we'll all wash. Won't we, Boris?"

"Yes," said Boris loyally.

She was wearing an old shirt of Dima's that Lala had given her, and pulled it about herself preparing to get up, but he would not let her.

There was no running water in Lala's apartment. He went downstairs to the courtyard pump, returned with a pailful, poured some into a shallow pan, warmed it on the stove and brought it to her. She washed first her face, neck, and arms, while Boris vanished modestly behind the screen. Dima knelt down, chattering half wildly in the reckless style of Lala but with superior talent, as he dried her feet and kissed her ankles. She blushed wonderfully.

35

There was no toilet, either, in Lala's place; he brought her a couple of tin cans that Lala kept for emergencies of the night, since she was not yet dressed to go down into the court.

Carmian was shocked by these primitive conditions in the middle of Paris but felt, remembering her own mother's erratic way of life, that she was a sailor and a soldier, and it was bigotry to protest against irremediable discomfort.

When Boris had emerged from behind the screen, Dima rolled a cigarette for each of them, licking the paper. They watched him closely.

Boris said, "We ought to have wine."

"*Slushye*, Boris! It's morning."

"After tomorrow night," he declaimed Biblically, "I shall no longer drink."

"That is probably true. You don't drink for six months at a time. After his gigantic binges, Cammie, he locks himself up in the room at Châtenay, and works."

Boris nodded tiredly.

"But the rest of us"—she objected—"we don't have his system."

"Ah, le Tamawak," said Boris, cast down and betrayed.

Toward noon he won the argument through persistent harassing and went out to get a bottle. Carmian paid absently. They all seemed gripped in a spell that was without time, without future. No one wanted to go anywhere or do anything, as if breathing were enough. Dima looked at her and patted her as if he did not believe she were there, and she knew that she wanted all her life to end now, for it could never be any better.

"I've never loved anyone before," she said.

"We'll die together and fertilize the earth."

Boris attended indifferently, but firmly, to his drinking.

Dima was a born storyteller, reminding one of long winter nights spent around stoves and fires in the old Russian *dachas*. He acted them out with his body, like a dancer, and since he could not sit still very long he was soon up like an arrow, swinging his arms, his hair ablaze in the ray of sun that had pierced the window at last— golden hair sticking straight up in back and falling down over one blue eye. They watched the spectacle in utter silence, bemused. He is beautiful! Carmian thought, her heart beating fast. He was not always. He had many faces.

36

". . . After the fighting they got bored in Berlin, so at night they all lay around the corners of a room on the floor in the dark and shot at each other to pass the time. *Kukushka!* they called it. In the morning they would find somebody who had been hit or killed and they would be very sad. After crawling on your belly through mud under fire, you get so bored when the fighting stops! Once at the front, on the push to Berlin from Poland where they liberated me, we were staying at a farmhouse. There was a cuckoo clock, and once they had seen it they had to shoot the cuckoo in the clock. But they did it like this: They lay down across the room with their rifles aimed and prepared to fire, when he came out. He said, 'Cuckoo, cuckoo, cuckoo!' very fast, shut the door quick—and got away. They had not been ready, so they held their fire, and being drunk they were very angry. Siberian sharpshooters, you know. They were not going to be outwitted by any bird. Then"—he tapped his forehead with an expression of dazzling revelation—"one of them suggested turning the minute hand *back* to five minutes before the hour. It saved them a whole hour's wait. They crouched down again: The cuckoo popped out and was shot dead before he could make a sound. His head hung down with all the springs dripping. Everybody was terribly sad. Some wept."

"How unsportsmanlike!" said Carmian.

"Oh, they were simple, pure men. When they liberated us from the camp the first thing they did was to rob the poor devils who'd been waiting for them of their watches, or whatever they had hung on to. Why not? They had nothing themselves. We were shocked and disillusioned, specially the Communists. But soldiers—in rags, with a violated homeland behind them? They got us out, and one doesn't demand morality of such men. I have nothing against the Russian soldiers. Later—after the fighting in Berlin—the commissars began to arrive with their brief cases. With the arrival of the jackals, it was time to scoot." He whistled piercingly through his discolored French teeth and smote his wrist.

"I took a plane along with other displaced persons. It was a service organized by the Americans. I'll never forget the pilot, an American boy. He had nerves of steel, though he was very tired. The plane was overloaded—I don't know how he ever got off the ground —because he let all the refugees take their belongings. They cried and screamed when he asked them to leave their boxes, bundles, and mattresses behind, so he said goddamn-goddamn and took off and landed us safely in Paris. What an infernal ride it was! Oh, let's not talk about the war any more."

"It was you who were doing the talking," Boris observed. "You talk very well, always did."

Dima paused, swept his hand through his hair and walked up and down. "I've got to act. I've got to find a place to live for the Tamawak and me."

The bearded mug of Boris plainly showed alarm. "Surely you're not thinking—"

"We have to live somewhere. You don't imagine we are all going to Châtenay together?"

Boris' eyes shifted to Carmian and lidded over. "Well, perhaps it will do you good for a while. You needed a change."

Dima laughed. "We are staying together forever. Do you want some tea?"

The black eyes grew flat and opaque, and Carmian knew he was against her now. But it didn't matter. It was much more difficult to assimilate happiness.

Dima came out of the bedroom with the rolled white paper that Lala had brought home the night before and hidden. He had forgotten the tea in the process of finding this instead, and he was excited. "Let's see what this is. It's heavy. *Bon dieu!*—but she is strong as a horse."

As it was laboriously unfurled, they saw a printed poster. He held up one copy, dropping all the rest which slid to the floor, and they read:

SALLE PLEYEL   17 Juin, 1950
GRAND CONCERT TCHAIKOVSKY
dirigé par

PAVEL ABRAMOFF
Moscou
Budapesth
Vienne
Berlin
Rome
Paris . . .
IMPRESARIO: OLYMPIADA DE KOUBIANKOFF

38

"Abramov!" Dima shouted. "Who the hell is he?"

"Her lover," said Boris.

"Ridiculous! She hasn't had a lover in thirty years. I don't believe she ever did—she hasn't the sentiment."

"*Olympiada*," Carmian breathed.

"Yes, that's it! Look at the size of her name, my God! She sponsors concerts the way other people play the horses. Every miser has his weak spot. She wouldn't lend me a penny, but she gives it to Abramov."

"He didn't fall on his head," Boris commented drily.

Dima was beside himself. "Once she produced *Coppélia*. At least she danced Coppélia herself. It was very funny. She was in a costume —well, I can tell you . . . part 1926, part gauze, part Lala. She had people throw flowers at her for the curtain call and hurled them back at the audience. It was like a snowball fight. My brother and I rolled in the aisles! I must see this concert."

"Abramov has at least *one* very important talent," Boris concluded. "He doesn't have to be a musician."

When Lala returned in the afternoon there was a terrible scene. She was in a bad humor. Boris was still there, for one thing, and apparently she had failed in one of her business schemes. She ignored Carmian. Dima confronted her with the affair of the concert. She was enraged. What right had he to go into her bedroom and pry into her effects? What had he been looking for? Money? There was no money in the house. Tea, he said. Well, he had no right to steal her tea. It was Russian tea acquired by her brother through secret channels and sent to her from the Belgian Congo.

"Egotist!" he spat at her. "What will Cammie think of you?"

"What do I care what she thinks? This is my house."

"And you are my mother! What kind of mother is that?"

"*Telle mère, tel fils*," she stated smugly.

"Don't get angry," Carmian pleaded, pressing his hand.

"You take them too seriously," said Boris. "I wish I had a cigarette."

"Now you're throwing a fortune down the drain on this fool concert," Dima raged. "I tell you every time not to do it, but you won't listen. Who is this swindler Abramov?"

"It's only two hundred thousand francs," Lala shrieked. "And he is a great artist. It is a great bargain!"

39

"Tartar!"

"They never came into our house except by the back entrance."

"Your own grandfather was a Tartar, with long thin mustaches. A rugseller. Hypocrite!"

"Tartars and Jews never came except by the back entrance," Lala repeated complacently, and then, *Rugseller!* He was a great man! He was at Court—one of the very few . . ."

Carmian looked at a man on the wall with long thin mustaches. He was very dignified and Oriental, with a flat cap upon his head. "What's wrong with Tartars?" she asked.

"I'll tell you what's wrong," Dima cried, as Carmian saw the cheekbone, the slanted eye, all the fabulous historic things, "her mother's name was Velikikotnaya—daughter of the Grand Cat. But the Biggest Cat is right there." He indicated Lala, jerking his thumb.

Boris laughed.

"You see?" Lala rebuked everyone tearfully.

"Listen to me," Dima said, "if you can afford to lose two hundred thousand francs—if you can afford to lose that—lend me two thousand francs till a week from Friday."

Prairies receded. Lala said, "You never pay me back."

"I will. Everything is changed now."

"No!" she said petulantly. "No! I am broke."

A new change came over Dima; he grew purple. *"Salope!"* he shouted. "We are leaving you now."

The exodus was carried out under some protest, but not forceful; she seemed actually to be tired by this time. Boris groaned resentfully under the weight of a suitcase and the burdens of a dispossessed man. In silence they walked a few blocks, then up a side street until they came to the first hotel. It was a narrow whitewashed building with clotheslines strung illegally across the windows. Across its front was painted in blue letters, HOTEL RIFF.

"Let's go in here," Boris said.

"Are you crazy?" said Dima. "The name is dubious, to say the least."

"C'est l'Afrique," Boris said, putting on his poet's expression. "I enjoyed Africa very much."

"This is Paris, and it's full of Arabs, and I've got my girl with me."

"This suitcase is heavy."

"Oh, let's go in the Riff-Raff," Carmian said.

So they went in and took an alarmingly cheap room and left the luggage downstairs to save trouble. There was an iron bedstead painted white, and a washstand. Rapidly Dima inspected the mattress ticking, rolled up the bedspread and threw it in a corner. They sat on the bed, Boris on a lone chair looking like a doctor making a house call, and Dima rolled three cigarettes. They brooded a while. It was not fun any more. He said, "Let's go to Olga's."

"It's too far," Boris said.

"Aren't you going to the syndicate?" Carmian asked.

"It's too late. I'll go in the morning."

"Olga is sick."

"Boris, *voyons!* She likes company."

"Then you go. I want to think. I'll meet you at six—the Dôme."

Olga and her husband lived in a tiny room in the Montparnasse-Convention district, on a lovely leafy street whose name Carmian could never remember afterward. Olga, also known as the *doctoresse*, was a pediatrician, or had been, for she was tubercular. She was a pretty brown-haired woman with a great deal of self-contained despair until she drank and the despair came out. She was the sister of Boris, whom she loved as much as she hated her husband. Her husband, Alexis, was bearded like Boris, with a falcon's face and burning dark eyes. He was an inventor and a prince; his name was one of the oldest of all the princely names of Russia. The room was littered with machine models, miniature boats, and firearms. While she welcomed them kindly, he paid no attention to anyone.

Obviously he was mad, for he knelt at the window with a machine gun, aiming it carefully at passersby.

"His favorite pastime," Olga sighed. "It's not loaded."

"He's just practicing," said Dima jauntily.

They talked of him freely, for long ago it had been assumed that he was deaf.

"For what?" asked Carmian, and wished she had held her tongue.

"He wants to kill them," Olga replied.

"Oh."

Dima said, "He could get ammunition."

"No one will sell it to him. I've seen to that. I've covered Paris."

"He probably would not shoot at all."

41

"The thirty-first time he might."

"Are you working, Olga?"

"A little bit—still."

"How is Fedya?"

"Terrible. Worse and worse. He hits me now; he hits everybody." This was her son.

"Olga," he said, "you must get out of here."

She nodded and took two hundred francs from her purse. "Get us some wine, Dimitchka. You know where it is. Anything you like."

"I can't take money from you, Olga."

"I can see by your eyes that you are broke, and I want it. You're my boy, a good boy. Nobody comes to see me any more."

They said some more things in Russian, and he left.

"You love him?"

"Yes, Madame."

"How wonderful! How wonderful!" Olga said.

Carmian looked past the machine-gunner at the silent street. All of Paris was full of leaves, on trees, in parks, on trellises. But this street was different. They were just one flight up, and looking down on it, at its neatly defined limits, block to block, it stood still as if going out of space and time, frozen in time, a painting by Utrillo. It had not the perspective or the colors of life, but of a painting—with the serenity, the harmony, proportion, of something made up out of a moment's desolation. A street to which people seldom came. But all kinds had walked here along the walls, under the trees, out of the fading perspective: nuns and murderers, lovers and revolutionaries. She could understand why it harassed the sick imagination of Alexis. To her it was a street to look into and dream, knowing that Dima would come back so that she could be happy for all time and soft with love. And if he did not come, still she would stay with the street, waiting. The street was not life at all, but the thing just beyond.

When Dima returned, Olga poured the wine and drank quickly. A red trickle ran down the side of her mouth. She said, "I am so happy for you both."

He muttered thanks in Russian.

"Don't speak Russian when you are with her, Dimitchka. She does not understand and it will make her feel insecure."

"Oh, no! I love to hear it. It's like music."

Olga studied her for a moment. "What an extraordinary girl!"
"She was an international child like me."
"Like us all," she said sadly. "But, Mademoiselle, you are so lucky to be an American. I wish I could go to America—to see the steel structures, the skyscrapers, the land of pioneers. . . . Such nobility, such magnificence."

Carmian quickly put away the thought of Boris' obsession reflected, with only slightly different trappings, in his sister. "Your street is far more beautiful to me," she said. It had begun to rain, and perspective had vanished utterly; it was all gray and soft, as if meant to be touched, all one and unforgettable.

"Ach," Olga said, "it cannot be compared. It is beautiful but not splendid. Tender but not glorious."

Carmian gazed at her suddenly with such sweetness that one tear dropped in Olga's glass. "Yes, that's it. But that's what I like, you see."

Sensing the wine, apparently—since he could not hear it through the back of his head, Alexis put away his machine gun and reclined ceremoniously on the couch which was covered with a kind of furry robe. They merely shifted a bit, making room for him, for no one wanted to sit on the only other seat, a hard kitchen chair. Olga filled an enormous jar and handed it to him. He drank, looking at Carmian like an archaic Turk—as if he intended to chop off her head. Then he turned to writing figures on paper: an invention he was working on.

Olga showed signs of beginning to weep in earnest. They left, uneasily, and went to a bistro for a sandwich.

"That was terrible," she said.

"More than Lala?"

"Lala is not tragic."

"She is comic. But she's a tragedy for others."

"What are their parents like?"

He grinned. "Sweet, gentle, simple people who don't understand their children."

"Ah," she said, and fought down an impulse to say: Boris . . . Boris is the Devil.

They met him at the Café du Dôme, where she bought a round of rum and expressed her wish to go back to the hotel. But Dima saw a Russian friend, and then an American he knew, who bought drinks . . . and it was long before the talking was over. Boris accompanied them to the door of the Riff Hotel.

"I won't see you again," he announced. "I'm going to Châtenay to work." He shook hands with her first, suavely, not making the mistake of many simpler Frenchmen. Then with Dima. But as he took her hand, bonelessly, she met the glittering hatred of his eyes.

She feared him ever after. But it was true, what he had said: They did not meet again.

6   Side by side, half dressed, they lay on the bed and scanned the flaky ceiling. Dima was still nervous about the bed. She was amazed at such fastidiousness in one who had looked as he did the night she met him, who had grown up in the dust-clutter of Lala. "I hate hotels," he explained gloomily. "I would like to take you to . . . somewhere . . ."

"You mustn't worry."

Algerian singing whined through the open window, a ceaseless lament intolerably getting nowhere.

"I suppose you're running out of money."

"Yes, I'll have to go back to Germany and get some more."

"I'll find work. I'm in good standing with the union, in spite of what happened, since they know I work hard. It's simply that I haven't been able to *act*—since I met you. It will pass. I used to like leaving home to go to work. Now I dread leaving you. Do you understand?"

"Oh, very much!"

His voice was flat and remote. "Boris should not have done what he did last night, attacking your suitcase for his *pinard*. I was shocked."

"He hates me."

"You think so?" with interest. "Don't fear; that won't change me."

"I shouldn't think so."

He said slowly: "If ever you will leave me, do it now. There is still time. It wouldn't hurt me now. I would integrate it into the part of me which dreams, until none of it would seem to have been real." With a loose wrist he traced spirals over his head. "It would all become the memory of a dream."

She propped up her chin to stare at him with the fiercest intensity. It was strange of him, and not like a man to share this particular pain of hers, a fear based on apprehension which sometimes brought about the thing one dreaded most. It came crashing back upon her now, a reinfection. Perhaps he was coming to prefer the dream, which could not hurt him, to the reality, which made him helpless.

"I could not leave you," she whispered with awful difficulty. "If you did—I feel—perhaps I'd die."

He held her tighter. "All right. All right. We'll do it together."

"Do what?"

"Live."

In the long silence he stared at the gas pipe that traveled along the molding and halfway down the wall. Like a giant blindworm it lifted its head and broke off abruptly into a jet. "Look," he said, "a trap, this Hotel Riff."

"Does that thing work?"

"If you want to kill yourself. If you were a little bit sad or a little bit drunk."

She gazed at it fascinated. He asked, "Would you commit suicide with me?"

She thought about it. Oddly enough, it caused her no fear. One would never be alone again: in order to be alone you must be alive. But you could not be together, either. She felt as if she had already lost her life, the good and the bad of it, by answering, "Yes. If you wanted to. If you had to."

"Now I know you love me," he said. "But think of it . . . no going downhill, no sinking into monotony, no panic . . . ever, ever."

"One no longer has even despair to believe in."

"No. But once there was an American girl. Her name was Maggie Toland. When I was about twelve she took me for ices in Montparnasse because she was lonely. We became friends and I loved her. She opened a gas jet like this one and died in a hotel room, and she had a million dollars."

She stirred, and said lazily: "Once I knew a little Russian boy in a Swiss school. A fair-haired little boy with deer eyes. There was something wrong, and I found out that his father had committed suicide. It was the first time I had ever heard of such an interesting event, and when I got back to America it was the first thing I told my father on the pier. I said proudly, 'I had a friend whose father committed suicide.' 'Why?' he said. I was terribly surprised at his lack of worldly knowledge. I said, 'Why? Because he was a Russian, of course!' "

"Yes," Dima said in a peculiar voice. "That boy could have been me."

She hugged him and kissed the inside of his arm.

So that was what had happened to the dark man in the picture.

He left early in the morning to go to the stage workers' union and came back at twelve-thirty with Jean-Philippe, who had been waiting for him outside the office of the *syndicat*. J.-P. had brought some money. They abandoned the Riff, leaving her luggage behind, and went to a *frites* place for steak and fried potatoes.

"*Dyevutchka*," he said to her through the fumes of other hungry people eating, "*je t'aime*."

"Say it in German."

"*Ich liebe dich*. You're right; it is better in German."

"What was the other thing? The Russian word?"

"Little girl. For you are that."

He had had no luck. There was no opening yet. His high sloping forehead was lined and his eyes were pale in the sun.

They looked at each other in a kind of hopelessness, but there was something yearning and tough behind it. Carmian said: "I finally counted my money this morning. There is just enough to get to Germany."

"Even after I get a job it will be a week, maybe two, before I get paid."

J.-P. piped up and said, "Isn't there something in Châtenay you could sell?"

"Indeed," said Dima sharply. "And everything I own stays there, understand?"

She decided, "I'll have to find a place to put my things. Then I'll go to Bonn."

They all exchanged glances. J.-P. said: "I'll find you a place today. I'll meet you at the Dôme—six tonight."

Life was getting a little out of hand and becoming a morality play. Boris was the Devil. But J.-P. was on the side of the Angels. She marveled at Angels and Devils, and all the lost children that they had been. And they in the middle, the lovers, inexplicably touching off strange emotions of rage, despair, heroism, all around them.

Dima took her to a telephone booth and called his wife at her office. She worked as secretary to a man who exported farm machinery. He kept Carmian beside him with the door open. He said into the phone several times that he was sorry. He listened for a while and said that he was not coming back. He repeated that he was not coming back. He agreed to a meeting.

White, but relieved, he explained that Denise had laughed at first. "She thought it was just another affair, another naughtiness, and told me to come home to be scolded."

"I don't understand her," Carmian said.

"Nor do I. I never did. If you ever betray me, I shall leave you. If you ever want to leave me, I'll let you go."

They wandered hand in hand along the boulevard Raspail under the great leafy trees. Her habit of turning to stare at people made him laugh—this unabashed contemplation in a grown woman who did not even bother to conceal her feelings, indeed sometimes incredibly mirroring one's own or even anticipating them; a dangerously responsive face. There she would go with her tall and graceful walk, although she was not really tall . . . or stand still . . . and stare, in her own eyes invisible. He never understood just what it was that arrested her in the particular dwarf, businessman, *poule*, tourist, child, or *clochard*.

Thinking of her as a child, he said: "When I was a little boy I wore a sailor suit with the name of a Russian cruiser in gold letters on my cap. I used to go to the pond in the Jardin du Luxembourg with my father and sail my boat."

"Why, that's funny, I went there with my mother! And once there was a boy with a sailor suit, and a man . . ." She clapped her hand over her mouth, and laughed, and gazed at him with round eyes. "I threw a stone at the little boy's boat—and he ran after me. He looked like you, exactly!"

"When was it?" he asked, feeling some impact of lightning.

"Thirty-three or thirty-four."

"It could have been."

"Oh, no—perhaps I made it up. Just now. But I asked what the writing meant on his cap, and my mother said it was Russian. He was a truculent little boy, bigger than me, but I cried when they separated us and my mother took me away. Was it you, really?"

"I felt I always knew you. Do you believe one can remember so far back without remembering what happened, but just the aura of a person?"

"Yes. Of course. That's what happened."

She threw everything in the pot—that's why he liked her. Plus her *tendresse* . . . But it could not be true! His excitement was unbearable: "The man—do you remember him?"

She hammered at her memory. Yes, the man had been dark with a military bearing (or was it merely the photograph on the piano that had inserted itself into the void?). It had been a cloudy day and they—the four—had been alone at the pond: no other children, no other parents.

And now the parents were dead. He gasped with the suspicion that there was perhaps a deeper reason for this mutual passion and the wish for death.

"After all, how many blond Russian boys of that age . . ." she began.

"Oh, maybe many. But I have a feeling it *was* us. If people knew!"

"They wouldn't believe us." She could not, herself.

"I believe it," Dima said. "I must believe it," as if it were a kind of drug that, once tasted, one must have access to forever.

But Carmian, remembering inside herself, knew—or dreamed —better than he the truth of it. Only because of its sanctity, she tried falsely to convince herself of its falsehood, for to be wrong in a belief was worse than to have none at all.

Those had been the years with her mother; a moment in an eight-year-old's wasteland. She had loved her mother but hated Paris and the lovers. And here she was back in it, returned to the scene of the crime. Straight to Port-Royal at first—where the concierge had changed, and from her balcony the square was full of ghosts, their footsteps and laughter—the swishing crowd and the fountain lighted up at night. In 1950 the square was dark, people who passed were isolated and somber, and the café across the street closed its shutters at ten. What had happened to Port-Royal—to everyone?

They had a drink, on the last of Jean-Philippe's contribution.

After that they passed a Uniprix, where she bought the least awful cotton dress for 125 francs, or about thirty cents, since the one she had been wearing was fit for the ashcan and there was no way of getting at her suitcase, which had spent the night in the office of the as-yet-unpaid Riff's concierge.

She changed into it in the ladies' room of the next café-tabac, while Dima gallantly bought cigarettes. It was blue-and-white stripes and bunchy in the middle, but it smelled of virgin cloth. She reappeared saying shyly, "I'm afraid it's a prison dress."

"You make a pretty convict," he said. He carried her old dress rolled up and tucked carelessly under his arm.

She smiled at him, he was such a tall, loping boy and so quick; in the rue de la Gaîté he crisscrossed the street, mindless, a waterbug, looking at the window displays. His curiosity had no bounds.

They doubled back through the Montparnasse cemetery, studying the stones, the names, the little temples and hovering angels. He promised her, as one would promise a holiday trip, to take her to Sainte-Geneviève-des-Bois, the Russian cemetery where his father was.

At five-thirty J.-P. was waiting in the Dôme. He had found them a good room for 450 francs on the rue d'Alésia.

Dima went into a pantomime of horror at the expense, but the matter was settled through sheer necessity. They picked up her bags at the Riff Hotel, Carmian paid the bill, and they continued their weary pilgrimage. She now had not enough money to get to Germany but told herself that a few hundred francs could be found.

They found it the same night in the person of a Russian painter who had known Dima's father. His name was Choukin, and he had an atelier on the rue d'Alésia near Plaisance. He was a saturnine man and painted workmanlike still lifes and street scenes which he occasionally sold. In the rough periods he had access to commercial work such as advertisements for the big firms (Gitanes, Cinzano) and lettering jobs for the small shopkeepers. He was excessively fond of red wine and had the habit of roaring his opinions; but his aspect was benevolent; he was a welcome relief from the shock of Boris and Alexis.

After the little session over red wine at Choukin's atelier, where

49

the few hundred francs were found, they all went and danced the musette in a bar on the rue d'Alésia. Here it turned out somewhat disconcertingly that Dima was a virtuoso. To dance did not fit the rest of him, at least in this disciplined way; perhaps because he gave the impression of dancing through life, carelessly.

In the morning she took the train from the Gare de l'Est to Saarbrücken-Bonn. The beat of the wheels was a wrenching away, leaving behind an uncertainty. She could not be back in under two weeks. They had known each other a week. There were pennilessness and joblessness and Châtenay to ruin her in her absence. She did not know how she could win, and held her head propped in one hand until a man in the compartment asked her if she needed more air.

Yet at the same time, underneath, there was this secret buoyancy —she knew! She knew it would be all right.

It took nine days to accumulate enough money (foreign bank accounts were blocked and she drew out daily the sum allowed for living expenses on a rather grand scale, while living in a student's room, a hole), change her hoard at the bank in Saarbrücken—an illegal transaction in which the bank was her willing accomplice (exemplified in the broad, admiring smile of the clerk: What brass he seemed to say) since it made a 30 per cent profit on the mark exchange, spend the night in Saarbrücken, and return to Paris. She felt rich but exhausted with waiting, anxious beyond endurance and her heart pounded as she arrived at the station one afternoon and went out and tried to hail a taxi.

There was none; it was hot, and suddenly she wanted to die.

"Cammie!" someone said.

It was J.-P. touching her shoulder.

"Jean-Philippe!"

While she fell on his neck, he struggled manfully to collect her suitcase and hail a taxi all at the same time. "You're tired," he said. "Come."

"I've got lots of money," she whispered to him in the taxi.

"Cammie," he said, "I walked all the way across Paris on foot to meet you. Dima asked me to, because he is working at the moment."

"Oh, he did? Did he really?" Then, ecstasy changing, she asked

"But Jean-Philippe, you live in La Motte-Picquet, don't you? Couldn't he give you . . ."

J.-P. the child answered her patiently: "*Il est inconscient,*" he explained.

Her heart shriveled. "But if he is working . . . Where?"

"I don't know yet. You are too serious," he said. "I like you both together, or I would not do what I'm doing. But you must know what you are doing. Don't mind me." He giggled. "I don't."

She sat back and they said no more until they came home.

It was bad to find no sign of him in the room, rue d'Alésia, nothing of him, for he changed clothes at his mother's and carried nothing. He might never have been there at all. She sat down and gathered strength before she could wash and change. J.-P. left to make a telephone call and returned with his zany air of cheerful efficiency.

"He was at the number where he told me to call him, you see? Don't worry," he admonished in a fatherly manner; "it was an interview, nothing more. He will be waiting for us at the Café Saint-Malo, rue de la Gaîté. We arranged everything so that you would not be alone when you arrived."

"I'm glad."

"You see, he loves you," said J.-P. merrily.

Dima was, unbelievably, at a table in the Saint-Malo, in an open-necked shirt with the sleeves rolled up. The sun had made him blonder. He scrutinized her quietly, as if he had not seen her in a year. She gave him a shy urchin grin, sliding in beside him.

They had gin fizzes, for which he announced his ability to pay, while they eyed each other. He had no job yet but had borrowed some money. The union expected something to open up any day; the summer season was beginning. He had been staying with Choukin who also fed him, having made a good sale recently. The concierge at the Alésia hotel had asked for the week; he had managed to put her off. *Voilà.*

"You look all in, *dyevutchka.* Are you hungry?"

"I'm tired. It's a hot, dusty trip, a toss-up between fresh air and cinders. All the third-class compartments are full of French soldiers who put their shoes on your lap when they fall asleep. When we crossed the border last night and the customs men came through I clutched my pocketbook, went out into the corridor as if for air, and started talking to a priest. He smelled brandy on my breath. I'm sure he thought I was trying to pick him up. But they didn't open my suitcase, and they usually do in third even if you're an American. Do you think it was on account of the priest?"

"You must have been terrified, poor girl."

"Yes, and then in the middle of the night I couldn't find a room in Saarbrücken because it was so bombed, so I stayed in an old air-raid shelter—a sort of haven for bums, I think. They lock you in at night, and there are no windows. It's like sleeping in a tomb."

"Have you still got your prison dress?"

"God, yes."

"I love you in it. You look about eighteen."

"Tell her about Abramov," advised J.-P. "That will cheer her up."

In her absence it had developed that Abramov, the conductor of the GRAND CONCERT TCHAIKOVSKY, was a former Red Army officer who had escaped to the Western sector of Vienna, taking a Viennese woman with him. She claimed to be his wife, but generally added that he had raped her first. Lala, in spite of her ancestral disdain for Tartars and Jews, had been inexorably drawn to him. His concert was scheduled a week from now, and he was in jail.

"In jail!"

"Oh, Lala is in a frenzy. She has to bail him out and is resisting; if she doesn't, there will be no concert and she has lost all her money. She is wild!"

"But what did he do?"

Dima hit his forehead with the heel of his hand. "Oh, cet Abramov! He was picked up in a police raid on a moneychangers' joint near the Hôtel de Ville. He had a valise with him which he would not open, saying it was full of music scores, invoking the honor of an artist and the dignity of art. When they opened it, it was full of nylon stockings."

"That Viennese wife is probably expensive," said J.-P.

"She is making him pay for raping her. Lala says that she wears the pants. They live off the Etoile with two telephones."

"A gangster set-up," J.-P. remarked.

"I wonder," said Carmian, "if he can play. Conduct, I mean."

"If not, somebody will cut his throat. For example, Lala."

"Never have I heard so much talk about money. Americans are supposed to be money-minded, not Europeans!"

"They have it," said Dima. "Why talk about it?"

He paid the check, they took J.-P. to dinner, dropped him off at the métro station, and took the bus up the rue de Rennes to Saint-Germain-des-Prés. Dima said: "Your first night home deserves a celebration. Are you too tired?"

"No longer." In fact she was so happy she could not have slept.

They met everybody. Marcel the Arab was there and a dozen other people he knew, including an American Negro poet, the millionaire widow of a French novelist, a Communist spy, and an old-time model turned prostitute. He drew the line only at pimps. Dima glowed, towering over everyone else; he courted excitement all the way to disaster, like his mother.

For the first time Carmian met a man dubbed Picasso, a little old bearded dark-eyed man, a self-styled anarchist, who of course painted. He was the beloved vagrant of the quarter, pushed a vegetable cart by day, slept under bridges, and wore faded checked shirts she had never seen on anyone but Americans; and that was probably where they came from. He was in the company of two faithful friends and gentlemen: One, M. Dupré, a writer of published works, an impeccable dresser in the bourgeois tradition, endowed with a pornographically inventive mind; the other a M. de Bérancourt who was related to the Bourbons and could be seen collecting cigarette butts when he fancied no one was looking, first maneuvering them as if idly with the tip of his cane and then stooping swiftly, delicately lifting them between gloved thumb and forefinger toward a temporary repose in his pockets. What these three of different Estates had in common was a question of some interest until you knew them for a little while. After that it clearly became a matter of age and impoverished circumstances; fiftyish Frenchmen with shared preoccupations: drink, philosophy, the arts, and noble bearing. Among themselves they fought mostly as to whether one should be patriotic or not.

Picasso offered them a drink. He was, of course, the noblest of them all. They had *vin rouge*.

"It's the blood of the good Lord," he said.

Dima asked, "Have you done any new paintings?"

"Yes," said Picasso. "I expect to sell one to an American for ten thousand francs."

"He paints houses and flowers the way he sees them," said Dima to Carmian, "and women marketing. I like the way he sees things. There are no complications."

Bérancourt rasped something unintelligibly detrimental, adjusting his gloves. Rubbing his pink pate, M. Dupré came hotly to the defense of Dima's theory, and they began quarreling. Picasso smiled at Carmian, remote as God in his art, bearded, tired, and dirty from his pushcart and bridges, about to return to some cloud perhaps where he painted.

Dima was impressed with the extraordinary sweetness with which Picasso treated Carmian, for he was regarded as having unspoiled intuitive powers, like a happy child or dog, *sans préjugés*.

She saw immediately that Picasso, like Jean-Philippe, was on the side of the Angels.

7   In front of the Café Montana on the rue Saint-Benoît, they met among the loitering sidewalk crowd of summer tourists, existentialists, artists, students, and fairies, Jerry and his friend, the Americans of the hotel-room spectacle almost two weeks ago. Jerry and Dima were cool; Carmian was affectionate; the other, whose name was Bill, invited them for drinks.

Dima withdrew from the conversation and paid for the next round, a sign of contempt for the company he was in. He would owe them nothing. And violence entered their uneasy circle in the form of a hulking habitué of the Montana whose name was renowned in ballet.

"Beell!" he cried in the heaviest sort of accent, "let me buy you a drink."

"Thanks, not now."

"I will buy you a drink, Beell! Come and sit with me at the bar."

"I'm busy," said Bill.

"But I loff you!" the big man cried. "Can't you see that I loff you?"

Bill instantly assumed the posture of the American whose manhood is under suspicion, and Jerry and the Montana's burly waiter took their cues. The four struggled through the crowd and out the door like a quartet in passionate embrace.

Carmian, feeling vaguely as though it had been her fault, looked at Dima. His face was cold, the cheekbones cruel in relief as always when warm color faded from his eyes, leaving them pale and slanted without the redeeming moisture or shine or sparkle that makes even cruelty less mystifying, less dreadful.

"So that's your American friends."

"You can't blame them. That man is a Russian!"

"There are no homosexuals in Russia. They get that way in the West."

"Nor whores either, I imagine."

"No, not today."

"Hah! You don't mean to say the Russian novelists' little friend has died out altogether?" She had grown angry. "What is the matter with you?"

"Probably your attitude toward your former boy friends. Why didn't you kiss them?"

"Yes, why not? I have friends who like me even though I don't sleep with them. *Better*," she added bitterly.

"You're a different kind of whore," he observed, "a spiritual one."

She wanted to hit him. It was a convulsion in her, but she was afraid. "You're a bully," she said stupidly. "You're no good."

It was the quietness in which she said it, the absolute conviction and acceptance of the fact that killed his consciousness of what he was doing. (*Words do not count*, was his belief, *but actions do*.) He slapped her as he would have slapped a man. Her head rocked. She almost fell off the chair. She grew white and stared at him, but said nothing. Some people turned to look and turned away again. In a place where the recently ejected ballet celebrity held forth, where the Turkish girl who lived overhead came down late at night in a fur coat which on occasion she opened to prove she slept in the nude—a slap was not very interesting.

55

"I'm going," she said, and got up.

He gripped her arm. Dima was paralyzed suddenly with the knowledge of what he had done. It had been an injustice. He was wildly afraid to leave the garish, shoddy crowd he hated so—and the lights—and be alone with her. They must drown what had happened here and all would be as before, poetic and innocent. He would see again her mischievous, sweet, bereft and grievous look that had made him recognize her in the first moment as his twin, as if they had come from the same womb. It was the reason he had left Denise, on finding his twin. *She* had never been of his mind, flesh and blood.

"You're staying with me," he said through his teeth. He propelled her to the bar, where a couple had just left two empty seats. He would anaesthetize her and let her drown the pain he had inflicted. Everything would be the same again. He had just got her back, my God!

She drank with him while his money held out. After a long silence he said, mostly out of nervousness: "I saw Denise while you were away. She is very upset."

"Really," she commented.

"She fell down," he repeated in his broken German, which she understood in all its shades. It meant: fainted. "The little one fell down," he repeated urgently, as if that would explain his behavior as arising from grief for the suffering of another and turn it into something higher, pure and remote from their own petty bickering.

Fell downstairs, her thought echoed, remembering how she had invited death at the age of three in order to capture attention, chasing the shadow of love on the wall that was rich and ripe like her mother but flitting ever ahead so that she could not catch up . . . misjudging the step that wavered, that was missing, not there . . . like her father, and there was the crash, and the pain, and no one to save her.

"She'll get over it," he said aloud, looking anxiously at her profile. Perhaps this girl would leave him. He could not bear to be left. If either of them did, it must be he—and he did not feel in himself the desire to abandon her.

"Do they?" she asked.

"In time. It's all a matter of time."

She thought: I show them my Sunday-school face, my dream

56

ng, listening, gullible exterior. They don't see the insult written behind my dewy eyes.

With intense fascination Dima saw her pick up her glass and fling it across the bar at the mirror. The glass itself was thin, luckily, he noted, and broke without extra damage. Also, no one happened to be in the way. She had done well.

In the resulting pandemonium, the cashier ringing the police which she did at least three times a week and the café employees bawling helplessly for employees higher up, she got off the bar stool and walked quietly through the parting crowd and into the street. He caught her across the boulevard on the corner of the rue de Rennes. Bravo! he almost said. Bravo. And he felt a deep relief, as though by her own action, of which he had not thought her capable, he had saved them for each other.

They heard the *pap-m, pap-m* . . . of the Paris police siren coming closer. From the *comptoir* of the brilliantly lighted Royal Saint-Germain across the street, they watched the raid of the Montana and drank a beer. Only the police seemed bored.

Then they started on the long walk home, for the buses and the métro were no longer running.

Two days later Dima got a call from the union. It was early afternoon. They had been resting on the bed. Jean-Philippe sat writing his book on his knees. Dima dashed back upstairs after communicating on the hotel telephone, dividing the remaining cigarettes neatly on the bed into three stacks, stuck his own share into a crumpled pack in his pocket, and announced that he would be back in an hour. "Stay with her," he told J.-P., bounding out of the room.

J.-P. went on writing. Carmian looked at six cigarettes like rows of soldiers on the bedspread.

Then she got up and cleaned out the drawers, went through her suitcases, straightening things. When it was all done, she pulled out a note pad and pen from the top bureau drawer, settled herself on the bed and began to write a letter to her father. Aside from her concern and her affection for her father, she had learned, on her almost daily rounds to the American Express Company, that not writing letters led inexorably to getting none in return. But she did not much like Paris, and there was nothing that she could tell.

57

She gave up and looked despondently across at Jean-Philippe. "*Ça marche?*" Although his pen was sweeping calmly across the page in unbroken rhythm and he was obviously in full form.

"*Oh, oui!*" With his self-deprecatory yet confident laugh.

She had never felt any curiosity to see what he wrote. She was sure that she would not understand a word of it, though her French by now was almost *du pays*. She had no doubt that it was obscure, intentionally of course, so as to hide the weakness that made clarity impossible: full of artifice, vanity, and the hollow laughter that pointed—intentionally—like a frantic clown to the never-to-be-forgotten, never fully understood, bitterness behind.

For he was not so dumb as Dima considered him to be. (But then Dima lived in a world of naïfs and children, whereas her world conversely was peopled with overshadowing adults.) She would remember the writing of his book: the steady strokes of the pen, the angelic faith, the belief in its destiny. Jean-Philippe would choose a posthumous fame.

"What time is it?"

He looked at his watch unperturbed. "Three-thirty."

In a great weariness of soul she tore up the letter to her father. It was blotted and her handwriting seemed to her unsightly, but she did not want to use the typewriter: naked print to reflect the empty spaces of things unsaid. She would buy a postcard at the Tabac and send him that, so he would not worry. God, she hated writing letters! Or anything, for that matter. Suddenly she realized that she was frightened; the lead in her limbs was fright, and the heaviness in her eyelids, and her sick stomach. Perhaps he was going to leave her. What did the Russians of comic tradition say? You are my father, my mother, my brother, my sister. . . . He was all these, he was everybody.

She flopped on the bed and opened the Russian children's primer that he had brought her from Lala's, or Shura's bookshop, or perhaps from Châtenay. She knew that he had seen Denise; perhaps he would go there tonight. After the dreadful scene in the Montana two nights ago, he might easily decide it wouldn't work and go back to an easier life—do the sensible thing. A painful sentimental dream, if you look at it that way, is preferable to suicide. But she had expressed a wish to learn Russian, and now looked at the book he had

58

brought her. She skipped the first few pages, exercises in the Russian alphabet (which she already knew due to the combination of odd gaps and knowledges that had formed her vagabond childhood—how can an American child know the Cyrillic letters and not the names of more than ten states?) and went on to the words printed in large type under the subrealistic pictures of household animals, mothers and children.

She was sure he had left her now and looked over at J.-P., and asked, "What time is it?"

"He will come back," said J.-P., writing.

She went on with her primer. *Koshka*, she read, for cat. *Sabaka*, for dog. *Matye*, or *Ma-ma*, for the lady with the kerchief around her head. The book was not really very amusing. She turned the pages idly. The poor children who read it must be very bored, she speculated. At the end there were pictures of little boys in helmets with red stars on them, shooting toy guns. The hammer and sickle waved. Stalin smiled from a platform, realistic but repulsive, as if someone had carved him from a box. Poor little boys starting off unwittingly, innocently, on furry Koshka, funny Sabaka, darling Ma-ma, to wind up later with the machine gun, the dictator, the red star on the helmet which was their reward, to fight other gun shooters.

She threw her book down. "He's not coming back," she said.

For the first time J.-P. looked at her as a father. "He is coming back," he said gently. "Don't worry."

"Do you *know*?" she asked the Angel.

He laughed—his joyous but hysterical, impertinent laughter. "He can't stay away!"

"How do you know?" she asked, desperately probing his secret.

"I don't know how," he answered, and went on writing.

Oh, Jean-Philippe. The pictures in the Russian primer swam before her eyes. She felt a listlessness, a fatigue, that tried to close them, though she could not sleep; for worms gnawed inside her. Her hands sank leaden on the open page. *Koshka*, she read, *sabaka*, *Ma-ma*, *Mamotchka*. Oh, happy childhood, not the red stars and the tommy guns . . .

Denise had threatened to kill herself. He had revealed that yesterday as they lay in bed at night, shunning the bedclothes in the warm air of the Parisian June, staring at the bulb on the ceiling as

doomed men do. She had been cold about it, in a flaring of dimly
sensed assault and injustice. In an emergency all her sleeping energy
and rampant languor united to make her strong: long ago, as a child
she had known that threats of suicide were intents to murder, not
to die. He had agreed that Denise would not kill herself (she was
not so sure, and conscience-stricken) and that all would be well in
time. She could repress a misgiving about his complacency—but
after all he knew Denise, and knew where she would go.

Volk . . . that was a wolf and he was snooping around the
henhouse till Pa-pa came out with a gun. On the next page was
a bear named *Mishka Patapovich*, an admirable creature, adorable

She could not close the silly book. Instead she thought, or tried
to think, about the trip to Germany which had evaporated, leaving
no impression, like a journey into limbo. Here, the talk of suicide
filled the air like locusts, like the thousand-bomber raid on Cologne
when, they said, high noon turned to black, and the noise made some
grow deaf, some insane, even before the things started dropping. But
stranger than talk of suicide here was the constant, fantastically impractical, exhortative and hopeless, hopeless, hopeless talk about
money. Oh, terrible Americans who confuse Communism with
ideology—they with their overflowing garbage cans.

She buried her face in the bedspread.

"He will come back," said J.-P., writing.

Then she heard the footstep, light and quick in the hall, and
there was an instant of anger. He flung open the door. His eyes
were awfully blue and first looked toward the bed where he had last
seen her, an anxious skittering look that settled upon her and knew
her and knew she was truly there and that grew luminous with con-
tentment. "I am late," he said.

Then he blazed with triumph. "I have a job!" he cried. "A good
job. Now watch—nothing can stop us now!"

"*Really?*" she said, pressing her hands to her breast.

"Really." He smiled at the archaic gesture and the little-boy
eager look; together they were very funny.

Really, she thought. He has come back to me.

"You are my girl," he said from the doorway.

J.-P. stopped writing and carefully wiped his pen, stowing his
brief case between chair and table. He was hungry and thirsty, too

60

8   Yet the fear did
not leave her. Desertion had to come, since she loved him and the
men one loved always left. No good to say they always came back
—one left only once. The rising spiral had to fall, the curve descend;
it could not rise for ever, nor level off: the climb had been too steep.
Thus, the cards were stacked. Her grandmother who had been
engaged for eight years and married for forty-six could have told her
that.

It was therefore no surprise to her when he called her at the
hotel on Saturday afternoon and asked her to meet him at the
brasserie on the rue de la Convention. She found him reading a
paper, his face unnaturally white and set, and she knew immediately
what it was about.

He was drinking a lemonade. She tucked her thumbs inside her
belt and said she would have a double Pernod, growing as white
as he. They looked at each other in the sun and were silent.

He said, "I suppose you know what I'm thinking."

"Yes."

"Perhaps you don't."

"I do. Go on."

"We can't live the way we have been. The room is too expensive. I have no clothes, for I won't go back to get them. Our
life is haphazard and aimless, no life for a working man."

He pursed his lips in a Frenchman's idea of expressing the sad
irony of life, where nothing is ever produced but *merde,* love being
simply a pastime sometimes leading to babies. But she saw more
than that: his gloomy stare, jaw set awry, distended nostrils.

In a flash of certainty, she asked, "Have you seen Boris?"

"You are intelligent," he complimented her, and smiled.

She made a sound of contempt. "I told you he hated me."

"Perhaps with reason."

Through her despair the anger glimmered. "No other man's
reason can or should be yours."

They sat back in ghastly silence, he reading *Le Figaro.*

61

Then he announced: "I have been thinking of going to Brittany some time in July or August. I'm tired of the city."

"Yes?" she muttered blindly, welcoming anything off the track.

"Will you come with me?"

She took a great gulp of her drink and raised an ashen face to meet his gleam of triumph. Victory, but a calculated one. Where had she failed?

"Will you?"

Blankly she said: "What of Boris?" (How *do* you deal with the Devil?)

"To hell with Boris. I didn't believe a word. There is no one, *dyevutchka*, but you and I."

This was love by mortification and she did not know how to say that in either French or German, and if she had, she would have said nothing. The bitterly coveted dream was hers again.

Dima's new managerial mood led to their moving from Alésia to the rue de Beaune in the Seventh, a block and a half from the quai Voltaire. Its best feature was the location, for Dima was again working at the Opéra, which had a new summer schedule and was within walking distance. He would go across the river to the Palais-Royal and up the avenue de l'Opéra. This was convenient since most of his work was at night and he rarely got out in time to catch the last métro back.

Jean-Philippe had found it for them. It was a shabbier and cheaper room than the last, with a small window on the courtyard, top floor. Carmian loved it at once, for its nearness to the river where the air was pure and its dimly Anglo-Saxon smell—this was a quarter of English tourists. She felt they would be happy here; it was good to hear English again, far removed from Lala and the Russians who seemed to cluster in the south of Paris. There was no trace of Russian or of Bohemian madness, but rather the holiday irresponsibility of the hearty kind, based on limited funds, that Britons and Scandinavians bring with them. The pits of hell were not here. Her heart gave a bound of joy at the presence of the northern Europeans, the breath of the air on the river, the musty smell of the bookstalls, the tar, coal, and oil of the barges—for she had no real alliance with hell, as Boris had perceived.

Dima softened. She saw it with incredulity and happiness. It was true, then, that love was to begin and not to end. And after a week in the rue de Beaune, it became quite clear. They were married to each other.

Hunting on the first day for the best grocery, the wineshop, the hardware store, the butcher shop, the dairy—all the tiny complications of gathering provisions in France—they started out together, then split up in order to divide the labor. He was working at night: but knew that she needed his help, for her French was still unequal to that ordeal. She went into the bakery as he disappeared around the corner, then into the Tabac. Then she stopped in the hardware store and bought a broom, some alcohol for the spirit lamp, and a pot. She started toward the hotel two blocks away, and heard . . . perhaps moments later than it actually happened . . . a woman's scream. It tore the mild evening air, reechoing like the klaxons of the taxis in the chasm of the street. She turned and saw no one, no sign of commotion, and hesitated, not knowing what to do. At the same time she heard a second cry, the shout of a man. She thought: It must have happened in the next block, and turned, her arms achingly full, toward the hotel, the scream haunting her.

She heard his voice: "Cammie!" edged with terror, and his feet pounding after her. He caught her up, broom, pot, petrol, bread and all—"I thought it was you!" he sobbed. "I thought you had been run over! I thought I heard you scream!"

"I heard someone screaming," she said dazedly, clutching the things.

"I thought it was you."

"Why—why?"

"Because you never look crossing the street. These narrow streets . . . It sounded like you!"

"No," she said, tears in her eyes. "It was probably a fight—an *histoire de ménage* someplace."

He looked at her long and rubbed his face as if he had been dreaming. "Thank God."

"Don't you think it was a fight?"

"Go on upstairs. I have another errand—I'll be up in a minute."

But he never did tell her what he found out, if anything.

J.-P. had been given the gate by Lala. She had tracked him to his current sleeping quarters in La Motte-Picquet and discovered why none of the Abramov concert posters had appeared on Paris billboards. They were all under Jean-Philippe's bed, loosely rolled up.

Jean-Philippe's eyes widened in horror, describing the scene. "*Elle était comme une folle!* I thought she was going to attack me bodily."

"All the same, J.-P., you ought to have affixed the posters," Carmian chided.

"I assure you I had every intention . . ."

"With the concert billed for tomorrow night?"

"*Eh b'en*, she wouldn't advance me any money, so I couldn't take the bus. Her manner of conducting business is more or less bizarre, as you know. I'm not going to go running all over Paris on foot to stick up her posters, *voyons*."

This spirited self-defense goaded Dima into pointing out that he went everywhere else on foot; that, J.-P. declared, was another matter.

"Well, probably no one will be there, but we'll go. She gave me tickets, but I wouldn't miss it for anything—even if I had to pay."

"Not me," said the secretary. "For me it is rather a question of avoiding her whenever possible."

"After tomorrow night, for Abramov too, I'll bet. He may find himself back in the jug."

"He's not a type to stay in long."

Their seats were in the balcony among the less prosperous Tchaikovsky lovers, many of them young Americans and students from the Latin Quarter. The hall, which was in Havre-Caumartin, was full, the balcony jammed with people sitting in the aisles.

"Heavens! How did she do it?" said Carmian.

"Too many people like Tchaikovsky." He was gleeful with anticipation, and she noticed the funny little click in his throat, like a touch of asthma, that came and went with his excitements. "Oh Cammie, if only you could have been backstage the time in London when she mixed up all the ballerinas' shoes just before curtain time. They had to go through a big basketful, weeping and cursing."

The orchestra was tuning up; the audience grew settled and subdued. Abramov strode to the podium. He was about five foot three, shaggy-haired, exhibiting a broad and charming smile before he turned his back and opened with a thunderingly energetic *Marseillaise*.

He conducted the Overture to *Romeo and Juliet,* the Symphonie Pathétique, and the Overture of 1812. His style was acrobatic and wildly unrestrained; he leaped, plunged, tore his hair, and during the crescendos flew in several different directions. Yet for some inexplicable reason he was good. At last slapstick was the winner in what had been a close race when, shortly after his plunge into the Overture of 1812, Abramov's pants began to fall down.

It was so much the sort of thing Dima had been expecting—the Marx Brothers quality that haunted all of Lala's artistic efforts—Carmian could not believe her eyes. That the suit was not his own and much too big for him had been visible from the start; only the courtesy of the audience had forestalled initial comment. When he began tugging at his waist and then holding one hand there permanently while conducting with the other, the inevitable conclusion was that his suspenders had snapped. Little by little the balcony audience underwent a metamorphosis from rapt listening to tentative, suppressed, and ultimately violent merriment which they attempted fiercely to conceal with rustlings, coughs, and the like. An American boy and girl on the aisle steps rocked together in silent seizures. Dima seemed about to choke. Carmian was doubled up. "*God,*" he told her, "it's better than the *Coppélia*—it's the best thing I've ever seen!" They caught a glimpse of Lala frantic in the wings, gesticulating.

At the end Abramov turned, spread one hand in apology, grinned, and bowed to receive an ovation. The musician had triumphed after all. He left the stand to get pinned up by Lala and returned for an encore, an orchestral version of the Andante Cantabile. Dima sighed like a child. The fun was over.

Afterward there was a *souper* with caviar, champagne, Lala, the Abramovs, Shura Gavrillovna, Dima and Carmian and assorted Russians. Madame Abramov was a stately beauty in a fur stole, a head taller than her husband. Lala's sister Shura was cool and phlegmatic and spoke excellent English; she did not drink, and left early: a woman of business who had invested her lion's share (so Lala claimed) of the fortune smuggled out by other sisters (Lala claimed) in a thriving Russian bookstore. They had done it with diamonds in cut-crystal glasses, an impractical means, thought Carmian, a seasoned smuggler herself, of conveying wealth across

65

frontiers and through customs. (The brothers apparently had stayed in Russia or vanished into tropical wildernesses.)

With Shura's departure, the atmosphere lightened and everyone except Lala drank a great deal of everything: Lala did not have to; her emotional pitch was fully equal to the highest stage of intoxication. Dima prevailed upon Madame Abramov to tell the story of her elopement with Abramov. She was delighted, pulling her stole around her splendid shoulders, although it was a warm night.

"He broke open the door with his boot," she began unromantically. "My husband was away on business—you can imagine my terror! There he stood, Abramov, dirty as a pig, in a uniform twice as big as he, staggering under the weight of the arms he was carrying: a cartridge belt, a rifle, a machine gun, and a pistol cowboy style in a holster at his hip. He looked as if he had been on some dreadful binge, but I suppose he just wanted to impress me. 'Come to bed,' he said. I said, 'You had better unload first.' He threw it all on the floor, clank-clank. The place looked like an ammunition dump. Three days later we fled the Russian Zone to the West."

"Now she treats me like a dog," said Abramov.

Lala pursed her mouth delicately, pretending not to have heard this shady narrative. But she offered pointedly: "Russians are not what they used to be."

Dima said, "Thank God."

"A gentleman used to kill himself over you before he would even touch you."

"Like that one who blew his brains out beside you on the divan?"

Her face lit up at this reminiscence. "Poor Volodya! No, he did not do it on the divan. Out of consideration for his hosts, he went into the kitchen and held his head over the sink. He had beautiful manners." She smiled archly and sadly at everyone. "He loved me too much! We were terribly shocked."

One agreed that the evening had been a brilliant success and kissed everyone solemnly on both cheeks as the party broke up. Lala was flushed with her victory.

It was only next day that she realized she had miscalculated and committed a financial error that cost her, with Abramov's tacit aid, her two hundred thousand francs. He had absconded. From then on 's name and any mention of the GRAND CONCERT was anathema.

66

In escaping from Russian madness to the rue de Beaune, it appeared that they had come straight to the Anglo-Saxon brand. The first sign of this was their meeting with Miss Fairbanks, the Honourable Genevieve Fairbanks, on the hotel staircase, while the *minuterie* went off. Hurled into darkness they exchanged mutual sentiments of sympathy and indignation, while Dima groped his way to the proper button, and then they parted with great affability. She was, Dima had noticed, the Englishwoman who typed all night with the door open on the floor below them, the fourth.

Sunday noon, Miss Fairbanks in a rusty black suit and a green velvet tam, was at the telephone in the concierge's office. She was thin, highly rouged and beak-nosed, at some age over fifty, and spoke idiomatic German in a loud, clear, British voice. She said that she had heard them conversing in German and how nice it was to meet someone who was something else besides English and French for a change. They replied that they were American and Russian and spoke German for the sake of convenience. They had both been born there, Dima elaborated, he in a prison camp, his wife in the foreign service.

How enchanting! she cried. Fancifully she added that then Germany was in a sense their mother, and they brother and sister.

In a sense, he echoed wryly. He strung her along as he did everybody, mostly telling the truth but choosing carefully from his store. As usual his intuition was right; Miss Fairbanks' father turned out to be a British colonel. They invited her to the particular corner bistro which had once been Marie Antoinette's private stable and sat on some kegs and drank apéritifs.

The world consisted of bright new blue mornings here, rare and clean, sharp in the air from the river, with the barge smells. Miss Fairbanks' faded blue eyes, like an old mariner's, went well with it. She saw suddenly that Miss Fairbanks had joined the little crowd, those agents of fate, J.-P., Picasso, Boris, who would not leave them. They were extraneous to their lives, yet they managed in some way to manipulate them, as though by being the lovers they were they had become both powerful and vulnerable, a mass still unformed with potentialities of unification and explosion, that attracted the tinkerer, the welder, the mover, the creator and destroyer. She did not yet know whether Miss Fairbanks was Angel or Devil, nor did she care much.

67

"We put her in our pocket," Dima said when they were alone at lunch. "You will see, she'll be with us day and night, like that crazy boy."

"I love J.-P.," said Carmian.

"I know," he said kindly with his peculiar sweetness when he was happy.

She watched the white bridges through the window as he read the Sunday *Figaro Littéraire*, bridges gleaming like ivory in the sun, the bridges of kings.

Miss Bixby was their next acquaintance. She lived on the first floor with a vagabond named Jo-Jo, an ancient spaniel, and—occasionally—Miss Fairbanks. The courtyard, an unnaturally efficient transmitter of sound, often carried their voices combined in contrapuntal discussion up to the top-floor window as from a deep well: the sharp, brittle soprano and the monotone contralto. Miss Bixby, of the Bixbys of Boston, had wings of dark-brown hair drawn soberly back from a pale and thoughtful brow. Miss Bixby too had a typewriter.

Dima, lying with his feet up the wall, commented: "This hotel is nothing but Anglo-Saxon women with typewriters."

"Better than Russian women with the ballet."

"More restful, yes."

Somewhere below, too, was a Swiss girl whose voice carried up in Mozart arias. They knew she was Swiss because Miss Fairbanks had said so. She had the sudden break from high to low, the swoop that broke your heart, the rich tone that Mozart loved. Carmian was jealous of her and turned her face to the wall.

He put his hand on her shoulder, feeling the flesh as a sculptor feels clay. She was depressed, he knew, but he did not know why.

She made a gesture of thrusting him off, repelling his arm, and he went into a rage. She stared horrified at his burning face. "Never —never do that!" he choked. "Words are nothing, but actions reflect the soul. It's the gesture, the action, that hurts, do you understand?"

Frightened, ashamed, she defended herself. "You slapped me once. In the Montana."

He gazed at her deeply, bitterly, but had no answer except to gather her into his arms.

"L'âge de virilité n'est pas gentil," he said.

68

shameless grin of a ragamuffin; it was shocking to see such mischief and wickedness in those rouged and powdered, ravaged, haughty features. It was like looking into Miss Fairbanks and seeing, instead of an English lady, Huckleberry Finn.

Jo-Jo gave them brandy and soda. It was Courvoisier, and they accorded Miss Bixby the look of respect that such hospitality evokes in most quarters of Paris. They talked of literature and the writing profession. Miss Bixby was doing a translation of Apollinaire. Jo-Jo refused to show them his poems—at first. To atone for his rudeness Miss Bixby asked if Carmian were writing, and Carmian said yes, a short story; she wrote long short stories and short novels that no one knew what to do with in America. Miss Bixby nodded in a melancholy way.

Meanwhile Miss Fairbanks had Jo-Jo refill her glass. Dima complimented her on her black suit. It was a Paquin creation, she averred, old, *bien sûr*, but still good. In those days she had had a public relations job, a vast apartment on the Etoile, and fifty pairs of shoes at one time. Then the war had come . . . the Germans. She was interned, herded down to the south of France. When she came back all was changed. She had some money in England, but the rotters made difficulties for her. They hated renegades, people who had the sense to stay away.

Carmian could scarcely believe her ears. She had never met anyone English who did not like the English. "Don't you want to go back?"

"My poor child, they are the most utterly impossible people! Smug, contemptible, mediocre. Frightful chumps, my dear."

"Genevieve," Miss Bixby chided calmly.

"Oh, I don't care!" said Miss Fairbanks, flopping back on the bed, crossing her legs and swinging one foot in the air. The spaniel slid to the floor, grunting. Dima twinkled at Carmian—a bright blue look of joy. To him, she supposed, Miss Fairbanks was a sort of British Lala, both springing from a Keystone Comedy of his own conceiving.

"*Qu'est-ce-qu'elle dit, la* Fairbanks?" Jo-Jo asked. It was plain he detested her almost as much as the spaniel.

"Da-arling, you don't really care what I say. I'm having a dreadful time writing my article and it makes me rather upset. Do fix me another drink, Jo-Jo."

Carmian had read part of her article. It was on the subject of saving money as a tourist in Paris and contained such helpful hints as: "Get a room in one of the smaller hotels. Walk-ups are cheaper than hotels with elevators. It may seem tedious to climb four or five flights, but one can grow fond of them—even when there is no need for slimming!—if the room is pleasant and has a good view." (Miss Fairbanks' own room had a sullen view of drawn curtains across the courtyard.) There was brisk chatter about resisting taxis and venturing down into the métro for only a few pennies. If one had the enterprise to apply for a worker's or steady commuter's ticket, the cost of transportation could be whittled down to almost nothing. "You will have to forego shopping sprees at Maggy Rouff's," she breezed on coyly, "and Balmain's!—and concentrate on the smaller shops or the department stores like Printemps, where Paris chic and quality can be acquired at prices to suit your purse."

This last had particularly impressed Dima in conjunction with the tip about workers' commutation tickets. He himself had never bothered to get them because they were based severely on *allez-retour* trips every day, six days a week. But best he loved Miss Fairbanks' comments on food. Here she evidently forgot her original premise and recommended the finest restaurants in town, with lingering descriptions of *spécialités de la maison*. "She got hungry," he had remarked, shaking his head.

"Jo-Jo," Miss Bixby murmured discreetly, "Suzie has to go out."

"Let her go," he growled. "That is her affair."

"I'll take her then. Poor thing, she is so old," she told them, "she has to be carried up and down stairs."

When they had gone, Jo-Jo said: "It costs her $150 every time they go to America. Suzie travels first class."

Dima asked: "Would you go to America?"

"You're not crazy, old man? She wants me to go, but that's not for me. I love Paris, I love the Seine. I'll die here."

"So shall I," said Miss Fairbanks.

"Perhaps; but in a different corner, please." He got out a loose-leaf notebook and began to read his poetry. There was the same sense of surprise as on the night of Abramov's concert when he had proved to be a musician. Most of Jo-Jo's poetry described the Seine, bitterly, hauntingly, and with a despairing love that left no doubt as to the many times when he had wanted to join her, be pulled away by her currents and dragged to the bottom.

Miss Bixby and Suzie came back. She served crackers and cheese, and presently Miss Fairbanks, replete, tottering slightly, climbed to her room. The brandy was gone. Jo-Jo, having read his poetry, abandoned serious things and announced that he was still thirsty. There was a polite verbal scuffle; Dima hung back in order to help Miss Bixby coax Jo-Jo back into the room, for his favorite exit was by way of the window. He stood poised on the ledge, hanging onto the balustrade, hailing people who passed below as those inside remonstrated with him. Then he dropped one *étage* into the street, as once he had dropped from a Gestapo jail, and was off. Dima and Carmian expressed their regret to Miss Bixby for Jo-Jo's departure, their thanks for a lovely time, and invited her out to supper. She declined sadly.

Later they saw him in the rue Bonaparte in the company of Messrs. Bérancourt, Dupré, and Picasso. They fled past.

"Why does Miss Bixby live in that dump of a hotel?"

"Because Jo-Jo drops out of windows."

"Why do we always meet such peculiar people?"

He looked at her. "We are not exactly the norm."

"I love them, but we must find an apartment, darling."

He swooped upon her, prancing like a colt in his optimism. "We will have everything in time! Be patient."

"I can't help feeling the gods will get angry first."

Didn't one have to be dull in order to survive? The fear of loss was ever so much more tragic than the dreary routine in which there is nothing to lose. Fate must be appeased. One could not laugh or love too much without retribution. The virtuous reformed are punished, not the bad.

He smiled to himself, but tenderly, sensing her fear. She was a sensitive one. Also, she threw everything in the pot: a gambler. That was why he loved her.

But she was worried about the thinness of it, the weakness of foundation. For if it was too weak, if it sank, and he and she with it, she would be thrown away.

Denise had been silent a long time, expecting his eventual, humble return with the patience of a strong woman. Now, almost a month after his departure, she called him up at the Opéra and asked him to meet her during the lunch hour. He arranged it for his day off and took Carmian with him.

73

"I don't know if I ought to," she said.

"Don't be afraid. She is not bad. And very intelligent. That's what counts. The worst combination is stupidity and malice, like Lala's."

"Perhaps this is more frightening."

He looked down at her thoughtfully. Her palm was damp and her upper lip beaded with sweat, but she showed no other sign of nervousness, walking lightly, skippingly as usual, chin high. She reminded him of the figureheads on the prows of old ships. Seeing her, Denise would know that they belonged together. In the street Parisians always noticed it.

"She will see at once that it's not just another affair. They never disturbed her. But Boris has been talking to her, and when she sees you . . . She has the character not to feel herself when she knows a thing. And she knows me well."

"But she's your wife! You talk about her as if she were your mother."

He laughed grimly. "That's the way she always treated me."

"Well, I'm coming because you want me to. But I don't like meeting rival women."

"Have confidence in me," he said. They ran after the bus and swung themselves up.

But he was pale as they waited in a small café behind the Opéra. He fiddled nervously with matches and watched the door, where there was a trellis with leaves very green in the sunlight and blowing. Then Denise came in, hesitated, saw them and headed straight toward them. She was small and slim but stockily built below the waist, with muscular legs; very trim in a summer suit with pearls around her neck and low-heeled sandals.

He rose. "Mademoiselle Wills—Madame de Koubyankov."

For a moment she looked outraged; her eyes grew liquid, flashing coldly, and she seemed about to turn and go. "I didn't know she was coming."

"No, sit down. I asked her to. I wanted you to meet her." (Persuasively, yet bashfully, almost proudly, as if he were saying: Look what I have here! See what I can do!)

It was outrageous. Carmian shriveled.

But precisely that blatancy and crude innocence appeared to soften Denise. She gave Carmian a critical, distant glance and sat

74

down across from him, pulling off her gloves. "Well, then, how are things?"

"Fine. What will you have?"

She asked for a menthe-and-soda, folding her hands on the table. They talked about his new job, about the boy, Lala, Boris, and the latest events in Châtenay. Her smile was extraordinarily sweet when she grew animated; it exceeded the conventional charm of her coronet of braids, her regular features, her modulated well-bred voice and large, dark, slightly hyperthyroid eyes. She seemed to brood over him tenderly, like a nurse, obsessed with his well-being.

She had decided to fight, thought Carmian in despair. Half Austrian and half French . . . how pretty she was! She sat in a longed-for obscurity until Dima, impatient with the deadlock, remarked, "Carmian speaks German too, as well as English."

"Really?" Denise said politely in German. "Are you of German origin?"

"My mother," said Carmian.

She kept her eyes on Carmian's face a little longer than necessary; they had a shiny round surface, like bulbs, like the dark eyes of a cat. Underneath there was the sense and expectation of victory, yet something compassionate too. Her eyes promised sympathy—if all went well.

She was powerful, and Dima weak. He still was baffled at her lack of warmth toward his woman, amazed that she was not happy for him—in spite of his perfectly normal awareness that jealousy was to be expected. Carmian prepared herself for the guillotine. No one as disorganized as they could win against someone as neat and strong as Denise. She could see a kind of blandness and vanity spread over his face as he listened to the caressing voice, not condoning but pardoning his prank. He was lost, she was sure, and she cast out. She hoped she would have the courage to walk out, through the door and under the trellis, without further ado. She did not begrudge Denise her success; a man's desertion was harder to bear.

As if sensing her acceptance of loss, Denise leaned toward him across the table with her ravishing white smile. "Let's stop all this nonsense now. Come home with me, and"—she sparkled with forgiving humor—"I shall spank you."

Carmian stirred imperceptibly, but he did not miss it and took her arm above the elbow, meaning: Hold on. It was the turning point, she knew, if there had ever been any reason for her misgivings, and her heart lifted.

"You are a terrible boy, you know. You were always a terrible boy."

"I am, I know it," he replied seriously. "I can't come home with you. I shall never come home."

"Why not?"

"I am going to stay with her."

"Is that your final decision?"

"Yes."

"In spite of your son?"

"Yes."

The three of them trembled at the table. "Then you want a divorce?"

"Yes."

She pushed back her chair and stood up, pulling on her gloves. Her self-control was nearly gone. Fury leaped in her eyes.

"Denise, we never got along."

She marched to the door. Carmian watched her go with a feeling of relief and deep desolation, thinking that she had behaved very well . . . thinking about the brave, straight backs of women . . . and imagining that it was she, herself, walking out under the leaves into the street.

10

The Korean war broke out. First there were the klaxons, the general excitement, and the Americans walking about with a serious, mobilized look, a kind of special halo that set them apart. One looked at them with pity, with admiration, or contempt, depending upon one's political views. There was Miss Bixby's sonorous missionary voice ringing in Bostonian French in the courtyard, sounding up the corridors and on the sidewalk, in the bistros and in the *épiceries*. She held political sermons in all of the shops of the rue de Beaune, rue de Verneuil, rue du Bac. Gentle, measured as always, but with a new ardor, she was listened to kindly and considered mad. Miss Fairbanks, too, was

76

volubly pro-American. Outnumbered by women, Dima sided with Jo-Jo and the North Koreans.

Dima and Carmian assured each other that it did not affect *them*, that the outside world was alien to them; but the truth was that it mattered more to them than to anybody that the world stay whole. The specter of a war between his motherland and the land of her fathers, though they considered themselves homeless, loomed fearfully in their eyes. It set them at war with each other, each following the pull of blood and roots, with the ferocity of civil wars and family feuds, for they had believed that they were everything one to the other, excluding nothing. The Korean War became the framework of a raging private one, a war of competitive verbal assault, of real or fancied hurts, of jealousy and rebuff. It was easy; in love all injuries are magnified.

The upshot was, during that first week, a battle on the corner of the rue de Lille. Dima had been doing some drunken and well-calculated scoffing and sneering at the Americans, when she plummeted into an abyss of rage and near delusion, crossing an unknown territory that made her lose her reason and behave as she might have wanted to behave in some wild daydream or nightmare of her childhood. She was the stronger, for justice was with her, and she would win—*little* as she was! She swung her shoulderbag round, twice, by the strap like a lasso, and hit him square in the face.

He in turn lost his mind. She saw the frenzy of her first open attack, forthright revenge, reflected as it flashed upon him that all the insults and harassings had not been forgotten, buried, but would fester and grow. She went at him, at his throat like an animal, to strangle the cruelty in his eyes, the black murder in his heart before he could get her. He was the Tartar face, the face of the steppes, under the street lamp the first night—

He laughed, incredulous, and beat her off with the flat of his hand. She came back at him, and he sent her sprawling. She came back.

"Stop!" he said. "Or I will kill you."

She came on wildly, without hope, and he knocked her down. The strap of her shoulderbag was broken; it lay in the gutter. He picked it up and tucked it under his arm. Then he picked her up and carried her to the hotel, half-carrying, half-pulling her up the stairs. He put her to bed. Already the welts and bruises were beginning to show.

77

She stirred. "I lost," she sobbed, "I lost. . . ."

"Go to sleep," he said, stroking her face and wondering what archaic battle it was that she had lost. He wet a towel and put it on her eye. Then he undressed her, himself, and lay down beside her until sleep came.

In the morning he had gone. Perhaps to work, perhaps forever. She did not know if she cared or not. She got up after a long time, looked at her eye in the mirror over the washbowl, washed and put on her freshly laundered prison dress; it seemed appropriate, and she remembered with sharp pain that he had said he loved her in it. After a while she felt unable to stand up any longer, lay across the bed, and started to read a red-covered German edition of *The Possessed* (*Die Dämonen*) that Dima had bought at a bookstall. He did not come home for lunch. She looked at a page of her unfinished story hanging from the typewriter, looked at her watch, and went on reading in a kind of coma. Later she had to reread that part.

He found her asleep face down, her rich hair spread over the open book. He put his groceries on the table. When she looked up he was sitting there strangely inert, his face gray, blue-shadowed. It was the face, she realized with astonishment and pity, of someone who was suffering.

"Let's try once more," he was saying. "It must never happen again. It has never happened to me before. It was inexcusable."

She nodded mutely.

"Will you try it with me once more?"

She nodded, tears welling up. They seemed to cheer him a little. "I brought something for your eye. Come, I'll fix it."

She let him apply a compress, staring at his hollow, stricken face with the free eye. He said busily, "I know you haven't eaten anything all day. I've brought you some food."

"Thank you. I can eat now."

"Do you like the book?"

"Yes. You are a Stavrogin, you know."

"Really? Why?" he asked, not displeased.

"I don't know. Do you remember where he goes as if to murmur something flattering into a harmless functionary's ear—at the party —and bites it?"

"Dostoevsky said, '*Der Mensch ist unergründlich.*' "

"Man is unfathomable. To whom?"

"To others and to himself."

78

"I don't believe that. I believe there is a reason for everything."

"Superficial scientific nonsense. I believe that a man can change —without apparent reason; that he is not always doomed to follow a track, a rut."

"I think most of them do."

"That's Balzac. Once a miser always a miser. How dull! How much greater Dostoevsky is!"

"Yes. Perhaps if one suffers enough—if one is forced to change, or die—one can change one's being."

"You doubt because you don't want to change."

Perhaps, she thought in her remorse. Perhaps that was true.

They began having most of their meals in their room, since this was cheaper and more convenient, and presently discovered that the mice who had been inhabiting the rooms of other people, such as that of the young couple with the baby next door, were democratically exploring theirs. When she saw three mice (or the same mouse three times) in one day, Carmian told Madame la concierge who sometimes came to the top floor with a broom and a dustpan to chat, for service was included.

"Oh, I'll fix that!" Madame said immediately. "I'll bring you something. They infest these old buildings, you know."

Carmian expected some chemical powder and the saddening corpses of little brown mice strewn about, so that she was almost relieved when Madame, with the self-satisfied air of the fixer, brought a cat.

"She is pregnant," said Madame unnecessarily, "and cannot run very fast. But she may frighten them away. Try her for a few nights. She will eat a little gruel, or perhaps some *moue*."

"A cat who works for her living," Dima commented, "even while *enceinte*. See how frugal they are, the French!"

A few days later he grumbled: "I think we ought to fire her. She eats too much and is friendly toward mice. She scratches me at night. She'll have the kittens in our bed—I can *see* that's where she plans to have them."

"She may feel bad if we fire her."

"I have no sentiment for this cat. She is too greedy and utterly absorbed in her condition. She did nothing about the mice and I'd rather keep them anyway; they eat less."

Carmian rendered her to Madame with thanks and lied that the mice had gone. This evoked exclamations of pride and satisfaction and the offer of a further loan of the cat, which Carmian refused.

In the course of her usual chatter, Madame dropped the hint that Miss Fairbanks on the floor below was becoming a problem of the worst kind for a French landlady: That is, she represented a financial hazard of frightening proportions, since she had been unable to pay her rent for two months and—worse—was continuing to accumulate a debt that even someone steadily employed would have difficulty in paying. Madame's problem was (1) that she could not let her keep a room which normally would be bringing in four hundred francs a day—in this, the tourist season—and (2) that she could not put her out altogether, since that would eliminate any chance of a settlement of arrears. The trouble was, she had been too softhearted, too impressed with the literary profession of Miss Fairbanks to be forewarned.

"I know that you are a writer too," she added ingratiatingly. "I've had many writers living here; they are not all the same. And of course your husband is working. He's a fine boy. You look very well together—sometimes my roomers remark on it: 'Who are the handsome couple on the top floor—are they German?' I always say, 'They are an American and a Russian.' " She giggled. "It tears them up. I vote Communist myself, but I am not overprejudiced." She swept the middle of the floor hastily, having changed the sheets, and departed with her cat.

Gradually it became noticeable that Miss Fairbanks was no longer on the fourth floor although somewhere still in the building, for they glimpsed her going in and out and heard her flawless Empire-bred tones emerging from the ground-floor *salon* where the telephone was. When they next met head on, she told Carmian that she had been demoted to a closet on the second floor.

She took it bravely in a soldierly manner, with an air, however, of hopeless disgust. "My dear, truly, my shoe closet in the old apartment at the Etoile was larger. It must have been a decent-sized room once, until they cut it in half to install the second-floor toilet. It's a hole, you know—I have to have the electricity all day long for typing, and Madame resents it. But she can't throw me out; she's afraid of losing her money. I should care! It's a great nuisance, though. I hear flushing night and day. There is only a thin wall between. The things one gets to know about people—preposterous!"

"Oh, *poor* Genevieve! I am sorry."

"Darling, it's all right," said Miss Fairbanks patting her hand. "After all I've seen."

Casting about for a nation to like, she considered the Americans her favorites really, but rather too well off. She hit on the Germans and at times spoke nostalgically of the Days of the Occupation ("During the Germans," as Lala put it) when she had been a staunch anti-Nazi. That did not deter her now. "Yes," she would say, "I can see where you got your bone structure. They were so good-looking, those first German troops who came in. They called them Hitler's Chorus Girls."

For some reason Dima did not let this rile him. He took her to dinner whenever he could, or invited her to their room for meals. Having nearly starved to death himself, he saw the signs of hunger as casually as a motorist a road sign, even when disdainfully concealed, and her spiritual façade amused him.

After Dachau he had been sent to Poland, where everyone went who was to be put to death, because he was a Russian *Untermensch*. A young SS guard had explained it to him. You are like an ox or a mule to us, he had told him naïvely, with the curious wish to instruct. That's why you're not treated as well as a Westerner. You may not understand it; you're not expected to. Another guard had kicked him one day because he was leaning on his shovel. Dima had lost his temper and spat at him. The guard had taken his revolver from the holster and pointed it at his chest. "No one will care if I shoot you," he had said, "and I think I will." Dima had looked at the empty blue eyes and down at the gun. "That is an Italian make," he had observed. "Where did you get it?" The guard had said, "That's right!" then peered closely at Dima as if in wonder, touched his forehead, muttered, "You're crazy," and had gone away. But they had beaten an elderly Czech professor to death with a lead pipe, for less.

In Dachau he had shared a bunk with an English flyer, a gentle boy of good education. The boy had been dying of hunger, being thinner and weaker than Dima, and had stolen from him a piece of bread that he had hidden under the straw mattress. One morning the English flyer was dead of typhus—for the bread was infected. "That boy saved my life," Dima said.

The reason why Dima was stronger, she learned later.

81

"The intellectuals went to pieces first. Then the Westerners started going. The Poles became informers and guards. The Russians were treated the worst—they were strong as horses. They didn't care whom they insulted and didn't care when they got killed. '*Na plevatye*,' they said—I spit on it."

"*How* can you like me?" she breathed, aghast.

"Germans? Ah—the old ones were good. I was better fed because I went on the *Bomberkommando*, picking up duds, pulling out pins. We all risked our lives but we got extra rations for it and didn't starve like dogs. We had a chance, at least. The old people threw us bread from their windows—it was a piece of that bread that poisoned the Englishman, poor kid. One old woman left sandwiches for me behind a gravestone in the cemetery we used to pass. She said I reminded her of her son who was fighting in Russia. I always knew she had left something there for me—and couldn't wait. One morning I got a fierce headache and thought I couldn't get out of bed. I couldn't understand it. I reported sick and did not go out on *Kommando* that day. That evening I knew, for none of my comrades came back. All five were blown up. They'd hit a live one."

"*Oh*," said Carmian.

"Sometimes," said Dima, "I think it was a terrible dream."

J.-P. turned up the next day after a puzzling span of absence. His father, the invalid, had died—an occurrence J.-P. spurned as a cause for regret. He was rather blithe about it but angry at his father's mistress who had got all his money after driving the old man to death. "He's well off by now," J.-P. laughed cynically, while they winced. He himself looked paler, if possible, than before.

He had come to take her to Gallimard, the largest and most august publishing house in Paris. This summer they were having a weekly affair known as "Le Cocktail Gallimard" at which champagne and food were served. J.-P. had connections there through his father. He would introduce her as an American poetess, and she need do nothing but smile and drink champagne while he went about the business of getting her book a friendly reading in the event that it might be translatable. Unfortunately, the party was that very afternoon, and Carmian, who was conscientious about visiting the public baths but less so in taking out the laundry, had nothing to wear but the prison dress—it seemed made out of iron, and felt like it. J.-P.

said that it would not matter, since poets were fully expected to be poor or eccentric, and wear twenty-five-cent dresses from the Uniprix.

Dima agreed to come too, as Monsieur the husband of the American poetess. He wore his white turtle-neck sweater, a gymnastic item that had come to him years ago through one of Lala's secret channels whereby she received things from her brothers left in Russia. It had been relayed to Berlin by a sister, Natasha, during the Russo-German Pact of 1940. It, too, was clean, although moth-eaten, and awfully dashing.

J.-P. carried his frayed briefcase with an air of confidence. Carmian's fears dissolved after a glass of champagne and a glance at the crowd. It appeared composed of serious intellectuals, beautiful models, eccentric writers like herself, followers of Jean-Paul Sartre in British surplus army coats, and literary bums. All were equally, frankly engrossed in drinking up as much of Gallimard's champagne and eating as much of its delicacies as was humanly possible before the amazing opportunity should be interrupted by a sustained conversation, or brought to a halt by the dictates of polite behavior when departure becomes inevitable.

Dima met a few friends, introduced her as "Madame," and wandered away. J.-P. introduced her to the reigning head of the house and a lovely, English-speaking lady of the foreign books department. Then they went back for more champagne. They met Dima at the buffet; the butlers were already on cordial terms with him. The air bubbled with Gallic conversation about art and men and women . . . in a heat of crowded bodies, brains, voices, gestures, *élan!* (But business was uppermost in their eyes.)

J.-P. led her out into the garden, where everyone walked about with a glass of champagne like, she thought, *Patterns*. There were Queneau and Jean Giono. Gréco was there, posing slenderly yet sad, in her Grecian sandals and long black hair. There were the poet Prévert and the musician Kosma, whose *Autumn Leaves* Juliette Gréco was singing. Carmian was gazing at her when an American came up and introduced himself. He told her he was a literary agent and that he suspected her of being a countrywoman.

"Yes, I am," she said with the involuntary sigh that always filled her whenever she thought she would have to explain to a stranger, or let him perceive in the end, just how unhappily non-American she was.

But for the short duration of their friendship she found that she never had to explain anything.

"I got my dress in the five-and-ten," she said with the *idée fixe* and the calm courage of an abundance of champagne, "and my shoes on the rue de la Gaîté, and I haven't had my hair cut in six months. Now, how do you know I'm American?"

"Your accent," he said unimaginatively.

"Oh, yes. I'd forgotten that part."

"But there's a look, too." He was improving. "It's a spectator's look, with an absence of participation, of greed, competition, avarice. Like innocence."

"You know, that's lovely."

"They all have it. Do you write?"

She was again invaded by fatigue. "*You* ought to write," she reproached him, and waved a hand in the direction of Jean-Philippe, who had disappeared. "That's my French agent."

"Oh! I thought he might be your husband."

"Really! He's only nineteen."

"Well, you can't tell. . . ." He laughed apologetically. "Maybe I've had too much champagne."

"No, that's *him* over there—" She looked through the French windows, spotted him in a large milling group, and pointed. "He's Russian."

"Well!" It seemed to cheer, or sober, him up. "Look, my name's Chedwick. I'm free-lance but I'm associated with a good agency. I'd like to talk to you sometime about representing you in the States—"

"I have a writing block."

He laughed sympathetically. He had sad brown eyes. "They all do. That's one of the jobs of an agent—make 'em write."

"You're fine," she said approvingly, and downed her champagne. "I bet you're from New England."

He gave her his card. Dima appeared and pulled her along in what turned out to be the first general exodus. They could not find J.-P.

"I've got an American agent," she announced.

Dima's eyes flashed. "Have you no shame? Exchanging addresses—"

"I have to, if I want an agent."

"What sort of agent?"

"Literary. He's—"

"How do I know what kind of agent he is—or if he is? He's an American—that's enough for me."

"And for me." She had remembered how she had been admired, petted, and courted, and her chin and lower lip thrust out in rebellion; her eyes grew bitter. Dear Chedwick.

He could not stand it. He cuffed her arm, mildly, but with fury in his face and posture. They were deadlocked in the heavy outer doorway of Gallimard, when a man in a gray suit brushed past them, also angry. He gave Dima the menacing gesture of a Frenchman, waiting briefly for retort, and said, "That is not the way to treat a woman, Monsieur!"

She was dimly astonished at the spectacle of a Frenchman interfering in a lover's quarrel. Dima spat on the sidewalk. "*Je vous emmerde*," he shouted.

"Do you want to fight?" the other yelled.

"Since when can't a man dispute with his wife?"

"When he acts like a brute," the man said. He waited a moment, and walked away.

Dima took her arm and said, "That was the poet Prévert."

11   Carmian had to go to Germany again. She did so philosophically; their money never seemed to last till payday, and they owed rent. This time she made two trips because she had not taken enough money for expenses on the first trip. She had tried to draw on a German bank in the French Zone, had been informed that it must be her original bank in Bonn which had once been under the monetary laws of the British Zone but was now under jurisdiction of the Free Capital, and was forced to return since she had not enough to continue on up the Rhine to Bonn. In the process she wasted ninety American dollars she had hidden from Dima. Now she had nothing. When they had accumulated enough for the second trip, this time through Belgium by the northern route, she returned after ten days with sixty thousand francs.

85

Meanwhile, he had begun paying for the divorce proceedings.

Coming home from Germany, carrying her suitcase across the beloved bridge, the Pont Royal, turning left on the quay and up the rue de Beaune, she saw him in his white gym sweater. He had a wonderful big back, for all his silken-gold hair and baby skin and the feel and smell of tender innocence. But here he was in conversation at a café table, with a Swiss young man, a student, with whom he had swum in the Seine—and drinking apéritifs on him. For the first time she was truly annoyed at what J.-P. called his *inconscience*. To go to Germany nowadays was triple torture: the time away from him, the loneliness, and the sense of loss. For everyone in and from that country whom she had ever loved was dead and gone in the past war, and worse—the most adored one only recently. The ones she met were jackals for her, those who had managed to survive on carrion.

The third day she let him lie alone on the bed late, while she ruffled her hair and paced up and down like an animal in a cage.

"Why don't you write?" he asked, quiet and strange.

"There is nothing," she said.

"Nothing?"

"You will kill me."

He watched her for a minute, then got up and packed his clothes into a bundle. "I'm glad you've done it soon enough. I'll go back to Châtenay."

"No!" The idea was horrible beyond words.

"Oh, yes," he answered smiling, his eyes that could be so blue, so tender and dreaming, or brilliant, turned into green Tartar slits, the wrinkles around them puckered up like an old man's with triumph and cruelty.

He went to the door, and he meant it. Perhaps the relief in the shake of his head . . .

"No!" she screamed, in rage, abandonment, and fear, hearing her own voice ringing endlessly in her ears.

"No?" He smiled with irony.

She rose, flinging her arms away from her body, and cried in German a peculiar cliché: "*You can't do this to me!*"

Something, as even she was aware, had happened to her voice. He narrowed his eyes at her. Her gesture . . . My God, her voice! The words had been nothing at all, but the sound!

"Oh, yes, I can," he assured her, smiling cruelly. But he listened:

86

"You can't!"

He looked at her for a long time, while she laid her hands on her breast, and her expression was unchanged.

A haze of doubt and pain assailed him. But most of all the voice: It was like the voices of Mozart singers, like the Swiss girl downstairs who sang arias from *The Magic Flute.*

It's real, he thought, with a voice like that. Straight from her guts. He threw his clothes on the floor, and lay down on the bed, folding his hands across his chest, so that they gazed stupidly at each other like two people crucified.

For one instant more she had her brilliant black eyes; then she slumped down at the table and held her head.

"Come here."

"No." She shook her head and spoke in quotes: " 'I must save my pride.' " She uncorked a wine bottle with the greatest difficulty and poured a full glass and drank it down and began to weep. "You've made me lose my pride."

"But I am here. Isn't that what you wanted?"

For answer, she wept into the crook of her elbow.

Her voice had changed back but he still heard the notes, swooping deep and dark from the heights of the soprano.

"You sang to me. Come here to me, please."

She came with tears wet on her face. She too heard the echo of what must have been her own voice and knew she would never hear it like that again.

"Il n'y a pas de retour," Dima would say. There's no turning back. He said such things when they were content. One night he took her to a movie on the Champs-Elysées. They came home across the Pont Royal, their arms interlocked, and she felt a sharp pain in her breast and disentwined her arm to see what the trouble was.

"What is it?"

"I feel so strange here. A pain."

"What kind of pain?"

"I don't know!" she said, terrified.

Simultaneously, they gasped.

They looked at each other under the lights of the bridge. And —there was no doubt—they both knew.

87

part

two

the river

12   The specialist
on the boulevard Haussmann said it was so, and congratulated Dima,
who blushed. He prescribed little vials, and after that there was a lot
of vial-cutting along with the *petits gâteaux* in bed, for contrary to
general lore she had lost her appetite and would take nothing but the
vials and little cakes, and could not stop sleeping. The specialist had
been so expensive they never went back. It did not seem necessary;
and things were bad enough.

Dima at first showed concern, which tended to break out in spells
of manic joy. He bounded up the stairs bringing home armloads of
Russian delicacies—caviar, *zilyotky*, sausage, herring, brown bread—
a difficult sight that caused her to swallow hard and close her eyes.
He had discovered a Caucasian delicatessen store behind the Opéra
and spent all his money there. When at his urging she attempted to

89

take a sip of *zubrovka* (a kind of souped-up vodka with a grazing buffalo on the label), her stomach declined with some violence.

He gazed earnestly into her face and asked her what was the matter. Sometimes she was a child to be fussed over and fondled, and sometimes he talked mystically of love. "*Mein Junge*," he called her meaning "my young one," "my child," ignoring by innocent omission of the final *s* that he was calling her "boy." His grammatical mistakes in German were frequent and hilarious.

"You are my child," he said, "and I am yours. I wish I had come out of you—but then I would always want to get back inside. I love your tummy and your navel because you were first nourished there —your life began there. That is where Cammie started."

She gazed back at him blankly with a certain fear because she did not know how to talk like that and did not know what was expected of her. But it was lovely to be the Botticelli Venus in the morning, in the squalor of a hotel room barely held together with bits of wire and string, like all of Paris, washing at the sink in her nakedness, adored for herself and all, all—so he conveyed—that he had been strong enough to capture.

Dima Mikhailovitch had been many things, more than just wild and implausible and full of notions: the snob little boy who had gone to the exclusive lycée in Normandy; the ballet student. Although he had tried hard to conceal it from her, she knew that he had been with the *ballet russe* under Diaghilev and had done a child's solo in *Petrouchka*, immediately after which he refused to leave the arena of applause but stayed, bowing and smiling, until someone dragged him offstage, bringing down the house. This had been during Lala's career, very brief, unfortunately, as wardrobe mistress, and the affair of the jumbled shoes in Covent Garden. Unlike his mother he had been much admired but quit because he was at the age where, Europeanized as he had become, he considered it sissified to dance.

But he was still a ballet dancer; the vanity, the grandiosity and grace were still with him; he danced, walking and waving his arms, prancing, attracting acclaim; but mostly he was the child who whirls round and round with the new-found ecstasy of being alive, though sometimes it stuck in his throat for a moment.

He had tried medicine but had been unable to go on, since he fainted at the sight of a surgical operation, and they'd had to carry him out cold. He had worked in a biological laboratory, another

Russian specialty that Lala had dabbled in during her long exile; as an antique dealer in a Paris flea market, and as a horse trainer for a stable near Châtenay. The last two had worked fairly well until Pierre Presnay and Jouvet gave him jobs in the theater and discovered his talents at stage decoration, for his eye was sensitive and infallible. Finally, during two summers, he had toiled as a fisherman on the Brittany coast, to get away. In Dima there were the proletarian and the snob, the exiled baron and the Paris urchin, and the artist hungry for fulfillment.

Carmian knew him somewhat by now, almost as well as she knew herself. He was capable of courage and action, though sometimes it was on the side of *bravoure* and a bit thin on top. Nonetheless, that did not detract. For herself, she could not think of a single virtue, the kind of thing other people called a virtue, that *she* possessed. She was a vegetable and only loved Dima. They would not call that a virtue—on the contrary—but it was her single hope. On a hot July night when their skin stuck fast so that a wrenching away caused them to wake in actual pain, as though they had been torn, they gazed at each other somnolently in awe. "We are growing together," he said, and laughed. "Our flesh wants to join."

Of course, this thought brought with it inevitable severance and loss, and was that the real emotion? He said, confidently: "I'll never let you be bored. You will never be bored with me and you'll never be able to leave me, because you'll never find another that you can love as much." That was the echo of her own voice in fear, the Mozart woman crying out: "You can't leave *me!*" (Because it is I—I—I.)

"We will go into the grave together," he said in his darling child way, and fell asleep.

"*Then*," she whispered to herself, "yes, then."

She was as happy as could be expected in the face of their highly questionable situation and the nuisance of throwing up. He reassured her that pregnancy and childbirth could only do her good, in line with his odd but not, to her, unacceptable theories, and promised that they would (1) have a beautiful boy baby, (2) move to an apartment, and (3) now really push his divorce proceedings.

"It's not the right order in which to do things," she said a little sadly.

"*We* can do it that way. You are too negative—you must be

91

more optimistic. We can do anything together. Mayakovsky said: '*Idyom! Idyom! Idyom!*' " He raised his right arm high, cutting the air three times. "In Russian that means, 'We go, we go—*Allons!*' He was a poet of the Revolution, full of youth and hope. It's a beautiful poem and goes something like this—'It is summer, the leaves are green, friends, comrades. . . . The roads of Russia are broad and straight—! Idyom!' "

"A simple poem," she remarked.

"Ah, you laugh, but it came out of his heart and its simplicity is paradise. The sentences are short and pure and march across the page, one under the other. You have to see it. I will buy you a volume of Mayakovsky as soon as you learn Russian."

She lay back and laughed weakly, but she had caught his fire. "Yes, I see it."

"Don't you see? He was saying: 'The present is new and the future awaits us. Let us not be afraid. There is no turning back.' "

"The present is the miracle."

"Yes, yes! And the future."

"What happened to him?"

"Ah, that is tragic, awful. He fell out with the Communists"—Dima admitted regretfully—"and killed himself."

"Ah."

"Don't think of it, darling." He fixed her with suddenly intent and bitter eyes, puckering his mouth, pressing his lips together and draining the saliva from them, as he did whenever some vague despair threatened. "Remember the poem, not his end. Remember the man he was when he wrote that poem. So joyous!"

"So joyous. His end was the ending to the poem."

"I wish I hadn't told you," he said.

One day Dima brought his son to see her. His name was Serge, a towheaded, brown-legged little boy who looked like him; a face that seemed naturally to belong to northern Russia. A thatch of hair fell over his eyes and he showed, like his father, like Lala, a crushing vitality, a supreme confidence and stubborn will, plus the inability to stay quiet for more than ten seconds. They took him to the Jardin du Luxembourg where he stuffed himself with ice cream and climbed everything in sight, while Carmian suppressed violent attacks of nausea. Jealousy, she told herself in disgust. Because he is not mine.

It did not help to recognize the fact that Serge gave her no choice—for he did not like her.

She decided, to comfort herself, that she was the dark burning kind like the man in the portrait, the tired kind. (How my father would have loved you! Dima said often.)

"How do you like Serge?" he asked that night.

"He's a very handsome boy."

"You see what you will have in a few years from now! Ours will be like him, only dark, with round dark eyes like yours, and a dreamer."

"You're so sure it's a boy?"

"Oh, yes," he said casually, and she rather thought he was right.

"After that we'll have a girl. It's worth it all. You'll see," he promised, sparkling, as if he were telling a child about Christmas. "What shall we call him?"

"Michael," she said. "In English."

"Michael, yes. Michael de Koubyankov. No, Michael Koubyankov. Michael Dmitrovitch Koubyankov. Do you want to keep the 'de'?"

"No," said Carmian, "I do not think it aristocratic."

"You are a princess!" he said extravagantly in his joy. "My father never used it and is buried without it on his tombstone. But Lala wanted everyone to know she was not a *muzhik*."

"Of course. Since he was the baron."

"Yes, yes." A slight frown had begun to appear on his forehead. "Look, what if it *is* a girl?"

She laughed out loud and then developed a small, sweet, baffling smile that he found not altogether unpleasant. "No . . . no. I think it is Michael."

"Michael," said Dima. "Michael."

July had gone by. J.-P. turned up regularly to take her to Le Cocktail Gallimard. She was delighted to go, for she found out that champagne did not turn her stomach, and the editors after reading her book were kind to her. They had decided that it would lose too much in translation, being of a purely Anglo-Saxon genre, to justify a Gallimard edition, but they were interested, very interested in her future. She agreed with them heartily; she had known it all along, but how could she explain to J.-P.? Chedwick was always there and kept prodding her about the long short story—or short novella—she was doing, which was now nearly finished, since she attempted to do some of it now and then. He had read earlier ones and liked them. He had sent them to the States.

She liked Chedwick more and more. Even Dima began to like Chedwick. There was that seriousness and honesty and gentle efficiency about him which, combined with the old boyish innocence, makes the cynical and shrewder European lay down his arms before the best of Americans. The three of them met sometimes in the afternoons and on hot nights in the Barbac, a rose-lighted tavern on the rue du Bac where she and Dima ate ice cream, drank beer, and played poker and dice on his evenings off. The hotel room had become very confining since Miss Bixby had gone to America with her spaniel and trunkfuls of canvases and old books. Jo-Jo had gone off somewhere else to await her return, and Miss Fairbanks at last had been evicted.

It was dreary. The evenings alone were hard for Carmian, and Dima had a heavy, shifting schedule. He got her tickets for a few operas, but could only get two for a much heralded, sold-out Furtwängler concert, which he gave to Denise.

He had told Carmian about the rehearsals and how the Meister went about it. "You must have it in the tips of your fingers, Herr So-and-So," he would say. And gently, "Let's try again," and that time it would be perfect. She was heartbroken that she could not go.

"She asked me weeks ago," he explained. "After all, I owe her that."

"All I get is *Aïda*," she said bitterly.

"I want her cooperation in the divorce, you know, and she is giving me that."

"Oh, I'm sick," she moaned, turning her face to the wall.

"But you have me! She doesn't, any more. Which"—he shouted, beginning to stride around the room—"would you rather have—me or Furtwängler?"

"Furtwängler."

He swallowed, and reminded her: "It's your condition. Try to remember you're not feeling well. In three months you'll feel fine."

"Thank you."

"Look—write to your father," he persuaded tenderly. "Think

94

how happy it will make him—a grandson! I know it, I feel it in my heart."

Suddenly she turned and opened her eyes with such an expression of wonder that he knew she had only just realized that she was homesick. (As if he had not been bringing her these impossible English things to eat, like white bread and marmalade, that you got on the Right Bank.)

"Do you think so?"

"Yes, I do. Kiss him for me. He will be my friend."

"Yes. My dear, dear."

Long ago she had prayed every night the classic prayer of the divided child: Please let them get together again. She had been the agent, the catalyst, the mover and welder, but she had failed. She had become the empty space between obdurate figures who would not be rejoined. The emptiness must be filled somehow and it took three—yes! The third would be Michael Dmitrovitch Koubyankov. She went to sleep dreaming of him.

The warm nights when she was alone she wandered down to the Royal Saint-Germain or surrounding bistros and talked to Dupré and Picasso (she had never been able to conduct a conversation with Bérancourt), to young Americans on the G.I. bill, to Marcel the half-Arab, and to enthusiastic long-haired young Frenchmen who were writing books intended to knock over time and space. *Bouleverser le temps et l'espace*: this was their aim. "What have you got left?" she asked naïvely, and they said, "The truth!" In ten years they would all be lawyers and manufacturers like their papas.

Toward midnight she walked to the Pont Royal and waited there for him, leaning on the parapet. She could not go back to a room in which he was not. He would come with the slow strides that meant he was tired, and content since he liked being tired, freed from his restlessness. They would stop for a beer and go home, Dima making a game of helping her up the stairs. "They are too many for you now. We'll have to move." She laughed. " 'I've grown fond of them,' " she quoted Miss Fairbanks. But often she mounted reluctantly, bewitched by the beautiful bridges gleaming moon-pale, the water rippling like ink.

One night she met Jo-Jo on the quay and they stared down into the Seine together. In Paris as a child, circa 1933, she had seen on the cover of a book a girl's drowned face and floating hair crossed by wavy lines of water. One did not have to read that book, for the story was plain on the cover. It was plain in Jo-Jo, too, the yearning. But his poetry kept him alive. He spoke of Miss Bixby who was now in Connecticut, which he pronounced as written. Suzie had not survived the trip—not even first class—and had rejoined her ancestors. This news, delivered with a funereal flourish, clearly pleased him, but Miss Bixby's absence had brought melancholy chords to his usual dry rasp. Even you . . . she thought, surprised. They stared at the drifting shadows on the Seine while he intoned some of his river-haunted verse.

He was not present at a formal luncheon of the Bérancourts the next day; it was well known that he scarcely ever showed up for appointments. Besides Carmian and Dima, Picasso and Dupré were the only guests. Madame de Bérancourt was dumpy, owlish, exasperated, but about twenty years younger than her mate, and it was said that she had married him for his title. This was hardly a startling conclusion, since Bérancourt was not only prematurely senile, but penurious, alcoholic, purple-faced, and incoherent, and wore gloves all the time as if he had wooden hands or leprosy. Luncheon chez les Bérancourt was strictly *pour rigoler*—for laughs—since obviously no Frenchman would have come to that junk shop in a courtyard of the rue Bonaparte for the serious purpose of dining, once he knew what to expect.

Bérancourt and Dupré had already finished the hors d'œuvres when Carmian and Dima arrived—fifteen minutes late, it was true. They squeezed, squirmed, and sidled their way to the table through a room littered with *objets d'art* such as African masks, modern sculpture consisting mostly of holes, dusty canvases, Chinese vases, and heraldic emblems. Madame de Bérancourt was serving a roast to which her spouse helped himself liberally, Dupré more modestly, before she whipped it back into the kitchen. She, apparently, did not eat.

As a host Bérancourt did better with the burgundy. He filled and refilled huge crystal glasses adorned with the family crest (as was the elegant silver) although stained with the wine of former occasions. Bérancourt announced, braying, that he never let his wineglasses be washed. Picasso arrived the last and was severely dispatched for more burgundy, which he preferred to food anyway, so there was no reason to pity him.

"What about the roast?" Dima demanded without ceremony—Carmian feeling more and more like Alice—when they had eaten the tomatoes, anchovies, and black olives, and waited expectantly for about five minutes as Bérancourt rolled a cigarette in his palsied fingers and prepared to relax on a full stomach. Dupré was telling an anecdote of a girl he had seduced on a green leather couch in an office in Manhattan.

Madame finally brought it in rather crossly. Picasso had been forced to skip the hors d'œuvres but seemed resigned to the loss. Presently Dima rose to his feet with baronial courtesy and complimented the hostess on her roast. She beamed surprisingly; his flattery, though rendered in the comic sense, was deplorably successful with ladies.

Bérancourt allowed everyone to finish eating before producing what he plainly regarded as the *pièce de résistance*, the latest edition of a Saint-Germain-des-Prés avant-garde magazine—in which a poem of his had been published. Carmian had never encountered so many people who unexpectedly wrote poetry. This poem was entitled *Rue de Rennes*, and he read it to them in a stately basso full of hoarse but sternly controlled emotion. It began: *"Elle est longue, la rue de Rennes . . . et ne tourne pas."*

That was about it, the theme being reiterated throughout two stanzas, some of the lines even differing one from the other. His audience drank thoughtfully. While it was true that the rue de Rennes, which linked the bistros of Saint-Germain and Montparnasse, was unconscionably long and dull, especially after midnight when the buses and the métro had stopped running, and a notorious trap for late drinkers—its poetic significance seemed obscure. If the poet had been drunk on the rue de Rennes, surely nothing could be more commonplace, especially (they thought) for him.

A road that was endless and did not turn, Carmian fancied: a gruesome parody of Mayakovsky's broad summer road. While Mayakovsky sang of hope and went to disaster, Bérancourt had nothing to fear. He was driven only by the hope of bed. What Carmian couldn't understand was why he had been impelled to write a poem about it, or the magazine to print it.

97

Unless, Dima later suggested, it had been someone's joke? In a sense it acquired a certain fame for Bérancourt, causing widespread speculation and becoming a rallying cry for late revelers. "*Elle est longue, la rue de Rennes!*" one would greet a friend, who duly replied: "*Et ne tourne pas.*"

The reading terminated, Dupré now jumped in to tell Carmian about the American publication of his book A *Frenchman in America*. It was prominently displayed in the window of the Saint-Germain Bookshop, and he thought it would interest her. She agreed politely and asked him the name of his publisher, whereupon she was struck with the horrid realization that here, in the flesh, was the unknown writer that a friend in New York had satirized at parties. Her friend had read the manuscript for another firm and, according to his description, it would have been more aptly entitled A *Frenchman in Manhattan*, or, simply, A *Frenchman*. So it dawned upon her that here was a man who wrote a travel book about a country of which he knew nothing and (though in France it might pass) had actually managed to get it published *in* America, the object of his ignorance, and for Americans. This, thought Carmian, was Success—as opposed to Miss Fairbanks' failure to get her article for tourists published. They had something in common, though: Neither of them stuck to the original premise, that of being connoisseur and expert—Dupré because although grandiose he really knew nothing, Miss Fairbanks (a more complicated type) because her real knowledge of living cheaply in Paris had interfered with her dreams, desires, and shame.

The wine began to affect her stomach unpleasantly, and she told Dima that she wanted to go. Their habit of talking to each other in German, considered by most a harmless eccentricity but often useful for purposes of domestic discretion, was lost on the company at this moment; they had begun one of their political arguments, Dupré the Gaullist, Picasso the anarchist, Bérancourt the royalist. Madame was gathering her forces to throw them all out, except for her husband whom rather absently she was accustomed to keeping.

Bérancourt's oft-quoted, rasping lament trailed after them. "*Quelle époque!*"

"Old butt collector," said Dima. "With his gloves."

"He has no insides," she observed in amazement.

"You are too fond of people, so you expect too much."

"You expect nothing. An hour's diversion, like Boris till he goes back to writing his poetry about sticks and stones."

"But this poem—wasn't it superb?" His glee was huge and unaffected.

"Utterly. We were all so good not to laugh."

"Yes," he sighed.

"Well, we can laugh—but I love Picasso." The gentle little anarchist, the humble painter, the bearded angel whom she thought of as a kind of allegorical opponent to the bearded devil Boris.

"Because he belongs to the upper regions, darling, as you and I."

She smiled, wishing she could talk to him in her own language. Aside from the extraordinary hazard of misunderstandings, their inability to communicate at their best made a vacuum. He could not read what she wrote; she could not read the literature he loved best in its native form; and they could not reassure each other as they would have done. Her French was spare; his German was funny. In settling on German, the advantage was hers, but he liked it better for the expression of love, since it was sincere if naïve, and lacked the professional polish and balderdash of French-language love that made them both shudder: the *chérie*'s and the *je t'aime*'s and the rest of it. One thought of the man and the mistress, not husband and wife. In Dima's mouth German was honest, halting, with the newness of children first tasting and testing their words, feeling the meanings, unable to hide behind the double-sense, the voluble truth concealing the lie. This is what gives foreigners their vulnerable air. It is difficult to hide, hard to dissimulate.

Their baby talk had been German, in part, for both of them. But German was also the language of the concentration camps, of the international displaced and the political *besprizornye*. She wished for his sake that it could have been another.

The enemies, of course, were the worlds of English and French, and the lives of each in them before they had come together.

"Boris hates people," she said. "You don't have to hate to write dreams."

"Some do. You're a romantic."

"If telegraph wires are the utmost—" She choked, beating her head against the idea of Boris, revolting. "If you can only associate with human beings for the pleasure of despising them . . ."

"Words," he said, "are his concern, nothing else."

99

"No—he hates."

"Perhaps."

Now that she had been able to tell him this, and win him to her, a feeling like that of a glider in the air came over her, buoying her up, relieving old pains and fears as a change in the weather relieves an old woman's rheumatism. Except it was better than that—she flew, for she was young.

"Darling," she said, "if *you* despise people, you will hate me."

"I don't care for anyone really but you." He bent to hug her. "We will have a new and beautiful life together." They went slowly up the dull-carpeted stairs and rested on their bed, for it was his day off. "What made you the girl you are?"

"I told you. My mother and father divorced. We moved every year, sometimes from country to country. I went to private schools. Sometimes we had money and sometimes not. My mother remarried, and I have a stepbrother somewhere whom I used to like, perhaps love. Nothing much."

"You loved your mother?"

"*Mamotchka maya,*" she murmured. "Oh, yes."

"I detest Lala. But she is the woman who gave birth to me. She put me on earth to live and breathe. She carried me around for nine months."

"With me it was different. She was pure in heart. The infant villain. You have to love a baby even if it is your mother."

Dima said sadly, "You had a child. But look—now you have a real one."

Frightened, aghast at what they had done, she crept closer to him for comfort.

That was the way it was, the nights, most of them, dark, rich and sweet. The days were bleak with loneliness and wrath and hidden terrors that disappeared silently, familiar demons, when he came home to her across the bridge. In the middle of August they moved to the Place Dauphine on the western tip of the Ile de la Cité which was not far off but seemed like another country. It was here that the demons moved in like unwanted relatives, bag and baggage, to settle and flourish, while she beat the air helplessly and cried and slept all day like an invalid, while he came home less willingly and less promptly . . . as people will do in such circumstances.

13 It was the usual smallish oblong room, but overlooking the Place Dauphine and only one flight up. This was the reason he gave her for taking it, but the truth was that he took the first one he could find and pay for. It was a relief not to have to climb five flights, and they both wanted a change from the hotel deserted by Jo-Jo, Miss Bixby, Miss Fairbanks, and even the Swiss girl who sang Mozart. He showed her the new room with persuasion, stressing all its better features—the window, the view, the blue-flowered wallpaper, a rather trim look with small attempts at decoration, homely touches designed to please foreign students and schoolteachers from Scandinavia. It was, he said, the kind of room you might see in Bretagne.

It was certainly wholesomer than Madame's mousetrap on the rue de Beaune, a place for chill autumn nights, but she was not happy. It lacked the warm and raffish charm of the Beaune hotel and gave in return a forbidding tidiness, processions of blue flowers on the walls. She had often been bothered by wallpaper, but this was the worst; it looked like bunches of poison grapes following each other around the room, maddeningly halved and quartered in places, yet smugly intent on their senseless regimentation.

She began feeling very ill and hardly able to get up during the day, restless and melancholy at night when Dima worked, ridden with the *nostalgie de la boue*: her longing for the streets and life, though it was going nowhere. The story was locked up in her typewriter; it had died. She could not write to her father. Her world was not green and young like Mayakovsky's—she knew his end. She was locked up inside and out, the baby growing and the window barred. She felt the baby as a hardness in her pelvis; her waist had thickened. She stared at herself in the mirror, holding her face, seeing a wasteland of wonderment, the desert stretches.

This was the beginning of the tumbling down of everything, of the house falling apart, the erosion of love, the acid of hate and suffering, and it seemed to happen quite suddenly—a natural calamity like an earthquake or a flood.

It seemed to her that he mocked and betrayed her, now that her trap had become his as well. She had found out that the divorce lawyer was still waiting for his first five thousand francs before he would commence action, and she nagged and wept until Dima told her it had been arranged. Later she discovered that he had possessed the sum intended for the lawyer, twice, and spent it on food, drink, and dice rolling in the cafés. He brought home the Russian delicacies, and for her the pasteurized cheese, jam, cakes, and white bread and butter that were the only things she could keep down; bland American food that he purchased in another store, equally expensive, near the Opéra.

He had herring and vodka for breakfast. She lay in bed and wept for her father, her mother, and smelled the herring with revulsion, glared at the soggy wrappings and butter papers he left around the room when he whizzed off to work. He came home later than had been his custom, sometimes not at all for lunch, and when he did arrive she would still—so it appeared to him—be crying. He started to cry himself, shaking clasped hands in front of his face, beseeching: "Don't cry so much! You will give me such a sad baby!"

"I can't help it."

"Darling, have courage," he pleaded, sweating, for he was working hard and had long hours during the tourist season.

He would go out the door, locking her in like a jailer while she worked at having a baby. He brought her food like a jailer, nourishing the life inside. That was all it had become. At night she crept close to the wall and turned her back to him. One cannot love one's torturer. He seemed to accept this philosophically and to have forgotten his earlier rage at gestures of contempt. But in daylight he looked at her coldly. She vegetated while he was gone, the weight of an alp upon her, waiting for night, his reappearance—and hope—or an outlet for fury. Jealousy gnawed its way through her like ants when she remembered his stories: The Breton fisherman's daughter who ran her own boat like a man, wearing a captain's cap. . . . The dancer at the Folies Bergères whom he had seduced behind the scenes while the show out front was blaring. She hit the pillow and the wall with her fist. How could she stand such a man? Most disgusting of all had been the story of his own seduction at fifteen, fresh down from a Normandy school, in a sailor suit, by a bored Countess in Passy who was the mother of his school chum.

To tell her these things! He laughed when she brought up these tales. "Oh, they weren't true," he said. "It was just to annoy you."

Most of all, and with greater pain, she remembered his story, indubitably true, of the red-haired, freckle-faced Russian girl who had ridden to Berlin with them on a Red Army tank, playing a guitar. She had jumped off the tank, unshouldered her rifle and fought with the best of them during attacks. She had gone through the whole campaign without a scratch, and she was known for her luck. Afterward she always played and sang songs of Byelorussia. She had lost her husband in the war against the Germans and had come along, she said, for the ride. The soldiers treated her with respect, for she was herself a Russian soldier and a woman to be left alone.

To Dima, she thought, Frenchwomen were objects of frivolity; Russian women sacred, untouchable; American women a source of interest mixed with baffling amusement.

He adored the daintiness of the Indo-Chinese.

She was jealous of all of them, staring with revolt at the blue wall-flowers. It was envy too. She envied the fisher girl, the dancer and soldier, whether fictional or real, who moved freely, their freedom making them elusive and desirable, able to hunt and be hunted and move through life. She was sick, in more ways than one, of being pregnant.

One September evening she simply got up and went out. She left a note for Dima telling him she would be at the Royal Saint-Germain. She met Dupré and Picasso and told them about her baby, since they looked oddly concerned. They congratulated her warmly, but continued to frown in a troubled way, so she supposed that she looked as haggard and gaunt as she had feared. The knot inside was taking all her vitality. She hated herself, the knot, and Dima. Perhaps, she thought, she could stop it while there was still time. The thought made her ill, and she swayed at the bar. Not she! Not she! What she started must end. She was stubborn, too. Smiling apologetically at Picasso, she was sorry for him; he had seen them happy together, exuding love, and he had believed in them. She had known a girl who claimed to have done it with Pernod, but she had not the heart for that; she had beer.

Everyone had gone away. Jean-Philippe no longer came. Their quarrels had made him sad. No one came any more; the Angels had left her, and these two looked at her with pity.

Dima was asleep when she came home and crawled into bed. In the morning, as she opened her eyes, he was fixing her with a furious glare. "What are you doing, running around by night in your condition?"

"I was lonely."

"So you left a note for me to run over and call for you after a hard night's work."

"I didn't say that."

"But you meant it."

"In America," she said with sudden asperity, "it is the custom to leave notes behind in order to let your family, or the people who live with you, know where you are. It is intended to spare them anxiety. If you took it in a different sense, it's not my fault. Even speaking the same language, people constantly misunderstand. How can I hope to make my meanings clear to you?"

He cuffed her on the side of the head. It was the most humiliating blow she had ever received. She was stunned until she had started screaming at him. "You misbegotten Russian! I've had enough of your brutalities!"

He was pleased, apparently, at her show of spirit. It drove her to cold anger. She said, "I am going to write to my father that I want to come home."

"And the baby?"

"I don't know"—wildly—"I'll go to Switzerland and get a legal abortion."

"How are you going to pay for it?"

"I don't know. All I know is that I need not take this treatment any longer. I don't have to do this to myself."

"That's between you and you," he said. "I'll gladly leave if you say so."

"This is a fine, manly time," she countered dryly, "to choose to do that. The best yet."

"I'm merely obliging you. Besides, I've had quite enough myself." He went to the desk, opened her typewriter, and inserted a fresh sheet of paper.

The Mozart voice had left her, and the will. After a while you have hurt each other too much, and there is no going back. He called her over to read what he had written. It said in French:

"This is to certify that Carmian Wills, American, was my mistress and that I, Dima de Koubyankov, am responsible as the father of her unborn child for all expenses incurred until she should leave the borders of France."

He said, "I'll get it certified by the police."

"Maîtresse," she quoted in disdain. "Sounds like a mattress."

"That's what it is, sometimes."

"Well, I'll see what I can do."

She was hard-eyed and thoughtful. He admired her. She was always better after a shaking up. Like Lala she was good in wars.

When he had gone, she lay quietly remembering a meeting with her friend von Kolmau, while they had still been living happily in the days of the rue de Beaune.

It was one of those extraordinary meetings—they had known each other in New York and since Germany—where you turn a corner and a face so familiar comes at you that you cannot recognize it until it has almost gone past.

Over some terribly strong coffee, he said: "This man gives up a perfectly good working wife—with a salary!—for another without? I don't understand it."

She laughed. He was an old European of the cynical school. He wore a monocle and did not mind if people gawked.

"Haven't you ever heard of love? Is it only in America that they ever think of that?"

"There is money in America. Have you any?"

"No," she replied, "but he doesn't seem to mind."

"Of course, the poor fellow is a Russian," von Kolmau reflected, weighing matters. "But how can it work?"

"Ugh! That's because you think you need sixteen servants in order to exist. Your conditioning. One can be in love and poor and happy. And there is always the hope. . . ."

"I don't know," he said frankly.

His fears had been justified. Not that it was merely not enough money, but not enough love, not enough. . . . Money had loomed large on the horizon lately, as always when love pales—the substitute moon. Dima was spending wildly, paying no bills. She was forlorn and loverless. Maybe really, she thought angrily, she wanted to be loved, taken, kept, without remuneration, as the infant screaming in the crib whose mother takes him slavishly to her heart. She was unable now to love Dima and his progeny, unable almost to move, act, eat, unable to do anything except make a try for raw survival.

14

An Angel came in the person of Miss Fairbanks. She looked wild, ravaged, and famished, and was almost incoherent until Carmian produced a pot of rice left over from the night before, some cheese and some bread. She devoured the cold rice standing up, and the human light came into her old eyes (old! Carmian realized suddenly) and she regained some of the wit, the breeding and poise which had been her original assets.

"Darling," she commenced, "you don't look well."

The hotel cat, ill received, who had been begging Miss Fairbanks for morsels now licked the quite empty pot.

Carmian experienced several lurches of seasickness. When her stomach had righted itself, she said, "I'm nearly three months pregnant."

Here was the mother she had wanted to tell it to. She felt— almost—as if Miss Fairbanks would turn into that big beautiful, unpredictable woman who had stood over her when she was small, who would either strike her or hug her and kiss her or sit down and burst into tears. It would be interesting to know which, at this news.

But Miss Fairbanks, although bearing a strong resemblance to womanhood, was not her mother. Her reaction was disappointing if soothingly sympathetic. "It happens to all of us, darling. Are you doing something about it?"

There was an old-fashioned Carmian (who sometimes laid her slim hands about her throat or on her breast in a gesture copied directly from the Victorian German grandmother for whom she had been named) that managed to live side by side with the gambling rebel, the hidden ragamuffin. She was shocked but rallied in a moment, aware that the fifty-nine-year-old Miss Fairbanks belonged to a smarter, slicker, shinier world than her own. Miss Fairbanks was the sporty English girl of a long-gone feminist revolt who said, "What ho! Caught again," and left it at that. She would never say: "Do you love me still?"

Trying to adjust to a new sort of mother, the only one available at the moment, she told this cool specimen, "Well, for one thing, I don't have the money." It was pretty lame.

Miss Fairbanks, reclining on the bed in her rusty black suit de chez Paquin and her little black slab of a hat that made one think she must have been very chic once, in spite of the spots and dust and hanging threads—Miss Fairbanks said: "Why, I had the best abortion in Paris once for practically nothing. I was frantic, my dear. It was a midwife who did it with a hatpin, and it worked like magic."

"God!" said Carmian. "It's supposed to kill you with infections and things."

"Why, no, I never had a moment's bother."

"Oh," said Carmian, sick and wishing for a doctor, a hospital, Switzerland—even a midwife with a hatpin, anything—but what was.

She offered Miss Fairbanks a glass of wine from Dima's bottle which she had unfortunately spotted. If only she weren't such a fraud. Tommy Tucker singing for his supper was all that Miss Fairbanks was. The knowledge was painful, but no one came any more, and she specially wanted a woman.

"Once I was dancing with Hemingway," Miss Fairbanks began her reminiscence, "and—oh, he was charming, I was wearing my best black tulle, it *was* so gay—and he escorted me back to my table and Henriette de Chavert, she was the wife of a financier then, she said, 'Genevieve, it seems to me you have gained a tiny bit of weight—around your middle.' Well, it was the very next day I had the appointment with the *sage-femme*. But she did spoil my evening, the bitch."

"My mother went to a ball the night before I was born. Champagne . . . you know. She said she didn't remember a thing."

Miss Fairbanks brushed such maudlin sentimentalities away. "Now I am worried about you. Don't you have a boy friend in America? Someone who can send you money? You are so lucky to be American and not filthy rotten English—"

"I like the English."

"My *dear!* Well, never mind that. Don't you have—"

107

"But," said Carmian, shamefaced, "sometimes I think I would like to have this baby. I can't seem to make up my mind."

The gray-blue eyes, color of treachery, reflected a chilly impatience. "Dima can never get you through this! Surely you must know that. You need someone else. Fight for yourself!"

Her opinion of Miss Fairbanks had taken a rapid turn for the worse. And yet—and yet—into those unreliable eyes crept orphaned spaces. Desolate eyes, forsaken eyes, what have they done to you? In them the Devil was not, or the transfigured mark of the Holy Sinner, but a pitiful truth revealed in light: Miss Fairbanks was *glad*, though she did not like herself for it. Carmian was on the side of angels, even erring ones, and of Goethe's light; but Dostoevsky was the beloved. She longed for a compassionate darkness.

When Dima came in, Miss Fairbanks got the sly, guilty, ingratiating look of a child who has done wrong. Dima hailed her sunnily and proceeded to torture Carmian.

Apparently it was deliberate, for he set about taunting her with elaborate sarcasm one minute, cold indifference the next, tempered with spells of deafness. Toward Miss Fairbanks he was inordinately chivalrous and kind, pressing vodka, radishes, cheese, and fruit upon her, even delicately suggesting that he had come upon a pair of ownerless shoes at the Opéra which looked as if they might fit her. She was thrilled; greed lighted up her forlorn face. "You're a da-arling, Dima!" she cried, kicking one foot up in the air. She had forgotten Carmian. It seemed he was trying to ally everyone with himself against her, and with his sharp instinct he had rooted out Miss Fairbanks' Achilles heel—her shoes. It was not difficult: a woman who boasted of having had fifty pairs of shoes once and now wore disintegrating wedgies held together with string, bloated by walks in the rain—shoes to shame the historic Paquin suit—shoes that even a Paris *clocharde* would reject. She had small feet and clearly they had been a source of vanity.

I hope you get them, Carmian thought, bitter and silent. She did not trust his promises. The wonder of his coming home to her across the bridge, when there was still no reason but desire, had weakened under the weight of small but incessant disappointments.

"Miss Wills," he disclosed with a Tartar smile, peeling an apple, "is leaving us to go to America."

Miss Fairbanks looked uneasy. Carmian asked him for the knife, which he tossed onto the bed beside her, and began peeling an apple of her own. She remembered how her grandfather had done this for her in a warm room where the clock ticked quietly at night, kindly, kindly, and they had loved each other. Now he was dead.

Here in this blue-flowered room her heart was cold. His stare was vicious watching her peel the apple, clumsily, seeming unable to complete it, as if peeling this apple would go on without end. Her hands started shaking . . . the knife slipped. In a ghastly silence he snickered with contempt. Suddenly she was trembling so hard she felt about to fly apart in pieces, when, instead of screaming, she flung the knife at him blade first.

It stuck in the wall next to his chair. She had not really wanted to kill him—for she could have. Her aim had been true.

Dima laughed, admiringly perhaps, perhaps in relief. Miss Fairbanks looked shocked and sad.

He quoted maliciously: " 'The passion for destruction is a creative passion.'—Bakunin."

It was true that this room was full of it. One wondered what monsters had been here to leave behind their generating aura, an evil mist. It seemed as though Boris had won.

Through September it grew steadily worse. Dima had plainly abandoned her, and she had nothing left but pity for herself. The question was who would leave first. These days he gamboled and hovered over other women with his hated charm, enjoying her rage, while she was the enforced appendage, the baggage to be checked and remembered when it was time to go. She walked heavily, not light-footed, soft-stepping, any more, as much weighted down by her soul as by the baby which did not show. He had a habit of forgetting that she was tired, striding quickly as he always did, annoyed that she lagged behind. But both were too paralyzed to change the situation. They could not move and had long ago broken the pact to tell each other the truth, so that imagined lies lay in ambush. If they could not love, at least they could hate. They were always short of money; the divorce papers were wilting in the lawyer's office; her visitor's permit was running out and they could not afford the necessary visa. Dima owed rent and would not tell her how much.

Bound together by hatred, they went one day to the Mexican Consulate to investigate the possibilities of Mexican immigration and divorce. He whirled upon her as she dragged uphill through the

Trocadéro park and berated her for her everlasting languor, for offices were closing. She hissed back at him that she could do no better. Then, as he sometimes did, he suddenly deferred. He told her that Boris had slept here, much as one would cite the sleeping quarters of General Washington. He described his impression of the unspeakable black beard rising and falling beneath a forsythia bush, but she did not laugh. The man at the consulate was discouraging, warning against paperwork, time and money. Dima would have to apply for a passport. He was a Russian exile? That might, he said in their kind of language, present difficulties.

Dima pursed his mouth grimly and narrowed his eyes. By this time she knew this look, and it was the one she feared most—the phantom of the concentration camp, or of the underprivileged foreigner beaten by the French police, whom no one deemed worthy of protection and inalienable rights. His pride in his nationality was strong but it was an anachronism, a defiance, an empty gesture flung at his persecutors. For them he no longer existed. The land that had harbored him, nurtured him, was France. Most second-generation Russians had become naturalized. Had he had Russian papers, they would have treated him better. But he had, as far as they were concerned, none.

"I have tried everything," he said to her bitterly, "and I can do no more. Nobody wants a displaced person."

"America does, I've heard."

"Oh, perhaps for propaganda. They want people who can tell them stories about the Soviets. I was never in Soviet Russia and I would not turn traitor if I could." He spat on the Place de Trocadéro. "I'll never go to America."

"You exaggerate."

"We started out with too many obstacles. I don't know what will happen. In this era lovers can be torn apart by even less than poverty, politics, and wars. They are all working against us, and we have no weapons, none."

"We ought to be living in the Impasse des Deux Anges."

"Yes, it would be fitting."

Privately she did think so, for something had made devils of them.

Sometimes she was accustomed to sitting in one of the circular niches of the Pont Neuf, where *clochards* slept by night and chatted by day, looking down on the black waters, wondering what it would be like if one had the courage to bear the leap and the first dreadful, bursting, splitting minute before everything broke.

However, she no longer did this after the night he came home and told her, breathlessly, that—*imagine-toi!*—he had just saved a strange girl from throwing herself into the Seine.

15 The hotel cat, a mangy scrawny abject animal, turned out not to be the hotel cat at all but a vagrant who slunk through the door whenever a roomer entered, bell tinkling, streaked shrewdly up the stairs ducking low past the concierge's door—and stayed, begging, rubbing his fur against the legs of tender-hearted ladies, scratching at the door of the Indo-Chinese writer who liked cats, exploring all directions where, he knew from experience, food might be forthcoming. His mind was a highly organized map of scents, both spiritual and physical, of good and bad will. He had superior intelligence, which was all that had saved him in the three or four years of destitution which had been his life.

When Carmian and Dima came home on autumn nights, now chill and fresh, they found him waiting for them on the landing. Satisfaction like love would come into the fierce, wary eyes; they would blink mildly and grow heavy with content as he followed them inside.

Although at first protesting, Dima began to like the cat, for the animal's will to survive and the enterprise and courage he put into it were admirable. He trembled all the time, fighting passively to escape the clutches of the law, and won. "*Quel débrouillard!*" Dima said. "A true Parisian. There is always a way."

"He reminds me of Miss Fairbanks," Carmian said. "He has her guts."

She called him Kitty, and Dima, in imitation, Kiri. He was one of the legions of rooftop cats, alley cats, café-counter cats, and shop cats that swarm over Paris, the kind that are castrated males with big heads and pleasant dispositions. They were usually tolerated and even well liked, but Kitty-Kiri was an outlaw. His emasculation had evidently been carried out with unnecessary brutality and incompetence, and he looked as if he had never even been loved by his mother. The law, in his case, was embodied in the harried face and puny figure of Monsieur le Concierge, whose wife was pregnant and who had the usual run of bad luck with the current crop of guests that is the concierge's personal fate. The cat messed the carpet and bothered the roomers, Monsieur threatened Carmian, and one of these days—if he could catch him—he would tie a stone around that cat's neck, put him in a sack and throw him in the river.

The cat was terrified of the concierge.

They decided they would save him, and in return he gave them his unswerving devotion. They were his. Only one night when they were out late did he deceive them. He showed up in the morning trailing perfume of a very strong sort. In the afternoons he continued to visit the Indo-Chinese, who cooked in his room. In fact there was a noticeable air of both food and seduction about that room, Carmian discovered one day when the Indo-Chinese invited her for a drink and a conversation about the international ordeal of writers. Roving bachelors that they were, the Indo-Chinese and the cat had much in common; they even looked alike.

It was Dima who first observed that Kitty-Kiri became unstrung when the atmosphere grew quarrelsome. He went from one to the other, anxiously, with distended gold-ringed pupils, using all his cat's wiles and devices to soothe, to becalm, and to draw attention back to himself. He enjoyed making them laugh.

"My word, he is keeping us together, the little bastard!" said Dima. "We can't let him down, can we—this Kiri-Kiri?"

No, he was one of the Angels, and when Miss Fairbanks next came with the driven starved look in her eyes, she could eat and talk without dramatic interruption. "Dears," she chirruped, "you look like two babies in bed."

She was tart on the subject of the Paris Salvation Army. "Imagine—they won't give you a bowl of soup unless you pay thirty francs! Of course it's bilgewater. Whom are they trying to save? Pretty costly, I'd say, that sort of charity."

"C'est les organisations," Dima said. "It costs them so much money to run it, everything is more expensive in the end. I never gave a sou to one of them. I prefer to give to independent beggars. Now in capitalistic America, there is the turnover, the mass production, that reduces the cost to the individual and permits of prosperity. The French haven't discovered it yet. They are hindered psychologically, as well as economically, because they can't stand waste and hate to spend."

"But charity!"

"Bah! There is no such thing."

"Disgusting," said Miss Fairbanks. "But you must admit the Americans—"

He was at his most didactic and insufferable. "A policy to win favor for themselves. Do they care about the individual? Their money goes into the grubby little hands of manufacturers who put it in their pockets, where it stays while those below wait for manna from heaven."

"There happens to be," said Carmian haughtily, "an organization called CARE which does care for the individual—among others like it."

"I do not believe in the charity of governments."

"Well, these are people—people who send in money for packages abroad. They are distributed and nobody makes a profit."

"Just citizens?" He was enormously impressed and pleased, accepting the news with simple trust and deferential grace. "I always knew they were a generous people."

"I must look into it," said Miss Fairbanks. She saw Kitty and picked him up. He looked trapped, uncomfortable, and finally fought his way down. She gave him an angry—and envious—stare. "You naughty thing," she said.

It was the way she had looked at Jo-Jo whose rival she had been, at J.-P. who returned her sentiments but was more secure, and, perhaps only once, at Carmian. The envy of the have-not for a successful fellow bum.

Carmian had a dream in which a cat was flayed, leaving a neat band of nakedness around the middle, and all the pains of such an operation were her own for the time that it took to perform—in a dream.

The low point had been the night of the apple-peeling and knife-throwing. It had shamed Carmian but had the curious, relieving and softening effect on Dima of the Montana incident. The old

113

well-aimed cruelty gave way to a kind of gentle humoring mingled with superiority. This made her very scratchy at times; at others wild with a rage and frustration that she tried to suppress, for he withheld from her any real hope of the future, and like someone blinded she was tired of peering into the darkness to see where they were going. Again she lamented that no one came any more; that she went nowhere, and hated her life. J.-P. stopped by, but shyly, without the gaiety of old, striving not to look at her as if she might be billowing and bulging in certain places. Clearly her condition was unsuited to his idea of her, and he was ill at ease. He reported that the Gallimard parties had been discontinued, not so much due to the end of the season as to the rapacity of the free loaders, who had been a hideous drain on the finances.

One night they were invited, through obscure but traceable channels, to a journalists' party—and there followed a scene it became increasingly difficult to believe in, although it was the kind of thing she had been used to from living with her mother, he with Lala, twenty or so years ago.

There were an American lady-journalist and a French Sécurité officer, referred to behind his back as the *flic*. The other human portraits distributed around the richly furnished, balconied room she never really remembered, as a result of the drastic behavior of a second lady-journalist, or boy, who shared the apartment with her colleague. For they were roommates. (It turned out later that both ladies shared the apartment with the *flic*, who paid for it.)

It was a rousing party, but Journalist lady I left with the French Sécurité officer after a cozy literary chat with Carmian, a talk combined with warmth and courtship, like soft enveloping arms, that alarmed and flattered her. The Journalist was prettily, tenderly interested in the coming baby and in Carmian's book, which she had read.

Journalist lady II, foreign but Americanized, did all the work. She was efficient and gray-haired, a rumble-voiced pixy, growing waspish with the number of drinks she downed, or bawdy—as she told a lavish story about her visit to a Lesbian house of prostitution, to the concealed distress of some American and Oriental students in the company. Journalist lady II kicked up her heels like Miss Fairbanks and began courting Dima. He laughed and humored her. She sang wildly: *"Du bist verrückt, mein Kind, du gehst nach Berlin . . ."*

which, one assumed, was a relic of the twenties. He seemed tolerant of this odd phantom of the concentration camp.

Then suddenly, or perhaps not, she attacked Carmian.

It was a shock. A woman presumably, American, even though slightly male, attacking her, *enceinte*. After her she's-impossible-what-do-you-want-with-that-little-bourgeoise kind of attack (reminiscent of the unexpressed thoughts behind Boris' deadly eyes), Carmian's eyes filled with tears of self-pity and rage. She said: "I'm expecting a baby. Why do you want to upset me?"

The men drew back into their corners and Dima smiled, crossing his leg.

"That's all you're capable of," said Journalist lady II. "You're no poet. You sit there with a good handsome Russian boy who loves you and you mope. You're a moper. Lots of women get pregnant and get over it. Wake up!"

God, Carmian thought, she's got it all wrong. But she rose to her feet in a surge of something that was more than the release of brandy, and akin to joy. She was shaking with it.

"You're a dope," said Journalist lady II over the rim of her glass, her legs flung across the chair.

"No, I'm not," she said, walking over to her. "Get up so I can hit you."

The party broke up very fast. Journalist II escaped into the kitchen. Carmian and Dima found themselves on the curb with two Canadians looking for a taxi, and they took it together.

"I knew you could handle her," he said.

He was so proud of her that he laughed when she screamed at the unpunished injustice of the assault, vociferated at the cat, and hurled herself off the bed—hitting her nose, not her stomach, and creating a bright red scratch there, at which he laughed twice as hard. In the end he stopped her from jumping out of the window, a thing she knew in her heart she could not do because she had failed to once before, at the age of eight.

Dima pulled her back, catching her in his arms, laughing but not unkindly.

It was laughable. Soon after, she awoke one day and said to him simply, "It's all over now." The misery was over.

"I'm all right," she kept repeating. "No, really I am." Perhaps he could not understand. He had waited such a long time.

"I think it was physical," she explained. For the scratching, fighting torment had left her. *Idyom!*

And then the baby kicked—Michael Dmitrovich Koubyankov!

"He's there," she whispered, holding her belly.

"What? Where?" Desperate, he put his hand on top. "I don't feel anything!"

"He's there!" she rejoiced. "Oh, he's there."

After that he waited for nights, while they pushed the cat off.

"He's there!" he shouted one time. "I feel him. My Michael! How he kicks."

"He is strong," she said proudly, "as you and I."

The early despairing days of love had vanished forever. Now there was the baby kicking and the interfering, jealous cat who sensed in them something new and merciless, for they could not die. They could merely live, and for that they needed the hope to love each other that had been so miraculously provided; they could no longer give him and his kind the heedless loyal love of brotherhood.

16   Dima had a nose for Russians; he was always seeking the home he had never known, never opened his eyes upon as an infant—those blind eyes unseeing but opened to the homelit stars that a German poet spoke of. So he roamed and sought, ever, in a foreign prison.

In a disreputable Arab quarter of La Motte-Picquet was a barren-looking bar with fly-haunted tables for eating, an unusually bewildered *patronne* behind the cash register, and a formidable Russian waiter clad in work clothes and a woman's apron who advanced upon occasional diners with one hand to his hip wherefrom he produced magically, as if drawing a saber, knives, spoons, and forks for setting the table. Not that the clientèle cared for exotic atmosphere; the waiter was simply a man who preferred to carry on in the tradition of a captain of the hussars, no matter what he was doing at the moment.

The restaurant would have been totally uninteresting, moreover depressing, if it had not been for the kitchen, a sort of back room, where Kupchik spent his nights. A small, bow-legged, madly hospitable ex-Cossack and the beloved of Madame behind the cash register, Kupchik took over the kitchen with its Russian cook and Russian waiter for the purpose of entertaining his Russian friends. It was a great honor to be invited there. Unfortunately, so many were that Madame suffered from *crises* of hysteria and went bankrupt during the same year. Carmian and Dima were among the lucky ones. The restaurant itself, a hollow shell, was limited nightly to a few impecunious surly Arabs; now and then a Citroën worker on his way home. Russians never paid. They were in back, singing and playing, while Madame fumed and drummed her fingers.

In back there were usually the ferocious cook, the no less ferocious waiter, and gentle musical vagabonds of all ages. They produced music with the help of an ancient, shoulder-length-haired violinist who had studied in Italy, a young balalaika player, and a guitar player named Yura; these at any rate could always be counted upon. Others joined with whatever was handy. When the music was Russian and very moving, the cook flipped his pancakes sometimes—in his enthusiasm—upon the floor, and the waiter beat time with forks and knives, pausing to rap the old violinist across the knuckles when he sang. The violinist was an intellectual, and very sensitive, but he took it in the interest of music, as it was intended, and would consume a great deal of wine, cheese, pancakes, or meatballs, to soothe his feelings. The cook was very generous and fussed only over the disposal of garbage, which was everywhere. Kupchik glowed royally. Only Madame, bursting through the door, unable to endure it any longer —showed any signs of low, utterly non-Russian commercialism. She always darted away, though, having voiced her objection. She was under Kupchik's childlike spell and did not want to lose him.

They admired Dima and accepted his little lady rather formally at first (there had also been a certain Cold War of the spirit to overcome), then more affectionately, for they were pleased by her good manners, her gravity, and her delicious laughter. Not, however, by Journalist lady I who was sitting out front one evening (one of those coincidences that make people say big cities are villages) with an escort who undoubtedly provided relief from the stuffiness of the *flic* —and cajoled her way into the kitchen.

This American woman, without even having had many vodkas, pulled up her sweater in order to display to her compatriot a black lace brassière she had just bought. Every man present blushed violently. Kupchik hinted strongly that night that he would no longer enjoy her company in the back room.

One night Yura came rushing into the kitchen in a frenzy, for he had lost a watch (he already had three or four, but not as many as when he had deserted from the Red Army in 1946) through a frightful misfortune. He worked at the Citroën factory and was paying for his watch on the installment plan. He had put it in his upper vest pocket. On his way from the jeweler's shop he had felt his pocket to see if it was still there, being pleased with so good a watch for such a good price, and behold! it was not there. There was a hole, he detected at once, in the pocket. Shocked to the bone, he felt the pocket below. And here was the terrible, unforgivable irony—the lower vest pocket, also, was unspeakably possessed of a hole. Through two pockets the watch had fallen to the street. Sobbing his tale in Russian, for he still spoke no other language, weeping and throwing a pound of Roquefort cheese on the table, Yura rushed out into the night to get himself a wife, he said.

Everyone was sober and sympathetic for a while and played sad songs as they ate the cheese. One should have a wife, they all agreed. There was a long, disorderly comparison of wrist watches and the usual futile argument as to whose watch came closer to keeping Greenwich Time . . . the cook's knife started becoming rather playful, as it had a habit of doing . . . and Carmian wondered what would happen if they were ever confronted by the mysteries of Daylight Saving Time. Dima bowed and they took their leave.

"I'm glad," she said, "you refrained from telling them that I don't sew up your pockets."

"They would consider that most ungentlemanly."

The last métro had gone and they walked an endless stretch up the Avenue de la Motte-Picquet—where she sat on the curb at the Parc du Champ de Mars with its beautiful grass, nursing her blistered foot as they both wept amicably—past the Invalides, along the Seine and all the quays to la Cité. "*I can't*," she said; the French shoes hurt. He said, inexorably, "You can." There was a bit of this in everything they did. He was sunny and cruel with bursts of grief like thunderstorms, or showers. She was dark as the night with its passivity, its deep rages, its silence.

One night the restaurant at la Motte-Picquet was closed. Kup-

118

chik and his lady had gone to seek a better fortune—together certainly, for Kupchik was a gentleman and cared little for the ups and downs; one had both.

It rained, it was damp; the little restaurant, Place Dauphine, so expensive in its orange light under the awning with the tinkle of silverware and muted voices, closed down too with the departure of the last tourist and no more kept her company across the square. The cat snuggled close at night for warmth. The dampness pervaded one's pores and clothes; once washed her hair never dried; it was like living on an abandoned island. Lala came, horrifyingly, one morning when Dima was gone. She showed extraordinary tact, saying nothing about the herring wrappers, butter papers, and empty containers he had left on the table—nothing even about the cat.

"You need care and must come to me," said Lala. "How much money do you owe?"

When Carmian had finally agreed to go to Lala's, since it was too cold, too damp, too cramped here—but on condition that it would be temporary—Dima admitted that they owed the landlord eight thousand francs. Moreover, the day that he and his mother had settled upon for moving was one of his full working days.

Enraged, Carmian said, "I can't do that alone—in my state or any other."

"Lala will do everything. She has no sensitivity at all. Don't worry."

"I won't leave without my cat!"

"Take him, darling. It will compensate the landlord for his loss. Be a good girl. Lala is good at that—she says we have been paying too much and ought to go to the rent control. I'll see you this evening, rue Maison-Dieu."

"Oh," she moaned, burying her head in the pillow.

He blew out the door on his way to make a living for Michael Dmitrovitch. He could not worry about a thieving hôtelier. Soon they would have an apartment, new clothes, peace, and it was up to him alone.

She felt utterly desperate. Lala would help her.

She did. She came up in the afternoon and packed swiftly and vigorously. The tiara of St. Petersburg and Moscow had been exchanged for muscle and brawn and a mulish determination. She bustled downstairs, carrying or attempting to carry everything, everything

119

herself—for Carmian must not; she was very strict about that. She made three trips unaided by the young concierge who screamed in anguish at his office door. But she had the power to frighten him, screaming back rapidly in a French he could not possibly understand except for her references to swindling, police, and rent control. It seemed to Carmian that he was the party to call for the police, but he merely pulled her into his office while Lala scurried upstairs for the last load, indicating to her that he would accept some items of value as a guarantee of future payment. Hastily, together, like conspirators, they pawed through one of her suitcases selecting material hostages as Lala came bumping down the stairs.

Carmian saved her watch, telling him it was broken, but Lala was too late to prevent his acquisition of some American clothing, a pair of high-heeled shoes, and a hand-woven Tartar costume that belonged to Dima. Lala was just in time to snatch the round Tartar cap away from the distracted man, continuing on down the stairs with the last piece of luggage, while Carmian tore herself away from him with earnest assurances, Lala calling imperiously from below. After these eternities, Carmian found herself in a taxi, baggage and Lala installed, heading for *derrière*-Montparnasse. The Kitty was nowhere in sight.

The next day she and Dima found him, a familiar gray little starving figure hunched in the shadow of the staircase. He leaped into her arms, clinging, not scratching, while she said, "No, I would not leave you, little one. Never, never."

Dima went into the concierge's office. His unfailing man-to-man charm worked wonders (and no doubt he would not have bothered to exert it had he not pitied the young concierge and his wife) in the offering of explanations and promises. He even invoked the sacred name of Michael Dmitrovitch Koubyankov, as the young man smiled palely.

Still incredulous he asked: "Who was the lady? Your mother, Monsieur?" Still haunted.

Dima shrugged. "I regret. However, my wife is disembarrassing you of the cat. We are taking him to my home."

The young man bowed, suddenly more animated. "You do me a favor. I hope he will not find his way back."

"He will not want to," said Dima. "*Au revoir, Monsieur.* We shall return. *Au revoir, merci.*"

On the street the cat clawed her, terrified, with all evident intentions of drowning himself in the Seine rather than to venture farther into the black unknown, so they took a taxi. Lala, on hearing of this, was in a dudgeon.

"All that expense for a cat," she said scornfully.

"You have never learned human kindness," said her son. "God will not be good to you."

"And to *you*—poor children?"

"God is good," Dima reminded her, smiling wryly and winking at Carmian. "He saves little Kiri-Kiris."

Lala sniffed at the bohemians of the Latin Quarter. One could not possibly explain that her establishment was the most stark, extreme, and utterly astonishing example of bohemianism to be found among all the relics and ruins of Paris. She thought it rather cozy and tasteful and spent whole days rushing about in it cleaning, raising clouds of dust, straightening the furnishings and rearranging the empty jars and bottles on the shelves of the old Breton buffet. Apparently Russians were mad about jars, bottles, boxes, and old rags. An attempt on the part of Dima to throw them out to make room for Carmian's smaller belongings evoked tearful cries of: *"Moi bonky! Moi sklonky! Moi karobky!"* It was like a song.

Dima translated the words as jars, tops of jars, and boxes—the staples of Lala's magpie instinct. Carmian grew resigned to keeping everything of her own in suitcases, including her toothbrush. She was afraid of losing it.

Slowly she got used to life with Lala, although the more she did, the more she felt inclined to stay in bed permanently, and chilly mornings helped. In Paris without steam heat (or even with) it was best to go to bed for the winter. Lala did not mind in the least; it gave her more room and scope in which to do her cleaning while she chattered at the girl or—if Dima were still in bed with her, the mornings he did not work—to fight with her son. Dima on these days resembled a fallen windmill. Lala bustled, swept, and muttered furiously. After a while, if she was unable to rouse him to violence, she would vanish into her room to rummage. Carmian remarked that it was real hardship to listen to constant fighting in a language one did not understand.

"She is not only mean but stupid," he raged. *"Elle est méchante et bête.* I would not mind the first so much, but I cannot bear the second, and as a combination it is unbeatable."

Carmian said, "She is kind to me."

"You will learn."

"She pampers and pets me when you are gone. She won't let me carry water—she brings me ice-cream cones."

"That's because you're giving her a grandchild. She collects them."

"Like bonky-sklonky?"

"And Belgian francs and sugar and tea and tin cans."

"How did you ever grow up?"

"Well, I went away to school. After my father died."

"But you know, she's better than I thought."

"Don't underestimate her. She is as full of ruses as a scheming child."

"If all she wants is a grandchild, I'm perfectly willing. . . ." She sat up suddenly and said: "I must get up. I *have* to. It comes upon me all at once, now. And here I am—not dressed and I can't wait. . . ."

"That's what the cans are for. Don't be ashamed, darling. This isn't America."

Her eyes widened in panic and filled with tears at the labor, the hopelessness of it all. "And then the water to wash—I can't—"

"I will get your water and everything you need. Don't worry. We'll have an apartment soon. I have a friend at the Opéra. . . ."

Eventually, the impossible accomplished, the mountain scaled, she stood dressed and ready to go out to market. He kissed her and left for work, holding a half-eaten sandwich.

She shopped in the rue de l'Ouest, renamed after a Resistance hero rue Raymond Losserand, which led to the Porte de Vanves to the south ending abruptly in a flea market and an open plain. Some days she went eastward on the rue Daguerre, or north on the rue de la Gaîté toward the Gare Montparnasse and M. de Bérancourt's rue de Rennes. The three streets were like a three-armed star-fish in the midst of which the rue Maison-Dieu was tucked away somewhere, unknown even to taxi drivers. She was relieved to be out of that hate-infested hotel with its terrible blue wallpaper flowers. Still, it was sad here in the south of Paris where no tourist penetrated, no American was seen. Hidden and lost, she did her two-carrots, three-potatoes sort of shopping, stoically bearing the displeasure of grocers (no foreigner had the right to parsimony), telling herself that penny pinching was almost endurable without the specter of a mounting hotel bill; that she had her Dima and her Michael at last, and that the world would reclaim them one day when they were three.

She was more than four months pregnant when she boarded the bus with Dima that took them rollicking across town to the Gare du Nord. She was taking the Belgian route again—it cost more but it was faster and easier. It had cost Dima his week's pay, and Lala was in a dreadful state; had she been Carmian she would have gone by cattle car.

The city lights flickered and glowed in passing. His arm tightened around her and he said, "You should not be standing." But the bus was crowded and it was always more fun in back, anyway.

Dima swept her up into the train, and her little suitcase, and ran alongside with tears in his eyes. They smiled and waved dutifully. She hoped the inspector would not look too closely at the expired date on her passport. She needed a re-entry stamp. A visa would have solved *that*, but they did not have the four thousand francs.

Ah, cette bureaucratie!

When shall we have peace?

Take care of the kitty—

Take care of Michael—

Be good—

Come soon—soon—

The wheels took up their symphony.

17 The baby hopped one day on a leafy residential street of quiet Bonn. It seemed to rear its head and poke—as if to look out precociously— and she almost fainted with tenderness. She addressed him in all the languages: My beloved, *moi malchik, mein Junge, mon petit frère, mon enfant. . . .* He was there as truly as if his feet were already upon earth. Your mama, she said, will take care of you. For the first time this particular heaven was revealed to her. *That* was what it had all been about! Of course, of course.

She patted him and herself, smiling, thinking that she and Dima were of the same wretchedness and of the same goodness, too, and that it was only right to make of them a third who would transcend them. She loved. What divinity it was to love something more than yourself! She went to bed eleven nights in her cold cheap room with hot bricks for her feet (there was a cold wind from Russia, the Germans said), warmed by love as the bricks burned, then turned stony cold. When she had accumulated the money allotted daily from her foreigner's account, she boarded the Paris-bound train, crossing the frontiers of Germany, Belgium, and France with equal impassivity as customs inspectors, currency and passport controllers came around —she with a thousand marks cash in her pocket, all of it recorded in fine German script in her passport. Sheer hell, she thought to herself almost gaily, primed with a little Schnapps for courage—especially through Belgium where there were two borders and you had to go through the whole thing twice. Of course, she had gone second class and they never looked hard at her. And all they could do would be to confiscate the money: but that would be like death now. She thought about Michael and Dima, listening to the beat of the wheels, sometimes sleeping, until finally the drab suburbs of Paris loomed; the factories of the district named Stalingrad, the tenements, and in the distance the ivory Sacré-Cœur on its hill.

There was no one waiting. She went the length of the station seeing no one until Lala met her at the *barrière*. Her heart smote her because she knew in a flash that Lala had not wanted to pay ten francs for a platform ticket, and also because she knew that something had happened.

In the smell, smoke and steam of the station, looking sharply at Lala's face, she revolted and thought: God, I hate him. I shall hate him until I die. For all the joy had died in her.

Lala, wearing a Russian hat of the thirties, was trying to hide her agitation, thinking of the grandchild, Carmian guessed. "Nothing is really wrong," she insisted, guiding her to a taxi, taking her bag, "merely a minor injury."

"What sort of injury?"

"Don't be nervous," Lala said, lighting her cigarette for her. "He is home and waiting for you."

"Can't he walk?"

"He broke his ankle," said Lala. "At the Opéra."

Even Dima did not descend to such a lie—to her. He explained to her that on the single night he had ventured out for amusement, he had got into a café brawl with three Arabs. The curious thing was that several years ago three Arabs had attacked him in the street in order to take his wallet and, as he told it, his anger was so great that he beat them all off, for he had just been paid; also, it was winter and he was wearing ski boots. Dima always won fights because he was bigger, and faster with his head and his feet. But this time he had tripped and fallen backward over a table; the ankle was fractured in two places. He looked at her with the objective eyes of the boy criminal who had done his worst and waits for the world to punish him.

With her coat still on, her suitcase on the floor, she covered her face with her hands. She said nothing. She had changed. His bad little girl was growing up. Suddenly tears stung his eyes so that he closed them in pain. "They insulted you," he said, although he had not meant to. "They knew us from Saint-Germain. That's why I lost my temper."

She was not interested in the Arabs. "It means . . . no work, no money?"

"Oh, we will have compensation, don't worry. In France these things are taken care of—I shall get half-pay for as long as—"

"Three months," Lala moaned coming out of her room, "and it's I who shall foot the bills again. Why was I ever born?"

"I have often wondered, but I never knew you did."

"*Hooligán!*" Lala screamed in Russian.

"There is someone about to be born," Carmian said coldly. "I went to Germany and slept with bricks to keep warm in order to get money. I come back to find chaos and destruction."

They looked at her in bewilderment. He poked his head up, she thought. He is ready and waiting, and taking all I can give him. They have got to help. She said: "What of the divorce? How will you pay for it?"

When Lala had retired to her room, he answered her. "Look, Cammie, you must give me eighteen thousand francs."

"I will go with you to the lawyer."

He smiled his ironical, slant-eyed smile. *"C'est toi qui commande."*

The cat crept up on them, courting, caressing, going from one to the other—as always when his security threatened to evaporate. Love me, he said with his soft kneading paws, don't desert me. She never would, and he knew it, choosing her stomach as his ultimate haven, the little mound that contained his brother.

None of this escaped Dima. In the dark he said: "He missed you. He was gone for three days and he has just returned. You must never leave him."

"When you save a life you are responsible for it. He knows that."

"You are kind," Dima said.

"What good does it do me? I'm not happy."

"We will be happy," he swore to himself in the dark. "We will. We will."

And the cat and the unborn baby, these curious allies, slept with her, while they twined their arms about each other.

Lala was given to saying that the cat would smother the baby. She was full of these sayings. The wrinkled gray-green eyes, their slant inherited from a droopy-whiskered grandfather, were foreboding, acquisitive, hungry for her grandchild. Carmian let herself be babied. Lala's potato purée and Lala's *ragoût de bœuf*, bought of her own purse, were—once the painful severance had been concluded—happily served and eaten. Lala showed her the trunkful of baby clothes she had mysteriously accumulated, some of it from Serge, some from the children of Dima's half-brother Kolya. "They will be yours," she said, with the sweetness of a prima donna tossing her flowers to the great conductor. Sometimes she came home carrying a dripping ice-cream cone, licked off the top and offered it to her —one child to another, beaming out of her Tartar eyes.

When Dima came home it was different. Carmian was the referee, that thankless job. Yet she was grateful when she felt him stiffen and tremble beside her on their bed, gathering himself together for the counterattack, and she put her hands around his neck, not caring for the old woman who tormented him, reminding him to keep calm—and he took up her hands and kissed them like a man reprieved from death.

The wooden chandelier above the three heads swayed like

the sword of Damocles, but when he was silent at her bidding Lala withdrew or fluttered about in fear. It was difficult to deny the substitute mother who brought childishly licked ice-cream cones. But Carmian knew whom she loved, and it was easier now—for her—that his rage went on Lala like the tide over a breakwater, leaving only the gentle swell and ripple. Dima knew the object of his anger.

Sometimes she wanted to scream at them: I'm sick of it! Yet she understood him, her twin, and knew all the anguish in the face of the photograph in which he held his dog against the world. And every day Lala became more pitiable and strange, as she studied the picture of six little laughing girls with their governess, fur-hatted, dark against the Kremlin. How long the road from there to this old woman, slightly mad, rushing headlong through the snowless labyrinth of Paris on her fantastic errands?

Dima had spent a lot of time in the cafés with his father. One night Lala, then rich and pretty, had dashed into the Café du Dôme brandishing a pistol, searching for his father's mistress. All the Dôme's sober customers had promptly ducked under the tables, convinced that a wild Russian woman would plug the wrong party, and among the cowering ones were Dima and his father who had pushed him under. Lala shot at the ceiling. Dima laughed, telling the story as if he had never been a child full of shame. Carmian knew. Yet it was funny. She woke up one night laughing about it until he put his hand over her mouth and stroked her and kissed her and put her back to sleep.

Laughing at Lala was part fury. Raging at her, Dima was like Prometheus, chained to their couch which sometimes seemed like an island of sanity in the cluttered living room. Lala, having achieved her aim, would raise fearful clouds of dust.

"If I did not have this ankle . . ." he menaced her.

"*Durák! Hooligán!* Tell me the truth, Carmiane, he has hit you too, has he not?"

"Leave my wife out of this!" Dima roared. "She has nothing to do with what is between you and me! I love her and that is all."

Just back from the country where she had been visiting Denise and Serge—always the time when Lala was at her most venomous—she would taunt and worry him: Serge had a cold, Denise a boy friend—

"What do I care? Why do you talk about her? You know it

hurts the little one here! Why don't you leave us alone, *duraká! Tu es toc, tu sais?*"

One day when Lala, whose obstinacy or curiosity had no bounds, was talking about Denise, Carmian stood up suddenly and raised her fist, her face red as fire. It drained suddenly, and she sat down—almost falling into a chair. Then, sitting upright, she swayed slowly from side to side, deathly white.

They watched her in horror. Lala went to her cupboard and poured some brandy she had been hoarding, and held Carmian's head, tipping it down her throat. "All right, children, now we will be quiet," she said. She got out her cards, for Carmian liked having her fortune told.

"A letter tomorrow . . . much love . . . success in legal matters," she intoned, with significant leers and simpers, while Dima fondled his girl, anxiously noting her recovery. Lala went into the tiny kitchen and cooked a *ragoût* for them, muttering to herself in Russian over the inadequacies of her utensils.

Sometimes she had a few of her countrywomen of the moth-eaten type in to dinner. They were usually princesses. Occasionally there would be a count, and Carmian came to know that a roomful of Russians will sit with unlighted cigarettes in their mouths, looking thoughtful, for as long as ten minutes or until somebody strikes a match. She undertook this job.

At one of these soirées, Lala's stew, served with exquisite anticipation and graciousness, had a rather unsatisfactory reception. Forks and knives were laid down quietly. The rolling voices were stilled for a minute. Shura's small lips were compressed almost to invisibility. Lala went on eating.

"Delicious!" she said in French. "How do you like it, Carmiane? It has a tiny flavor of—*je ne sais quoi*. However . . ." She finished every bit. Only later they learned she had accidentally dropped a bar of soap into it.

In Lala's house there was a railroad-station atmosphere (Compagnie des Wagons-Lits et Express Européens) of waiting, as people came and went and one played at cards, and Dima lay waiting for his ankle to heal, and Carmian waited for her child, and Lala waited to grow rich on some scheme or other. It was an impermanent air—the best one could do for the time being—one had to make the most (or least) of it. Now and then the thought did occur: Would the train ever come?

Carmian and Dima played poker and sometimes drank the cheap champagne and made love when Lala was not there. They played for high stakes: You win, we do—I win, we don't. She played the rôle of fate, and he of desire. It was a game of laughter and argument in which nothing was sacred. Dima always won, and Carmian put on a show of sulking horribly. The beautiful game did not escape Lala's shrewd eye, but she let it pass. One of her virtues was an apparent lack of jealousy. She lusted for change and excitement.

A dozen children, six girls and six boys, Carmian thought looking at the picture of the bland swanlike girl—how they must have fought! That house in Moscow, and the one in St. Petersburg, must have been a hell for governesses. Lala would repeat their names for her amusement, in singsong, counting chronologically on her fingers: Lala, Olga, Kolya, Tolya, Nina, Dima, Nadia, Alya, Talya, Shura, Vasya, Stasya. It was a nursery rhyme.

One day when she had gone off the deep end again, home from Châtenay, she said something in Russian to Dima, who glared at her. It was morning and he was barely awake.

Carmian roused herself like someone coming out of a dream.

"I know what you said!"

They stared at her. "You what?"

"You have a letter from her for him. She asked you to give it to him, and you said you would show it to him in the other room. What is in it?"

They stared a little longer, Lala rather pale, and Dima burst out laughing.

"She's learned Russian, my girl!" he cried. "*Now* what are you going to do?"

"Oh, we shall tell her, of course, it's no secret—" Lala stammered, discountenanced, red-handed. "Of course, of course! Come, we'll buy champagne to celebrate. . . ." She dug into her purse.

Later they sat eating and drinking gaily, Dima with his foot in the cast propped up on a chair, Lala wildly feeding cake and champagne to the cat. And Lala, as an even more extravagant gesture, kissed her new daughter-in-law on the forehead. It was Old Home Week.

18 Lala displayed pride and complacency over Carmian's Russian which had suddenly become vocal, like a two-year-old's burst into his mother tongue after long silence. She took the credit for this phenomenon for herself and coached her informally throughout the day.

Carmian's further rewards included learning the text of Denise's love notes of which Lala had been the faithful bearer. They were written in excellent French (*le style littéraire*) with a conciliatory affection that placed the writer upon a pedestal of virtue and wisdom as well as wit, youth, beauty ("I gazed at my reflection . . .") and maternal gratitude ("At least you have given me a magnificent son").

It was amazing to understand almost anything that was said in any language. Among the three, the language dodge was seen as outgrown and simply discarded: if necessary one could write notes or whisper. Lala understood German well and spoke it badly—a formula that applied to all her languages except Russian. Her French included such monstrosities as "voyla," "kom il fot" (the *c* was clearly a *k*), "to-wah" for *toi*, and "Konciergeka"—to whom she referred without benefit of the preposition, as the English speak of "Cook." Konciergeka was mentioned often in the most unflattering terms, for she owned the chickens in the courtyard, caused mail to disappear, was a red-hot Communist, and detested Lala.

Only Lala's pre-Revolutionary Muscovite Russian was bell-like, ultragrammatical, and precise, with a sliding and caressing feel, like her sugar candies going down. It was beautiful to hear although not remarkable in content. All Lala's talk seemed to end with "*patóm, patóm*" (later, later) or "*y tagdaly*" (et cetera), staving off interruptions or unwelcome discussions to clear the way for certain tales that began: "*Ona skazala . . .*" (she said). Carmian had found out that these she-said stories were usually traceable to Shura or Denise, and almost always odious.

Lala had a language student, a prim young engineer who lived with his parents and three sisters in a two-room apartment near the Ecole Militaire. They had been looking for another apartment for seven years, he said with a shrug, the well-adjusted cynicism one expected from him; consequently he was prevented from taking a bride. He was interested in Russia and Soviet science, he told Dima. Plainly he wanted to emigrate. He never told Lala anything. He paid her to teach him Russian.

Most of the time, however, he was paying her to eat cake. She would not accept money because he was a poor student, so he invariably came with a large round cake in his briefcase—a bulge that Lala, hanging out the window, spotted on the avenue du Maine. Carmian was sorry for him, since he had logic, a definite goal, and material progress ever in mind, while Lala's greediness was simply a passion for rubbish, a fetish, a child's game of pebbles. Defending himself, the student always came too early in order to allow time for the seizing, praising, cutting, and eating of the cake (so that there would be time for lessons). She also went about grinding and preparing her Congo coffee, at the same time rushing about pulling the couch together and slamming the door to her own room, where Dima and Carmian had been banished with threats and exhortations to dress the moment the young student's step creaked on the floor boards outside.

"My children!" she simpered in apology.

"Oh, I know how it is!" he would always reply. And then, hopefully, he would continue further chitchat in his fluently terrible Russian.

Meanwhile behind the door Carmian's mouth watered, and Dima, peering through the slit, said triumphantly, "Yes, he has a cake."

"Well then, let's go." Coffee—how good coffee was! "Which do you like best?" she asked, pulling on a dreadful sweater. She had no clothes any more.

"The cake," said Dima, and swung himself out on his crutches.

"Where is my daughter-in-law?" Lala cried theatrically. *"Idi syudá, Karmianka!"* She clapped three times.

Carmian finished combing her hair and emerged, feeling a little like someone in Outer Mongolia. She took her place beside Dima on the couch, holding his plaster-cast leg in her lap, and they followed the progress of the weekly lesson with suppressed giggles. The student obviously considered them bohemian and somewhat stupid. Lala passed the coffee and cake interminably with gracious smiles and gestures, her usual diet being dry bread out of a tin box that rattled like walnuts, and unsweetened tea. The student was an excuse to celebrate, and Lala loved an excuse.

"—You know each other? Kamitchka has a pure Russian accent which I want you to listen to closely, Piotr Stepanovitch. Say: *porokhod*, Karmianka."

"Pa-ra-khód," Carmian obliged, munching. Evidently he was struggling with the intricacies of the Russian *o*, which they pronounced as they pleased, mostly like *a*'s. The boy was still trying to make *o*'s out of them. He looked at her with reproach and disfavor. An American had no business speaking Russian.

"Perfect—you see?" said Lala, clapping her hands. "Now, say: Vye—tye—byelyi. Na!"

This was the hardest, the vowel that seemed to exist in no other language and made one suspect Russians had an extra opening or secret passage in their throats. She primed her inner ear, hearing rich, larded Russian tones; syrupy ascent descending on a note of implacable regret. She formed a sound with her tongue and palate three times and again won approval. The student was furious.

"You have the vocabulary," she tried to appease him. "I'm just a parrot, you know."

"You are very good, Kamitchka," Lala said, slapping down Dima's reaching hand before she passed the cake platter, first to Carmian.

No matter what else she might do—it was strange—Lala loved stuffing her with sweets.

"Now we shall read," Lala declared after three-quarters of the hour had passed and she had swept away the crumbs. The student read on, entirely unreformed by the recent example; it was all French to him. Carmian felt sad thinking how much he must hate her, and Dima seemed unable to suppress a ridiculous desire to talk to him about politics. After several interruptions, in resignation, the student packed his briefcase and chatted a while with Dima. His political views and sympathies were rather personal—strictly confined, one might say, to the framework of an engineer interested in finding work. He was very analytical and well informed; grandiosity was not in him. Possibly he hated those barbarians whose language he was painfully learning and whom he was going to have to live with. But, he said sighing: "Africa is dead. America is saturated." After he had gone, shaking hands endlessly, hurtling (perhaps falling) down the stairs as so many did, they were rather glad. He was a ghastly bore.

"You liked his cake," Lala remarked. "You must admit, he is a polite young man."

On a full stomach and a brisk sunny morning, they nodded warmly and agreed again that he was.

They were sitting in Chedwick's apartment on the rue de Vaugirard, watching in silence as this funny woman, Chedwick's landlady, poured them each a glass of homemade cherry liqueur. She chattered shrilly and appraised: "Your wife is expecting a baby, Monsieur?" felicitating them. It did not show much yet, but Frenchwomen always knew and got up for Carmian in buses, as if they had X-ray eyes. Only once a conductor had noticed and loudly ordered gentlemen to rise. "Madame is a *little* bit tired," was the way he put it.

Dima performed their share of the introductory ritual, patter, patter, patter, complimenting Madame upon her period furniture which was Edwardian and rather horrible except for the handsome desk; Carmian could see that he coveted the desk. Photographs of a fierce-mustached man stared down from all the walls. "My husband," she explained, touching the gold pocket watch she wore on a chain hanging down over her stiff bosom to her waist. Her snapping black eyes rolled alarmingly, the eyelids fluttering. "He was a motorcyclist and was killed in an accident. Twenty-three years ago!" She pulled a handkerchief out of one leg of mutton sleeve and hurried out of the room.

"Her clothes, my God," he muttered in German.

"What do you think she wants us for?"

"Maybe Chedwick didn't pay his rent."

"She looks crazy to me."

"She's out of Balzac. The liqueur is not bad."

Madame returned with a dish of cookies which she placed beside Carmian. Then she reseated herself in the majestic armchair in front of the desk, arranged the folds of her red velvet gown, and began: "I am aware that you are curious to know why I sent for you. I had expected you earlier."

"The letter was forwarded from a previous address. We came as soon as we got it."

"I see. I found that address among Mr. Chedwick's things—also a manuscript which I take to be the property of Madame."

"He returned to America, then!" said Carmian.

133

"Yes, he returned to America," Madame echoed somberly.

"Why didn't he tell us? We haven't seen him for two months."

"There was good reason, Madame." She sighed. "I shall tell you."

There was more arranging of folds and nervous pattings of the bird's nest she wore on her head, fingerings of the watch on the chain, until Dima said rather rudely:

"*Eh bien, Madame, si vous seriez si gentille.*"

She spread her hands supplicatingly. "First you must understand my position—as a woman alone, a widow struggling along on a small pension with all this to keep up. I took in this young American to share my apartment—in all propriety, you understand. He was most courteous, most discreet, a gentleman of high moral and mental caliber. He was in letters and I have always had an interest in literature. We became, I think, good friends. I took the place of his mother, so to speak. Well, Madame, Monsieur, it was only in September that I discovered he was gravely ill. He developed seizures which on occasion caused me to find him lying unconscious on the floor of his room. Oh, it was terrifying!" She clutched at her bosom. "I am not well myself. I have heart disease. Many times I thought that I—"

"Didn't he have a doctor?"

"Under the circumstances I thought it best to persuade him to depart immediately for his native country where he would be cared for, where he had relatives. He did not know how sick he was himself. I—a widow—what could I do in case—"

A cold suspicion crept over them. "He is dead," said Dima.

"*Oui, Monsieur.* He was too feeble to pack his own things, so I did. I believe he was barely conscious. I took him to the airport myself. Then, a few weeks ago, I received this letter from his parents"—she picked it up off the desk—"informing me that he had died in mid-ocean of a tumor of the brain."

For a moment they did not move. Dima rose and bowed shortly, his face stiff. "Thank you for telling us. I wish we had been called."

She stretched forth a hand in the fantastic sleeve. "No—wait, Monsieur, I beg of you. The letter of Madame Chedwick is in English, naturally, and although I managed to decipher some of it—my English has been all but forgotten. I understand that your wife is an American. Monsieur Chedwick had spoken of her and her talent to me. I wonder, Madame, if you would be so kind as to translate this letter for me before you go. It would be a great service."

Dima eased himself down, the creases around his eyes hardening as Carmian read a testimonial to the gullibility of a heartbroken mother from Pennsylvania. Chedwick had been their only son. She thanked his good friend for caring for him so well. He had often written home of Madame's generosity and kindness. She would never forget . . . and so on. Was there anything she could do for Madame in her gratitude to allay her own grief?

Madame's little dark eyes sparkled with triumph and tears. She made birdlike exclamations: "But how nice! . . . The poor mother! With parents like that, no wonder he was such a good boy! The things he used to bring me . . . so generous!"

Carmian folded the letter, handed it back to her, and said, "So you are reassured, Madame."

"Yes, thank you, my dear."

As they were being ushered out, Carmian turned. "You should have sent him to the American hospital."

Now relaxed and off her guard, the lady shrugged. "If anything had happened . . . the expenses, *les ennuis* . . . You understand me, Madame. A person in my position could not possibly."

There were only two things to do. They took the alien course of leaving in silence. Carmian ran down the stairs, with him right behind her, muttering, "Let's get out of here before I throw up."

"You should have done it sooner so you could spoil the rug."

"Poor Chedwick, poor Chedwick, how could he—" She leaned against the portal and wept suddenly.

"Think of the motorcyclist's mustache," he advised.

As a matter of fact, it helped.

The elderly surgeon from the *Assurances sociales* who treated Dima's broken ankle was another motorcyclist, a bearded one in a brown leather jacket and crash helmet, possessor of the loudest vehicle Carmian had ever had the misfortune to hear. It was his habit to look at the clock every once in a while and pop a pill into his mouth; he kept different kinds in different pockets. He grumbled savagely that their clock was never right, which made it necessary for him to dig after his own curiously elusive timepiece, but met Lala's coquetry head-on with the utmost courage and nobility, scattering compliments, although he would not be inveigled into staying for tea. He would pound down the stairs like a man possessed and go roaring off as if competing in a *course nationale de motos.*

The next time the doctor came he was less offhand than usual. Dima's ankle was swollen, it hurt, and he demanded to know what he had done to it. Dima described the activities of the day they had gone to Chedwick's: a visit to his lawyer, a stop *aux Assurances,* a visit to a sick friend. . . .

"I strictly forbade you to go out," the doctor said fiercely.

"*M'sieur le docteur,* my wife is pregnant and a foreigner. She cannot do these things. I had to see my lawyer or else the divorce would be put off till next year: already it was very late. As for the *Assurances,* they do not send money and we have to eat from time to time. My signature was needed in one case and—as you know, not even Frenchmen can deal successfully with those people. An American could hardly—"

"You have delayed the cure for a matter of months," said the doctor wagging his beard. "Perhaps your leg is not important to you, *tant pis.* But you may be left with a permanent limp."

He retaped the ankle, popped a pill in his mouth after checking his watch, threw a contemptuous glance at Lala's clock, and departed. His motorcycle racketed down the street as Carmian gazed at Dima's sullen eyes, horror-stricken. Thank God Lala was not home! He turned his face to the wall but let her hold him round the waist and bury herself against him as much as she could. The cat, as susceptible to scenes of affection as of strife, jumped up to snuggle in the crook of her knees.

"You see what happens?" he said bitterly. "It is too much. It is all much too hard for us."

"I should have done all those things alone, and I'm ashamed."

"You could not. It is too hard. You—" he laughed briefly. "God."

"It was hard for Chedwick too. Think of Chedwick."

"I was a dancer when I was a kid," he mumbled, and she knew he was crying.

"Chedwick was alive once," she said, she did not know why, kissing his fine gold hair and the wetness in it.

136

19 What Dima
called *la bande Rajensky* invaded them. Shura she already knew:
cool, plump, quietly *haute couture*, and colorless, except that she
wore a great Russian Cross on her chest—with good reason, one
gathered after hearing Lala's stories. She had much to be thankful
for. Then there was Kolya, or Nikolai, a big broad shaggy-haired man
shorter than Dima, with stern and pleasing but angry features. He
had Grecian beauty to begin with, but life had given him a sour
look. He arrived at Lala's in overalls and a turtle-neck sweater with
axle grease on his hands, for he was an automobile enthusiast. Dima
said that he had the soul of a mechanic. This was Dima's half-
brother, older by the ten years he had spent in Russia—a circumstance, Carmian thought, Dima was unlikely ever to forgive him.

The bearish person was civil to her to the extent of bowing and
saying, *"Bonjour, Madame."* He had one of those voices she had
grown used to that seemed to rumble up from the guts, and a Russian
accent. He inquired after Mama and after Dima's health, to which his
brother responded coldly, offering him a glass of wine. Kolya refused.
He did accept a cigarette rolled from the stale tobacco of old butts
that Dima kept in a tin.

His father had been a high Imperial officer, of course, who had
died prosaically of pneumonia at the onset of the 1917 Revolution.
According to Dima, they were an unimaginative lot, of Baltic ancestry, concerned only with material acquisition, impervious to the
arts, made to live in little houses in suburbs, tinker with motors, and
emigrate to the United States.

His own father, the man with the dark burnt eyes whose picture
stood on Lala's piano, had been a true aristocrat from a renowned
family of warriors and landowners. Mikhail's brother had owned three
thousand acres in Poland and given little dinner parties for twenty
with a footman behind the chair of each guest until, one day in
1939, his two sons had been found murdered and castrated on the
estate as the Red Army rolled westward. ("Not land we want, but
blood. Even Christ cannot get you out of the grave.") Dima had no

use for his uncle's high living and would probably never have mentioned the tragedy if it had not occurred to him, off and on, that he need not have been poor. Dima had been heir to half of it. His uncle had no children, any more. Only the parents were left. They lived somewhere in Germany in dire straits, and Lala sent them a package sometimes.

"I wrote to him to get out of Poland," Dima would say. "Pack up, save what you can, and come west as fast as possible. But he would not listen. . . . He didn't want to lose the land."

The antagonism between Dima and Kolya was poisonous and to her unbelievable. They were civilized and had to content themselves with bristling and a lidding, in Kolya's case, of cold eyes; while Dima's hot eyes bulged. But the air was thick and it was not hard to imagine them breaking their fetters and getting at each other as they really wanted, perhaps always had. Lala used Kolya to discipline the rebellious Dima. "I'll tell Kolya," she would scream. "He will come down here and give you the beating of your life!" Dima would laugh, enraged, although clearly he thought this quite possible in spite of the fact that he was as big and half a head taller. "He will not! He doesn't give a damn about you, foolish old witch!"

So their childhood loomed up before Carmian, that had begun in a St. Petersburg mansion for Kolya, in a German internment camp for Dima.

"But what did he *do* to you?" she asked.

"Do! He is a brute, an animal. He would trade in his wife for a new car. Whatever goes on in his mind I do not know—but it's not thinking! And this creature is my . . . my . . ."

"What did he do to you when you were little?"

Suddenly he said: "He used to frighten me. He would jump at me out of dark places and shriek and flap his arms. Once he took me out back of a chicken coop at night and scared me and watched me cry."

"He was jealous."

"I was only a little boy."

"Lala made it worse for him. He didn't have his father."

"I suppose," he said moodily, but with the grace he always had of examining an idea without prejudice.

His animosity did not extend to Kolya's daughter, Eliane. She

138

was seventeen and vapidly but lushly pretty, blond, doe-eyed, and best described in Hollywood terms, such as "gorgeous." She looked as if she had been made in California and could scarcely avoid winding up back there even if she wanted to. Dima afforded her the bemused and baffled, indulgent treatment he always gave these accidents of nature, but he was rather kinder to Eliane since she was a nice child. Her stupidity was tempered by good will. He gave her a hundred francs before sending her home on the bus, though she towered over Carmian and had the overripe mouth of an Italian film star. It was like Lala giving Carmian a lollipop.

Eliane was a runner-up for the French Women's Basketball Championship and bore promise of becoming a fine athlete if her other, more valuable assets should remain undiscovered that long. Lala doted on her almost as fanatically as she doted on Serge. Serge had the advantage of being a boy and younger and the son of Dima (who in her questionable heart had always been her pet, no matter how she raved). The day Serge came, Carmian thought she would throw up. Lala's fatuousness, and his exploitation of it, was sickening, and Carmian thought: I won't let her do that with my son.

Serge needed no babying. Under his straw-thatched top the blue eyes were pools of mischief, greed, willfulness, contempt, and extraordinarily bad behavior well planned in advance. Carmian did not like him, nor he her. Apparently their relationship was not to improve. But his father loved him, and the attempt to get along, to be nice, was oddly mutual between the son and the woman who had stolen his father. Perhaps Serge thought that some cooperation would be of material benefit to him; perhaps he wanted to please Papa. But inevitably when they looked into each other's eyes, the brown and the blue, equally wide and innocent (she was all of nine years old at those times and just as innocent as he), they knew they were enemies.

Thus, once, he stuck out his little boy's arm and poked her in the eye. Never having been hated by a little boy before, or any small animal, the outrage, the shock, was worse than the physical pain, which was considerable. She would rather have been hit in the eye by a man, whose fist would be bigger. As things were, Serge's fist inserted itself neatly into the socket and left a shiner that lasted an intolerably long time. In fact, she could scarcely see for several days.

Dima was very stern with Serge, but Carmian, looking at Serge through clots of blood, thought, "Boy, I do not blame you in the least."

While Lala crammed him with sweets and affection, Serge rattled on happily in his parrot voice, showing off his Russian, his argot and his impudence. His French was spectacular. *"Te casse pas les nénettes, Papa,"* he would toss off airily, his mouth full of cookies. He was tolerant of Lala, but when she bothered him he said: *"Tu m'énerves, alors, tu m'énerves, Lala."* When he grew tired, like any small boy, he always brought up his nerves to explain things, and to his mother, who was the only person he feared, he often cried: "I couldn't help it, Maman; it's my nerves!"

When he had gone, Dima said: "Don't look like that. I will love your son more, since I love you."

"No. No. I wouldn't ask you to."

"He will be a miracle," Dima said, dreaming, staring at the icon of St. Gleb with a sword in his hands and a halo round his head. "A demon and an angel both. A genius."

The little one kicked hard and she laughed. They edged closer together with the delicacy they had and had discovered in each other. The cat clambered up, turning round and round on Carmian's stomach before he settled.

Later, she used to think that everything would have been all right, in spite of the broken ankle, in spite of the pennilessness that was the natural climate of Lala's house, in spite of Lala herself and her fancies, in spite of a divorce that appeared to grow more unlikely as time passed . . . for without these impediments she knew that Dima and she would have been happy. She used to think that it would have gone well if it had not been for the visit of Denise de Koubyankov.

On the dark staircase, back from her shopping tour, she heard Denise's voice. It was a pleasant and melodic European voice, but now strident, haranguing. A woman who wants to be boss, she thought angrily, a dominating woman. She had come from the rue de l'Ouest with potatoes, carrots, bread, and half a pound of good horsemeat. The baby was suddenly heavy. Dima opened the door and said: "Come in! What are you doing here? Darling, I won't let them mistreat you!"

"No, no."

"Come in. Please!"

"She came without telling me—they—"

"No, I won't."

From inside, Denise screamed: "No, if it's she, I won't see her! I will not see her!"

Carmian gave him her bundles and went back into the darkness of the hall toward the stairs. "I can't," she said over her shoulder, apologetically.

"If you come," he hissed, "we'll go together into the other room! Don't you see that will send her away?"

But there was Lala. Somehow, lately Carmian had grown weak and she preferred to flee, even from him; she would risk nothing, nothing at all, not a moment's insult and hate. It was very important not to.

"I won't see that woman!" Denise stormed, inside.

"Have you no faith in me?" Dima begged.

To her lasting regret she turned her back on him, went down the dark well of the stairs and started to walk round and round, up and down all the sad streets, the gray streets of Paris she had come to know.

It was November and it was damp and cold. She walked down to the rue Daguerre and thought of the ancestor of the photograph and his era. It seemed a better one. She looked across at the rue Froidevaux, now dark and lonely, where Dima had lived as a rich little boy when his father was still there. It was a beautiful street, with a cemetery wall; it held the march of saddened feet for which one weeps. She had known such streets before. But children can do nothing.

She became terribly cold and went into the bistro off the rue Daguerre and had a hot rum. She had another . . . and the fish-hawker's cries and market lights and the dreadful sadness for the dead mingled together like Christmas. . . . The living were not to be pitied; they could have rum.

She walked home slowly in the cold. She had a sore throat, but Lala had given her a woolen scarf which she wrapped around twice, and a small Russian fur hat. Her coat, which she had bought in Germany, came almost to her ankles since she had lost weight. She looked like a refugee from Omsk.

From the staircase she heard Denise's voice again and turned and went down the stairs again without waiting to hear any more. She walked until she found a bench to sit on.

The next morning, after a night of walking, homecoming, and idiotically boring explanations and placations, she was happy to see that she was about to miscarry.

"Oh, no," Dima said, "no. It's something else." He mopped the floor with a helpless air, mopping up the water that had burst out of her.

"Yes," she agreed, "it must be something else."

He limped on his crutch to the kitchen and started heating water for washing. Lala was giving vent to her medical opinions, all hopeful, for she did not want to lose a grandchild. She refused to tear up her old sheets and rags, almost coming to blows with Dima while he tore them out of her cupboard and did it himself.

Strangely detached, Carmian saw their anger and horror quite happily until the pain started, and then she began to pay for her moment of triumph and revenge. The pain was awful; it could not be worse, or it would kill her. But it was something else. It was of course Michael, who was getting lost too soon. And after that she could only think, Michael, Michael, Michael, I love you, I love you. . . . And what could one do? What can a child do?

I love you. I love you.

And always will, she thought, straightening up in spite of the cramps, because right then she knew she had lost him. For ever and ever.

There was pain in a series. The first night Lala, having got over her shock of the torn sheet, gathered her up in her strong arms, bandaged her and tucked her in beside Dima. Whenever the pain stopped, Carmian threw her arms around his neck and they slept. The second night it began again. At two o'clock Lala dressed her in all her warm clothes and took her to the nearest hospital.

As she left, Dima said, "It's not Michael. . . ."

She gave him a smile so sweet that it seemed to him to be happy, and he turned his face to the wall.

"*Viens, viens!*" Lala said in the doorway. "Karmianka!"

"*Je viens*," Carmian said.

"Cammie!" he bellowed, seconds later, but they had gone. And he lay stone still, letting the tears wet his flat Russian cheeks.

20

It appeared to be the middle of the night, and the young doctor looked sleepy. He examined her excruciatingly and called in another and they stood there confused, regarding the American girl gravely, and the unintelligible peasant woman, Lala, with utter bafflement. She had dressed in her worst clothes. At any rate, it was all very odd.

"It's a tumor," the girl said politely, smiling through her pain. "They said I had a cyst there once. That was in America."

"*Evidemment*," one of them said, chewing his lip, meaning "America."

Lala smiled too, nodding at the young men in their white smocks, as if that would make it true, that there was actually nothing wrong at all.

"You are in pain, Madame?"

Suddenly she drew up her knees and lost her breath.

"Please give me something. Everything will be all right if only you—"

They immediately gave her a shot of something and shrugged, separately, with different expressions that she did not care to remember. Only there was this puzzled look. Why didn't they know?

"Go home now," said one, "sleep, and come back in the morning if you are no better."

They were very tired.

"*Au revoyar, Messieurs les docteur-rs!*" Lala sang on the way out. She had no pride.

"You will be all right," Lala said as they walked out into the night of Paris. It seemed warm, although that could not possibly be true. Dark, soft air like her mother's kisses felt dimly. She was happy, the warmth curling round and round in her stomach like a cat. . . .

"Can you walk?" said Lala.

It was funny, Lala's penny-pinching, and she smiled because she was so happy and at peace. "*Je suis heureuse*, Lala," she said.

"You will be all right. Hold on to me, Kamitchka."

"Michael."

"He is all right."

"Dima?"

"He is waiting for you."

She walked through the soft dark night as strange and silken as her mother's hair, holding on. The night was lovely. She could hardly stand the beauty of it. And lovelier still was being brought home to her beloved, whom she had taken to her heart the day he was born.

"I am you. You are me," she said.

"Are you all right, Kamitchka?"

"*Da, da*," she said carelessly.

It was the *night* took her home, took her home . . . to the tear-stained boy, and she sank into a loving sea, blissful for eternity.

"*Mort, vieux capitaine*," she whispered into his ear just before she went to sleep, laughing back at some lovely laughter that had not occurred.

And the awakening.

At eleven o'clock she was sitting upright with an expression of sheer amazement, then suddenly bent double.

"Help me!" she screamed at Dima, who was beside her.

"Darling—"

"Help me!"

Lala, suddenly, was already out, getting a taxi. He dressed her like a baby with the clothes that she always left at the foot of the bed. She rocked incessantly, ghastly and sweating. She pounded her fist, furious. Fury was the only answer to that kind of insult—that pain.

"*Dima!*"

He picked up his crutch and hobbled to the window.

"Dima! Dima!"

"Wait, Cammie," he said quietly. "I see Lala in the street. The taxi is coming. Now it stops. Get up."

She saw the poor cat grow limp and crawl under the bed.

She said to Dima, "I'm sorry," and kissed her hand to him, and then she was in the taxi, and it bumped unbearably.

"Lala—" she begged hoarsely.

"Hush. We're almost there."

They swung around and bumped and swung around, and she hung on, until suddenly she said: "Lala, look! The lion."

It was the stone lion of Denfert-Rochereau, curled up, proud on his pedestal with an arrow in his flank. She remembered him from long ago, as the taxi swung around him, bumping hard, and she moaned and Lala bruised her arm.

"He's *gone*, Lala!"

"Sh-h," Lala said, and touched a knotty hand fleetingly over her hair.

"Michael is gone, Lala." And it was the end of everything. Even Dima existed no more.

They walked into the place slowly as in a nightmare; once out of the taxi it seemed as if the world had slowed down. The young woman at the desk took out papers and a pen and started to write meticulously, asking questions as she went along. She had got up to her father's address when Carmian, sitting on the edge of her chair, cried sharply, "Lala!"

"She is in labor. May she go now?"

"Madame, we need the facts, if you don't mind."

Sweat broke out all over her and she started to plead, as the inmates of prisons and concentration camps must do when pain overcomes reason: "Please, please, please."

The young woman looked disgusted. Lala smiled worriedly but rather sheepishly. She was not a very good champion, having lived as a refugee too long and with a stored-up fear of thirty years of persons just like this one. She bowed abjectly to authority.

"Lala!" Carmian gasped. Her heart was bursting, although she had never been a coward, never. . . . "Please, please."

The young woman put down her pen. Someone led her away into a room full of cubicles and calm, pregnant, waiting women. They revolted her. She was weighed. Then she lay in a cubicle until a big rough woman in a white uniform with the face of a butcher came and thrust a hand inside her. She yelled and pounded the mattress and insulted her, the hospital and France, in gutter French. The midwife gave an extra twist to her hand, and withdrew it, pushing her down.

"Behave yourself," she said.

"*Sadique, vous!*" Carmian screamed.

Then there was another room, and three doctors came to do exactly what the midwife had done, although more objectively, and they stood in consultation through the oceans of her pain. They were very unkind and very cold. "How long ago did the water break?"

"What are you doing?" she cried, almost unconscious. They looked like men who would give a dying soldier a cigarette, a crippled horse a bullet. Why did they hate her?

They stood over her, censorious, tight-lipped, shrugging, conversing. But at least, she sensed through her haze, they were seeking the truth without the desire to torture. It was an improvement over the midwife.

She was guided into a ward by a sly young nurse who asked, "Where is your husband?"

"He broke his leg," she said, and the nurse laughed.

Lala was gone, she suddenly realized, but she did not miss her much. In the bed next to hers a woman smiled at her sweetly.

At some time, not long after, everything changed; the world stopped being grotesque and grew kind, all at once. . . .

The pain had stopped. It simply did not come back. She climbed off the bed and went to the lavatory. Returning, she met another nurse and said to her: "The cord is coming out. Will you help me, please?"

This one, miraculously a human being, looked alarmed and took action.

After that everything went swimmingly, and Carmian became the darling of her floor.

21   The thing was . . . the baby would not come out. He refused to leave, and clung to her, even dead. It became a rather crucial affair in the hospital after she had been transferred to a private room with powder-blue walls, a lovely white bed, and a large window. A jolly, muscular mid-

wife came and kneaded her abdomen, and pummeled it, but nothing happened. She vanished to return with a doctor who gave directions. They left, and a nurse appeared, who shaved her and brought a basin, hot water, and towels. The doctor came back and did some kneading himself. Another doctor came in. The midwife pounded and pummeled. They enjoined her to be patient, to relax. She had the desire to laugh, although the pain had started again through all their combined efforts.

At last she felt something rubbery—as they bent over her—being pulled out, and gathered from their remarks that the legs came first. "Ah, the broad little shoulders!" a nurse cried enchanted. As if he were alive! she thought—and he is merely rubber. A tiny rubber hand touched her briefly, with all its fingers, and fell away. Then the head. She braced herself, swam into unconsciousness and back. It was over. Yes, it was over.

"It's a boy," the midwife told her.

"I know," said Carmian, lying limp. It was a boy.

The doctors and the nurse left. The midwife picked Michael out of the basin with some forceps and held him up for her to see. "Do you want to see what he looks like? *Il est beau,*" she said.

Carmian turned her head slowly, against her will. He was curled in the fetal position and covered with blood. He was perfectly formed with round little buttocks and a fuzz of black hair on his head.

The midwife dropped him back into the basin and started cheerfully to clean up. "Did you do something?"

"Do something?"

"Yes. To bring it about."

"No."

"Oh, that's too bad. Well, you will have another. Now we must wait for the placenta. It will come by itself in about twenty minutes."

Carmian struggled to her elbows. "Madame—"

"No, no, lie down! You must not move. Do you understand?"

"Yes. What will you do with him?"

The woman gave her a pitying look. "What does it matter? He is dead."

"Are you sure?"

"*Oui, ma petite.* He has been dead for days. Now lie still and rest. It's almost finished."

Carmian lay still, looking out the window at a leafless tree. She felt nothing. It was like lying in a coffin, a grave. The last line of one of Zola's novels came into her mind, about a girl buried in a cemetery of a suburb: *"Jeanne lay facing Paris for ever and ever."* Feet first as Michael had come. As she lay now.

The rest of it did not come despite more pounding and pummeling, and in the evening she was wheeled into the operating room. She accepted the gas mask willingly, and gulped in order to forget her straddled legs and the mirror that showed her her bruised part and the men in white smocks who peered at her and into her. It was insufferable. She wept with rage, unable to brush away the tears, as she waited for oblivion. *"Un, deux, trois, quatre . . ."* Somewhere between seven and ten she lost consciousness, hearing a voice say sharply, *"Ne bougez pas!"* Why should I budge? How ridiculous! she thought. And he did not only say it once: it became a broken-record thing, angrier and angrier, mounting in intensity and insanity: "Don't move, don't move, don't move, don't move . . ." ad infinitum until she submerged.

She had a beautiful dream. It was a nineteenth century dream, rather murky and D. H. Lawrence, a Lawrencian dream with a bit of Henry James, too. She was being wheeled on a stretcher through a railroad station accompanied by servants of an unparalleled devotion talking in whispers. Although she was hopelessly crippled, paralyzed for life, she reclined luxuriously, for she was beautiful and rich. She was precious to everyone around her, a priceless charge. She breathed the air that had a freshness of stars, and stars came out of her mouth. The chill of fine linen caressed her, and their whispers, their care, and the lovely air. She was a millionaire, of course, and therefore they must be careful of her. But that was all right. It was lonely but it was her fate. They wheeled her down through a tunnel and up again to a platform where her coach awaited her and she was lifted up tenderly into the train, placed on a couch of red plush with antimacassars at each end. . . . *Wagon-lits, Express Européens.* She was going to the south of France.

There she sat in a wheelchair in a garden of heavy, perfumed flowers in the night. The air bathed her like water, her satin skin and liquid eyes. He came and covered her with a shawl.

"Dima," she said.

He did not answer. He was in blue denim work clothes and his expression was flat. He shifted her a little, making her more comfortable, but said nothing. He did not understand.

Perhaps he behaved in this way because she was an invalid. But she was rich!

"We can start a new and beautiful life together!" she cried—in English, hearing herself, shivering at the music and intensity that had poured out of her. A *new and beautiful* . . .

But he disappeared among the flowers as big as babies' heads. He left her. . . .

She gazed at the midwife bending over her, the jolly plump one. "You don't know where you are, *ma petite?* You are in the hospital."

She stared at the powder-blue walls and the moldings. "Yes, I remember."

The nurse smiled roguishly, patting her pillow and straightening the bedclothes. "You just embraced my husband."

"*Your husband?*"

"He is the attendant who wheeled you in. You were speaking to him in English."

Oh. So it was he, this attendant, who had left. "Oh! I was thinking of mine," said Carmian.

"I know. It is nothing. You will sleep now—after a little *piqûre.*"

"What is it?"

"Penicillin every three hours."

"Ah." He had not left her. It had only been this attendant. On the other hand, she was not rich, not precious, not ever so beautiful. She would have to walk again, and more.

"I shall sleep," she said.

"Yes, *petite.* You had a bad time," said this woman, so unexpectedly that two large tears rolled out of Carmian's eyes as she smiled.

They became, to her astonishment, very kind. They were careful to alternate sides with the needle as she grew sore. The constant waking and lying still was a torment, for she was not supposed to shift from her back. The next morning she asked for a cigarette. The young nurse considered thoughtfully. "Well . . . since you don't have your baby, perhaps. You can at least have that little comfort, eh? I'll get one from the attendant."

She brought back three and lit one for her and opened the

window a crack, adjuring her not to tell anyone, especially the doctors. (After that, Carmian smoked whenever she wished in the presence of anybody.) At noon with her lunch they brought her a quarter-liter of red wine in a baby bottle and she sucked it through a nipple lying down. Everyone had wine with meals.

She sucked the *pinard* staring through the wide window on her left at the leafless tree. She had become the baby. It was sunny weather, *fin d'automne*; pillowy clouds sailed by, leaving spaces of amazing blue, and she was glad they had left the window partly open to dispel the aroma of Gauloises. She preferred to look there, anyway, rather than to her right, through the door, where ugly women passed to and fro waiting for their live babies to be born. The uglier they were, the lustier the babies' cries. After the ninth or tenth, Papa could retire on the *Assurances sociales*. It was profitable if one had enough of them. But I, she thought, lost a baby in France. It was like losing someone in a war, in an alien country, on a battlefield.

The woman came to clear away the remains of her lunch, and a nurse came with penicillin. "Where is your husband?" she asked conversationally.

"He broke his ankle."

"Ah, that's too bad."

Shameful and horrifying tears sprang to her eyes. This was to happen over and over again as if she were a human faucet, and at the most unsuitable moments. "Poor little one," said the kitchen worker.

"She grieves for her baby," said the nurse.

"Could I have some matches?"

"I'll see."

Lala came with oranges, cookies, cigarettes, a book from an unknown American friend, and a letter from Dima. The letter was cheerful, the kind one writes to a child, with *I love you*'s running across the page and drawings of the Kitty in a melancholy mood. Lala also, after some hesitation, produced a few hundred francs that Dima had sent her. The old girl was rather nice, beaming in her deplorable attire (her second best)—the shapeless hat, moth-eaten coat, and wrinkled stockings—until she began to show an interest in the details of the operation. Carmian waved her away, but Lala was not to be stopped that easily. Undaunted, she asked the nurse: "The child was a boy?"

"*Oui, Madame.* He would have been a magnificent boy. It was a great pity."

"Did they burn the little one or put him in a bottle?"

The nurse remained silent.

"I would rather not have him pickled," said Lala. "I used to work as a chemist, you know, in a laboratory near the Parc Montsouris."

Then she went away after injunctions to Carmian to lie flat so as not to ruin her figure, kissing her on the cheek and blowing kisses from the doorway.

Carmian, in her window-gazing those bright November days, felt that her heart sailed upon the wind outside, aimless, high and free, stirring the bare cold branches. A *new and beautiful life together,* she heard the singing of her own voice in the dream. Every time a nurse came in, the involuntary tears shot into her eyes. They cooed to her in the shrieking, batlike sopranos of Frenchwomen: "Ah, she feels bad, the little lady! She is unhappy!"

"It's nothing," said Carmian. "It is the reaction. Do you have a small light, perhaps?"

They lit her cigarettes, saying, "Don't let the doctors see it."

When at last a doctor did come, she was smoking her third cigarette after lunch and finishing the *pinard.* He ignored it, sitting down on a chair at the foot of her bed. It was the third day. She assumed that he was a doctor, although he wore a business suit and carried a pad which he placed on his knee. He had a long, sad, worried face, so perhaps he was not a doctor after all. What had they sent her?

He took down the elementary facts of her identity and parentage. She handed him her passport which Lala had brought, and he thumbed through it patiently; it baffled even the police with all the visas, the *aller-retours.* Then he inquired into her medical history. To appease him she mentioned that she had had pneumonia once, wishing she could dig up something more interesting.

"Did you have prenatal care?"

"I went to a specialist twice. Then I no longer could afford him."

"Did you know that there are clinics all over Paris, as, for example, in this hospital—for that purpose?"

"No."

He sighed. "Did you do anything to yourself?"

"Once I fell on my nose."

"You must tell me the truth," he said sharply.

She gave him a dangerous look. "What do you want to know, Monsieur?"

"I believe that you had an unnecessary abortion at five and a half months."

"Abortion!"

"That is the medical term for any miscarriage under six months. Now please lie back or you will hurt yourself."

She lay back and stared at the ceiling through the damned tears. "So that is your bureaucracy and your medicine. You can't tell if a woman wanted her child or not. I wish you would leave me alone."

After a long pause his voice reached her mildly. "It is rather inexplicable," he said. "We have spoken to your husband and to your mother-in-law also."

"There are acts of God and those of the devil," said Carmian. "Leave it at that."

"Too much whisky, perhaps?"

"You flatter me. I can't afford that here. More likely your *vin du pays*."

He smiled, shaking his head. He rose and bowed, tucking his pen into his pocket. "I understand you are a poet."

"I should think," Carmian said, "that the doctors who operated could tell you all that you wish to know."

"I was among them," he replied. "That's just it—there was no clue. I wish you good day, Madame, and good luck."

Would there ever be a stop to these interviews in bed? The branches stirred, the clouds sailed. She took Dima's letter from under her pillow and reread it. If only he had come, hobbling on his crutches, being carried, anything at all.

Other inquisitors came, government officials from the look of them. They were a little less personal and therefore less offensive also less memorable. She answered their questions automatically. Most of it had to do with money and the hospital bills. She referred them to Dima Koubyankov.

On the third day, also, she discovered that her breasts were full of milk. There was no end to these horrors. She had been totally unprepared for it, and nearly panicked. The jolly midwife came and bound them up, stuffing the bandage with cotton. "Don't let them

152

get cold," she warned, "or you will have lumps and that can make complications."

"Lumps!" she cried, and the treacherous tears welled up.

"Only if you do not take care. See! The little belly is quite flat. You are doing well. After today the penicillin stops."

"Oh, it hurts so! I can't sleep! Then can I go home?"

"But no! It would not be wise. You must rest for a while."

The tears flowed evenly in rivulets down her chin, neck, and bandaged breasts. She was thoroughly sick of the tears.

"*Ah, mon Dieu,*" the midwife said. "*Toujours elle pense du petit bébé! C'est pitoyable quand-même.*"

"*Elle est mignonne,*" said the young nurse in the doorway.

Did Frenchwomen never lose their babies?

Overwhelmed with their affection, Carmian asked for the usual match.

"*Mais les docteurs . . .*"

"One of them even lit my cigarette himself," she begged.

"Well, in that case . . ."

At night she heard them giggling in the corridors, being pinched by the male attendants, flirting, gossiping, scandalmongering, rustling and twittering, their quick feet whispering along the polished floor. They were happy.

It gnawed inside her. She'd had enough of the clouds, the sky, the lifeless tree, beautiful as it was. The little, big-brown-eyed Michael (she knew how he would have looked) was gone, and it was time to go.

On the morning of the fourth day, with the nurse protesting, she got up out of bed and almost fell down. She walked around the room for a bit holding on to things and went back to bed for a nap. Then she got up and slowly dressed. Her belly seemed really all right and smooth-skinned as before, but she had a great deal of trouble with her swollen bosom and decided finally to cover the whole thing with just her sweater. She had been slender and buxom, but this was disproportionate in the extreme, since the rest of her had grown very thin while the top half inflated. Also, to complicate matters, it leaked. She drew on her corduroy slacks, put on her socks and shoes, collected her brassière, Dima's letter, the book, her cigarettes, passport, money, and overcoat. She combed her hair. "*Me voilà,*" she said to the apprehensive nurse.

"You ought not to go yet, but I suppose if you feel strong enough . . . *La penicilline est terminée.*" Plainly she was off the doctors' charts.

"Oh, I must! I shall take a taxi."

"Wait," the nurse said, and returned quickly with a paper that Carmian signed; the responsibility was her own.

"Thank you," she said, "for all the cigarettes and everything."

"*Eh bien, bonne chance, ma petite dame,*" said the nurse.

"I shall return to bring you bottles of champagne."

The nurse laughed. As she went down the corridor, walking carefully—she had to be very careful—she turned back to smile at a cluster of them, chirruping in the manner of the French who believe that no foreigner can possibly understand. "*Qu'elle est adorable!*" they said, and waved goodbye. "In her trousers!" they said. "She's a funny one!" They laughed sweetly, like birds.

She refused to listen to the squalling sounds of babies, descended, and emerged into the air; walked through the hospital grounds, passing the gate to come out into the street. It was the wide, wide, honking world. . . . Oh, heaven, it was Paris! And suddenly she thought she would faint, clinging like a midnight drunk to a lamppost. I must not, I must not; it would disgrace them, she thought, and an empty taxi drew up like magic. It took her in and they careened away from Port Royal toward Montparnasse. But when in Denfert-Rochereau they swung around the Lion of Belfort, the lion unchanged, high on his pedestal with the arrow in him, she threw up her arm to cover her eyes.

part
three

the room

22   The door was
unlocked. He was lying with his head at the foot of the couch, arms
crossed, chin puckered, snub-nosed, staring at the ceiling. As if that
were not offensive enough, he was wearing the Tartar cap that Lala
had wrested from the concierge in the Place Dauphine. Her heart
sank when she saw the cap. Would he never stop playing the tough
boy-urchin? Then suddenly he had torn it off and held out his arms
as she stumbled across the room and fell on his chest.

Not only was she flat-bellied, but he saw instantly that her
physical grace, a length of ankle, wrist and arm, delicately molded
and beautifully joined, had come back into its own; his light-stepping
girl was back again. When her sobbing had stopped he asked: "You
are going to leave me, aren't you? Don't be afraid to tell me. I won't
blame you."

She shook her head, speechless.

"You can tell your Dima. Look, we are alone. Tell me why you're crying."

"Poor little boy."

"What is it?"

"I can't leave you now."

"I thought that now—"

"No, no," despairingly. How could he misjudge her so?

"Why are you crying?"

"Michael—have you forgotten him already? I lost him. He wanted to live, but I couldn't hold on to him."

His chin trembled and he wiped his eyes. "You are so deep. I never knew you were so deep."

"You didn't?" she asked, mortified.

"I thought you would leave me."

"Oh, how little you know!"

"You love me. You love me."

"I hate you. Why didn't you come to the hospital?"

"Darling, you know why, my God."

She covered her face with her hands. "Why did you have to fight those three Arabs?"

"Don't start that."

"It wouldn't have been so bad if you had come."

"Was it very bad?"

"A soul has been lost!" She wept, like a child, grinding her knuckles into her eyes. "Poor little boy, poor little boy."

"Come," he said, sniffling and businesslike, "you ought to be in bed, not on top of it. I'll undress you; lie still. I bet you left the hospital much too soon. Lala put your pajamas here. . . ." He hopped to the buffet holding the foot in the cast off the ground. "Go to bed and I'll make you some tea."

"I don't want anything."

"Some bread and cheese?"

"No, please, no."

He smiled at her wistfully across the room. "What a joy to have you back!"

"That's why I came."

In his arms she felt rocked as in a ship's cabin, a sailing ship. The tin cans on the kitchen floor were not so harrowing, the bills on the sideboard not so ominous as once.

But something was missing. "Where is the cat?" she asked.

"I was afraid to tell you."

"He's gone?"

"The day after you went he disappeared. I looked for him through the window for days, darling."

Her heart grew cold, remembering his signal, three bumps of his big round head against the door, at night when Lala was asleep—and how they would jump up to let him in with stifled laughter.

"He was afraid of Lala," she burst out angrily. "She chased him with her damned witch's broom and sent him down into the street all the time on account of her precious floor."

"She thought of him as merely a cat. You know how stupid she is."

"That does not comfort me. He was afraid of the street. He was a small frightened soul who had been abandoned and never forgot it. Life was too hard for him. The moment I turned my back—"

"Don't excite yourself. He is smarter than Lala. I think he will return."

She tossed and muttered restlessly, for she was made of pieces of broken glass and there was too much pain.

Lala did not come home that night; she was in Châtenay. But the cat did. There were the thumps of his big round head, imperious against the door. They woke—and waited—and again it came: thump, thump, thump.

"He is back," said Dima in a hushed voice.

"You're dreaming—"

He pushed her down. "Stay—" and hopped to the door and opened it. Kitty walked in. He was starved and scraggly and ate up what was left of the bread and cheese: a Paris cat who liked cheese but would not drink milk. They watched him admiringly from the couch, before he leaped up and turned and fretted and curled up on Carmian's stomach.

This time her insides plunged. He sensed a change that was bound irrevocably to mortal desolation, and shifted to a place beside her, pressing close for warmth. He never slept on her stomach again, for something had been lost; it was clear to him who had been born a loser.

Lala came home in the morning, and for once Carmian did not mind the peering, darting arrival of the crafty wrinkled face, astonishingly developed from the long-stemmed flower it had once been, like something left too long in the dark—endives or mushrooms. Lala promptly bound up her breasts, criticizing the nurse's handiwork, and her middle—while Dima moaned quietly for "all that waste of milk." Relentlessly, Lala turned her round and round on the wide stiff bandage. "This," she said, "is what I did for all my daughters-in-law, and see how slim they are. A lady must keep her shape." Then she bundled her back to bed beside Dima, much as she put her boxes into cupboards. She approved of Carmian for leaving the hospital on her own, calculating happily how much money they had saved, and it did no good to point out that you had to have some money in order to be able to save it.

Dima was getting only half his working salary, and spent it on food. He demanded that Carmian be fed on best-grade horsemeat, eaten raw; he had a theory about horsemeat and invalids. There was no doubt that it worked. She grew stronger. Occasional bottles of the cheap champagne soothed her feelings, although it did not dry the fountain of tears. Neither was allowed to stir out of the house, and Lala was stern about making them stay in bed. "Think," Dima said —"all this time. We will never be so lucky again."

"We can't even make love," said Carmian, inconsolable.

"Not yet."

The cat walked all over them snicking and snucking grumpily, massaging them with his paws. "He is jealous," Dima observed.

"He is beautiful now—that shining fur."

"And see how grateful he is, the prima donna!"

"That lovely rich fur," she repeated, as if she had made him.

Lala, a demon in the mornings, raged through the house with a broom, scattering dust and cursing hideously in her native language. "The cat has done something under the commode," she would say. "Remove it at once."

But when they tried, she would not let them. Lala carried the buckets of water upstairs and down. She brought home whole logs which she chopped on the dining-room table with a heavy ax, as the chips flew and they watched guiltily, protesting.

"Mamotchka," Dima appealed, "she is sick. I am lame. Do you want us to die?"

"It's not the work. *Koshka!*" Lala whimpered, choosing the only possible victim. "She makes my life unbearable."

"He."

The cat, also having learned Russian, crept quietly under their bed. "Please," said Carmian, and began to cry.

Dima buried his face in his hands. "What have I done?" he wept.

Lala went into the kitchen to make some soup. The cat came out again. By afternoon they were laughing.

Every morning Lala strapped her abdomen tightly as if the fate of nations depended on Cammie's fine figure. She gave her little animals stitched by a Russian woman, a pink lamb, a gray elephant. She read her cards to Carmian and bought champagne. It was then that Carmian discovered the cards were true but at the other end of the telescope: a grave illness was sniffles, an important communication a simple letter, true love a kiss, and success and happiness lasted but for one day.

She remembered the Riviera dream in the hospital; summertime on the rue de Beaune . . . when they had fought the Korean War at the corner of the rue de Lille . . . the pink and orange nights in the Barbac—poor Chedwick!—and the time they were so hungry— she had been so hungry with the baby, God!—that they walked all across town to Lala's for food or money and she was not there, and they finally got some rotten apples from a friendly Arab for nothing. And had sat in the Luxembourg watching little children.

Michael. How would she tell her father that she had lost a baby in France? And how would she ever digest the regret? She lay with her eyes tightly closed, and Dima talked to his mother, mainly asking her to shut up.

I dreamed you had the loveliest angel's voice, he had said to her once. And once a silver trout had leaped out of a stream. . . . A little Russo-American had died.

They seemed to have an understanding these days, the mother and the son, even presenting each other with a certain respect.

"*Elle est en choc,*" they would say to each other.

Carmian knew she was supposed to be in shock, but when the hospital man came she felt fine, although worried about the bill. It was in the morning and, of course, in bed. Lala banished herself to her room in God knew what fears . . . one of them being that the bedspread was dirty.

Carmian was quite used to this by now and answered his terse but deferential questions briefly, fierce-faced. Her testimony was that they could not pay yet, and that the American Embassy was on no account to be notified. Dima pledged his salary. The man took a look at his plaster cast and prepared to depart after papers were signed and courtesies exchanged, although Lala's faint moans beyond the door had caught his ear and plainly intrigued him.

The gray man left with a bow. They never saw him again, never paid, and never heard anything further about it.

Not knowing that, Dima asked: "Why didn't you dig up a complaint? He asked you for a complaint."

"How can you complain about death?"

"But the things you told me—"

"Not to them," said Carmian. "I couldn't—haggling over—God!"

"You are too sensitive."

"No—no, but it's my business, no stranger's."

"He was merely trying to help us with the bill."

"Would you let him look at me naked in order to help the bill?"

"No."

"I'm sorry. I am stupid about this thing. But it is a dream, all a dream, and I dreamed it, and I must defend myself since I believe in nothing."

"I believe in you," Dima said. "You are my country and my religion."

She said, "I love you as much, but differently."

A yearning for the English language overcame her in the evening. She wrote: *We smell our mother's dresses in our dreams, and hear the light voice of our father, a lost young man younger than ourselves. And awake deprived, and violated.* The apartment was full of these scraps of paper, which Lala was very good about not throwing out.

23   "Ne couchez
pas avant Noël," Lala kept warning in her deplorable French. She had an idea of her son as part overgrown child and part stallion. This being one of her gentler fantasies, they let it go without retort.

But she softened. The night before Christmas Eve, with a twinkle of the gray-green eyes once famous in Moscow, she vanished into her room early after many kindly hints and smirks, not knowing that they had been unable to desist the night before. And how lovely it had been—again! This night they slept wrapped up together like children. After all, one could not make love just when she wanted you to.

During the holidays they ate oysters and drank champagne that Dima bought in the rue de l'Ouest, for he was up again and hobbling with a cane. He did not mind shopping when there was money; it satisfied his natural extravagance. Broke, Carmian did it, picking up carrots and potatoes wrapped unwillingly in newspaper (she always forgot the net market bag) and braving or avoiding the hostile eyes of the petty grocers, depending on how she felt, as she counted out the francs. She trudged through the snow and slush in her long German overcoat and Lala's Russian hat, the refugee from Smolensk, feeling some amusement but mostly worse; indeed, intolerable self-pity. One day, trudge, trudge, rue de Vanves, there was a sentence that someone else was repeating that would not leave her: *They cut a dead baby out of me,* it kept saying. How sad, she replied, I know, I know. The specter of the baby rose and loomed, and rose again. And her bound-up breasts hurt, and it was cold and her eyes teared.

It had become better since they could walk. Lala left them alone during most of the holidays. Dima had revived an old radio full of static and was incredibly adroit at finding either Haydn or Mozart. His attitude toward them was tender and personal, not only for their music; he told her stories about them more intimate and illuminating than ever any about his father. She was fondest of the one about the raffish old genius with his head full of music and wine (*"Morgen kommt der Weinachtsmann"*) trundling through the Vienna streets with the children running after him to whom he fed bonbons: the one who named his symphonies "Clock" and "Surprise."

At times there were Lala's guests, always good for a laugh, these moth-eaten princesses, but Dima was somehow cruelly ashamed—the illustrious names notwithstanding—as if they had no right to be living any more.

Three days after Christmas, when they had an American painter to dinner, in a sudden access of fury Carmian picked the cat off her lap and hurled him across the room. The American, a gentleman, gazed helplessly at Dima. Carmian buried her face in her hands. She apologized, blinded by tears.

"She can't help it," Dima explained, petting the cat.

The American nodded seriously, for he knew what was meant. The cat fixed her with a luminous black stare. It was the beginning of an estrangement between them, when he began to let himself be lured by Lala, avoiding his place on their couch and finding a little lair on the second shelf of the bookcase which was covered by a tiny faded curtain, truly a doll's house. The cat left Carmian, and it hurt her quite as badly as though he had been a child.

Drunk on New Year's Eve, she ran away from Dima down the rue de Rennes, Tamawak-style, swinging her shoulderbag by its strap, and he limped all over the quarter looking for her in the rain and in the morning his ankle hurt so badly he could not get up. "You've done it again," he said in a toneless voice, shielding his eyes with his long fair arm.

"In the Royal," she said achingly, "I went downstairs just before twelve, and then I heard shouting and the lights went out and I knew people were kissing each other for the New Year."

"Why did you run away from me?"

"I'd bungled it. I wasn't there to kiss you. It was like an evil omen."

"You must have more confidence in yourself. You *are* someone, you know; you are someone. Have you stopped loving me?"

"No . . . no." His kindness in spite of his pain made her weep. Ordinarily his grim, strained face and smudged eyes would have frightened her, but he had given her no cause to fear him in such a long time, having Lala to keep his demons occupied. He would complain for ages about this New Year's Eve, though only sullenly, like a nagging wife.

But he had not forgotten her sick melancholy since the *faussecouche* and what he imagined to be the rage of empty arms and a scratchy emptiness that she was bent on filling up with wine. On cold evenings with the stove smoking—while Lala's ancient radio thrummed to the songs of Kosma (*Les Feuilles mortes, Les Enfants devant la porte de la nuit*) which seemed to embody their relationship from its doubtful and desperate beginning—he planned a vacation trip with her over a cracked map of France. The map being Lala's, it was not merely old but went back as far as the eighteenth century. But most of the cities and provinces were there. He thought of Hendaye near the Spanish border, or Perpignan, although the trip was too expensive. He suggested various Atlantic Coast towns, and Brittany, which Carmian rejected: it reminded her of their summer plans bogged down in the Place Dauphine, the blue fungi on the walls and her morning nausea.

Lala sneered, dipping a crust into her tea. "And what do you propose to use for money?" she inquired.

"It's none of your business, but Cammie's father sent her some."

"How are you going to pay the hospital?"

"I'll see to that," he said grandly. "She has been ill and needs a vacation, so she shall have it."

"Perhaps if she hadn't traveled so much, the baby—"

"Shut up!"

"After all," Lala sniffled, wiping her nose with her knuckles, "he was my *petit-fils*."

"There will be another *petit-fils*."

Carmian gave him a helpless and adoring look.

"We have to pay the gas and electricity. I can't do it alone!"

"But not on her money—that's not going for bills and groceries. Listen, darling, what do you think of Lille? It's foggy there but it's pleasant, and it would be a change."

"I don't know," she said, subtly feeling another hope slip away.

"You depress her," he accused his mother, "as if she were not depressed enough in this—" He waved his arm around the room in a lassoing movement describing abomination.

"You depress me, too!" Lala shrieked.

"*Dima*," said Carmian.

"*Muzhik, razboynik*," Lala muttered, calming down. "Listen to me, Karmianka. Save your money for an apartment in Paris and for a vacation take a little trip to Sainte-Geneviève-des-Bois where his father is buried. There is a Russian village with a church and dachas just as in Russia. When he gets his divorce you can be married there by a pope."

"A cemetery?" said Carmian, frowning. "That isn't exactly what we—well, cemeteries are everywhere—"

"We'll do that in the spring," Dima agreed, "but now we'll have our trip. Lille? We could easily stay a week or ten days. . . ."

And so the discussion went, while Carmian dreamed secretly of sun and the Riviera. Of course, they never took any trip, but she hoped to the end, while the stove smoked and they sat shriveled and sunken in winter discomfort, rolling cigarettes on the table that served as a chopping block; the trunks of trees had to be removed before one could eat upon it. The cat sulked behind his curtained shelf. Across the street under ragged political posters an elderly couple foraged nightly through garbage cans. Sometimes the man paused in his search to besprinkle the whitewashed wall.

A persistent cold damp did not improve their tempers. Dima's ankle continued to ache, and Carmian got chilblains. Lala agitated ceaselessly about the gas and electric bills which lay pinned together on the buffet under the painting of the fish. Feeling her hair cling slimily to her neck, clogged with smoke, Carmian protested, between coughing fits, against the stove. "Either get it cleaned or stop using it," she said, "for God's sake! I'd rather be cold."

Lala replied spitefully: "As you wish. I cannot afford to buy wood any more." She now visited her sister Shura more often and got another crack at her job in the bookstore, although owing to the pique of customers utterly forgotten in the heat of their quarrels, profits had steadily declined whenever Lala was employed. She spent longer week ends in Châtenay with Denise and Serge. It was warm there, and she had Serge.

On coming home she would rush without a word into her inner chamber, there to rummage among the crates and boxes and in her secret caches. She always emerged in angry tears with accounts of tea and sugar missing, along with the coffee and cocoa from her Belgian Congo supplies. Sometimes this was true, sometimes not. Since they lived on less than fourteen dollars a month from the *Assurances*, anything was possible. Dima shrugged indifferently; this was the side he tended to laugh at without breaking into fury. But to Carmian so much noise, solely, was ill-making; for that she dreaded Lala's razzia-like appearances. Lala's second step was to bring forth detailed, malicious reports of *"ona"* and *"malinki"*: Denise and the little one. She intrigued endlessly to acquire Serge for herself and thus far was still on Carmian's side, hoping that she might persuade Dima to take him or sign him over to her—though her manner was cooler since the memory of Michael had been mislaid among the persistent clutter of her preoccupations, like some once cherished object in her room (the pearls under her bed). As for a replacement, in view of their sad situation, she saw small chance of that. She now labeled her chest of baby clothes "For Eliane." Dima's brown-eyed little cousin was only seventeen but ripe; her passion for basketball would soon give way to another.

Carmian and Dima had a month together before he went back to work. In truth they had no money at all except what he borrowed from her, since his sick pay which was half-pay—even that had been held up *aux Assurances*. Carmian was troubled. She asked: "On what does a sick man live if he has no one?"

"Why, nothing," said Dima.

Lala was very upset about having to pay her prewar rental of ten dollars a trimester—since it was so little, she never expected to and saw in it an affront, furious at having to tip the concierge.

"I am obliged to give Konciergeka three hundred francs," she moaned, "or she will withhold the mail."

"I'll pay you back," Dima said wearily, "when I get my money."

"*Les Assurances qui viennent,*" she scoffed. "That will be the day." She flounced out on her way to Passy, and the room grew still.

She popped in again: "Don't forget to pay the electricity and the gas—or they will turn them off!"

Then she was gone, the key turned, and Carmian begged, "Oh, when can we move?"

"When I go to work."

"It's lonely without friends."

"Friends?" He laughed, hugging her. "Darling, they will love us better for our absence. I've done it often. You're there every day and they're bored. After being away for six months, a year or more, you suddenly come back, and they can't get enough of you. *C'est la sensation qui compte!*" he said.

"But this isn't a concentration camp—"

She stopped. There was nothing more to say, because of course it was, in a sense. His prison was akin to her wheelchair of the dream. The bed, their island of refuge, had become a ship plowing through uneasy seas, for suddenly one wanted motion, no matter how painful, how delusory and hopeless.

She would give up the anonymous love, the sensuous comfort, the strange starlighted hush of that haunting memory as a condition to be desired, if only he would help her.

In the dream, as a part of her death, he had left her—and be-

165

hold, he was back! Together they would break out, for she knew urgently that they must.

Those cold winter evenings when they were cloistered, she was treated to many curious bits of Dima's philosophy, a hodgepodge of the ruthless, the innocent, the whimsical, and the chivalrous, picked up from the gutter, the theater, the cafés, and the concentration camps. He believed in the virtue of carnivals, circuses, street music; of Henry IV, François Villon, Stendhal and Bakunin; and that there were no prostitutes in Russia, a factor he attributed to the national character.

This was too much. "Pah!" she cried. "Have you forgotten all Russian literature?"

He side-skipped nimbly with the bland expression that accompanied his recognition of a *gaffe*. Sometimes, in a lighthearted mood, he would kiss his hand after one of these and say, *"Adieu, belle théorie!"* There was nothing graceless about Dima when proven wrong, which was roughly half the time because his imagination prowled and flitted ceaselessly, and nothing was too wild, too improbable, to say. He had no fear of ridicule—mainly because he did not care. She had begun to feel the true solitude underlying his gregarious behavior and to know that he was deeply antisocial. Something in him did not belong to the human race.

His contempt ("It's sensation that counts") engaged her horrified fascination. He illustrated his idea of shock technique with the story of an American model or showgirl who had fed the pigeons in front of the New York Public Library stripped to the waist. "Of course she went to the jug, but who cares? The *pourrie-presse* took it up and she was invited to come to Hollywood. That's the way to do things."

This was genuine admiration. But just as earnestly he could extol the regenerative pioneer traits of America, the wide land; or presage for it a Roman decline and fall. Consistency was not his forte.

Always in his enthusiastic ramblings he returned to the subject of Russia. The United States and Russia alone were young pioneer countries and matriarchies; the power of women flourished in young and wealthy lands with hope in them. He spoke of the wide prairie

166

spaces of Russia and his desire to see them, since this largeness was in his blood untainted by the French insistence on limits and adoration of things in miniature ("*petit, petit, petit* . . ." until one felt squashed by the littleness of things and its cult of babies, cats, and penny-pinching). "We cannot be avaricious," he proclaimed grandly.

"What of Lala?" said Carmian, whose fifty dollars had gone down the drain.

"Well, when it does happen to them, it's worse than anybody's. Like Russian syphilis."

"What?"

"Or Russian puritanism. No immunity."

Carmian reflected that this extremism seemed to be true of practically anything the Russians did, one way or the other. "Are many Russian ladies mad about empty jars and bottles and old rags?" she asked with real interest.

He slanted his eyes at her good-naturedly. "Now, you know Madame is a magpie, brainless and meaningless. It's kind of a crazy child playing house. Grubbing and saving is different. Germans want to die with money in the bank and funeral expenses paid; they only want to acquire and keep."

"*Sparsamkeit*," she said, and truly the word had an iron-clad ring: *spareness*.

"The French have avarice, which is more grasping. They really do intend to rob their fellow man and live on his entrails. They mismanage, that's all. They haven't the American genius."

"Or wealth. But the Germans don't cheat you," said Carmian. "A porter will always tell you what you owe. And it's always the same."

"That's why they go to war."

"They are very Protestant."

"The Germans bore me," he said.

"I understand you. But there are some compensations. There are no penises in the urinal—on the walls, you know."

"How do you know?"

"At least not in my own urinal, in my own house. They have no right to draw their crudities in that one downstairs."

"No, poor one, *dyevutchka maia*. They are swine, the French."

"Well, about urinals."

"They don't understand puritanism. Russians can be very puritanical. Shura for example—"

She groaned. "Never mind. As an added insult, when you pull the chain, you find yourself ankle-deep—"

"Listen, go get us a liter of red."

Then commenced one of those childish squabbles they were noted for. "Why don't *you*?" she said.

"Cammie, I shine your shoes for you. I find the things for you that you are constantly losing—"

"Who wouldn't—here?"

"I do the best I can," he said tearfully, holding his face between his palms and swaying from side to side.

"Oh," she said on a dark note, scornfully. "I do not consider anything that we do while living here of any value."

"New Year's Eve you not only ran away from me—you kicked me in my bad leg!"

"I do not believe that," incensed, and terrified. "If I should have done so, it was an accident."

"I want to rest my leg so I can go to work. The doctor said it was doing very well."

She whipped her coat off a hook on Lala's door.

"*Vin d'Afrique*, twelve per cent. And some cigarette papers, Zig-Zag."

She left him carefully unrolling the fortune of ancient stubs he kept in a tin box. Bonky-sklonky and karobky, she thought; they serve a purpose if one has something to put in them, even the dried harsh tobacco of too long ago.

When Lala burst in two days later, it was not in her usual state of bitchy misanthropy. She sat down heavily, casting down her market bag full of flowers and country fruit, as they stared apprehensively from the bed.

"Poor Fedya!" she said. "Fedyosha—do you remember him?"

"No," said Dima.

She was breathing hard. "Yes, you do. He was our cousin from the line Rajensky whom my brother took to Africa with him. A fine young man, Fedya, although small, rather short of stature, which never happened to the men of our family."

"Ah, that one."

"He was swallowed by a snake."

"*Pardon?*"

"A boa constrictor. Here it is in the French newspaper. Shura found it. Read it. Poor Fedya . . ." She babbled on piteously while he scanned the clipping and Carmian composed her face into lines of dismay.

He read it aloud: " 'While strolling through the jungle one evening, two Russian émigrés, Feodor Alexandrovitch Rajensky, former officer of a Cossack regiment related to the Governor of the Belgian Congo, and a friend (name unknown), encountered death and mutilation in the form of a huge female boa constrictor. When found by a local searching party, the unknown man was discovered lying bruised and semiconscious, in the underbrush. It is surmised that he lost consciousness when lashed by the serpent's tail. After dissection of the boa, M. Rajensky was revealed fully clothed in a state of complete preservation within the beast, who lay not ten feet away in deep, digestive slumber. The boa constrictor is known as one of the most dangerous of jungle creatures. The wounded Russian comrade had not yet recovered consciousness upon receipt of this report, although he is expected to recover.' "

"Fedyosha!" Lala exclaimed, weeping.

"Obviously," said Dima, "this stroll into the jungle was with a bottle or two."

"It's that other one," Lala contended hotly. "The bad one. Name unknown—indeed!"

"You can't ignore the snake. But my God, only a Cossack could be swallowed alive nowadays and be so indigestible!"

"In all his clothes," breathed Carmian, who tended to get caught up in little things like that.

Lala began to laugh, streaming tears of sorrow and laughter intermixed. They laughed wildly.

"You starving children," Lala said after a while, wiping her eyes. "You need a good meal. Wait—I shall prepare you something!"

And it was veal. Oh, the luxury of dinner in bed! And mashed potatoes, too.

24

"I think Russians and Americans ought to get along together," Dima said.

As she dressed, the idiotic tears squeezed past her eyelids. He watched her sympathetically. "You think too much about the little boy."

She sighed brokenly. "Such a waste . . . It was such a . . ."

"Tell me about it."

"Oh, the mechanics were very dreary. Besides the pain. No mystery, just rubber and plumbing. But the emotion—was—"

She cried steadily for several minutes, although it was by now all past and no longer part of her breathing and a weight on her heart but just a sadness sunken into a grave—while he kissed her and cajoled her and finally called the cat, the cat who had taken a sudden liking to *him*, Lala having proved unfruitful.

"He doesn't love me any more," she wept.

But he crept out from behind his concierge's curtain. *"Tiens,"* he said, and threw the cat into her lap. "I'll make some tea."

Miracle! The cat stayed and purred. She wept some more, quietly, finished dressing, and smiled at last as they were sitting over tea and crusts. "He has forgiven me," she said.

"Who would not?"

She looked long at his slim face with its wide cheekbones and narrow, restless eyes. "Do you regret it all?"

"Il n'y a pas de retour, ni de reculement."

"Seriously."

"There is no going back."

"But the person—the person left—"

"I should not have divorced my wife if she were not young and perfectly able to find someone new. That would have been cruelty. And—do you know—I'll never divorce you—unless you get on your knees. You're mine," he explained as if he had just created the phrase. "I couldn't enter a strange woman."

An old familiar hunger gnawed at her, so that part of her was soothed and caressed, another part desolate.

He grew shy and barbarous when his natural optimism was threatened. He sprang up and became declamatory, and his fine blond hair blazed as it had on that day last spring with Boris. How beautiful, Dima!

"Once," he said, "I was on a Berlin streetcar (this was before the C.C. when I was there just to look around). I saw two young girls, very pretty. One of them smiled at me. The other one had a yellow star on the breast of her coat. She was trying to hide it with her pocketbook, standing of course. When a place became vacant I took her by the shoulders and sat her down, standing before her. No one dared look at her after that."

"You loved her," Carmian said with jealousy, bending her head like a woman in an opera.

"No, no. All Germans were enemies to me at the time—but something caught at my heart."

Basely, she gave in to what had not become misery and produced the lament: "*Hélas!* I had no yellow star."

"Quite so," he agreed clinically. "Perhaps that's what's wrong with you."

"To you I'm just a God-damned German."

"No," he demurred. "A matter of sentiment purely."

"I spit on your sentiments."

"That is not polite."

She was raging, and proceeded to walk up and down like a sick tiger, and it was true that she had an odd walk for a woman, a sailor-like swing and Indian prowl combined. He loved her walk.

"I am tired of your depraved countesses, your hawk-faced French-women, and sad Jewesses and all the many little women in the world you remember and want to protect."

"You're anti-Semitic," he suggested vilely.

"I'm anti-Russian and I've had enough of you." She began packing her suitcase.

It took a long time finding everything. He was the detective and finder of things in this house where small objects were invariably lost. "Listen," he said after a long silence, his throat clicking, closing nervously as it did when he fought Lala—"you're not pregnant any more; you can go. But . . . But I ask you to stay."

"I don't like it here."

"We'll move—end of the month."

171

"I don't like you."

He came at her, and for a moment she thought he would hit her in the face. But she had an ally stronger than he. The cat rubbed against her legs, making sounds of distress.

"*Eh bien*," she said sorrowfully and sat down, for a long time immobile. The cat crept up on her lap.

"He loves you," Dima said, and went to make some tea.

Michael, Michael, Michael, she thought as she always did when the cat took his place.

Over hot tea she remarked, "We were so happy when we wanted to turn on the gas."

"In that hotel. Yes, the Riff. But listen: we shall be as happy as that once again, and happier still—for we shall live."

"What," Carmian asked the next morning, "took you to Berlin before you had to go?"

She was part boche, he reflected, and systematic in her crazy way. "I was a Nazi, of course," he confided.

He tortured her with this notion for some time, making up an elaborate story of early fascist tendencies and subsequent revulsion. His humor sometimes took that form. Gradually it transpired that he had been transported as a worker, along with his brother Kolya, to alleviate the German labor shortage. He had been a postman and had happily driven a horse and wagon around the suburbs of Berlin delivering mail and numerous packages to the population. The housewives had always given him a *Schnapps* when he brought a package, and he was always drunk and warm in winter. It was after that, on a visit of leave to Paris which he spent distributing phony ration cards on street corners ("come one, come all") that he had been caught by the Germans in a more menacing way and retransported to Germany, or rather, Dachau.

After a year they had decided that he was ready for the chimney, since he was obviously more Russian than French and capable of spitting into the faces of guards, and they had sent him to a death camp in Poland, from which no one returned except those last-minute ones in the path of the onswarming Russians who were primarily interested in wrist watches but who nonetheless saved their lives.

"The Germans, you know," Dima said, "some of them fed us, the older ones. But I needn't tell *you* that, eh?"

"*Enough!* I suppose," she spun dreamily, staring at the ceiling, "that you loved the Jewish girl on the streetcar. And suffered all this for her. And suffered . . . and hoped to see her some day. Was she pretty?"

"Very."

"Oh!—I don't know if I'm jealous or sad. Help me, tell me . . ."

"I love you, Cammie," he declared sensibly. "She was a poor, sweet little kid. As for Jews, well, they're everybody else. Though I don't much agree with their Old Testament. Justice, justice. *Putain!* Balancers and weighers, the Old Jews. Right and wrong. Hogwash. Just as crazy in the head as somebody who claims not to know the slightest difference between the two. Look, the intellectuals were the first to go. Well . . . But *les schleus—enfin!*"

Schleu was a modern version of the World War I boche, an insult derived from the name of a primitive North African tribe. However, she did not let it stick. "No justice?" she bridled, remembering Boris. "There certainly is."

"Justice—there is no poetry in it, and rarely even truth. It is merely a plan. When I was a boy I knew a girl named Miriam. I think that she was beautiful. We ate grapes and made love on the floor."

"And?" she asked coldly.

"There is truth in action, not in theories."

"I think I should like to keep a few theories."

"Of course," he laughed, teasing, "it's not for nothing that you are a bit *schleu.*"

"Shut up."

"My tormented girl."

"*Steppenhund!*" she said.

It was a stupid argument, but they did not get on very well that day.

"All you do," said Lala, "is lie on the bed all day and quarrel. Especially when it's red wine. The white becomes you better."

"*Ne l'emmerdes pas,*" Dima warned her, leaving. He was in a foul mood because he had to go all the way to the Stalingrad quarter to procure a paper that the *Assurances* were clamoring for.

"*L'amour,*" Lala shrugged, "men. I was never interested, no matter how many ran after me. Just so they treated me with respect."

"God," said Carmian, muffled, into the pillow.

"When you drink red wine you quarrel. When you drink white wine you are affectionate. When you drink tea you go to sleep. When there are no cigarettes—he fights with me."

"You exaggerate."

"Oh," said Lala, pursing her mouth and crinkling her little Eastern eyes: "I have watched you. It is the Cold War—as they call it in the journals, between the Russians and the Americans—*tout à fait!* And it all falls down on me in the end, since he is afraid to offend you too much."

She showed no inclination to leave the bedside, and Carmian felt her nose twitching. Unfortunately, Lala's motives were, if not inscrutable, heavily camouflaged, and she had this animal cunning that Carmian was quite unable to meet. Moreover, Carmian did not have the trapped animal's advantage. Lala was quite odorless: an amazing feat considering that she never bathed—at least not in her own house. But deviltry was in the air.

"I do not blame you, Karmian. I know my son. You must listen to me: The trouble with him—he is not working. He has such nerves! When he is working he uses up his energy and calms his nerves. When he is idle, you or I must suffer."

Carmian remembered his bland and tired, dreaming face after coming home to her across the bridges, the peace in it, and she was silent.

Bent on propaganda, Lala seized her advantage ruthlessly. "I see you know! Then you must encourage him to go back to work."

"He's been sick!"

"Of course, but he can work now. He is perfectly able."

"Maybe the doctor should decide."

She swallowed her tea and cradled the cup. "Has he never hit you?"

"Yes," said Carmian the naïve, for the moment losing sight of her true ally; then furious at herself for her betrayal.

"*Voylà!* It was a mistake to ever let him get away with it. A first time—and there is no end!"

Carmian simmered. "I saw him kick you once," she recalled, "in the shins. You must have let him get away with it the first time."

The point seemed to escape Lala, but one never knew with her. "He has always been that way. It's his nerves."

174

"Those nerves that Serge talks about?" (She heard him still, piping, *"Ce sont mes nerfs, Papa!"*)

This was the only subject that could touch Lala and pierce the rhinoceros hide. She decided to turn it upon Denise, squinting across her teacup, a seeress. "I'm afraid he will share his father's fate, as Dima shared his father's, Mikhail's, even perhaps to the ultimate end."

Chilled, Carmian rolled a cigarette. The gypsies are out again, she said to herself. "What makes you say that?"

"The men of that family have been doomed. Violent, angry. Dima's father left him in death on account of a woman—and so Dima leaves Serge on account of a woman. No, no—don't mistake me—perhaps leaving Serge's mother had more to do with it than finding you. She is so harsh to Serge at times, no wonder he has nerves."

It was a fine interpretation of what ailed the Koubyankovs, mainly that they married the wrong women, and remarkable for Lala except that she remained Lalaesque in not recognizing that it threw her into the same pot as Denise. Carmian decided to help the parallel along.

"And Dima—why his nerves?"

"He ran down the street one day," Lala said sadly. "We were living in the rue Froidevaux—before we became poor—I think that he—"

She stopped and looked at the girl as if she saw her for the first time. The mantle of hair hid most of her. The languid hand propped up her chin, and above the slender skyward nose was revealed a Grecian eye, haughty, sad, critical . . . accusing?

"Don't set fire to the bed," she shrilled. Carmian put out her cigarette.

"He was eight years old," Lala went on more quietly, "and he ran smack blind into a post, running, playing with other children. He was passionate and wild, always. It was a street lamp. He fainted and they brought him home. I put him to bed. For a while afterward we feared he was not normal."

The damned tears started out of her eyes as she felt the blow that had finished his joy. *Blind joy!* That was like Dima. Rapture of a little boy racing up the street toward death of some kind.

God, she still wept about everything, hell, hell.

175

"And do you know—all his life, since then perhaps, he has not been"—Lala dipped a crust into her tea—"*kom il fot.*"

"Nor have I since my early misfortunes."

"Ah, but he is stronger than you. Therefore it is you—"

"Physically."

"It is you who pay. You are in love, but a mother is better able to judge."

She shrugged, bored.

"How you have changed, Karmianka. But aside from that"—a world-weary wave of her hand—"I have simply been present at times in his life when you have not."

"That's true," said Carmian, struck with this extraordinary piece of logic coming from Lala.

"Apart from his *nerves*, he is very strong. When he arrived home from the concentration camp, he crawled in. He was a skeleton, gray and feeble, so I did not recognize him. We had thought him dead. In six months . . . *na.* You see him now. He gets into mischief when he does not work. Did you ever wonder what he did while you went to Germany on your errands?"

There was a greedy glint in Lala's eye.

"Of course."

"Did you know that he saw Denise?"

"Yes!" said Carmian, and the cat came out of his chamber to settle quietly on her lap.

"*Tak,*" said Lala, eyeing the cat with malice. "You have a cold, a Nordic, temperament. It would disturb me very much."

(Don't you see how she baits her trap for you? She heard herself telling Dima after one of those sniffling, whining parodies of a mother's martyrdom. But now the bait was for her, and she got a nasty taste of it, a whiff of poison, waiting.)

"I trust him that way."

"Do not believe in men."

"Must I then believe in women?"

"I merely know," said Lala, smiling, "that Denise complained he . . . wanted her too much. When they were together, naturally."

"She had a lover."

"Perhaps that was for something else," she remarked piously. "When I was a young woman I liked to flirt and to be admired, protected. I never liked the rest of it."

Feeling like Lala's homemade berry liqueur which, bottled, had a tendency to explode and had once knocked a hole through the ceiling, she bent her head, stroking the cat as if he could ward off her destruction.

"He is like his father. Women are foolish," said Olympiada de Koubyankov, "if they believe men."

And looking at that once lovely, stupid face, turned shrewd with age as beauty left it, Carmian thought: She's not just guessing about those trips. She knows. She probably bedded them down together as she did us. Because of Serge.

The cat made funny, distraught noises as though he were trying to talk, and crept up higher, closer. Through the fog of her anger she felt his rich silken fur and saw the eyes of black and gold and thought, foolishly but passionately: I saved you. I made you. Behold what I've created! How you do love me!

Dima was obliged to return to a certain bureau of *Assurances* near the Etoile for a paper which they had not found at Stalingrad during a wait of five hours. No Koubyankov apparently had ever learned to use the telephone, thus expending much time, energy, and rage. Even if so, their lot would hardly have improved. The telephone, if answered, was a steadfast purveyor of unreliability.

Next day he asked her to come along. On hills reminding her of the Trocadéro Park, he asked her to slow down, although his mood was jaunty, his spirit unbroken.

"You *used* to run," said Carmian.

"I'm crippled now!" As an afterthought, he whimpered slightly. "*I* was, then!"

"The elephant never forgets. But you're so pretty. I always loved you, but I like you better now. You not only have a shape—but a soul you never had before."

"It was always there," she said dryly.

"How vengeful women are! It was you who tried to sink my boat in the Luxembourg pond. Walk slower, Cammie, damn you."

"You think you made my damned soul?"

"No; but your shape." He grinned. "That is, I improved upon it as I promised you."

"Only a minor god," she snorted, headstrong and full of rage. She slowed her pace, fighting her ruined heart of dreadful yesterday.

177

"A household god," she taunted, "who thinks about the shapes of women."

"I kiss your feet and shine your shoes," he said, watching a Parisienne go by, "and only yours."

Since this was a serious statement and a declaration of faith in his huskiest voice, she was silenced. People streamed along looking at them as they always did—because of their odd, restless, reckless air, more dispossessed than foreign. They were looked at together, rather than separately, by both men and women, in ways that were curious and friendly. It was a phenomenon in Paris, as it would have been in New York, where even freaks did not receive this attention. Usually it was very pleasant. They could speculate why. Because we are good-looking, Carmian thought. And Dima: Because we are free. And neither was right.

After waiting for him for an hour and a half on a bench in a dark hallway, she sighed and picked up her package of Gauloises. She knew what it was like inside. Bureaucratic birds in a cage, all twittering, and a director in an office.

He appeared at that moment, in his beret, limping—she could have sworn—a little more than usual. "Where are you going?"

"To the Tabac for a drink."

"You drink too much."

"Of course."

"Listen, the rôles are reversed now and I'm the helpless one. Doesn't that satisfy you?"

"I'm not looking for revenge."

They sat in silence for about a quarter of an hour. "It takes a long time," he said finally. "I thought I would wait with you. Why are you so strange?"

"No, no, Dima."

"Cammie, what is it?" And he shook her rudely.

"About Denise. You made love to her after . . . me."

He looked aghast. "Did Lala tell you that?"

She raised her eyes in a dangerous look that he knew, all her own, of perplexity and distraction, as if she had lost something, or forgotten something never quite to be recalled. He feared it more than any attack, since then she was not to be reached.

"Cammie! You know what a liar she is! Why did she—"

"And you?"

178

"I love you! How could I do that to you or to me?"

"I don't know," she said. "It's a feeling I have that you did and it's like a knife and I want to get out of here."

"Shall I take you home now?"

"No."

"I am pure," Dima said, "and honorable with you."

But he was white and his hand trembled on her shoulder as he left her when the clerk called his name. "Wait for me, Cammie!"

She smoked another cigarette and left, asking someone the way to the métro and taking a train to Passy. It was raining.

25 Von Kolmau

was so startled to see her he kept offering her cigarettes from gold and silver boxes, gazing all the while at her middle.

"Oh, that—I flunked," she said.

Kolmau's eyes grew a little more hollow. "Well!" he began, crossing brilliantly polished, pointed shoes. "What have we now?" He always expected much of her in the realm of disaster.

"I really don't know."

He was a man who had fought in Russia during the First World War, escaped from Germany in the blue-ribbon year of 1933, losing *all* his money, which was considerable; he had lain in French concentration camps with a frozen leg, crossed to America by way of Portugal, starved in New York, and re-escaped to Paris. By origin he was Protestant, Catholic, and Jewish. "How do you keep your good humor?" she asked.

"I take out my spleen on others through the written word. Are you writing?"

"Mine isn't the kind for spleen."

"It was pretty good, though. How is your Russian? The boy, I mean."

"Limping around with a broken ankle which won't heal."

"I can see you'll be happy together. Does he still have herring and vodka for breakfast?"

"Tea and crusts."

He went to his decrepit, ornate and authentic Bavarian buffet and took out a glass, which he filled with an impressive brandy. She gave him the smile with which she rewarded everyone who comforted her in this expensive fashion—though she loved him, von Kolmau, entirely on his own merits and would have even if he had been unable to offer her anything but coconut juice. He was a strange father-confessor who advised her not to be moral about things. Only the moral behave immorally, or think that they do.

She told him a current story about a South American million-airess who had bought a houseboat in order to have a party on the Seine. But the combined weight of guests and liquid supplies had proved too much for the poor old thing; it buckled and sank at the height of the festivities, and had to be dredged for long after. A marvelous party, everyone said. Most of the guests got to shore.

"How is Lilly . . . Lally . . . ?" he asked, pressing an éclair upon her.

"Terrible, terrible. I left *him* at the *Assurances*. Lala told me he slept with his wife last summer."

"What could be more proper?"

"But he was mine!"

"My dear girl," he said, "if he is *aux Assurances* you will probably never see him again, so your problem is solved."

"No, it isn't. You ought to tell me he *didn't* sleep with his wife last summer."

"*Immensee*," Kolmau mused. "I thought you might grow out of it some day."

"That is very unsatisfactory."

"My poor broken children—he with his leg, and you . . . The Nazis cut off your growth. They were the product of disenchanted *Immensee*, but naturally you couldn't grow in their direction. So you stayed a romantic nineteenth century girl, which of course is part of your charm, at least to me."

"I am not so German as that," she said haughtily.

"Germans, English, Americans: they are all the same." He waved enigmatically. "Another brandy?"

"Yes, please." She brooded. "And Russians?"

He cleared his throat, and answered brightly, "They are not the same."

She laughed like a child and ate another éclair. He smiled. He was the Western World, monocle and all. He was, yes, he was home, and if he was crazy it was the kind she was used to.

"But do you know, I am pleased, Cammie. You look well."

"Better?"

"It was better that—" he paused with unaccustomed delicacy; it arose, she knew, from nothing less than his kindness and tenderness.

"The baby lost?"

"Yes. A blessing," he said, even taking off his monocle to mop his brow. He looked weary and old as he did so, for the thing held up his eyebrow.

"No," she said gently, "no. Now if *I* had come from a family of bankers—"

"It would still have happened."

"Well, I just thought if we'd had some money and bought specialists—although I despise it."

"Of course you do, since you never had any. Money, I mean. Do you need some, by the way? I'm not quite as poor as you, you know."

"No, no. Give me some more brandy, please. My people were interested in the Arts, primarily." She reproduced a sweet synthetic smile and a La, there! expression.

"That was not so bad," he observed judiciously, and cryptically, too.

"It's the historian in you."

In the métro station at La Muette, she said: "I'll be perfectly happy so long as I don't wind up at Châtelet. I never can find my way out."

"It has nothing to do with your itinerary on this occasion, my dear girl. Now look." He pressed her bare, rather dirty hands between his pearl-gray-gloved ones, kissed her on both cheeks and said, "Now don't destroy yourself, for I'm fond of you and you're a good girl, no matter what nonsense you may do."

"Imagine being condemned to the labyrinths of Châtelet for life."

"I can."

"I feel so much nicer," she said, "and I love you, dear," and disappeared into the subway train waving at the slim man in gray spats and gray Homburg hat and gray gabardine coat, eyeglass flashing.

She ran home, ran up the rue de la Gaîté and across the avenue du Maine, the soft gray rain falling on her face. She reached the house, opened the big front portals, went through the courtyard past the hated W.C., up the stairs plunged eternally in darkness, and thought: Not *Immensee*, no, no—Gorky. But one did not like to tell the worst.

Lala rushed to open the door for her. Carmian heard the scuffling of her feet, and behind, inside, the sobbing. She stopped in the middle of the room. Her boy had his head down on his arms and was crying: "No, it's not she! Why do you say it is? She has left me!"

"Dima, Dima," Carmian said, kneeling down, laying her wet hand on the back of his neck humbly. "Dima—"

"It's you! It's you!"

"Dima."

"I thought—"

"Don't cry," she wept.

"I thought you—"

"Never. Never."

"*Och,*" he breathed, and buried his head in her lap.

"Oh, darling, I am sorry."

"Don't ever listen to her. She thinks only in terms of paying the bills. She will do anything—"

Lala said, white-lipped, "He tried to poison himself," and raised a small blue bottle.

Dima picked up his coat and rushed out, in the joy of his redemption, God knew why.

Carmian could scarcely believe her eyes and ears—the ludicrous horror of it all. "Do you mean to say you keep poison in the house?"

"I was a chemist," Lala said proudly.

"Well, I mean—are you *still?*"

"I have samples—"

"*Lala!*"

"Do you see now that he is like his father? His father's fate is his own, and his will be Serge's. He thought you had left him. He started to take the poison—and we fought. Then he smashed the picture." She burst into tears.

Carmian lifted her eyes toward the broken glass of Lala's centerpiece, the frame containing her life's history. Everyone was in it but Mikhail, who smoldered from his old-fashioned frame, bitter and unfathomable, in Lala's inner chamber—on top of the piano amongst the crates and boxes. Here in the living room, behind broken glass, were the six little girls with their governess in the snow, laughing in Moscow. Lala, Lilla, Olga, Lola . . . There were Kolya, Eliane, and their relatives. But where there was a star of splintered glass, and where the blow had been struck, were Denise and her son, Serge.

In their silence they heard Dima storming up the stairs.

"He loves you, Madame," said Lala—astoundingly—bowing as before a princess.

Carmian threw the poison down the toilet, since Lala could not get rid of anything.

She was aware of a titanic victory, after subterranean struggles in which she had conquered. Lala became her ally now, as defeated nations do. No more talk of Denise's virtues. She had been beaten. But Carmian, quite unused to such a rôle, was somehow forced to become Lala's fellow conspirator, the strong often being putty in the hands of the ambitious weak. Lala now accepted Carmian as the strongest one and went about her business as usual—which was getting Serge. "If . . ." she kept saying. "If Dima were more forceful." But she would not elaborate, not yet sure of her ground.

Instead she told Carmian a story.

As always, it started off innocently. Mikhail and his friends of the days of Montparnasse: Modigliani, Soutine, Foujita and the model Kiki, and the numberless Russian artists and poets . . . resurrecting the international café life that Carmian and Dima, apart, had shared as children, and that had made them posthumously brother and sister. Lala played this violin very well, and Carmian was a good audience. Why, at any time, during the Exposition coloniale, for instance—wasn't it in 1933? (the shivering Negroes in woolen sweaters so much more interesting than the carved wooden beads that her mother bought)—at any time he might have been sitting, eating ices like herself beside a lonely, loving, desperate parent at one of the marble-topped tables of the Dôme, the Ronde, or the Capoulade.

She knew the color and texture of those childhood nights when they should have been in bed—the orange-yellow-pink excitement of it all, and underneath the knowledge of despair, the gnawing of pity. And it had stayed with them so that every neon light in the

183

now emptied cemeteries of Montparnasse (so called because everyone had died) was a Lorelei beckoning to happiness and death at the *comptoir*, where Mummy and Papa had filled the air with their misery and abandon that you had not been old enough to share, and you talked to the ghost of Modigliani.

"Was it not wrong for a boy—that life?" asked Lala.

"Yes, I suppose. Yes."

"Do you know how his father died?"

She had not been listening, but only remembering, so that now she showed her alarm and started to undress, getting into old American pajamas.

"The way his father brought him up!" Lala moaned, leaning her eyes on her hand and peeking—one could have sworn—through the fingers.

"Well, we all—"

"His father hit me many times. How do you think *he* learned?"

Carmian took the tin box from the buffet and started to roll a cigarette. As she lit it, it blazed toward her nose and was suddenly docile, sending out smoke.

"I hope that is not his last tobacco."

"If it is, it is," Carmian said coldly, determined to keep her advantage.

"I was merely thinking of you. His temper! His father was the same way, selling my jewels, never home, not working . . ."

"Lala! I am tired."

"I too." Gently, Lala said, "Shall I tell you about the funeral?"

"Okay, tell me about the funeral." She smoked, sick, and growing sicker with dry sharp bitter things that had once at least been moist, live tragedy. It was funny too, as everything around Lala, but not very. Dima's father had taken poison and died. At the funeral two widows had made their appearance, both in black veils: Lala and the Danish mistress. The cortège; the Russian Church rue Daru. The glares exchanged, beneath veils, between factions. And suddenly the awful unforeseen—the wild, twelve-year-old boy with his blond hair all over his eyes, leaping up and throwing himself upon the coffin, snarling like an animal.

"He clawed," Lala said, "he banged his head on the wood and bit it. He tried to pry up the nails with his hands, then with his teeth.

He wailed, trying to open the coffin. They had to carry him out of the church, kicking and screaming like a wildcat."

"Oh, my poor boy," she mourned, hands clasped between her knees.

"What a scene, Karmianka! My sister Shura . . . You cannot imagine."

"They were taking his daddy away."

"Karmian, look at me."

She lifted dry, bitter brown eyes. "He wanted his daddy."

"You are just like him," Lala declared, not untenderly. "But how you will suffer! Put out that cigarette before it falls on the table, and" —sighing—"I shall go to bed."

Soon he would come home, soon.

26 Dima's union had sent him to work at the Folies Bergères. This was unfortunate in more ways than one, for he considered it a demotion and a great bore, laughing wryly at her question whether it was not enjoyable to be surrounded by so much handsome female nudity. "I tell them to get the hell out of my way," he said.

Now his work would be always at night, and Carmian found this a hardship without precedent. She was afraid of the evenings with Lala. Dima gave them tickets to the show which his mother viewed appreciatively but somewhat blankly, preferring to regard the whole thing as the naked gamboling of children, future Elianes upon a stage (though not so beautiful), while Carmian could not keep from blushing for some reason—seeing this kind of entertainment with Lala made her want to sink through the floor of the box.

In February the lights went out in Lala's flat. It was a disaster equivalent to war, seemingly irremediable.

No one had paid the electricity bill, and the bundle of communications from the State-owned company that controlled this facility had gathered dust on the buffet. A month before, Lala had left a five-thousand-franc note pinned to it with a stern injunction to Carmian to see that it was finally paid, and had gone off to Châtenay.

Thereupon Dima had seized the note and run off with it to his lawyer, who had been regretting the necessity for dropping the divorce case for the coming year with increasing acerbity by post. Konciergeka had never seen so many bills, and delivered them faithfully, including his back union dues.

Dima, suddenly anxious to marry Carmian, had faced the enraged Lala with a clear conscience. "This was more important," he said, "so as not to lose the whole year. I will pay your electricity and all I owe you besides, as soon as the *Assurances* . . ."

"*Les Assurances!*" Lala shrilled the loathesome word. "I wash my hands of everything!"

But not before she had tinkered with the meter, mysteriously tapped walls and inspected wires, and resorted criminally to that last dodge of the Parisian of arranging for free electricity before the bill grew any steeper. You went to jail for it, but her patience had burst its bonds. She had learned her electricianship in czarist Russia where sheltered young ladies of good family took such a course along with their music and French, to the timeless bemusement of any Westerner.

So it happened, the bill having completed its life span, that Carmian while alone one night was plunged in darkness. Luckily there were candles, which she found by striking innumerable evil-smelling S.E.I.T.A. sulphur matches, whose fumes were supposed to kill you slowly, on the buffet. She reassured herself that the gas, also, had been turned off, lit some candles, and sat down to wait for Dima's return in four hours.

At about nine o'clock there was a tap at the door, and she admitted a small round person barely discernible as a frizzle-headed blonde—or perhaps her hair was gray—with some sort of matted fur around her shoulders and an air of vagueness. At her feet, attached to her by the end of a joint leash, were two grubby little gray poodles. "Madame de Koubyankov . . . ?" she stammered.

"She is out. I regret—"

The small person stood irresolutely gazing at a guttering candle.

"A little trouble with the fuse," Carmian explained delicately. "Do you have a message for her?"

"No . . ."

"Would you like to sit down? I don't believe she will be home this evening."

"No, thank you. Tell her I'll return."

"Certainly," said Carmian. "Good night."

Dima took the news of the electricity with equilibrium. He was more concerned about the gas and getting a spirit lamp on which to cook. "All you think about is your stomach," she remarked bitterly, thinking of the hated darkness.

"I'll have it paid for in a week. Don't you worry. They'll turn it on again."

Lala discovered her loss in the morning, when she entered the dark little hole of a kitchen and snapped on the switch.

"*Elektrichistva!*" she shrieked, uttering what was to become the most unpopular word in Lala's house. "Where is it?"

They kept silence, holding their breaths.

"*Et le gaz*—Karmian!"

"They have departed," Carmian answered, shrugging. "They have been cut off."

"Ai—ai—ai!" said Lala, and proceeded to unfix the meter, by candlelight, so that the inspectors would not know.

"In America," said Carmian, "you could make a lot of money."

"What good would it do me—with a bandit for a son?"

The walls rang with her laments for days and weeks, but on that first morning of deprivation, scandal, and disgrace, she was as nearly quiet as she could be, working quickly and efficiently. It was the shock, no doubt.

To divert her, Carmian told her about last night's visitor whom she suddenly recalled—unhappily reminded that she had forgotten to ask her name. Of course, it was equally true that the person herself had forgotten to leave it.

"She looked as if she were doing an errand for someone. She was walking some dogs. A Russian, I think. I'm sure it was not important."

"Dogs," Lala pondered, throwing herself into the mystery. "What sort of dogs, Karmianka?"

"Poodles, little fat ugly poodles."

"Somebody's maid," Dima suggested.

"A *Russian?*" said Lala. She was not to be put off; she dearly loved company. Tapping her teeth, she inquired: "*Ell avait l'air—comment?*"

"Fat and short with curls and a ratty old fur."

187

"Poodles. Was she blond with dyed hair?"

"Well, I couldn't—" Carmian decided not to mention the lack of light. "Yes, I suppose so."

Lala screamed, "La Princesse de Natterkron!"

Dima collapsed with laughter.

"Oh, I'm sorry! I thought she was somebody's—"

"One of the greatest families of Russia, Madame! Related to the Galitzins! Well . . . well, I can't blame you. You could not know. You say she looked that terrible?"

Lala was beginning to preen herself on being better preserved than La Natterkron, when she remembered the misfortune.

"The electricity, *mon Dieu!* Were the lights off? Did she notice?"

"I told her a fuse had blown. Perhaps if there had been light I'd have known she was . . ."

Dima patted her admiringly. Lala sighed. "It must be paid without delay, do you understand, Dmitri? Or I will throw you out of this house. Karmian may stay if she likes. But you go!"

"Oh, shut up and leave us a little peace," said her son.

"*Svolitch!*" she retorted, a non-aristocratic word meaning garbage.

So long as Carmian knew, the electricity was never paid, or the gas. Lala received no guests after dark; candles were prized as once had been tea, coffee, and sugar; and only the cat was indifferent, prowling with distended pupils by candlelight.

The chilblains itched and burned. In the afternoons the sun threw pale rays into the room, made lovelier for the dread of their early passing. There was no more Mozart or any other music, or descriptions of missing persons—Carmian's favorite—from the dead radio. At night the only beauty was the grillwork at the window and the golden rings in her cat's eyes; she wrangled with Lala over his meat rations (he disdained *moue* and other entrails) and sneaked food to him on the sly. There remained hope to amass the sum for the reopening of the electricity and gas, until—

One day when Carmian was again alone three men came to the house on rue Maison-Dieu, from the municipal company, and went to work with screwdrivers, wrenches, and hammers. When they left, all the equipment for receiving gas and light went with them, the entrails.

"But Messieurs," she had protested, pointing to the box high on the wall that they were working on, "one will want to reopen as soon as one can pay the bill!"

"There is an extra charge for that, Madame. The reinstallation. After a period of three months the fixtures are taken down."

"How much?"

"Seventeen hundred francs, Madame."

"But that's not very amiable! We can almost pay now——"

"It's the law," they said, shrugging.

She stared at the results of their formidable labor, the wires and screws and tubes and casings which they carried off with them as she led all three to the door. "It's a disgrace," she remarked.

Shame or not, they failed to respond, with the boredom of men hardened to their job. She hoped they would fall downstairs, but they did not.

Lala had a few things to say about how she would have acted if she had been there, and intimated that if no one had been at home —why, they could not have got in! But even her spirits were lower than usual. She could not produce the appropriate fury and spite. This was a monstrous thing, for though half the necessary money now reposed in a cookie jar, an additional seventeen hundred francs made the whole endeavor unbearable. It was just too damn much money to spend on electricity and gas. All hope of earthly light and heat left Lala's house with the departure of the three workmen.

"O la, la, la, la, la," Dima would say sometimes, and his mournful exclamation was so clearly an echo of his mother's name. "She has the money," he would rage, "to do it all."

"Well, we *live* here. We ought to move."

"There isn't a place anywhere. Do you want to go back to the Riff-Raff Hotel?"

Carmian almost said yes. The failure of optimism in the Koubyankovs shocked her. They with their windmill hopes, their blindly rushing ways and bottomless energy. It was really a problem, then, if even they foundered.

Even the cards—that were bigger than life—were no longer possible. It was astounding how many things failed with the light. They had thought that he had played the rôle of Desire and she of Fate, whereby she had always won. But possibly she had been merely Life with its puny miseries, and he the Dream denying hopelessness, bravely dealing.

No Beethoven, Haydn, Schumann, Schubert, and the Russians. (To Carmian the music she liked was always Beethoven, which amused him.) Not even the terrible French National Symphony Orchestra, who sawed away steadily looking at their watches, being first and foremost government employees and future *rentiers*. No more Papageno, Papagena . . . *"Ein Mädchen ging im Wa-alde . . ."*; and Genghis Khan; Tamburlaine; Taras Bulba.

Music and light were gone, so they fled after hours—quite naturally—to a bar.

There Carmian found a German engineer who would transfer marks into francs at a 20 per cent higher rate than the banks, who stole from both sides; and she had been planning another foray into her mother country. It was a Danish bar between the avenue du Maine and Montparnasse, a region where girls stood shadowed in corners even while it rained and spoke softly to Dima as he passed. At the Danish bar they drank Tüborg and Carlsberg, dark and blond, and after a time they were there every night. It was easier to spend money as it came by the week than to save it in order to stay in a dungeon.

But the Danish woman who owned the bar fell in love with Dima and let them run up a mean-looking bill over drink and dice. The Dane was overly fond of beer herself and often had to be dragged upstairs by the hair of her head when the Spanish husband, an ex-prizefighter who did not drink, grew moody. As money got scarce, or invisible, they began to avoid the Danish bar, taking another side street on their trips to the boulevard Montparnasse. The last they saw of her, she was taking the air with her Boxer dog and a very black eye. She greeted them wanly, without rancor, for which one was grateful.

In Montparnasse drinks were cheaper, and local Russians could be persuaded to buy a few *rouges* on hearing still recognizable accents of their homeland.

Thus they encountered Choukin once more.

He was at the *comptoir* of that grave, that cemetery, the Café du Dôme—the scowling man, the painter with the moist dark eyes, who had financed her trip in May or June and let Dima sleep in his atelier. Looking at him, Carmian decided he had never been repaid. But he was also the kind of man who did not care. He behaved as if he had seen them yesterday and invited them to the studio in the rue d'Alésia where they admired his latest—and best—painting, still wet, of oysters on red velvet. He broke out his Moroccan wine, pouring it sloppily into large tumblers as he reminisced about Soutine, Foujita, Modigliani. . . . And Dima sat like an angel dreaming of his father.

Carmian was not listening either, dreaming of a warm May night when she had met Choukin. In one of the bistros she had danced the musette with a nimble, merrily inscrutable, big Russian boy, whose inner darkness was her own. The particular love, mixed with the smells and sounds and textures of that bar, that night, surged over her again. Now it was different and saddened by familiarity. He was beside her, as known to her as herself, and perhaps as hated; no longer an accident to her heart but everything she had ever loved and hated all one. Mother, father, sister, brother . . . A unity had come about, whether happy or not, for good or for evil, it did not matter. The thing was to be One. They had married themselves. It was true what they had surmised then. And they had the innocence to believe in its power and its virtue.

Dima had lines of strain across his forehead; his golden hair had thinned. Carmian since the loss of Michael had grown a streak of white down each side of her face. The children were not the same, nor had they aged by merely a year. Choukin knew it. He waved his arms, talking about the Revolution and his desertion from the Russian Navy in Odessa 1919 . . . a true orphan, a *bezprizornye*, a brother.

27 Another week passed, punctuated by her trip to the public baths, and turned into March. The *bains publiques* in the rue de Vanves were distinguished by a hand-printed sign in the window stating a revolutionary concept: "It is healthy to bathe and harmless even after repasts." She would stay under the hot shower for the allowed twenty minutes or more and walk home with wet, flapping hair in an icy wind. For some reason she never caught cold. The misery was too consistent; perhaps it hardened one to spend a winter as cold indoors as out.

But now the weather changed to rain. . . . The frog-swallowers and chain-bursters practiced their art among the shining puddles of the Place de la Gaîté, encircled by a gawking crowd; the *poules* stood waiting under umbrellas at night. Anticipating spring, Lala brought home a bird in a cage who peeped nervously, hopping and fluttering, at the mesmerized stare, the tentative claws of the cat. She hotly defended her whim but forgot to feed it, a chore that was performed by Carmian and sometimes Dima out of compassion. "Birds!" was his comment. "She has another in her head—that makes two."

Lala screeched, "I also have the right to have a pet!"

"Then clean his cage."

"I clean the whole house!" she wailed. "Everything I do—everything!"

"You're jealous of Cammie's cat because you know he hates you. How infantile you are!"

"Hates me! I who cleaned up his messes! That's the thanks I get!"

"Has it ever occurred to you," he asked her, "how few persons have ever thanked you?"

"You—no. Your father—no. But Kolya—I shall tell him how you mistreat me. He'll whip you for me if I tell him!"

Dima turned pale. He gasped for air, his eyes bulged, and his throat closed with that disturbing little shutter sound that Carmian always heard. Suddenly, she had it. She knew that Kolya, ten years older than his half-brother, had beaten him up. It had the ring of an oft-repeated threat received in childhood terror. It had been Lala's weapon.

Carmian took his reddening neck between her pale cold hands, leaning against him, in silence. He recovered a little. "Kolya feels the same as I," he growled hoarsely. "He despises you. All the men you ever knew despised you."

"Ha!" Lala laughed falsely, throwing back her head. "What do

you know? Your father was jealous of me! Why . . . (etc., etc., etc.)
I had six Cossacks fighting for me under this very table!"

Flushed and triumphant, she let them drown her out with their
bitter incredulous laughter. One could not stay angry at anyone so
preposterous. It was very frustrating. And apt to drive any little boy
quite mad.

But that had been long ago, and the black bombazine bosom at
the Préfecture de Police was another matter and another kind of
ordeal. Carmian, facing the stout, aging lady bureaucrat across her
littered desk as she thumbed through the shady-looking passport with
its interminable visas and German hieroglyphics, sweated coldly and
hoped.

Lala had warned her, afraid of harboring a delinquent, for the
thing was four months overdue. *Carte de séjour . . . carte de séjour*
. . . Lala had harped. It was terrible, criminal, unforgivable. (Only,
one could not afford the visa. If one could not even afford light to
see by, gas to cook by, how could one pay an enormous price for a
little piece of paper? And that to stay in a country one wished all to
hell anyway?)

Carmian told the bombazine bosom everything except about her
contraband German currency activities, hoping that the Bonn bank-
er's notations in his relentless fussy script would go unheeded, perhaps even scorned in the whole frightful mess of seals and stamps.
Perhaps she was only interested in entries and exits. Carmian waited,
holding her breath—but the baby had done the trick. There had
been a noticeable softening of the official features at that point in
her tale. Now she put on a grave and serious bedside manner, joining
the tips of her fingers over the historic document (which clearly
shocked her) and told her about an American student whom she
had just recently banned from the country for less. She could expect
the same treatment; or at the very least a fine of six thousand francs.

Carmian paled. It was approximately what one owed everybody:
the light company, Lala, the lawyer, the hospital, the Danish bar—
in effect, an unpayable sum. To be thrown out of France! *Dima!* But
the iron bosom seemed oddly to belong to that vanishing sort who
helped orphans and lovers in passing, even as once J.-P.

She leaned forward, tapping a pencil, with a piercing stare.
"You were lucky to draw me, Mademoiselle, rather than one of the

gentlemen in this room. I will do for you what I can, which is to let you go home. There you will pack a suitcase and take a train to the Belgian border—Mauberge, I believe? You can take the next train back, as long as you have your exit stamp. With your exit and entry stamps you are entitled to stay in Paris another three months."

Apparently the crime was not cumulative, once you had fooled the officials into giving you their little stamps. All past sins were then forgotten. Carmian nodded, in awe.

"Then come back here and get your visa and stay out of trouble," said the lady, handing her the offensive object and the tattered piece of paper that had once permitted her to register at Paris hotels. It was bisected by a strip of Scotch tape, reminding her unpleasantly that once, in a rage at Dima, she had torn it in two.

"Thank you, Madame."

"I warn you to take the trip at once and not to let this happen again. Be sure to receive the stamps of exit and entry. The entry stamp is of the highest importance. Do not forget."

Carmian understood her better now; she was maternal. "But will they let me cross the border—when they see—"

"I hope so for your sake," the angel in black said dryly. "There is no guarantee."

"*Au revoir, Madame. Merci!*"

Lala simpered, smirked, and puffed up with relief when she heard that Carmian had escaped a fine of six thousand francs.

Dima was furious. "What if they don't let her out—or in again?"

"As long as they let her out," said Lala, "she is safe. With her money in Germany, she doesn't have to come back—"

He burnt her up with a look. "Witch!"

"I mean at once!" she wailed.

These hissings continued, off and on, until she left with half of Dima's pay in her pocket. It cost money even to be illegal. Less, that was all. She stuffed a small suitcase with plausible things, and they rode a bus through the morning mist to the Gare du Nord. She bought a second-class ticket, one way. Dima's embrace was warm but distracted, and he had a tic in his left cheek.

"Perhaps you had better stay overnight," he said.

"No, no—"

"Well, if there is no trouble—"

"I'll be back tonight at seven. You be here too."

194

"Yes, seven-ten. I'll be here. If you're not here—"

"I will be."

"This is the last time I'll ever send you away from me." He swung himself off the train and smiled, making the curiously old-fashioned V-sign as she pulled out.

The ridiculous conspiracy of the thing—the spy-novel note—had kept her on the verge of laughter until now, although hysterical. Alone, a cloud descended, chilling her heart. Surely Madame de la Préfecture had not thrown her to the wolves?

She remembered other trips tinged with terror; the priest in the corridor to whom she had glued herself at Herbesthal, deutsche marks burning in her pocket . . . and all the frontiers she had crossed since with the help of a little Schnapps and an American face. She tried to remember who was tougher, the Belgians or Germans—was it coming or going?—and could not. The clothes were awkward, they should not be so European; it set up a confusion and made them look at you twice.

Then she reminded herself in her tired, muddled head that this was purely a concern of the French. No one else would be interested in their ciphers once you got that far. And once you got past the first one—*out*—it would be all right. Perhaps he would be nice, or angry at the government. Sighing, she settled down for the five-hour ride as they clacked through the glistening suburbs, their ugliness shrouded in fog, the Sacré-Cœur like a big white misty woman high over Paris. The train stopped in a dreary outlying district, where a man entered her compartment, and gathered itself for the long, fast run.

Her traveling companion was the kind of Frenchman who seems, by a studied air of astuteness and penetration along with a stock of ready-made wit, to be innately wise—a fallacy—although she thought him rather sweet in his rumpled brown suit. He immediately unpacked a sandwich made of an entire loaf of bread and a bottle of *rouge*, which he insisted on sharing with her. She knew him to be a type apt to get sticky with foreign women, convinced of his ability to impress them and hard to shake off, but accepted gracefully enough, glad of the diversion. Anyway, she was hungry. Munching and drinking out of his tin cup, she was soon laughing her high childish laughter at his jokes.

But the thing that stunned her about him was when he flashed

195

a pass at the conductor, called him by name, and explained to her that he was a railroad engineer on a holiday; furthermore, this was his run. He knew everyone and talked with every trainman who came through. She paused, cup in mid-air, to wonder if she could . . . and shook off the temptation. Madame would be certain to disapprove of such a confidence. But maybe he could help her. Or if he could not, would he betray her? She lapsed into moodiness, wrestling intolerably. Dima would know, but she did not.

At Mauberge, which was the French border station, he got out to accompany her to the passport and customs queue, remarking that he wished to stretch his legs. Her own buckled quietly. And sure enough, as her friend lounged chatting in another corner, a French official leafed through her maze of exit and entry dates with infinite patience until he had extricated the last, pertinent one. He looked at her and went off to consult his colleagues. They huddled with sinister porings and head-shakings at the end of the room, while she waited to be sentenced. Oh, Madame de la Préfecture. And how fast it had happened, how ignominious!

The engineer approached with a face that was composed of canine alertness and reproach. "Madame," he inquired sadly, "if you are in difficulties, why did you not tell me?"

"I should have, Monsieur; I regret." She described the trouble.

"Wait here," he said.

It ended, she could never remember just how, in a wild dream during which she was reluctantly, severely, permitted to board the train once more and continue on it across the Belgian frontier. The stamp was there all right, but cleverly blurred and on the wrong page, leaving its discovery and proper interpretation, like a work of art, to the next inspector. They had washed their hands of her.

The engineer eyed her mournfully, saddened at the lack of trust in one so young and gentle. "I know them all!" he said, waving her gratitude away. The Belgian inspector gave her his entry stamp without further ado, and she descended with the engineer at Mons, where she elicited the information that the next train back to Paris would leave in half an hour.

"You're not taking the next one back?" the engineer echoed, incredulous.

"Oh, I must."

"But it's the same train!"

"My husband is expecting me."

"But really—excuse me—foreigners are crazy. You should stay in Mons overnight. I will take you to a hotel."

"Oh, no, really, thank you so much."

"You can send him a telegram, and we will have dinner."

"You have been so kind," she said firmly. "Monsieur, I will never forget you."

"He is lucky, but you are not wise," he declared, shook her hand, and went out into the city. She bought a few packs of Belgian cigarettes, a return ticket, and boarded the train.

There rose in her mind a picture of the Rhineland beckoning to her with fluttering flags: Money was there, and comfort and leisure and light, and no Lala. Freedom was there. The fleeting specter of a life without Dima filled her with desolation, as if already, one without the other, they were lost and grieving for all time. Something lured her, so that by a razor's edge it had to be this train, no other; and he would be waiting in the station for her as he had never done. If not this train, she knew she would be going northeast, in the opposite direction.

Alone in the compartment, she resorted to the rather ludicrous tactics of changing from her German *Lodenmantel* to a three-quarter-length camel's-hair coat that an American had given Dima. It was long in the sleeves. She turned them up, took off her hat and stuffed it together with the overcoat into her suitcase. Well, the day had grown warm.

The train started rolling, Paris-bound. She breathed deeply. Somehow there had been a narrow escape not limited to matters of frontier officialdom. Where it is difficult, sometimes impossible, to leave love—it is equally hard to turn back once a step has been taken, if only a geographical stride, meaningless in itself. The momentum alone could carry one to the threshold of Dima's resolution: *Il n'y a pas de retour.*

We have to fight everything . . . so hard, she thought with anger and pity. That's the way we are.

The same Belgian inspectors came through. The passport man did not seem to recognize her in her altered costume, but the currency man eyed her suspiciously. She gazed back at him with the virtuousness of one reformed, fortified in the knowledge that she carried no more than fourteen hundred French francs and some

197

Belgian cigarettes. But she was in for a shock with the advent of the customs officers.

The train due 7:05 at the Gare du Nord was a half-hour late.

Dima's fair head reared above the waiting crowd. She saw him right away and ran to him, letting herself be hugged and kissed.

"My God, I thought your train was never coming!"

"It was *me!*" she cried. "I did it!"

"I thought so. I knew it." He wiped his forehead and blew out his breath as they moved toward the street. "Listen, did you get the entry stamp?"

"Oh, yes," she said, breathless. "They recognized me but let me have it anyway." She paused. "Although I don't think they like me too much. But the Belgian customs—the Belgians—couldn't understand why I had spent only a half-hour in Mons. Naturally I could not tell them and they couldn't figure it out at all—you'd think they would put their heads together—being on the same train even if they are different nationalities—so I said that I had gone to see friends in Mons who had moved away!"

"*I* should have thought of something better," said Dima.

"Naturally. Well, they spent the whole time looking through my suitcase for dope and diamonds."

He snorted. "With your face?"

"Maybe that's what international smugglers look like. At least they didn't have one of those matrons undress me and look—"

He laughed and squeezed her shoulders as they waited for a bus. "I have you back; that's all that matters. My God, I missed you; I was so scared." On the bus he said: "Lala will envy you bitterly. It's the kind of role she would have wished for herself—only *with* diamonds."

"Ah, Lala. Listen, there was a railroad engineer . . ."

"Yes, of course," he said, looking at her as if he could not look enough. "Come, we'll have a drink in Montparnasse."

Paris smelled of the spring night. She was torn between joy and the dread of her bondage, observing him sideways as they rode the bus hand in hand on the back platform. It did appear that he had changed profoundly. It was his philosophy, and perhaps he was right in this too. People changed. He proved it. And she . . . amazed that, after taming the savage, she should feel a curious wildness in her own breast.

"To an engineer!" said Carmian raising her glass, and everyone drank solemnly without the slightest notion of what she was talking about.

"To an engineer," they said.

28   Hurot was a painter of Choukin's vintage but unlike him in every other respect; he was abstemious, ascetic, and taciturn except when discussing his art. While Choukin's broadness and versatility could be—and was—called characterless (except for his best, such as the oysters), Hurot was uniquely the creator of fragile, doe-eyed girls in dreamlike mists. His girls were all adolescent, touchingly beautiful, incredibly romantic, and tremendously saleable. Choukin did not consider them worthy of mention. Hurot, uncaring of the financially inspired envy of Choukin and all the rest, continued to paint his girls one after the other, with the narrow devotion of a monk at work in his cell. He loved them passionately.

The visit to Hurot occurred one afternoon when Dima, in a desperate attempt to think of something amusing to do, had a flash in which he recalled not only Hurot's name and earlier cultural hangouts (the Montparnasse group) but found his studio much the same as a dog would, by instinct, looping here and there, nosing in and out, until they came to a heavy oaken door in the quarter. Hurot admitted them after a while, and Carmian entered a vast duplex atelier by means of skirting a small grave.

Hurot's considerately guiding hand at her elbow—perhaps he was used to people falling into it—she looked back. It was a grave, all right, sunken into the studio floor, with dirt, a vase of flowers, and at its head a natural stone. He acted as if it were not there. Dima proffered the banal courtesies, but his face was all broken up, the eyes slitted and crinkled, betraying extremes of self-control. Hurot's grave was clearly not suitable for discussion or inquiry. Was some loved one in it? She started at what seemed to be a pile of bones nearby but recovered sufficiently to perceive it was plaster. Perhaps the grave was merely an object of beauty to Hurot.

199

The walls were equally discouraging. They were strung with broken dolls and instruments of torture among the objets d'art. The whole ground floor was a museum of the master's fetishes.

Upstairs it was paintings, and cabbage in the sink. There he made some horribly bitter coffee and, strengthened in this manner, proceeded to show them all his paintings—the best, he said, but he could not have missed one of about fifty on hand—with minute analytical comment, while the cabbage wilted in the sink. It stank badly.

The prospect of further evenings chez Hurot lacked a certain appeal, so they became almost nightly visitors of Choukin in the rue d'Alésia. On Dima's working nights Carmian went alone, taking her cat, and waited there until Dima called for her around midnight. The candlelit nights at Lala's had become intolerable, especially since Lala had started to pinch about candles.

In this period of gloom, in the direst poverty as a result of the Belgian trip with its expensive entry stamp, the Koubyankov nerves were badly frayed. Not to help matters, a visiting dog of the larger sort smashed Lala's windowpane. She, never really an animal lover, took on even more than usual about this catastrophe since she hated drafts, although the change in room temperature on windless days was negligible.

Heated or not, it was still a railroad-station waiting room: one was going nowhere, and from that above all they suffered abominably. Lala could or would not get back the electricity, Dima could not meet the payments for his divorce, Carmian had no place to go except to Choukin's. Apartment hunting was hopeless even if one could pay. It appeared that only Americans got apartments; fairies, and important people. One had only to remember, with a sinking heart, the language student and his family, to despair. They were blocked and deadlocked in each other's impotent grip.

One night Carmian came home after an impromptu party with some Americans in Montparnasse. She showed the effects of this by unfortunately crashing into Lala's buffet in the dark, knocking down some bonky-sklonky, and Dima, in bed, began slowly, furiously, to revile her. But it was Lala who turned the trick. She came out of her room and when Carmian in several sorts of blindness bumped against her, she seized her efficiently by the shoulders and hurled her head first toward the bed. Above the bed was nailed a bookshelf which hit her squarely in the bridge of her nose and caused an amazing amount of excruciating pain.

While the pain lasted, Carmian became a savage. She suddenly desired to kill Lala, and the first thing to do was to get her hands around her neck. However, it was dark, which was the thing that had caused the damage in the first place; it was hard to find her.

"*Je vous tue*, Lala," she warned, starting after her (for the polite address persisted, pain or no pain). Lala screamed heartrendingly and tore away from the groping, almost clutching hands, and slammed the door behind her. As an afterthought she pushed some heavy piece of furniture in front of her door. Carmian sat down and laughed, and began to cry.

"Go to sleep," Dima said. "*Tu as le mauvais vin.*"

Lying down beside him, she announced, "Tomorrow I'll not be here, and don't look for me."

"You drink like an Indian," he said sleepily.

But in the morning, seeing her blackened eyes and swollen nose, the always ready but not unmanly tears sprang up, and he accused his mother: "What have you done to Cammie? See what you have done to my girl!"

"Nothing!" Lala shrieked. "You did it! You did it! Don't listen to him, Karmianka!"

For, it was strange, she was in terror.

He growled, "Take care of her," and went to work.

That night Carmian did not come home. And no one looked for her. She took the cat.

The cat always followed her down the street, like a puppy. He loved her. He followed her all the way to Alésia, although he must have known that his rival was waiting there to taunt him and spit at him: Choukin's cat. He would jump on to the high windowsill and sit there contemplating suicide, while she stood below, cajoling, calming. He was like a child. He had become less of an animal and more of a martyr (it was laughable but sad) and a saint. His eyes glowed seeking her and the truth in her.

Carmian was full of anger, except toward the cat, and for him she felt impatience, pity, gratitude. You and I, she would say to him, the orphaned of the world. We found each other by the Seine. "Now hurry—*viens, viens vite!*" And she snapped her fingers.

Choukin's door was opened wide, casting rays of light on the garden, the gnarled but fruitful little tree. The atelier looked lovely, like a stage, and Choukin took up her cat in his arms, and inside was M. Garashoko, a Japanese artist who visited here for purposes of argument and to sample the African wine. Garashoko had a French wife and six children whom he supported by being, among other things, a master imitator. He had sent innumerable Renoirs and Cézannes to the United States, as originals.

She said, "I just thought I'd . . ."

And he said, "I know. You're in the dark over there," and gave her a tumblerful of his ruby-red wine. In the light it was jewels and blood, warmth and sweetness and hope in the stomach; it was like love.

Some time later when she opened her eyes the Japanese had departed . . . and some time after that she was by some mysterious circumstance stretched naked on the bed, and, worst of all, Choukin lay horribly beside her. He seemed to be half-dressed, but she could not really see because a red veil came between them—not before she had caught sight of his cruel and avid eyes—and she slapped his head away. Then she twisted her body in so violent a revulsion that he almost flew off the bed, tensing herself as he came back, this time in anger.

"No woman ever did that to me!" he roared, and for a moment of rage Choukin's broad flat hand hung suspended in air like the guillotine, and murder was in his face.

The hand dropped. "Go home," he said.

She slapped him again, and his mouth fell open. Then she found her voice: "*What have you done to Dima?*" she screamed.

"Nothing happened, you silly child."

"Garbage of the devil!" she screamed in Russian, weeping because her heart was broken.

Much later she was to remember his wonder and dismay at the bitter, bitter tears for her boy; for, hard as he tried, he could not comfort her. And Choukin, the Russian, began to love her.

His love was chaste and compassionate. What was fearsome was that, in some compensatory way, he had to grow to hate Dima.

At Lala's they sat in a draft from the broken window while she arranged pussy willows in a vase and chattered about the *babki* she would make for Russian Easter. The cat was shedding fur and had a bald patch on his neck; the area surrounding Carmian's eyes had turned yellow; the bird had died. Dima had never asked her about the night she had stayed away.

Everything was all right, really. Except something had happened, just a little thing. And she dreaded to hear the first dim ominous rolling thunder of an avalanche, started by the first slipped stone, that small death.

She showed a sudden aversion to visiting Choukin's atelier, which Dima simply accepted. For all his pretensions to Russian bearlike shrewdness and treachery, he was uncorrupted, a choirboy. His purity shamed her.

It was time for an angel: Semyon Semyonovitch. He came out of nowhere after an absence of more than a dozen years, looking like a tall old Apache Indian, possessed of a beautiful falsetto voice that sang its way through less than ordinary sentiments and observations. He had been *précepteur* to Dima, a male nanny and governess, a kind of parent, and had taught him how to swim, shoot, and ride. This, of course, had been before the death of Baron Koubyankov. Before that, he had been hetman of a Cossack village and ridden at the head of his men in flowing white robes. He was a peasant; but the warrior was in him. He was no serf.

Instantly his small Asian eyes saw a love affair, a serious one. His "Madame" to Carmian was as mellifluous, as full of echoes of the faithful servant, as it was to Lala whose paid servant he had been. In his deepest register it sounded like, "Modoma."

"He has accepted you," Dima told her.

"Hell," she said.

"Yes," he pondered rather bitterly, "the aristocrats of the modern world are the Americans."

"Not you or me."

He looked at her with that puppy look. And the warm lovely world was their bed, where they might kiss and comfort each other. The trouble was that there were always so many people in the room. It was a thoroughfare.

Sometimes, when they were alone: "I am so jealous of you," she would whisper, softly into his ear.

And he: "I love you. Don't I always say that I love you?"

203

"Yes."

"Ah, yes."

"Will we go to America—or somewhere?"

"Patience, *dyevutchka*."

"Will we ever be in peace?"

"Yes," he said, "yes, yes, yes. And I love you so terribly."

Choukin came with his dark diabolic face and his dog eyes one afternoon when Dima was working at a matinée. Lala and Semyon were there, and they all sniffed at each other suspiciously, Russian-exile fashion. The air was thick. But Choukin, with his superior intelligence, summed up the situation and lost no time in getting under way. He bowed deeply over Lala's roughened hand.

A minuet took place. Lala had an archness at times that reminded Carmian of the German Karla Maria Anna—the graceful hand held high, the little finger crooked, the laugh and sparkling eye. Choukin's voice was deep and throbbing in the telling of amusing stories. He looked at Carmian, and she was glacial; Lala chirruped; Semyon sniffed. Choukin rummaged in his mind for Russian pleasantries, while Lala rummaged in her room for tea, evoking in her excitement the flatteries, the silken sofas, the low-cut gowns of her youth.

"Semyon Semyonovitch, prepare the tea!" she sang, depositing a box of the stuff in his helplessly outstretched, massive hands.

"Modoma—" he groaned, his Cossack voice at its very saddest and deepest.

"Semyon!" Imperiously.

Outraged, imploring mutely, he obeyed and disappeared into the kitchen.

Choukin looked at Carmian.

Lala then rummaged for a box of sugar, which she placed on the table with a smirk of apology. "We live very simply here," she explained in what Carmian thought was a marvel of understatement.

He nodded solemnly. "The only way, *na Parizhye*," he declared. She chattered on. She had forgotten Carmian. Semyon, his chore done, withdrew into an Asian stillness. Choukin smoked heavily through a cigarette piece held, palm up, between thumb and forefinger.

Lala continued in her role of the ingénue: "You know, I never smoked. How they used to smoke at home—in Moscow! But I never developed a taste for it. You are a sailor, you say? Odessa, 1919? Ah, we were escaping then; and my husband and I were separated. I had Kolya, and Dima was on the way. My husband exchanged his officer's uniform for a simple soldier's, and we met in Germany and Dima was born. To get milk—it was so difficult! The poor child was born in a prisoners' camp and had to return, alas, during the Germans. He has had much to bear. You know my son? But of course—since you are a friend of my daughter-in-law!"

"Yes, yes," said Choukin, flushing darkly.

"Madame," Semyon suggested with irony, "more tea?"

She smiled at him sweetly, "*Spaciba*, Semyon Semyonovitch."

"*Diable!*" Choukin said later in the rue Maison-Dieu. He mopped his brow. "What a woman."

Carmian was silent.

"I'm surprised she let you out."

"I have errands to do."

"I think—that in a curious way—she is afraid of you, you child."

"We have had our differences. Now, what have you to say to me, for I must go."

He looked at her for several moments and said, "Forgive me."

"I do," she replied stoically, and held out her hand.

"That is not forgiveness."

"What do you want?"

They went into a vegetable store where she bought carrots, potatoes, and leeks. "Your love," he said.

"*Soixante francs, Madame.*"

"You know whom I love."

"*Merci, Madame!*"

"I don't mean that love. I mean the love, for instance, that you give to your cat."

The street felt moistly of spring; the air washed her cheek. "My cat does not harm me."

"I was a fool, but worse."

She bit her lip, frowning.

"I knew the night you wept and could not stop. Will you be my friend, now that I know you?"

"Yes, of course," she said, shuddering involuntarily.

He bent to kiss her hand, and went away.

29 If Hurot was,

plainly, a lover of death—Choukin at least was alive. With the coming of the Russian Easter (Christ is risen!) Choukin fussed and fumed and feverishly painted Easter eggs.

Carmian's laughter offended him. "The master!"

"*Khristos voskres'*," he said dourly.

"*Khristos voskres'*!"

Thus they had been greeting each other all morning in the Russian houses of Montparnasse and Convention and in the rue Daru where, across the street from Shura's bookstore, the Russian church reveled in its greatest day, the day upon which "a lady may kiss a beggar," and people swarmed in and out exchanging Easter eggs with kisses before adjourning to the bistros. Christ is risen! At home Lala unveiled her *babkis*, her *paska* and *kolachi*, before the round, covetous eyes of her grandson, and Dima babbled dreamily about the spring solstice and ancient barbaric rites and crocuses and the sap renewed in the birch trees of that ever-lost country, much in the style of Mayakovsky. Easter was, it seemed, another Russian madness—like Christmas in New York, she considered.

"Your eggs are beautiful," she appeased Choukin. "Dima will come later. Serge is there. Dima is bringing some vodka for tonight."

Choukin was giving a party.

He waved her to a chair with the mixture of gruffness and softness he always showed toward her now. "There is nothing to do just yet." A burnt-out stub protruded forgotten from his mouth. His cat, a big-headed eunuch, brushed against her, fur rippling. The sun streamed through the slanted windows on the dead stove and the pieces of coal scattered around it. The cat miaoued, and she let him out into the little garden with its high wall and path and tree. Nothing . . . nothing of horror had remained from that night. For somehow Choukin had managed to erase it for her, and it was like something felt from afar, read at midnight.

"In America," she observed, "where they heat their houses, Easter is not quite such an Apotheosis."

"Ah, it pays to suffer."

All afternoon he pottered and fussed, drinking red wine, until the atelier was quite clean, the unhung canvases stacked out of the way (just in case), the tables pushed together and bedecked festively with flowers, bottles, glasses, fruit, nuts, cake, and the eggs. Choukin was a natural host, but it took a lot out of him. He had a few nervous crises in spite of the wine, and collapsed, allowing Dima and Carmian to finish the job. When at last all was done and night had fallen, in the calm, fatalistic hush before the arrival of the first guest, they all sat back, breathing easier, drinking wine, and surveying the scene with satisfaction.

Needless to say, they were not in a state of complete sobriety when the party began; but neither was anyone else. There arrived the Japanese painter named Garashoko; a Russian entrepreneur who did a thriving trade with obscure African natives; an American painter; a Princeton graduate with his French girl friend; and a red-haired Swede who was reputed to have been the innamorata of the Sicilian bandit Giuliano. They were a handsome and charming assemblage duly admiring Choukin's eggs and imbibing his vodka, slowly, at first.

The Princeton man was Dima's find and lifelong chum of the week before, a tall, dazzling boy who caused Carmian to wonder at how extraordinarily American some Americans can look. Was it more than just a way of looking out at the world? She could see what had attracted them to each other. Dima was the Russian counterpart. Since the American painter was a big man too, the three towered above the little Japanese, while he observed them not at all balefully, but as he might have looked at gigantic children. When Choukin, anxious as a society hostess, had them all sit down, he placed Carmian between the Japanese and the Russian, the French girl between the two Americans, the Swede between himself and Dima. It was a master stroke of international diplomacy. The Swede had brought along some knitting, and sulked doing it, and one could not help wondering if she had not also sulked and knitted in some mountain cave with Giuliano, as shots rang outside.

The Japanese drank lustily but preserved the oriental self-control, choosing to be observer rather than observed. It was remarkable in one so small, the amounts of vodka that he put away without apparent effect. No one lagged, except possibly the melancholy Swede;

the Russian businessman soon took to his balalaika as the pace of the party increased. Brimming with laughter, Dima sought Carmian's eyes across the table. He had told her about this Russian, who lived in Lala's house in the rue Maison-Dieu with his wife and children. Carmian glanced at him with compassion and comradeship: he shared with them the same black, creaking stairs, the same disheartening W.C., the same redoubtable, Communist-voting Konciergeka who hated White Russians. The little Russian himself was, however, a cheerful type. His export business consisted of buying up old theatrical gear and collecting discarded gala clothing—mostly top hats—which he sent by mail order to inhabitants of inner Africa who wanted to dress like Europeans. He conducted his own advertising, of a rather florid and mendacious nature, and made a modest profit. The Waughish aspect of his undertaking escaped no one but himself; he was a child of the steppes, displaced perhaps but quite at home in his own skin, so much so—the rumor went—that he was apt to make love to his wife at any time the spirit seized him, regardless of company. Since there was only one room, visitors, at such times, shrank toward the door, while babies crawled about and their father beckoned hospitably from the bed in the direction of food and wine set out upon the table, indicating that he would be right back.

Choukin beamed on his guests, especially the Swede and Carmian; he was in fact so full of vodka that he failed to notice the most interesting group of all: the French girl and the two Americans. The Japanese had seen it from the very beginning, when the party was still at the Gallic stage of hauling out identity papers in order to establish a conversational truth. Dima had, and Carmian knew he was prepared for the worst, from the grave sweet look he wore, a tender mien of gazing into distances. The French girl, alas, was flirting with both Americans, who had decided that they did not like each other. Quite suddenly they were on their feet. The girl obligingly screamed, although this was unnecessary. The table overturned. Dima ran round to prevent what augured bloodshed.

Carmian stared frozen at the litter. The scene was reminiscent of their own earlier days of *Schrecklichkeit*, when they had been the bad ones. Not to be the offender gave one a surge of noblesse: Dima reasoned calmly with the painter and the struggling Princeton man. All smaller persons had taken cover except the French girl and herself. Now the Americans were both fighting Dima . . . She started blindly into the fray with some idea of protecting him.

"Get back, Cammie!" he said.

And suddenly—of all things most humiliating, most terrible—a woman, wound up in a ball of fury, flung herself upon Carmian and began tearing out her hair in fistfuls.

She gasped with pain, staggering, for the French girl hung on. She was the bigger, but this small creature was full of strength and venom. To push her off only redoubled the grip on her hair, so Carmian struck her a blow on the back of the elaborately curled coiffure. She knew what was coming next, of course—the teeth—and felt them sink into her hand. . . . Then Dima saved her. He threw the girl to one side, after prying her off. "*Va-t-en!*" he hissed. "Don't touch my wife!"

She cowered, shrieking like a bat. Choukin pulled Carmian toward the back of the room where a screen guarded his cubbyhole kitchen. The noncombatants left silently, while the fight went on and the police siren came closer, *pap-m, pap-m, pap-m,* in the Easter night of the rue d'Alésia.

Dima had kept them from almost killing one another. All three men were bloody, but the Princeton boy most of all, and his shirt was in tatters. The siren put an end to it. They all went out in order not to incriminate Choukin, through the darkness of the garden, and joined a small crowd milling in the street who were also waiting for the police.

"What's this about?" a *flic* demanded.

Choukin had the Russian's fear of cops. Someone, perhaps a neighbor, answered for him: "A brawl. *Ce sont des américains et des russes.*"

"Everyone is bleeding!" a woman cried.

"It's finished now," said a man.

"Oh, that." The *flic* laughed, no doubt putting it all down to the Korean War. "Let them fight it out between themselves." He rejoined his colleague in the car and drove away.

The crowd laughed and disbanded in front of the big *Perrier* poster on Choukin's street wall. He, crushed, disappeared without speaking to anyone.

Carmian and Dima found themselves alone with the American painter, who insisted on taking them home, with a stop on the way for beer. They sat holding their heads in a bistro corner, their wounds hidden under their jackets. Dima's hand, caressing her as he lectured the young man, came away with a bunch of loose hair.

They stared at it in dismay. "The devil!" he said.

"Am I bald?"

"A little—on one side."

"Bitch!" The American was concerned, although pretty soon his friends were laughing. They were tough and knew it, and the nobility of guiltlessness lay upon them as a kind of harmony.

"Why did she have to do that?" The young man frowned savagely.

"Why did you have to ask her for a date?" said Dima.

"Choukin—all his pretty Easter eggs," Carmian mourned.

"Ah, the Russians with their *mauvaise electricité*. It short circuits. I've seen it before. It infects everyone in the room."

"No, no," said the painter, "it was my fault—and his. I'll make it up to the Russian. I'll see him tomorrow."

"He won't want to see anybody."

"But that girl—I don't understand—"

Carmian had been wondering hard about this herself. "Maybe she simply saw you both fighting and thought she had to fight someone too. Join in, so to speak."

Dima said, "She didn't like you, that's all."

"But what did I—"

"You have"—he smiled—"a haughtiness sometimes, Kamitchka. But you do not even know it yourself, for you are a princess."

"You two are swell," said the painter. "I'll make it up to Choukin, you'll see."

Later that night the Princeton man heaved a rock through what he thought was their window. Unfortunately it was not. There was a great outcry from the neighbors and Konciergeka, to say nothing of Lala, until the matter was sufficiently explained and adjusted, but not before Dima had searched Paris for the culprit and made him pay up, talking to him like a father—for the poor boy was as patched as a quilt.

Meanwhile, broken windows in the rue Maison-Dieu had reached a new statistical peak.

The spring solstice. Christ is arisen!

Khristos voskres'!

And the big Old World lay nursing its bandaged head like all of them, no better than they.

"Choukin's party" and "The assault of the French girl" became household words like "The dog who broke Lala's window" or "Hurot's grave," provoking gusts of unreasonable laughter.

Lala testily echoed the cops: "*Amerikansky y russky*—what can you expect?"

"But it was not that," said Carmian.

"You are my children," Lala replied with dignity and that false sweetness, for she could not resist pointing to the cat, saying: "And this one is half and half."

Dima blazed: "Madame, when we have a better product to offer you, we shall be far away."

"Good luck," Lala replied, but she trembled pouring her tea.

"*Khristos voskres', Mamotchka.*"

"*Khristos,*" Lala answered slowly, "*voskresye.*"

Carmian sat unbudged, for she could no longer show her rage.

Semyon, however, spoke for her. He glanced up from his copybook, transfixed Lala over the rims of his spectacles, and sang vibrato: "*Madame!*"

"Mind your own business and write your poetry!" Lala shrilled. "You don't understand anything at all."

"I understand decency, Madame."

Her eyes flew open, fluttered on the brink of incredulous humor, and narrowed swiftly. She plunked her elbows on the table. "Is this the way you address your mistress, Semyon Semyonovitch?"

"We are in the democracies, now," he countered with equilibrium. "I left your service it is eighteen years."

"You are a *muzhik* all the same."

"I know bad manners when I see them," the old man said.

She left the table and started cramming in her kitchen, muttering Russian insults. She did not want to throw him out, obviously, as he still did a great deal of work for her, carrying water, sweeping, and sometimes cooking.

He was engaged on a series of epic poems of a political character, alternately celebrating Truman and reviling Stalin. He worked persistently, licking his pencil, undeterred by the guttering of candles and the constant interruptions of Lala, who taunted him ruthlessly. When Dima and Carmian were there, he read his poems aloud. It seemed that his quarters near the Porte de Vincennes had grown uncomfortable since the advances of a one-eyed landlady. This lady had a frightful temper when repulsed or even slightly neglected, which was evidenced by her disability, for her husband had shot her in the back. It had gone through the back of her head, which had healed nicely, and with her black patch she was still a handsome woman. But Semyon was a poet and had no time for her; besides, he was getting old.

He read his poems sonorously, letting his Cossack-choir voice roam up and down, swell, slide, and fade, with an undercurrent of tears or slow menace. His Don accent baffled Carmian, but she liked the sound, and recognized the recurring "Stalin . . . Truhmann." Roosevelt came up once in a while, but Roosevelt was dead, and Semyon had made the adjustment rather easily. They were all just figureheads to him. Once when she tried to point out to him that Truman was neither heroic, poetic, nor elegiac, phonetically or in person, she came up against a blank wall and never mentioned it again.

That it was epic was plain because of the many verbs, third-person singular, in the past tense: "Stalin said . . . Truman said . . ." argumentative, and, on account of Russian grammar, all rhyming: like a Greek chant.

Semyon also liked to discourse on Pushkin and Lermontov, his other heroes. He was really a singer, for he did not care a fig whether she understood the sense of it or not, although he read to *her*. Dima grew bored after a while.

("*Koshka!*" Semyon would warble to the cat. What a beautiful voice he had! What a beautiful voice! "*Kot*," someone would correct irritably; for the cat was supposed to be male.)

"No wonder the Russians take you for one of them," said Dima. "Really, you are crazier than some I know."

"I like to listen to him."

"It's so bad."

"But I can't understand him," she said. "Don't you see?"

30 The big painter
had kept his word, and Choukin's shattered vitality was somewhat restored by an elaborate apology plus a few thousand francs,
for which a whole case of African wine was directly purchased.
Choukin was proud but could not very well refuse the peace offering,
since he had spent all of his money on the Easter party. He split two
bottles with the American—his rage having given way to tides of
affection—and declared his willingness, nay, desire to lend him money
at any time that he might be needy. Which attested to the good
forgiving heart of Choukin, for three of his canvases had been
trampled or otherwise injured in the battle.

Semyon and Lala glaring at each other across the table by
candlelight reminded Carmian of the endless disputes between
Choukin and Garashoko, in which the first charged like a bull and
the other circled wilily, Judo-style, nearly always emerging victorious.
Choukin got his revenge by making fun of Garashoko's accent, although his own was by no means unassailable. He referred to his
friend as "*Zaponais,*" dropping the pronoun, in a kind of pidgin
French featuring Garashoko's confoundment with the letter *J.* They
argued mostly about painters and the Russo-Japanese War. Also a
little bit about France, for Garashoko hated France just a touch less
than Choukin, being married to a daughter of France and having six
French children to feed.

Just for fun Carmian introduced into one of their Russo-Japanese
arguments (Port Arthur, the defeat of the Russian Imperial Navy, etc.,
etc.) the hideous alien note of Alaska, and Choukin sprang to the bait.
A three-cornered quarrel ensued, the three corners of the world, as it
were . . . fearful enemies, and the African wine was rapidly con-
sumed as voices rose and clashed in the heat of old patriotisms.
Carmian queened it; she was sitting on top and knew it; so did they.
While Choukin flayed her for Alaska, Garashoko set about remembering the last war very vividly. Particularly a scene in which the Americans fled from the brave Japanese:

"Take place in jungle. *Beaucoup d'américains . . . très peu*

213

zaponais. Americans very rich, much material. Zapanese poor, very poor, no big guns left, no ammunition. But—"

Here he paused and significantly tapped his brownish temple—"*Zaponais pas bête.* Zapanese soldiers have drums which when turned round and round make noise like lion roaring in jungle. Not so dumb." He jumped up to illustrate, advancing on the terrified Americans in the manner of a rather brisk Italian organ grinder, roaring under his breath. "Americans all run away," he concluded peacefully, sat down, and unobtrusively put away a glassful of wine in one bend of the elbow.

"Indeed?" said Carmian. "*Sans blague.*"

If he thought Americans were rich and dumb, Japanese poor and crafty, she was not going to disillusion him. Choukin gallantly opened his mouth to brand him a liar and a charlatan, but snapped it shut again, remembering Alaska. She reopened the subject of the Russo-Japanese War. Garashoko proceeded, dangerously, to the Cold and the Korean wars. She drew a line between the Imperial and Soviet Russias. Choukin bellowed his disagreement (sharing Dima's view of an expansionist, imperialistic rather than ideological homeland—in which they both declared themselves Russians, not turncoats). However, he could not be brought to argue with any eloquence about the Cold War. He would only upbraid her for Le Plan Marshall. Where was the money? Did they stick it personally into the pockets of the manufacturers to make sure that none of it sifted down to the poor devils?

Eventually Carmian scored a mean coup against Garashoko for being so smug. She mentioned that the Japanese seemed quite happy with MacArthur, Marshall Plan included, and acknowledged Choukin's smile of malicious congratulation (for it was really Garashoko they were after). The injured small nation needling from the sidelines, pitting the tyrants against each other. If she dragged him over to her side, she would bring Choukin down on him. He struggled to maintain his neutrality at the risk of uniting them against him, or of being left out of the discussion entirely. He was a good juggler and they observed his feats with admiration, waylaying him wherever possible.

It was a good chess game, over maps, on warm spring nights in the rue d'Alésia, while Carmian stroked her cat and waited for Dima to call for her on his way home, round about midnight, bounding in

214

the door, shaking her heart as he had the very first time. Dima said, "In this world one must choose sides." But the truth was that none of them except herself had chosen, and they were in no-man's land.

Not so Semyon. He had a good reason, for his children were in the Soviet Union and he had not seen them in twenty-five years, not since he had left, on foot, to go to Paris. Semyon had arrived in Paris one day, taken off his cap, mopped his brow, and looked about him with a simple, uncompromising gaze used to great distances and sighting the peasant villages of the Kuban. His comment had been, and was still, uncompromising:

"I never knew they were so dirty. Everything jammed together, and garbage in the streets!" Where were the gleaming palaces? He was like the immigrant who settled bitterly in the slums of New York once the dream had worn off and it became plain that no gold was found in the streets, but plenty of garbage.

Semyon was not one to give up: he wanted to go to America. First, however, he wrote letters to the Soviet Government asking permission to send for his son. These were never answered, though he wrote them for years—until he finally heard through a woman of his village that the family had been dispersed, son, daughter, and son-in-law, throughout Russia, to north and south, lost to one another and probably imprisoned. The Cossacks, addicted to uprisings, were often treated this way by the régime.

He continued to write his odes and indictments to himself, scribbling by Lala's candlelight. He asked Carmian to get him a job with the American Army. It was strange that an old man such as Semyon, who had lost his children, should fight so hard for his future, care so much where he died. Why, it's over, old man, she thought.

"I have no influence, Semyon."

"You are American, Madame?"

"Yes, of course."

"Well!" He laughed richly, showing all his long teeth and throwing out his long arms.

"You have to be in the Army. I am only a traveler."

"Was your father not in the American Army?"

"Oh, but no one remembers. They are all other people now."

"You tell them who you are and you speak for me. I am a good worker. I cook, scrub, anything. I know horses—no one knows horses better than I. I love the Americans—tell them that. I worked for the first troops when they came here during the war."

It was hopeless, like trying to explain that Truman was not the antithesis of Stalin, a sort of modern emperor, the American Czar.

She bit her lip.

"You are a wonderful, a beautiful girl. Dmitri Mikhailovitch should be proud of you. You should not be—in this place. She is not kind to you. But I am your friend, Madame; you may believe me."

He was, in fact—divulging one day that he had been searching for an apartment for them. His long strides carried him relentlessly all over Paris, through the tunnels of the métro, up and down stairs, into many houses. So far nothing had been right for them, but he would continue: he would find something.

"Good," said Dima when he heard of Semyon's project. "He can live with us, the old preceptor. He'll be the first cook I ever had who didn't drink."

"You, Madame," Semyon addressed himself to Lala one evening: "Why do you live in—this? No light, no water, no space . . ."

Lala raised her head proudly in an antique gesture of noble sufferance. "It is my home, Semyon Semyonovitch, and the only one I have. I am grateful for a roof over my head. If my children do not first destroy it for me, I shall die here. Their cats, their dogs—"

"That dog wasn't ours," said Carmian.

"A dog, nonetheless."

Semyon's voice rang high as a bell. "You have money, Madame! Your sister Alexandra Gavrillovna lives in a mansion—"

"*Durák!*" she screamed sharply, not only on account of his impudence—she had fought again with Shura. "You put your long nose everywhere it does not belong! Now go fetch some water. You can write your poetry after that."

He looked at her over his glasses, unmoved.

"The young lady here, with no warm water in which to wash, no light by which to read. I think she is not very content."

"Then let them go elsewhere," said Lala. And shrilly: "Semyon!"

"Twenty years ago you paid me," Semyon said bitterly, but went to get two pails of water from the courtyard pump.

While he was gone, Carmian said, "Don't be offended."

"At you? No, Karmianka. But he is a shrewd peasant who does nothing for nothing, as tricky as a bear. You will see. Now: What is the word for 'bear,' Kamitchka?"

Her lack of rancor, even considering that she was the least vulnerable of human beings, had its winning side; still, Carmian bolted for the rue de'Alésia on the nights when Dima worked. The rue Maison-Dieu had a dreadful Tweedledum and Tweedledee quality at times.

Garashoko, who apparently had thought nothing of the extremely occidental behavior at the Easter party and its subsequent wreckage, was so disturbed at a flare-up between Dima and Choukin that he disappeared for three weeks. His own life was not of the most regular and he looked with tolerance on fights, drunkenness, and illegality; but Dima's deliberate rudeness to Choukin left him smoldering and shaken.

That evening in a warm silken May they had been talking about art and forgery.

"Picasso!" said Choukin, shoving forth his underlip. "Do you know his secret, Carmiane?"

"Do you?" asked Garashoko.

"Of course. Ask the children—they know. It is so simple. Carmiane, put your face close to mine. Closer. No, don't blink. Open your eyes wide. Don't focus. What do you see?"

"Four eyes. No . . . five."

"Now turn your face slightly—so. And I turn mine."

"Yes, yes!" she cried. "The profile. I see it. But you know, my eyes are different one from the other."

"How so?" he said, displeased.

"Well, one is higher than the other. One sees things in a kind of cool blue; the other in color."

"Which eye do your prefer?" Garashoko asked agreeably.

"I think the low colorful one."

He laughed. "She is a painter."

"A child," Choukin growled. "That is why she proves my theory."

After a tactful tumbler of *rouge*, Garashoko said: "Picasso—*mais alors*, no one can do him."

Choukin started to flail the air. "He floods the market. Plagiarizing himself."

217

They began an impassioned discussion of painters in whose style one could paint, when necessary; a craft they understood very well, both having done Renoirs, Corots, Cézannes, and sent them to America.

"Matisse!" said Choukin, and went on to elaborate: the grand old man, half mad, the wife and lover. According to Choukin, who burned for truth and the exposé so fiercely that he was at times given to inaccurate statements, it was the painter-lover who was now Matisse. He signed the hallowed name, holding the old man's wrist, and the wife cashed in.

It was an evil story, and Garashoko, who had the conventional morality of a safe-breaker, shrugged, and preserved a firm silence. As an artist he had high morals.

Carmian saw an old man by a river, painting, with a straw hat. She doubted Choukin and came out of her dream to say, "I love your oysters," for she had been staring at the canvas across the room.

"Do you?" he asked, crumbling, shy and trying to smile.

"If I were rich I would buy it."

"The greatest compliment," said Garashoko approvingly.

Choukin was flustered. "Give me your glass, Carmiane. Where is that cat? He has been a very bad cat all day. He is jealous of yours."

"Painters . . ." muttered Garashoko. "They have to live."

"Vertès," Choukin ranted gratefully. "Take Vertès!" and went off to look for a book. "A good craftsman, you know. Now he does something called—"

"Shocking Pink," Carmian recalled, refilling her glass.

"Ah, yes, he went to America."

The door opened, and Dima stepped into the room from the garden.

He brought the garden air with him, a freshness as always. He was fresh as a baby and his skin was as fine. His shirt, a heartbreaking blue, was open at the neck, and there were his thinning hair combed back, his slim face delicate with tiredness, his eyes in shadow. He was handsomer than when she had met him, and terribly—she suddenly noticed—sadder.

He looked a sad twenty-two. So did she. It was their failing. They had failed to grow up somehow, and it showed in their eyes like clouds leaving a space.

"Don't you ever knock?" Choukin asked gruffly, interrupted in his dissertation meant, of course, to lead to the relentless undoing of Vertès.

Dima looked at him as if he were not there. His glance brushed Garashoko and sought her in a rush while she recovered her breath, he seemed so beautiful to her. The desolation went out of his eyes, they softened, and he said mildly, "Good evening, *dyevutchka*."

The mildness should have warned her, but it was very hard to remember, to know and be warned when he did not even know it himself. She merely had a sense of uneasiness that he had not greeted the others first. For a long time they had been safe in a kind of cocoon that no one dared touch, permitting them to favor the outsiders, nearly ignoring each other, in public.

"We were talking about art," she said (the feeling of guilt moving in upon her from that almost forgotten, unhappy night at Choukin's).

"What is that?"

"Picasso, Matisse, Choukin, Vertès—"

He pulled up a chair beside her. "Dead," he pronounced. "The modern art gallery is the automobile showroom."

Choukin bristled. "And who is the artist, may I inquire?"

"Collective. There are no artists any more."

"Are you condemning us to death?" she asked, shocked.

"No, to the factory only."

The Japanese smiled, but Choukin, whose childishness had somehow persevered through revolutions and wars across the decades, was beside himself. He appealed to her:

"Can you live in a world without artists?"

"No," she admitted, "I can't."

Garashoko shifted gently on his chair. At the same time her cat made clucking, scolding sounds and sprang off her lap, stalking uneasily around the room.

Dima had won his round; and he was just beginning.

31

He did not stay long. There was an attempt at conciliation. Choukin poured him a glass of wine and made passes at turning the thing into something humorous. Dima, his eyes misty blue, did not smile. "You take me for an idiot," he said quietly, squinting through cigarette smoke.

Choukin in his old and spotty corduroy jacket, his cigarette in its holder suspended Russian-style between thumb and forefinger, was devastated. But he rallied. "No, Dmitri Mikhailovitch, that is your province. I respect my brothers."

"Then I should like to know whose wife she is—yours or mine."

Garashoko rose, put on his stovepipe hat, bowed to Carmian, shook the hand of his friend, and left. They watched him go in silence.

Unfortunately Choukin lost his temper. "Neither," he shouted. "She belongs to herself! She is a true and loyal woman to you because she loves you—but whether she knows it or not, she belongs to herself!"

Dima laughed nastily. "You romantics," he said. He turned to her. "I have come for you every night after work, but I find that for my pains I am only losing you. I'll not come any more, and I am going now."

The cat jumped nervously onto her lap and clung there. She bent over him stroking his fur. There was something she must do now. Get up and go with him. But she was numb and did not want to fight, and couldn't move.

He hovered over her. He said lovingly, "Look at me," and as she raised her head he clipped her lightly but smartingly on the chin so her head flew back and her eyes filled with tears of anger.

"Judas!" Choukin roared his fury helplessly, for Dima was too young and strong for him. All he could do was kick back his chair with his lame leg. "Get out of this house!"

Dima flung him a glance of humorous contempt, unutterably wounding, and said, "*Adieu*," stepping out into the garden and closing the door.

They were alone together. Insects hummed in the garden and leaves shivered, perhaps with the passage of Choukin's hunting cat, and somewhere a radio played. Choukin was breathing hard, the color of burgundy. "Brute! I should have sent him spinning. If I were ten years younger, Carmiane—I swear—leg and all—big as he is, the imbecile—"

"But he's no imbecile. He likes to play the part."

"That is imbecilic in itself."

She was frightened; she seemed to be living with the stranger under the lamplight, the Stavrogin biting the ear of the functionary, the motorcycle delinquent. A year had been spent on him, thrown away, that might have been saved if she had gone to London instead, Italy or Spain. And why that particular night on that street corner of Paris, of all places—May the twenty-first of that particular year? For they had been born to be each other's poison, there was no doubt. They had seen each other at once, in a kind of staggering, and embarrassing, brilliance.

She warmed her hands on the cat's fur as on a stove.

"You must leave him," Choukin said.

She shook her head slowly, obdurate, as if it were an idea long harbored and fiercely resisted.

"You ought to go back to America. You don't belong here."

"I don't belong anywhere."

"Or to Germany," he pleaded.

She laughed.

"At least you have property there."

"All I have there is dead."

"What"—he raged—"what have you here but cruelty and unkindness?"

She leaned her head to one side as if her neck were tired. "I have—I have him. And some dust."

He scowled. "That baby. But he never was."

"Well, he went into the air of France. Through him I belong here. I never had anything as good as him before."

"You mean to say you've struck roots here."

She laughed. "I hate this place."

"For a dead baby—"

He stopped abruptly. He grew sententious and declared, "Well, if you call being miserable a way of life, then I won't say any more. I merely warned you, Carmiane."

"Thank you," she said honestly.

"I wish I were your father right now. But I suppose that would hardly help. What are you going to do tonight?"

"I'll go home in the morning when everyone is up."

"Do you want to sleep here? I'll sleep on the balcony. There is a mattress up there."

"Let's go to the Dôme."

Choukin was long acquainted with despair. He said, "Okay. I'm broke, but we'll breathe the fresh air en route and back."

That morning Dima was home, and Lala. The flat seemed filled to stifling. Dima said nothing to Carmian. She sat nursing a hot cup of tea, her pupils small in large haggard eyes. Lala had time on her hands and said acidly: "She does not seem very well. I'll cook dinner for you."

"Don't bother, Mama—"

"You are a man after all; you must eat! I know what it does to your nerves when you don't eat."

"Oh, be quiet," he said wearily. "My nerves are not due to my not eating."

"You must eat," she repeated stubbornly, and incarcerated herself in her cell of a kitchen from where issued mercilessly a cacophony of pots and pans and mystic noises.

Carmian sat on the couch cupping her chin in her hand. They no longer had the power to move her. She thought of the round smooth, bloody baby with the black fuzz on his head . . . the curve of a buttock and square little shoulders. *Quelles belles épaules!* the nurse had shrieked as he came out. She had not seen his face, and wondered what it had been like. A soul had been lost, and that is in the face. But perhaps one could not see . . . so early.

"You're depressed."

She nodded indifferently.

"You got drunk this morning."

She nodded.

"Can't you speak? You brought the cat home. I admire you for bringing the cat home."

"He follows me. I think he thinks he is a dog."

"He has the disease of you."

Tired, she lay down facing the wall. He shook her gently. "Sit up. Don't let her see you like that."

She sat up.

"Choukin is a demon," he said. "You thought Boris was the devil, but you see he leaves us alone."

"Boris was on your side."

"We can't have sides if we want to stay together. Choukin is our devil now. He doesn't know it—they never do—but he is."

"I have to have someone on my side," she said.

"Do you want to stay with me?"

"I don't know."

She met his bulging gaze steadily until Lala entered with the stew that she had evidently cooked for him the night before. She gave them all equal portions of rice; most of the meat to Dima—to herself none. He transferred half of his own share to Carmian's plate.

"No," said Carmian, distressed.

"You must eat!" said Lala. "You work hard and you are a big man!"

"Can't you see how thin the girl is?"

"She doesn't need what you do."

"If her father saw her now," he said slowly, burning, "I should be ashamed."

"Ashamed of whom? Ashamed of me?"

"Never mind who. Isn't shame enough?"

"Lord!" said Carmian. "Good Lord." She put down her fork and looked about her with wide-open eyes as if she had never seen the place in her life. She started for the door, and there was a brief struggle.

"Sit down," he ordered, "and eat what is on your plate."

She sat down quietly in deference to Lala, who after all had cooked dinner. But the tiger must prowl in his cage, though he cannot kill.

"I have never caused anyone shame before," she protested.

"Trollop!" said Dima. "You don't know yourself."

"Sh-h," Lala said. "Be still and eat."

It was unbearable. Carmian choked on a forkful of rice and became aware of a sharp pain in her throat and more—a hair-raising sense of danger. Dima was patting her back. . . . She flung his arm aside, full of horror: something was sticking in her throat. She bent double with the monstrosity of it and thrust in her finger. It was only where her tonsils had once been, and she drew it out with the help of her thumb, gagging. They all sat staring at it. It was an ordinary straight pin.

"A pin in the rice," she explained blankly.

Lala burst into peals of laughter.

Maddened, Carmian spread the rice with her fork. "Look—two more!" (Pins in the rice, soap in the stew!)

Dima bellowed, "Are you trying to murder my wife—witch?"

Lala laughed immoderately, which was not nice of her. But she rendered them helpless. The trouble with Lala was that you did not know where malevolence and stupidity parted. It made her a never-failing source of humorous anecdote while corpses, mostly figurative, piled up around.

It grew upon Carmian that she must leave indeed, as Choukin had said, for whatever was sinister here had now gained admission and festered in her. She tried very hard to deny it, while all the time it grew. She clung to the memory of forgotten voices, their own lost warnings to each other, and those of Angels: Don't listen, don't let anyone get between, don't lose to the jackals. But in some bosoms love is killed.

She was unequal to the destroyer Lala but not ready for destruction. One night she put on her summer dress and observed the graven bones of her neck and chest with dislike and melancholy, fastening the strand of pearls around the slim neck where it rested on the wishbone as stripped as a chicken's, rather bumpily. At least, though she was no longer a poet she looked like one.

Dima shined her shoes and dusted her off. The dust of the rue Maison-Dieu had a peculiarly cloying quality and invaded pores and suitcases alike. All one needed were the trains coming through. They descended the stairs eternally plunged in blackness and groped their way through the courtyard and the heavy portals. They went to a Russian movie in the Champs-Elysées, then passed a shooting gallery. She was undecided about the rifle; he chose it for her, and she smiled at him, standing well back from the booth and leveling—more a warmth, a blaze, than a smile—and fired. He laughed and began to enjoy himself.

They reloaded her rifle, and once more. She got tired of hitting the ball bouncing on the fountain and the clay pipes and concentrated on the red concentric targets. The drafted soldiers standing about grew angry and went away because she was a girl. Dima took his turn, shooting as fast as she did and away from the booth. Between them they won a doll and two bottles of champagne. The concessionaire, although fascinated, indicated his regret that he was unable to entertain them longer.

"You see," Dima said, "together we can do anything. We can outshoot Korean veterans."

She felt fine. She looked at him—he wore the old blue shirt and khaki pants inherited from some American—and said, "I don't know if that's so good."

"But you feel better."

She slipped her free hand in his, clutching a bottle. He said, "Cammie," under the lights stringing far into the distance, loping along with the rest of their prize, "Cammie, you need a little success."

"Never mind that. Let's move away from Lala."

"Semyon is looking. I think he will come up with something, the old man. Will you wait just a little?"

She hesitated. In his joy and exuberance he kissed her and said, "We are one. Isn't that strange?"

"Yes," she agreed, staring at a lady in furs with four poodles all streaming by, "it's strange. Like incest."

"Incest!" he said delightedly. "Yes! That's what it is. We have the same blood in our veins."

"The bother is, one *hates* one's self, too; and therefore one's flesh and blood."

"But one is one's self for ever," Dima said.

"As long as one lives."

"It is for ever," said Dima.

32

That spring the national strikes had emerged in full dress. She could never forget how he looked at the Gardes Mobiles with the contempt and fear, almost horror, of one who has lived under the boot of their kind. Trucks full of demonstrating C.G.T. workers rolled quietly through Montparnasse and turned up the rue de Rennes. There did not seem to be enough noise to go with all the police, the crowds, the stopped métro, and buses, everything stopped. At one time during the general strike the gas and electricity went off, gratifying Lala, who, when it finally came to her attention, remarked with familiar logic: "You see? Now think if we had spent all that money on those back bills!"

For half a week the garbage piled up in the streets: it was the worst, it could cause revolutions—and quietly the trucks reappeared before the rats became boldly visible instead of merely rattling the cans at night. But the transportation strike went on and on. Carmian walked to the American Express to get her mail (none of them trusted the Konciergeka—or one another—and had their *postes restantes* in various parts of the city like fugitives). Dima talked happily of the *Fronde* and the Parisian *frondeur* spirit, going back to the storming of the Bastille. Independence, bravery, solidarity! It made him rejoice to think that something was happening, something that one could understand, unlike the bowed heads and grumblings of latter years, the smell of decay and death; the fear of war from the East and other intangibles.

"It looks so routine," Carmian said. After a while he acknowledged that it was disappointing, even tedious, as the haggling was carried on, and comforted himself with vivid descriptions of better strikes when the world, although full of terror, had been less boring.

The Parisians had all the provocations necessary for bloodshed, they felt. In one year, since Carmian's arrival, prices had doubled. Even the black market did not help any more, assuming that one had dollars. The métro had gone up three times, and Gauloises twenty-five francs. In accordance with the verity that it is expensive to be poor, they now bought Gitanes, merely ten francs more and not worth saving. Their disappointment in the peaceable, if enduring, strikes was related to their own long sufferance through the winter and spring: the endless afternoons of sitting in the chaotic dusty offices of the *Assurances sociales* wedged between pregnant women, restless children, cripples, and the unemployed, while on the other side of the long counter the government clerks gossiped and chattered like birds in a cage, sublimely indifferent to the waiting crowd. One waited sometimes for four and five hours and refused to be sent home at five-thirty, whereupon the nervously sweating director came out of his cubicle and made a speech pleading for greater cooperation and greater efficiency for the good of France. Whereupon the waiting crowd rushed the counter. Then the birds in their cage, with many twitterings, awoke from their stupor and—usually—all was accomplished in the last half-hour, for which they were paid overtime.

Since the strikes, no money had been coming in from the *Assurances* and it was the worst time yet, for, owing as much as they did, they could not live on Dima's salary. The divorce was finally, irrevocably put off until next fall after the summer adjournment of the courts; they had missed their payment. So was the hunt

226

for an apartment. And other, minor luxuries describing man's rebellion at being asked to live by bread alone, such as toilet paper.

Thinking of all the long afternoons, the sunbeams filled with dust on dingy desks, the benches in dark corridors, the pursed, refusing mouths and the languid eyes who knew one's eventual inevitable fate . . . in offices in Trocadéro, Stalingrad, Convention . . . Carmian said: "Ah, your leg! And all because you had to fight three Arabs. God."

"I had everything before I met you. Do you forget? I am in rags now."

"You had to leave everything. She wanted you at least to get your clothes."

"I didn't want them! I don't do things that way. Once you burn your bridges they are burned. It was lucky she was young enough—if she had been forty I would never have been able to—"

"Oh, you are noble. But I wish that you and I had met at forty."

He threw her a dirty smile. "So you regret it, eh? It's too much for you."

"No," she said.

"Liar!"

"Well, perhaps too much. And also too little. I think that you will be a better man—and I a better woman."

(For someone else?) The thought came between them. They stared at each other in bitter thought. When you love it is desperately simple:

"If you have no faith in me I can't live with you," he said.

She sighed. "I've had quite a lot, you know."

He shook her angrily. "Don't look so hopeless! Give a man a chance!"

"I know," she said suddenly and swiftly, touching his arm. "It was not your fault."

"You miss Choukin. Is it that? Tell me the truth!"

She was speechless, horrified. For all the languages that they communicated in, none seemed able to impart the true condition of their souls.

Dima lost his job. It was hilarious—a story which he later told with his native sweep and gusto. There was a ballet sequence in the new show at the Folies Bergères: the touch of dignity to soothe

227

the collective conscience of the Anglo-Saxon majority, or its wives. (Backstage Dima would say, "Out of my way, bitch," to the tune of screams and cackles. But the prima donnas hated him.)

On this particular night he was drunk when he came to the theater. He slapped them jocosely on their rumps and was inordinately merry. Something had happened to the technician who worked the spotlights, he forgot what, and he found himself upstairs in his place. It was great fun. He knew how to do the thing—the only trouble was that when the ballerina came on, who needed a moving spotlight, he saw more than one ballerina. He saw two, and sometimes even four, or eight. Which ballerina was the real one? It was an intense problem, more than mathematical, and he tried them all out, one after the other as they plunged across the stage, with the result that the *première danseuse* found herself dancing in the darkness followed by a will-o'-the-wisp, a jack-o'-lantern, that danced better, or at least livelier, than she, outdoing her and always a bit behind or to one side of her. "Come, *chasse,*" he muttered under his breath, while colleagues around him had given themselves up to hushed, hysterical laughter, "*now*—find her! We've got her!" Her dance was not seen that night. Dima was very angry with himself. For all he knew, she might be Lala as Coppélia in wisps of gauze; she was a phantom. But he had his job to do. His eyes, his damned eyes, insisted on multiplying:

"*Now,*" he said to himself, "*now,*" as all the angry ballerinas went on dancing. She danced like hell. He saw that much. So he had not done anything really very wrong.

She was furious, and he lost his job. How little they had appreciated his efforts! The cigar-chewing man who ran the place climbed upstairs to fire him before the show was over, the same one who night after night looked the chorus line over and pointed a stubby finger coldly and pronounced: "Tonight—that one."

When he left, the ballerina was still fit to be tied, which he thought she should be anyway. "*Adieu, bel argent!*" he waved blithely to the cigar-chewing man, departing. But he felt heavy somewhere. Cammie . . . Cammie would damn him.

But she did not. She laughed, and once again he was happy. Of course, he was now blackballed by the union. It was, he reflected, the only time he had ever done such a thing. He had been a good and steady worker.

He wanted to sleep on the floor. Lala gave him a cold compress on his brow. But Carmian held him close to her in bed. "I love you," he murmured to her sadly. "Oh, I love you, Cammie."

"Dima, Dima. The hell with the job. It will be all right, my poor."

"She danced badly," he mumbled just before going to sleep.

Having no money in Paris, not even a franc, was sometimes more fun than having the money one worked for to spend. There was time to investigate the city. It was a city to walk in; a city which J.-P. could cross on foot to meet a girl at the station; a city of which Boris the poet had said Biblically and in tragic measure: "*Un homme marchait à travers la ville . . .*" It was full of beauty, and in odd places of despairing joy. One laughed all the time; it was comical being penniless as life is comical when you forget death. Around which corner did it lurk—annihilation or the next sou?

They were dizzy with freedom and each other's company, once again constant. First they made a pilgrimage to the hotel lodgings in the rue de Vanves of a Moroccan peddler, bearing old clothes, knick-knacks, and some tea and sugar pilfered from Lala who thought she was being robbed even when she wasn't. So one might as well. The Moroccan was very black and wild and lived with his drab, almost toothless young French wife and their baby in a single room on the top floor. Together—he with his stiff bushy pompadour, she with her floppy felt slippers and servile smiles—they made an interesting pair. But their baby in his basket was unbelievable. He did not wake up, although his breathing certainly indicated that he was alive; and this while the corks popped, the wine gurgled, the father bellowed, and the mother cooked noisily under the lines of washing strung from wall to wall, flapping in the faces of bewildered risers, an eternal dreary obstacle.

It smelled heavily, unpleasantly, of stew, the sort that might have mutton fat in it. Dima tried unsuccessfully to dissuade the Moroccan from opening a second bottle. He was wary of that heated blood thick with an old anger. But their host burned with reckless hospitality. He clung to them, to Carmian's eyes, to Dima's neck, as if they were the very last people left to him on earth, while he recounted the woes and injustices done to his kinsmen. He told how the Moroccans had won France's battles for her, fighting in the front lines on dope, drink, rape, and courage, only to be sent back home as colonial slaves—these loyal warriors—while the Algerians, getting along on idleness, thievery, and syphilis, were granted the French passport and the status of Frenchmen. He showed them his purple scars, wounds of the First World War, and his papers, and beat his breast tearfully in a dreadful rage, while his wife got sentimentally drunk, and Dima's eyes, now slow and dreamy, roved round in search of a casual knife—just in case. The man was so big.

But it was not necessary. His present love of them was real. Some other North Africans dropped in, ducking the hung laundry, and the stew was served. They were not allowed to go for some time: it was a question of honor. When they finally did it was in a glow of solidarity, a compulsory Francophobia. Of course, money could not change hands in such a situation, and Dima presented gracefully the clothes, the trinkets and Lala's tea and sugar to Madame with his compliments. They broke away under a barrage of affection and breathed deeply outside, in the lovely gray evening street.

"You and I," he observed. "What a pair!"

"Americano-russe."

"What would happen if we went to America?"

"It absorbs everyone."

"It is like Russia: the land takes you."

She thought of the endless white birches on Mayakovsky's rutted road. *Idyom.*

"With us it's the culture, I think."

They stopped there, at an impasse they knew very well, for he would say, you have no love of your land but only of wealth; and she would reply, you have only your *land*; there is nothing else.

They walked silently together, loveless and alone, his arm around her waist. It was a state they could not bear.

"The worst," he rallied, "was the closeness, the smells."

"No, the baby."

"The stew. I could not stand the stew."

"No, the Moroccan!" she amended. "The Moroccan!"

"Yes, you are right. He is tormented, *le pauvre type.*"

"So brave—you can see it. Even if he did cut people's ears off. Still, everyone is tormented. Isn't that so? Why does he worry me?"

"Well, he isn't pretty," Dima said after some reflection.

"Oh, that's it! Of course," she agreed, "of course."

The scarred warrior.

Next was the *antiquaire,* in their search for grub. He had an antique shop near the Etoile and owed Dima some money long forgotten, now recalled in the dearth of tobacco, meat, and wine. Lala's bread crusts and tea, her occasional bursts of cookery while wrestling with the spirit lamp, were hardly sustaining, although she probably would not have let them starve to death. They migrated on foot across Paris, up the Champs-Elysées among the great and grandiose, the echoes of Napoleon and the vibrating tread of conquering armies gone to dust, or those dispersed, lingering like a dream under the imposing houses.

"Are you tired?" he asked her several times.

"No. I am sick of sitting in cemeteries. There is air here."

"Yes, it's good."

"Now we can walk alike. Have you thought of that?"

"Ah-ha! When I was lame you gave me a dirty chase, never waiting."

"When I was pregnant—"

"Yes, yes. I was a brute. But you made me suffer for it."

"We walk!" she cried, and skipped a little, overcome with joy.

"Wouldn't you rather ride, like those?" He nodded at an American automobile as big as a house, with an army license plate.

"No, no, no, no."

He smiled, half-maliciously, glancing at the car. "Ah, *l'Occupation!* You have your nerve about you, you others, you have."

"Army," said Carmian.

"Go 'ome," he finished, and kissed her abruptly in the middle of traffic while horns honked.

Lozière, when they found him, was shaving behind a Louis XV screen that almost hid him from the window-gazers. He greeted them without surprise and told them his tale of woe. His wife, upon ruining him, was divorcing him and had usurped his apartment, so that he was forced to reside in his fancy shop, cook, wash and shave cowering behind a screen, and sleep in the bed of Marie Antoinette. The thing was like a golden tub or swan. The legal details of his misfortune were complicated to the point of idiocy, and one did not want to dwell on them.

"*Dis-donc,*" Dima remarked, "*mais c'est une histoire américaine!*"

Lozière nodded dolefully, giving Carmian a sidelong look.

"Yes, my wife is American. You noticed?"

"Yes. But she looks different from the others. What happened to—or—pardon; it's none of my business—"

"I am getting divorced from Denise."

"Ah. I congratulate you. That is to say, on your lovely young lady, of course."

"You find her so?"

"*Charmante. Une belle tête*," said Lozière.

They observed her judiciously for a moment.

Lozière wiped his face with a towel and led them out from behind the screen to the front of the shop, where they sat about in Empire chairs, being stared at by window-gazers most of whom bore the stamp of wealth. When the face seemed preternaturally American, or promising at all, the countenance of Lozière assumed a beaming hospitable expression. His features were naturally benevolent but melancholy, and changed easily.

"You don't happen to have *deux cent balles?*" Dima inquired during a lull. "We could get a little lunch. . . ."

"Ah, *mon cher*, I regret," said Lozière, smiling at the window. "I am utterly broke. I shall have to sell the shop. I only hope to get rid of a few things first in order to meet expenses. What happened to your job?"

Dima told him about the spotlight and the ballerina. "It's a dog's life," said Lozière. "The country is falling apart."

"Rotten. Carmian and I are going to America."

It was the first she had heard of this, but she nodded loyally.

"I envy you," Lozière said.

As they sat there chatting about nothing, intently thinking of ways and means to acquire the necessary few hundred francs, someone entered the shop. He seemed to be an undertaker, yet on closer scrutiny of the Homburg hat, the hawk nose, the umbrella suspended from the wrist (*obviously* not a pimp), the patrician became evident. Carmian glanced with hope and felicitation at Lozière, sorry to note that his eye was dull. His welcome, however, was cordial enough. The stranger turned out to be a friend and a count as well, with a number of names. It was clear that he had come for reasons purely social, possibly to borrow money, and with the grace and astuteness of the aristocrat—looking at their downcast faces—saw no necessity

232

for harboring illusions, much less bringing them out into the open. He accepted a chair, joining their camp.

Dima had been growing very hungry, his churning metabolism being the kind that does not stand this well, but the count diverted them beautifully for a while. He talked in noble language *à la* Comédie Française with flowing gestures of his vast Etoile apartment, which he was trying not to rent to Americans, and his grown son and daughter who would not work. They prefered to sit in a mausoleum freezing in wintertime and dining on a small dish of peas, he said. The count, too, looked hungry. He had a few projects on the fire. . . .

She was wondering idly if he wore black as a widower, when it happened: A lady came into the shop. She was plump, foreign, and rich, and for a moment it was doubtful whether they intended to eat or merely cajole her. She was a hapless Scandinavian. Lozière, without damage to his Hamlet side, remained a French shopkeeper. The count, for all his authentic nobility, had been a lawyer (now disbarred) and was an eloquent spokesman for his friend. It was, Carmian thought, extremely unfair, and when the lady left, Lozière had become the possessor of fifteen thousand francs in return for some bric-a-brac—money he seemed to consider as a sort of divine dispensation. He redisposed of it with boundless generosity. They had cold cuts and wine during the rest of the afternoon; the Sèvres porcelain and crystal glasses were ruthlessly stripped from the window; prospective customers came and went unsmiled at.

"You see, we have everything at hand," said Lozière, chewing.

One felt quite warm. They all agreed to visit him in his native Anjou in July, and still later after more *fillettes* he told them of his secret plan to emigrate to America as a barber, or coiffeur. In the evening they drifted to a Bal Musette. One could not always mope and wait. It was most restoring.

33 Dima wangled a job from his union as a replacement. The job was brief and out of the ordinary for theater personnel; it was setting the stage for an international meeting of mayors. For about a week he traveled up to Trocadéro, having first to borrow carfare from Lala, and draped flags, bunting, and like symbols in and around the Palais de Chaillot. The C.G.T. was very excited about this meeting, and for that reason only—he surmised—had dropped the grudge against him. Temporarily only. But he was able to witness the gala affair itself and reported to Carmian that the Mayors of the World favored champagne, whisky, and vodka, but for the Russian contingent, which drank Coca-Cola.

"Mayors of the World unite!" she said.

When the mayors had gone home, there was again nothing to do but walk the streets of Paris. The Jardin du Luxembourg had not changed. They watched the pond, holding hands and thinking of their father and mother and of the time when they had met in childhood. Children played around their knees with the usual misguided choice of small animals. She smiled at them wryly. He thought of little Michael . . . and the other, older one. . . .

A Russian in Montparnasse said: "Your father did not suicide himself once. He did it twice."

Dima's mouth disappeared, drawing in. "My mother—"

"Yes," the old Russian agreed cruelly. "Who could live with her? But I meant that he was a tormented man. Only a Russian could do it twice."

"How?"

"Ground glass," the old Russian said dourly, and left them with the drinks he had bought at the bar, for he could scarcely stand up.

It was the anniversary of the start of the Korean War. A year ago they had fought the Korean War in the rue de Lille. Now they wandered together up the rue Delambre hand in hand. Dima was crying to himself, his face screwed up in a child's grief.

"The ground glass?"

"No, the obscurity."

"Everything is—that happened so long ago."

"Lala! Lala might as well have killed him herself—as she nearly killed you."

"The pins in the rice?" She laughed without conviction.

"No," he rebelled, "she does not have the stature to kill anybody."

"Don't fight with her when we get home."

"She is viler than nothing." Tears streaked his face. *"Une emmerdeuse, c'est tout."*

"She was pretty when she was young."

"Too bad," he shouted. "The life of a man was the price of that prettiness."

"Listen, the Danish doctoresse loved him."

"Yes. She sent me to school, after."

"So he did it because he was he, not because of Lala."

"Perhaps because of me . . . Cammie, he did not know what to do about me."

"No, no. He did it because he was a Russian."

Her simpleton's remark appeared to mean something to him. He seized her in the Place de la Gaîté and gave her a passionate, salty kiss. "Ah, you're funny," he said.

Dima ran into Choukin at an art gallery. Still angry at his mother, he apologized for everything to Choukin, who accepted with a profound pleasure ill-concealed by sullen martyrdom. Gazing at a Dubuffet, he inquired after Carmian. Dima, with the cynical smile he was wearing for the occasion (in one room was the *vernissage* of a Bostonian lady who painted bullfights), stated that she was well and had gone to look at the works of her compatriot, or drink her punch.

Later they pooled their francs toward another dinner in the rue d'Alésia; it always turned out *more* that way, like the self-perpetuating wine at Cana, although one could have sworn nobody had a sou. They stayed all night keeping Choukin company while he lettered a poster proclaiming a new African rosé wine called ORANOR. This was to be affixed to the front of a wine shop in the rue Didot in return for a cancellation of debt plus one case of the advertised product, which had been going badly. The owner hoped fondly that Choukin's poster would get rid of his overstock, that is, what of it Choukin personally had not drunk.

It was a hot night. The cat, whom they had picked up in the manner of conscientious parents, ambled home with them at dawn, trotting faithfully behind them. They paused, sitting on the steps of the boy's public school in the rue Asseline, resting hand in hand in a curious resurgence of their first painful love, in the center of a storm

235

and waiting for the light and the heavy air to break. Their eccentric animal rolled over and over in the dust of the gutter, his eyes on them in revelry, defying the spectator rooftop cats he had always feared. His joy and pride and silly bravado were unspeakably human and grand.

"Such a coward," Dima said.

Triple roll and somersault. "So happy," said Carmian.

A thunderclap came, and the cat rushed terrified for her lap. Another—then the downrush of rain, laughter, and they ran after him hellbent as he wriggled through under the courtyard door on the rue Maison-Dieu, afraid that maybe the God of those rooftop cats he had sassed was going to get him after all, for such is vainglory.

Of course, this sweet idleness could not go on. One day Dima went to work at Citroën. A refugee Russian, as his papers denounced him—he was relegated to the open hearth along with other foreigners and second-class citizens like the Algerians, the Senegalese. He came home and wept.

Carmian knew then that it was intolerable.

Lala produced her cards and chirped falsely: "When you are married everything will be easier. The cards say so. They say you will soon have dealings with the law. . . ."

It was hardly the time to dangle that bauble.

"What kind?" asked Carmian.

"Shut up, old woman," he said through his tears to his mother.

"Move!" Lala screeched at the cat, and pushed him rudely off her chair.

She smiled, through lips that had done this often, and tried again. It was a curious, curling smile like that of a comic villainess, innocent by its transparency (and even children are allowed to witness its sort).

She told them a long story of a young Russian who had married a poor American girl who turned out to be rich, once he got to Wisconsin. Then, applauding her own story with her winsomest smile, while her son gazed at her with the eyes of a man who had chewed ground glass, she removed herself graciously to the next room to play, among crates of tea, sugar, and coffee, the piano. She played her own composition—a Hoffmanesque waltz which was not bad, except monotonous, badly played, with all the archness, trills and ripples.

Still, it had a tune. He relaxed. He said dryly: "*Une composition de jeune fille*," and fell asleep.

There was no more Citroën.

On a certain morning Lala, pursing her lips on her way to the bookstore in the rue Daru, remarked: "He becomes nervously ill when he does not work. It is organic."

"*Oui*," Carmian said toughly, with a tired air. Dima was asleep.

"You have changed," Lala observed sweetly.

"Me? Why?"

The door slammed. After the bookstore she would go to see her grandson and tell her daughter-in-law what a bitch the American was—as she always had, even before the cards had been cut.

They went and laughed it all off in Alésia, helping Choukin affix the poster ORANOR. Only slightly embarrassing were the thirty-year-old Tartar slippers which she wore on her feet, because her shoes no longer had soles. In spite of her determinedly serious bearing, at first—even in a quarter where people shopped in carpet slippers, she became the object of snickers and stares.

"Pay no mind," Dima advised.

But it was like being a freak. Like being taken for a Soviet spy by Semyon. Lala had got fresh recently on account of Semyon. It was this way: Carmian had gone with Semyon to the headquarters in Paris of the United States Army, and they had refused him. Their suspicion, in fact, their very impersonal detestation of Semyon, that devoted cook of the First Army (just as personally detested by the snooty Russian girl at the desk), had horrified him so that he had been driven to suspect her, the daughter of an officer of the Armya Amerikanskaya, of the unspeakable.

"La Libération," he kept saying in shocked Russian into the air, "we did it together, they and I."

"Semyon," she begged, running after him along the rue Grenelle to catch his arm (he had made her get up at 7:00 A.M. with the same obstinacy of the cat banging his head against the door until admitted), "Semyon, you did the latest war with them. I am from the Old War, or my father was, and know no one now, as I told you."

His Indian face was wood, with the artistry but not the grandeur of stone. It was peevish. He could not accept his doom.

237

"Did I not tell *you*—to tell her—so that she might tell to them —that I have loved the Americans, fought with the Americans? That I could cook, sweep, ride, and fight?"

"This new young lady—" Carmian began, and stopped. "I told her that, Semyon."

Some time later in the ghastly maze of Montparnasse-Bienvenue, underground, he faced her with his terrible look of suspicion and betrayal: "Did you tell her, when they were hungry and dirty I fed them and they called me their Russian papa?"

"I told all that and more. The young lady is not interested. They do not hire Russians since the Korea. Did you see them all waiting? They will get no jobs."

"But I had you," said the old hetman, in a way that made her feel he would never write poetry about Truman again.

She was silent.

In himself he discovered a last ray of hope, however, and fixed her with suddenly crafty eyes. "Perhaps it is that you are not trusted by the American Army."

She felt bad. She wanted to stamp and scream. Idiot! Peasant! Well—

They had lost a good worker, and she a friend. Semyon disappeared into Paris.

The pointed Tartar shoes stared up at her in reproach. Dima had laughed about it. Choukin had laughed. Even she had laughed upon the wooden corpse of old Semyon.

You cannot, after all, make the stupid understand?

She held a wobbly ladder while Dima stood on it and tacked, Choukin tacking from above, flattened on the roof: ORANOR was coming into life. Choukin's head reared over the parapet like a gargoyle's. It began to rain. Hammer in hand, he blustered and cursed as the wind fluttered the poster and succeeded in tearing one corner. He had the artist's conscientiousness. But the *patronne* of the wine shop declared herself satisfied and gave them each a brandy as well as the case of Oranor to haul away. She commented upon Carmian's shoes and ventured that they were very chic. In the rain they had turned a fascinating mottled pink; going barefoot would have created less of a stir.

238

"Not bad, all the same," Choukin fussed across the street, gazing upward with pride.

Carmian, still bent with laughter and streaming at the eyes, read the fine letters for the dozenth time and said, "Listen Choukin, now you can go back to your Oysters."

"Ah, the Oysters. Art is an accident. But this is to eat. Come, we shall eat and drink in style!"

"No, no," said Dima, "don't be an imbecile. We'll eat at your atelier."

"I have the wish to drink at a *comptoir*," Choukin said grandly. "My shoes—"

"I love your shoes; they are a thousand years old."

"So is la Miss Wills," Dima said, "although she claims but three hundred. *Allez!*"

"*Allez!*"

"The cat," Carmian said. "But the cat."

Choukin, overcome with wine and success, went to sleep early. They went home, slowly and happily, to discover that the cat had been missing all day. That alone was what Lala would tell them. Nor did he, in the night, come home, his round stubborn head hitting the door until he was let in.

"He is out chasing women," Dima said.

"But," she worried, "he is not that type of cat."

She rolled about in the night, saying, "Kitty!"

"Hush, darling. Sh-h," Dima whispered, for it was he who knew something dreadful was about to happen, and flexed his arms in the dark.

34

The cat whimpered in his hiding place, hissed, and sprang out. He stared at her from the table in the candlelight, eyes gold-ringed with pain. She stared back in fear, the hair rising on her own head, at the wild, black-and-gold, imploring eyes.

"Kitty," she whispered, sharply awake.

But when she touched him he shrank. He hissed, and it rippled along his body like a caterpillar.

Dima had found him three days after his disappearance, huddled in an ashcan. The children had known him by his little collar, and told where he was.

Now, nights later, still nothing showed. Dima was again at work. Lala was gone—Lala of the diamond tiara; the woodchopper, wiresplicer, nurse. For once Carmian, terrified, wanted her.

A week ago Dima had brought in a *bouvier de Flandre,* big and mean and lost, who had been haunting the neighborhood, probably dumped out of a car from the country and abandoned. The dog had vented his rage on the tobacconist's cat, whom he bit neatly in the neck as she dozed on the curb in the sunshine. The tobacconist was inconsolable. So they had heard, yesterday.

Three days ago at the window, where her cat had always sat watching the life of the street, lifting his upper lip and chattering, rambling on like an old woman (for which they mocked him pleasantly—what other cat could talk?) he had arched his back, fur stiff. He clung to her, scratching. Across the street in full view the *bouvier de Flandre* was trotting toward them, watching for cars. The cat wet her as she held him scratching in her arms, and she knew.

She watched him across the candlelight.

Ever since then and his return from the ashcan, he would crouch, helplessly, and do nothing that might infuriate Lala, or relieve his bladder. Inside his little house, the curtained box that he had chosen for his domicile, he bit softly, desperately, on cloth. Tonight he had hissed.

The golden eye of the cat stared at her, somehow askew, as though unhinged; his tongue hung out. She touched him gently. His gasping ceased, and he turned tiredly away. Then she saw the lump on his haunch, touched it, felt his flinching and his pain, and delicately kissed his eyes. *But tomorrow is Sunday!* No help on Sunday!

"I know, I know, I know," she murmured to the small demon he had become, as the clock ticked and he looked to her for help.

Dima came in from the last métro.

"It was the dog—the dog you brought in," she stammered.

He examined the cat and talked to him tenderly.

"The dog. The tobacconist is right—he's a killer!"

"Be calm. Tomorrow we'll see."

"Tomorrow is Sunday." She lay back, tears welling out under her eyelids. She knew Death.

But early in the morning he was hunched in his old place, the windowsill with the scrolled ironwork that had permitted him to stare for hours, safe and protected, down into the street which he feared, watching the passing of cars, dogs, and children, with the lively avidity of a concierge. She called to him, and he turned to her: he blinked a little in the sunlight. His oriental eyes lengthened and grew somnolent upon her.

"See how he loves you," Dima said.

The cat reproduced his fowl-like gossip, articulate, querulous, snicking and snucking grumpily. Dima chattered back at him. "He speaks like a *Parigot*," he said.

"We've kept each other company so many nights."

"Now you can dry your tears."

He had grown beautiful, sensitive, like the silken texture of his fur. In the mangy, hunted creature a new intelligence had been born, illuminating his actions and his beautiful eyes. She had wanted to annihilate his melancholy. Perhaps last night had been a thing . . . nothing more . . . a panic.

"Come here, *petit*," Dima said to her, as she brooded at the window.

But there was again the end. She stared in horror. The swelling lump had burst, releasing a stream of blood, pus, and water that trickled from a hole down the wet fur. It seemed to have relieved him, but the sight of his pain was unbearably exposed.

They bandaged him up with Lala's medicaments and trembling hands, as he whimpered.

Carmian left him at a veterinary's in the rue de la Huchette on Monday, after they had realized, tacitly, that he was beginning to die. He had lain with enormous weariness on the dark far corner of the bed all of Sunday. He gazed at them with his old haunted look of the hotel, worse than when they had fought or disagreed, or when Lala had picked up the broom preliminary to chasing him out —but with an approach of abandonment, his old tragedy; a return to the terror on the hotel stairs and in the alleys. He could defend himself from no one, and he took the hard, slow way to die. The street had killed him, its natural victim, finally, in the shape of a murderous abandoned dog. He no longer clambered from one to the other, burrowing into their laps and the crooks of their arms for appeal. Since he had lost, there was nothing more to dread. And perhaps the event of death was easier to face than the hotel terror with its threats of the Seine.

When Dima left on Monday morning she stood fully dressed in the middle of the room. The cat stared back at her, still waiting, probing his own chances of healing, the dark cat's eyes turned inward, troubled and resentful. She went and sat down beside him. "Life," she said, stroking the lovely fur where it was not bandaged. "At least it was only a dog. Or God. Or nature. Not one of us."

She went to Konciergeka and borrowed a square wicker basket.

He was reeling round the floor when she came back, trailing his bloody bandage. She rebound the widening red hole in his side while he twisted to look at it, trying to lick it in worry, fretfully, and gave him some milk he did not touch. The street, the cars and children outside, interested him no longer: Only once did he turn his round head to stare down briefly at a barking dog. A king might have looked that way at his executioner, or a man at his killer.

He trusted her. But on the bus, pushing his head up against the lid, he began to moan. The sound was so terrible that people grew restless.

"*Il est malade*," she explained to a whisk-broom-haired old woman sitting beside her, in a loud voice. "He was bitten by a dog."

"*Ah ça!*" the old woman began. "I had a cat once . . ."

Suspicions of vivisection left the air; she received sympathetic looks, cluckings for the cat. One was minutely sad for such a small animal. He moaned.

"Baby, baby," she murmured as he lifted his sick head and rebelled at death.

And off the bus, crossing the park: "I won't leave you, baby, no, no, no . . ." He struggled to shift, to turn around, tipping and swinging the basket. She thought it would break her arm. She set it down on a bench, dropping beside him, as he pressed his forehead hard against the wicker and stared out at her with unutterable loss, though not betrayal. Not betrayal.

She carried the basket in both arms now, through a green-leaved park in summer.

There were other sick animals in the waiting room. But after a while that was too short, a doctor, a Martiniquais, lifted her cat out of the basket and set him on the operating table where he stayed on his legs, wobbling like a new born colt, head hanging. "He's very thin," the doctor said.

"We found him sick in a garbage can—" She had never been very good at talking, specially in French, if one did not know her.

Besides, the doctor would not let her. He was calm and unreadable and did not want stories. His prodding hands, strong with big flat nails, were neutral. The cat began to struggle.

"Hold him," he ordered.

She held him, covering his eyes, and he made no sound. The doctor squeezed the wound: a red, then a pink clot of flesh mushroomed out of it, which he brushed away with a piece of gauze.

"It's a hernia," the doctor said. "He can't cure that by himself."

Released, the cat lay weary under her hands.

"He is about four years old, young enough for the operation if he is lucky. He will have to remain the night. Call for him in the morning." He began to wash his hands.

"I—I—" She forgot to mention the dog, only trying to tell him it was a cat she loved. The white back was forbidding.

The assistant came in, a sullen, rather sloppy young blonde. She inspected the cat with loathing, picked him up and dropped him like garbage into his basket. From the next room came wails.

"*Chat de gouttière*," remarked the nurse.

Carmian's only, wild desire was to placate, and to get him back. "Please," she said, "he is not a gutter—"

The girl pointed to a sweater inside the basket. "Will you leave this?"

"Yes. Will you—please—"

She minced off with the basket, and from the other room a wailing began, higher, deeper, than the previous wails.

The doctor said, "*Au revoir, à demain, Madame.*"

Carmian stood stock still and listened.

It was her cat who was crying. He was screaming deep in his belly: his desertion, his agony and protest. It was mortal grief, and unendurable.

"Please, Madame . . ." the doctor said.

243

(I have not abandoned you—)

His sobbing followed her out. She sat on a park bench with her fingers in her ears. Doctor, could I stay overnight? No, for a cat is only that. But the green leaves of Mayakovsky, on the roads and boulevards, in the park, were also for him. Life, life and continuance. Never, never had there been such a sound.

I'll come back for you tomorrow. I'll come for you tomorrow! Hear!

And he was dead. He was dead in the morning when she arrived at the Hôpital des Petits Animaux in her best summer dress and new red espadrilles, trembling.

"*Le pauvre bête,*" the assistant whined in her thin French voice, having changed overnight from a surly drudge to an ingratiating hypocrite, "*il a tellement souffert cette nuit qu'on a été obligé de lui donner une piqûre.*" Perhaps it was the presence of Dima, who stood broadly above her.

Carmian broke out crying openly like a child.

"Why the needle?" Dima asked in a menacing voice.

"Punctured kidney. No hope," the doctor said, washing his pale brown hands at the sink. "Unless, that is, you had wanted to graft."

Carmian stumbled to the outer office, unseeing. "*Chat de gouttière,*" she sobbed. "That's why they didn't think he was worth a new kidney—"

"Fifteen hundred francs," the blonde said coldly, now at the desk.

"Nothing," Dima said. "We came here for a live cat, not a dead one."

She watched them go in outrage, helpless. The doctor did not come out. He did not seem to care.

"You care more for money than—" Carmian began, dragging herself into the street.

"He's dead, idiot. Do you want to pay for that?"

"And if he could have had a new—"

"If, if. I don't know. I wouldn't have had the money."

"I would have given everything—I would have—"

He brought her a rum on the boulevard, then another, till she stopped weeping. They sat dully on a bench in the Jardin du Luxembourg, the garden of their childhood. The Lion of Belfort rose again with the arrow in his flank and the pain.

She said: "I saved his life. He was my responsibility and I failed him. I am going to find the dog and take him to the police station."

He was shocked. "No, no."

"I should have stayed all night. I should never have left him. I should have . . ."

He used shock treatment. He said, "You kill everything you love."

She stared at him in a kind of black relief. "I'll leave you, Dima."

"Yes, with the cat dead, now you can."

"Yes."

"Salope!"

"Well, it's better, isn't it?" She looked at him narrowly from her tear-streaked face. "We haven't done so well, have we, after all?"

"Whore," he raged. "If I didn't love you."

"Too late," she wept afresh. He took her hand and steered her home.

But she did as she had promised. The next day the dog was still prowling the neighborhood, hungry and baring his fangs at the approach of a human being. She went to the *poste*, after some thought, and turned him in. He was taken away. It was a bad thing that someone had to do.

part
four

exile

35 Carmian pre-
pared to leave. They did not take her very seriously until she got a
check from her father and began to repack her suitcases. Everything
had grown so dusty.

"Karmianka, you are not leaving!"

"Certainly I am leaving."

They were thrown into confusion. Lala collected her wits, hastily
and crudely, as she did everything. She began to describe lyrically
how fine it would be if Carmian went again to Germany to get out
her money bit by bit from the blocked account, and Dima stayed
behind working in Paris—a nest egg—now that he was again in good
standing with the union—and then, little by little . . .

"*Merde!*" said Dima morosely.

"*Le divorce*, marriage, the apartment, babies . . . Babies!"

"*Nyet*," said Carmian, packing. "Exit Karmianka." She had a half-liter's worth of courage under her belt in the form of *rouge ordinaire* and had lost her manners once and for all. There was an afternoon train from the Gare du Nord. First to American Express, then the train.

"I am going with you," Dima said, looking blue-gray as on the morning after their battle in the rue de Lille.

"I am going in twenty minutes."

"You will lose all your money!" Lala implored.

"If I stayed here it would all go on electricity and gas that never stay put," said Carmian.

"I am going with you," Dima repeated, and started packing his bag.

"Have you no sense? Carmiane, you will lose everything. Dima, you will never get a passport!"

"Get me my papers, please, Mamotchka," he said.

After much violent searching and rummaging in her room, she found the necessary papers. His birth certificate, made out in Cyrillic script in the camp at Kassel, proved to be three years older than he had fancied all his life. He threw her a look of disgust and dismay and shoved the thing into the back pocket of his dungarees.

"You cannot go to Germany looking like that!" she screamed.

"I looked worse the last time. Listen, how could you lose three years of my life, *nom de Dieu!* Ah, never mind—"

"You know I was never good at figures! Besides, you look it." She wrung her hands and gave herself up to despair and a rising murmur of Russian, with tears to come. "These dreadful children!"

She calmed herself, swallowed, and persisted: "The Germans are very particular about their clothes."

Dima choked. Carmian packed sturdily, not listening.

"How," Dima suggested bitterly, "am I going to tell the Sécurité that I am three years older than I am? They are not exactly my mama."

"It's all that terrible cat," Lala moaned. "I fed him, I swept up after him, I—"

"He could not stand the street!" Carmian shouted, whirling around. "You swept him out with your damn broom every day."

"My God, my God," Lala wailed behind her hands. "Don't let her hit me, Dimitchka!"

They snickered dryly, without mirth.

"This is the thanks I get—"

"Thank you, thank you," said Carmian.

Lala suddenly did the most amazing thing. She dropped on her hands and knees and began searching the suitcases. She was rearranging, she explained, so that the clothes would not wrinkle; stuffing towels into sleeves and such, methods that Carmian who had grown up traveling had never seen. Meanwhile she felt around the cracks and side pockets. Apathetically they watched her. Carmian, feeling plundered, sat down and rolled a cigarette in newspaper, hoping only that she would not crumple things on purpose. If only she would pack, that was fine.

Lala kept up a running hysterical monologue, digging, pushing, packing, digging. But she put everything back in place, and better than before.

"You see?" Carmian remarked calmly. "There is nothing of yours."

"What do you mean?" Lala screeched. And to Dima: "She is insulting me!"

"'Voir, Maman," he said severely, and took the suitcases outdoors.

"Where will you stay—*en attendant les papiers?*"

"I don't know. *Au revoir,* Maman."

Lala, beaten, was silent. "*Au r-revoir,*" she replied.

There was a young man named Yves Manach, a Breton, sharp-featured and sadly undernourished, with a musical voice of an incomparable courtliness and melancholy when directed toward women, bartenders, and policemen. Sailors and ships were not in the memory of those brown dog eyes. He came from inland Brittany, not a rover but of the tribe who stay clinging to the harsh land, and stay to the end. Manach was a frail but tough and stubborn soldier defending his bitter acre, his seat on the train, his cheap room, his place at the bar, his place wherever it was.

A translator of six languages named Antoinette had left him her atelier, one of a string of them corralled in an enclosure in the rue Colas, to fix up. Manach was a very good fixer. He was hammering and painting busily around the room and the upstairs balcony, while his guests settled their baggage and sat around aimlessly, thinking of a liter of rouge. They had run into him in a bar in rue de l'Ouest (Raymond Losserand, A.D. 1945) where Carmian knew an aging whore named Solange whose striking attributes were that she whistled piercingly between her teeth and loved her job, besides trying to get her man out of prison. Dima knew Manach vaguely. They both knew Picasso, Dupré, Bérancourt. Kiki de Montparnasse. He knew of all the great in whose shadow Dima had grown up: Modigliani, Foujita, Soutine. The new great: Sartres, Prévert, Queneau. The ancient great: Villon, Ronsard. These were the true friends of Manach, it was plain. He would not leave France even in spirit.

"The French are nothing but *embêteurs,*" Dima said. "Since Napoleon they have done nothing but sit on their asses and pat themselves on the back. Except for the painters—the smearers—that was the last loophole for their creative energy."

"But what do you want, old man—nowadays?"

"*Eh bien,* even the best of French art springs from foreigners—Russians mostly."

He was a sly one, full of bearlike ruses.

"We have given," Manach sang plaintively, glancing at Carmian in a reference no doubt to the Statue of Liberty, "shelter. And we have been richly rewarded—in some cases."

"Not due to your generosity," Dima sneered, "nor charity."

"*Mon vieux,* I am a Frenchman," Manach reminded him from the top of the ladder, jabbing the paintbrush at his chest, his thin appealing face strangely enlivened by cream-colored spots.

"Well, you are a Breton. What I mean is, they take all the credit."

"Why not—if we take them in?" said Manach.

"The trouble with you is that you're half dead."

"Yes," said Manach in a personal way. "But it does not delude me into thinking that the poets and thinkers of France are dead."

"Paint your wall some more, *va!*" He laughed. " '*Victor Hugo, hélas!* '"

"Dima, you are a bad boy," said Carmian.

"Is there no wine?"

She affirmed this commiseratingly. "And we go to the Préfecture tomorrow."

"You'll come with me," he lowered at her. "Won't you?"

"Yes, I'll come with you." He was as reluctant as a hooky-minded schoolboy, as jittery as a horse smelling blood.

"No wine?" Manach was reminded, appalled. "But then I must stop work!" He descended the ladder, wiped his splattered face, making a nice blend, and went to prowl the streets as was his nightly custom.

When they came down from the balcony in the morning, a kind of hayrick in its present state, Manach was snoring gently. The light streamed through the elegant blinds, illuminating an abandoned ladder, a forlorn bucket of paint. Dima drew water for her (like his mother, he never washed and remained sweet-smelling) from the pump outdoors under the terrible protruding eyes of the concierge.

"'Jour, Madame!" he called to her blithely in his gutter-urchin voice between the geranium boxes—the hypocritical respect, the cheerfulness tinged with sass and *je m'en fous pas mal.*

The old toad grinned and nodded back, unconscious of irony. How could he do it? She trembled before these witches out of Grimm. But at least it was no longer chez Lala. No more Russian mutterings and changing humors, hints at conspiracy and references to Denise, screams and threats involving financial horrors.

She washed out of the pail. "You are so clean," he said.

"Now you," she commanded, while Manach snored.

He splashed his face—on second thought applied a little more water—and shivered drying himself. His fine, fair skin like the tender skin of dirty little boys shed dirt without benefit of water and manu-factured oils, though often like Manach he'd had paint spots and smears of grime.

"Hurry up with your primping. '*Opp-la,* do you hear?"

Yes, the Préfecture. He was going after all. She had wondered.

On the way he was silent, odd for him who had always tried to frighten fear away with blusterings, boastings, and laughter. When they entered the turreted fortress on the Ile de la Cité, the courtyard reminiscent of prisoners' rounds, crawling with *flics*—his natural blond flush paled. When they arrived at his floor, the ninth, *Deuxième Département pour Etrangers,* he was green and shaking.

Here, where she walked with confidence although angrily, it was his time to tremble. It was hot but not hot enough to moisten his forehead; the sweat was cold. It gave her no satisfaction, and revenge was not sweet, to think that she had suffered in his realm unnoticed until she might have fallen apart like a broken doll out of fear. She pitied him as once before—yes!—in bed at their first hotel when the *flics* burst in during passport inspection.

"Like a concentration camp," he whispered in the corridor.

"Dima! Just because you lived in them—you were born in one! This is only in order to obtain a travel permit."

"They will never give me one," he hissed. "This isn't the ordinary department for that. I have a number . . . they beat me up."

He grew incoherent and turned toward the stairs. She pleaded, keeping a grip on his sleeve: "But that was political and those politics no longer exist. They are abhorred. These are different people!"

"They will never give me one. It's on the record. I am a criminal according to the law."

He trembled so violently she said, "Then we'll go home."

"Will you stay with me?"

She hesitated. "Not with Lala."

"Not chez Lala, I swear!"

"I'll stay with you."

He wheeled about and strode down the corridor so quickly that she had to run to catch up with him. But in the opposite direction. He had infected her, and her knees had a peculiar tendency to wobble. The gray grimy corridors, the stale air, the haunted look of passing strangers who did not want to be seen, shabby, hopeless, and caught in the machinery like night-flying insects, fluttering in the grip of alien laws. They had the look of Slavs, peasants in shiny suits. No one demanded here but only fawned, cringed, and finally accepted the ax: Out. She remembered her own fright with the bombazine lady of the Belgian trip. But that had been *civile*. This was police. Shady foreigners.

Dima, surprisingly, got better treatment. He did not have to wait. He was ushered immediately into an office with a deadly name, partly faded and illegible, on the door. She waited outside, smoking old tobacco home-rolled in Zig-Zag that would not stay lit.

I hope he fawns, she thought. If he would only fawn.

She was glad that her papers were for once in order. Sorry only that they looked so unprosperous; his threadbare suit, her now frayed espadrilles with bits of the hemp sticking out. She had meant to trim them. They did not look like people going off on a holiday.

She thought with extreme irritation of her shoe trouble that had, even, nothing to do with money. She had *le pied anglais*, long and narrow. The shoes of a short- and square-footed homogeneous race . . . it was too impossible. The toes bitten mercilessly, the heel lost in air . . . you would have to be so rich. Godammit, and no cigarettes.

The door burst open, and Dima, flushed, his hair ruffled up, beckoned to her, tall in the doorway. He seemed curiously ecstatic as well as nervous. The windmill had come out in him; he swept her inside, where a brown-clothed gentleman sat at a desk pawing through a dossier.

"Monsieur Duraudon—*ma femme*, Carmiane," he presented her breathlessly.

"Monsieur," said Carmian, nodding.

The brown eyes were sharp but he had a worn, sad air; a sad policeman was somehow very sympathetic. More than that, he looked positively, disturbingly, familiar.

They took seats. He went on with his paper-pawing. Where had she seen him before? Dima winked surreptitiously, and then she knew. It was his special *flic*, his personal bloodhound, who had pursued him around the seventh, sixth, and first *arrondissements* all last summer. A shocking revelation.

But he seemed to like Dima. Perhaps he was even a little sorry for this great big *enfant terrible*, this crazy lost oaf of a Russian whose senseless activities he had been forced to observe. He coughed gently.

"There appears to be a disparity in the date of your birth. Which is it, 1922 or"—he held up the Russian document from the camp at Kassel, heavily embossed, impressively larded with the titles of parents and godparents, witnessed by a Greek Orthodox priest and sealed with a coat of arms—"1919?"

"The latter of course." He blushed violently. "My mother made a mistake—an accident of memory."

M. Duraudon raised his eyebrows. "Three years. That's quite an interval, considering the nature of the mistake, M. de Koubyankov."

"Ah, my mother—*vous savez, Monsieur* . . ." The shrugged

253

shoulders, the attitude of despair sufficed. His interrogator took up the next matter at hand.

"You and Madame Wills are not yet married, I observe."

"My divorce has not yet been accomplished, Monsieur."

"There has been enough time." Dryly.

"I have had financial embarrassments, you understand. We have both been ill, with obligations."

"I know. There is a hospital bill which has not yet been paid. Also a small affair of eight thousand francs in the hôtel Place Dauphine. I suppose you recall?"

The air grew heavy with a sudden collapse of hope. Dima opened his mouth. "It was impossib—" His throat closed; he breathed quickly and hard.

"You understand that we cannot very well let you leave the country under these circumstances."

"*Oui, Monsieur.*"

A pencil tapped. "How do you propose to live in Germany?"

"My wife—Mme. Wills—has holdings there."

He gazed at her sharply. It was a curious situation, she had to admit, quite incomprehensible to the official mind. So this was retribution. The final impasse, the click of the trap, the dreary end.

Dima made his mouth disappear, then jutted out his lower lip, and made an effort. "I expect my divorce to come through in a couple of months, when I shall be able to make the final payments. Then I shall marry my—I shall marry Miss Wills."

He squared his shoulders and glared at the pondering man behind the desk. "She is an American citizen of good standing and an artist, Monsieur, even if her personal circumstances of the moment are not of the most fortunate. As for my former wife, I have been unable to contribute to our son's support, but I intend to do so when the divorce is made final. In the meantime I have left her all our joint property without a single exception. She manages . . . far better than I, Monsieur."

"Yes," M. Duraudon mused, tapping the pencil on the desk, "that stands in your favor. Also that your papers are in order." Carmian caught a sidelong glance and looked away.

He rose. "Very well, I'll arrange for your passport, Dimá, on the condition that you meet your obligations at the first opportunity. I

254

shall see you on your return." He gave them a smile, wan, amused, and cynical; a brief bow. "*Enchanté, Madame.*"

"*Monsieur,*" she said.

"*Je vous remercie mille fois, Monsieur.*"

Again there was a smile from him, a lovely one. Then, seated at the dusty desk, a dry police officer, M. Duraudon resumed his immemorial role. "Nine o'clock Monday. French passport section. That is all."

Dima walked on air, his cornsilk hair waving in a breeze from the Seine. "You see how he is, my *flic?*" he exulted. "Did you hear that he called me by my given name at the end?"

"Yes," she said.

"All the same, he is a good fellow."

It was nice for him to have his policeman-father, although his impressionability, his weakness, irritated and alarmed her as always. She was used to living warily in a world of terrifying adults. But Dima lived among permanent children, a self-imagined giant of enlightenment and cunning. When he reverted to the child, his deflation—because on such a grand scale and so unexpected—caused her to suffer secondhand a kind of vertigo even worse than the balloon-like flights, for one never knew what was coming next, or where one would land.

Dima went to get some back pay, collect his passport, and say goodbye to his mother. Carmian waited with Manach. It was a sweltering day. She opened the neck of her blouse, fanning herself with an avant-garde magazine. Antoinette was very literary.

"You are too thin, Cammie," Manach remarked.

"Yes, it's humiliating. But light, too."

"The events have got you run down. You must be careful of tuberculosis."

"Not me," she laughed.

"I have a present for you," said Manach. "Wait."

He went outside and returned with a square wicker basket.

She closed her eyes quickly, as if in prayer, before opening them on a gray-striped kitten who seemed to be part Persian and part owl.

"You like her? I thought that, after losing the other, you would like to take this one with you. It will do you good, a little bit of distraction, amusement. The concierge's cat had a litter. This one is the best. Do you like her?"

"An aristocrat," said Carmian, watching her.

"She can travel," Manach said. "She is ten weeks old. Why do you laugh?"

"Nothing, really."

"Don't you want her, then?"

"Of course I do, Manach," she said.

Dima was swollen with pride and joy—more than ever bounding. For the truth was this: Not only did the French Government think so much of him as to assign to him a special *flic* of such superb qualities; the passport delivered to him bore the subtitle *Réfugié russe, protection française*. His francophobia and the post-Napoleonic decline were forgotten. He was a favored son, albeit a stepson. He talked of it half the night, delirious with the warmth of his passport. Acceptance plus protection—is not that akin to love? France loved him.

He wanted Carmian to be happy too, and showed her his new *carte d'identité*, a better-class, green one, in which the line following the question *married?* had been left blank. It would help in stuffy hotels.

"Your *flic* really was a help," she remarked.

"Perhaps he just wants to get rid of me," he said gaily. "Did I tell you what Lala said? Lala is very hurt that you did not come to bid her goodbye. She says, 'What have I done to her?' "

"That's very funny. What did you say?"

"I said—"

"Okay. Then I suppose she did the Cassandra."

"Better than usual. *What is that?*"

"A cat," Carmian said stiffly, "that we are taking with us to Germany."

Manach, expectant, looked up from playing with the kitten.

"*Mais non, alors!* If I see another . . . ! *Sans blague.*"

"Manach gave her to me as a present. She is beautiful, isn't she?"

"Yes. Yes, she is. Manach, you are a *chic type*."

They celebrated their departure until Manach put them on the Belgian Express the next night. Leaving the suburbs, the train thundered along the tracks. It was almost unbearable to be so safe, so well armed with documents and the right sort of things. Opposite them in the empty compartment, the kitten sat, released from her basket, poised and aloof, her bushy tail discreetly curled round her feet, absorbed in what seemed to be a trance of self-adoration.

"She is not," Dima observed, raising a pint of cognac to his lips, "Kiri-Kiri."

"She is a snob."

"What did he do—give us a freak?"

"Just pretend she's not there."

"Shall we throw her out the window?"

"Oh, not yet."

The conductor, taking their tickets and bracing himself, grinned at the kitten. "Mademoiselle is comfortable?" he inquired.

The absurd creature started licking its paw with infinite composure. They laughed. The door scraped shut.

"Tell me frankly," Dima said half an hour later, "do you like her, darling?"

"No," she admitted, "not much."

"I think I loathe her."

"I hate her!" Carmian decided, and laughed tears at his mystified face while the train slowly left all France behind, rushing toward Germany.

36

The Rhine was gray at dawn, startlingly broader than the Seine, eerily smooth. The passing current flowed like pale oil and would be in Holland before noon. They crossed the bridge, staggering with weariness under their burdens, to Beuel where, a man had told them, lodgings could be found at this hour.

The Rheinhotel he had named was indeed open and they entered piously, after first draping Dima's raincoat over the sleeping kitten in her basket. The bigness and space were always strange after France; one did not scrape elbows or bang knees in tiny doorways, twisting passages, or among crowded tables. There was lots of space here, also a curious lack of the human species: they hid. One would not dream of picking a cigarette out of the gutter (now) or scanning same for lost currency. It was what had fascinated Boris: like looking through the dead eyeless windows of ruins.

They wolfed bread and cold cuts grudgingly served by the fat wife of the hotelkeeper. An old woman was mopping the barroom floor and it smelled of Clorox. After their long trek and a nasty quarrel on the steps of the Bonn cathedral, where they had rested briefly, a full stomach began to change the color of the world. The kitten, like a parrot in a covered cage, was silent. Now all they needed was sleep. They consulted the *Wirtin.* The price staggered Dima, although he would have given their last mark for a bed, as the lady well knew, examining their drawn, tired faces. ("How you look!" Dima had spat at her on the church steps.)

They filled out the forms with the help of some beer. She wanted to be paid one night in advance.

"*Comme elle est conne, alors!*" he raged.

"Oh, all hotelkeepers."

"This one is a *boche.*"

Perhaps the *Wirtin* was disquieted by the legend of their passports. She was cold of eye and not stupid. The nationalist in her screamed suddenly at the woman on her knees across the room: "Idiot! You have been in that corner for five minutes!"

"*Ja, Frau, ja, ja,* I finish," the scrubwoman said, moving on, crablike.

"They are so lazy," said the *Wirtin,* essaying a smile in which there were traces of arsenic. She met with no response. "*Kommen Sie, meine Herrschaften!*"

"Right off we have to run into *her,*" Carmian said on the stairs.

She led them to a vast clean room with twin beds, at fourteen marks a night. Her trained eye glanced swiftly over their prewar luggage and the raincoat under which the kitten mercifully slept. She was the kind who would not want animals or children. She made an attempt at refined conversation, bobbing her braided blond head up and down with ersatz vivacity, showing them the closets, the plumbing, letting the hot water run. For a moment Carmian feared she would start to help them unpack, Lala-like. Thinking of the kitten, they grew very nervous.

Dima did not waste what he called his "noble air" on her. Only his bad German. "Excuse us, Madame"—that got her—"my wife and I are very tired. . . ."

She jumped as if she had been seized bodily. "Yes, of course, do excuse me. You come all the way from Paris, don't you? I wish you a good night." She withdrew after a sweeping glance like a scythe, a sweetly frigid smile, and closed the door.

"She has a bad history, that one," he said. "She reeks of the concentration camp."

"You overestimate her. She was a block warden."

"Spies are all the same."

The kitten woke up and started to mew loudly. In a panic, imagining an ear at the door, they stuffed Mademoiselle into the clothes closet; there her mewings were still audible but dampened. Carmian began to unpack their toothbrushes. Dima stood against the door listening.

"What are you—"

He shook his head.

Carmian took some sausage slices out of her skirt pocket and threw them into the closet with Mademoiselle. The mewing stopped. Dima opened the door as if he had suddenly lost his mind. He beckoned.

The little scrubwoman was outside, dark and scrawny, wispy-haired, lifting a finger to her lips.

"Talk Russian?" Dima asked her in Russian. He had an infallible eye for ex-inmates.

"*Polska*," she said.

"Come in, Pani."

She listened over her shoulder without turning her head; then, satisfied, entered.

"Dachau?"

"Auschwitz," she replied, oddly using the German name.

"Dachau," he said to her—"Oświeçim," and pointed to himself. She took his hand to kiss it, but he laughed silently and bowed low over hers instead. "We have a problem," he said. "A cat. I could almost see her smelling it."

"She did not find—"

"No, no. It is in the closet now."

Her face grew grave and shut. "Be careful. They are terrible here."

259

He laughed contemptuously. "Pani, this is my wife, an American."

The burnt eyes stared at her as softly as they could, as you gaze at a child. "I must go now. If they knew I was here . . ."

"Why do you stay with them?" asked Carmian.

Well, she had never made it back to Poland after the slave labor. Her children were dead and no one else wanted her. These people kept her because she scrubbed the place from top to bottom for her board and keep plus thirty pfennigs a day. The Pani was terse, but her eyes ignited like hot coals.

Carmian offered her two cakes of lavender soap, which she accepted with an expression almost of joy and secreted in her apron. She refused cigarettes, wished them good night and glided from the room, soundlessly closing the door.

"You know," said Carmian, frowning deeply, "she could give us away to improve her standing with the *gnädige Frau.*"

"I thought of that. But she is our friend. You'll see."

"Or their enemy."

"Yes, my girl."

They slept blissfully through the cool German day and all the next night without leaving the room. The daughter of the house, a glass-eyed slimmer copy of her mother, brought them cold cuts and beer for supper. Her hair was carved into amazing waves and troughs. On her departure they again released poor Mademoiselle from her closet, ate, drank, and resumed slumber. The kitten slept curled up on their bed (its twin untouched: "Shouldn't we rumple it up a little?" Carmian brooded), and on the following morning it came to pass that there had occurred a most unfortunate, a calamitous accident. For the shiny new burgundy quilt was very wet over an improbable area.

"*Merde, alors,*" said Dima. "Kiri would never have done that. The floor perhaps, but not that."

They gazed starkly at the damage. "If she sees that, we'll never get out of here without paying for a new quilt."

"We shall have to stay here till it dries."

"They think us bad enough already for sleeping the clock around."

"What do you care? We're paying."

"She doesn't like us. We're dirty foreigners."

"What can she do?"

"Throw us out and take our money, that's what she can do."

He was galvanized into getting up and prowling. He was hungry. Damn these eternal traps! He raised the back of his hand to the kitten primly licking her plume-like tail. "*Salope*," he remarked. "*Tête de vache*."

Carmian hit on an idea. She draped the quilt over the bed lamp, which was large and solid like everything else in the room. Lighted, it radiated a gentle heat. "You're a genius," he said.

There was a knock on the door, plunging them into silent panic. Happily the door was locked. "It is ten o'clock," came the crisp announcement. "Do you wish breakfast?"

"No, thank you. My wife and I are going out this morning. We will leave by noon."

"Very well," she replied, venom clearly audible through the door. "But the room must be cleaned."

"Of course."

Her steps receded. "*Putain*," he hissed. "Don't look so terrified, darling. We'll get out. I've been in worse."

The kitten had not mewed, which was extremely lucky, for she had a merciless way of demanding her rights. They dressed right away, as if to cover the vulnerable flesh, forgetting the quilt. By the time they smelled it, it was too late.

The fateful place was quite dry, and burned. It was a large, black, disastrous and undisguisable hole that stared up at them while they stared back in horror.

Carmian found her voice somehow and heard it saying: "I never knew electric bulbs were so hot."

"There is a lot you don't know."

All right, she thought, all right. Her bones were like jelly. It was not an auspicious beginning to the German adventure.

At that moment there was a knock, and she sat down, knees buckling. But Dima went to the door, opened it, and admitted the Polish woman.

"I come to clean."

"Pani—look." Carmian showed her the charred quilt. The shriveled face was bitter and disapproving, glancing at the cat.

"Much trouble," she said.

"How much?"

"*Fünfzig—siebzig Mark*."

It was what she had thought. "*Nein. Unmöglich, zuviel*."

Pani spread her hands. Dima spoke to her hopefully in Russian. Had she an idea? He would probably have offered to give her the money outright, rather than to the bitch downstairs, if delicacy had not stopped him. She was impassive for a long time. They watched her nervously, imploringly, having shown their cards. The difficulty was that, Pani being in the *condition humaine* that she was in, one did not know whether suffering and homelessness had weakened her fiber or strengthened it: Was she truly a friend?

Suddenly she decided; they hung on her words. "You go down. Eat in restaurant. I clean room. You say you leave for one o'clock train, you pay bill, you come back upstairs. Then I tell you what to do."

"But the quilt—" said Carmian.

"She inspects the bedclothes to see nobody steals. But later. She does not come up until I finish cleaning rooms and stairs, so she can see if I scrub well same time. She does not like stairs—up and down."

They descended, assuming an air of tourists preoccupied with a timetable as they neared the restaurant. The *Wirtin's* figure, as she presided, bore ample testimony to her aversion to stairs. However, she would give them intent scrutiny and run her finger along the banisters. After choking down a dignified luncheon and attending to the bill, they dashed back up.

Pani met them on her knees. She was scrubbing. "You go now," she said. "I stay—scrub and scrub. I am slow. Very slow. You go to Hauptbahnhof across bridge—left, left again, then right. They will send someone after you. A boy on a bicycle. Be quick!"

"You," Dima worried. "Pani, I cannot—"

Carmian pressed the remaining bars of soap upon her, since this seemed to please her so, producing them rather magically from her pockets and saying, "Thanks—thanks."

"Be quick! I scrub, I scrub the stairs already third floor." She was off on her hands and knees at a sound from below.

"Pani—"

"You are my children," she muttered moving up a step on the next flight. "Now go." In Polish, or whatever it was, this sounded quite normal.

"Christ be with you," Dima said, bowing with his hand over his heart.

The room was clean as a whistle. The kitten was in her cage;

262

her crime negligently hidden under artfully pulled-together covers, as if left that way by the occupants. They could see Pani's line of defense, pleading a stupid, unsuspicious nature whose efforts did not go beyond elementary rules: and she might get away with it. But she would not have a good time. She would keep her job only as a more valuable piece of property even than the quilt, an irreplaceable source of cheap labor, and weather the kicks.

Carmian took up the cat in her basket with the raincoat thrown over, the typewriter, and the small suitcase. She staggered down, steadying herself against the wall. She made for the front entrance, traversing the bar, where a few beer drinkers had gathered, under the *Wirtin*'s nose—afraid they could hear her thoughts. "*Auf Wiedersehen!*"

What they did hear was the kitten. She emitted a piercing mew. "What was that?" someone asked.

The landscape grown purple before her eyes, Carmian kept going, rounded the street corner and deposited her load, waiting. Shaking slightly all over she immersed herself in reading an announcement in a windowed box, one of those strategically located public servants like mailboxes, *ancien* domain of *Der Stürmer*. The quality was still as bad, but perhaps the message had improved. She could not say. She read the words and could not figure out, somehow, what they meant.

After ages he emerged. He had been going to cover their retreat once she got the cat out, and he seemed in a hurry. "The whore of a daughter came to check up just as you left," he said. "Don't run yet."

They zigzagged along a few short blocks and started to run. It caused some notice, but they might have been running for a streetcar.

"Now the bridge," Dima said. "It should be northwest."

"No!"

"Are you having whims—now?"

"Listen, by now they've sent the boy on a bicycle—or a cop—and they will all try the bridge."

"Where then?"

"Let me just . . . see . . ." she said vaguely, exasperating him, she knew, to the point of apoplexy.

Was it childhood knowledge, a memory that stirred just under the surface? At any rate, he knew, was silent and followed her. The kitten mewed and squealed interminably in her basket, pitching this way and that. Blindly Carmian followed her nose to a part of the Rhine bank, where there was a ferry stop.

"What a woman!" he remarked, mostly to himself.

"I've always thought there was a lot of dog in me." She concentrated on the insurgent kitten and young boys passing on bicycles. Lurking in the little quayside park, they fell flat behind a hydrangea bush just before a particularly determined boy rode to the edge of the river, peering blankly about. The kitten mewed. He rode off and they watched him crossing the Beuel bridge at an energetic clip, where he would have caught them possibly three-quarters of the way across. He was followed by a cycling policeman, who decided to turn back just as they boarded the ferry.

They sat in utter stillness for a long time behind the broad friendly back of the skipper. The Rhine was gay and choppy in their wake, like the proud-plumed tail of Mademoiselle, signaling triumph in the breeze.

"My God," said Dima, "it was like the war."

"Poor Pani!"

"But you know"—he laughed—"I planted ten marks in her apron pocket and she never knew it."

"It's not enough."

"Enough is being treated like a human being, *dyevutchka*."

37 The majestic blonde who picked them up, disconsolate in a Bonn restaurant late in the afternoon, was a Belgian married to a local actor with a noble but sentimental profile. He was out of work at the moment, and she hard put to it to satisfy her appetite for the best grade of beer, so that a foreign couple talking half in French, half in German, interested her keenly. Astutely she summed up the boy: brash, buoyant, brazening it out. The girl was more difficult. She was English or American (one had known so many after the war), looked as if she might have been ill, and presented an air of mild distress. They were charming

264

together, thought the lady, and could be fun as well as profitable. At the girl's feet was a cat in a bamboo cage, mewing angrily. Frau Habemeyer's collie, probably used to being her alibi, sniffed all around it. The little cat hissed and arched her back exquisitely, which gave Frau Habemeyer the opportunity to reassure them in pure bruxellois while calling off her dog in medium-low German. They responded politely across the tables, warming under her rather raffish spell, and invited her to join them since it was difficult shouting across a *Bierstube* in French.

So they went to live at the Habemeyers'—on credit, of course, until Carmian could get to the bank and unblock her account. They had a large clean, expensive room, but not as expensive as a hotel room, into which members of the Habemeyer family burst at all hours of the day and night to get their clothes, for it contained the only closet. They seemed to imply that it would be stuffy and thoroughly inartistic to object to this, and after Beuel anything was an improvement.

Ducking the Beuel pursuers and policemen in general gradually ceased to haunt them as a permanent picture of flight. There was never any necessity for going to Beuel, unless one happened to be a traveling salesman. The wide river was in between, the river that had halted Caesar when the red-haired Teutons menaced him from the other side, beating their shields and shouting.

They went to the grandmother's grave in Bonn, high up on a steep hill; a little cemetery. Englishmen had been buried there circa 1900. The chiseled stone was legible but dead; no one came any more; no one was left. One knew, a stone had died though someone still raked the leaves.

On Carmian's grandmother's grave the leaves had fallen and rotted for six years. "But she has no stone!" Dima was shocked.

"We've been eating it."

"Oh, we shall get her a stone. She is lonely."

"Yes, she is lonely."

The Mother of mankind stretched out below, there, the mother, suckler of men, lying dead but still nourishing, below. Mother, the almighty, the big mother's body sprawled passive, inert, under the soil. Powerful as ever, turning to earth. But insensible, caring no longer for her children, indifferent as the universe. Grievous, bereft and large-eyed, she stared down on the fallen leaves. ("Grandmother, how long is an hour?" At four in her sailor hat with the broad blue ribbons hanging down. And it had been explained: As long as it feels. Grandmother, how long is eternity?)

Carmian spoke to a man raking leaves. "Is someone in the office now?" He nodded, and they climbed the hill to a cottage.

"Karla Maria Anna Reth, born Kardinal," she was saying to the keeper of the books. She spoke to him of the leaves and eventually a stone (though why would you want to put a stone on her breast?) and he asked her what to do about the empty plot beside that grave, and she said she would see.

"Karla Maria Anna," said Dima as they descended. "Car-Mi-An."

"Oh, yes! Didn't you know that?"

"I had forgotten."

"She died at the end of the war. When the coldness in her legs traveled up to her heart, she put her hair in curlers, pulled the sheet up over her face and died."

"A job," Dima said, "a job like any other."

She gave him a look of grandmother-iron.

"I've seen it done well and also very badly," he said.

The old Czech intellectual whom they had beaten to death with a lead pipe? The Russians shot for spitting in the camp-guard faces? The young Englishman who died of typhoid in the night, apologizing? Surely an old lady weighing eighty-six pounds, in a lace-trimmed nightgown and looking like a child, was not of their caliber, also dying alone and without a whimper. But Carmian remembered when she had run her household like a general in the field and had survived the things that are unsurvivable.

She handed the caretaker ten marks to tidy up the place. She said, "Dima, I'll sell the empty grave next to hers."

"Your grandfather's?"

"He was buried somewhere else on account of the war."

"No, no." It distressed him. "Don't jam her in between some Schmidts or other. Girl—you don't sell graves!"

"It's good earth; it's clay," she said, but she wasn't talking about the price, although he gave her a horrified, searching look.

True, it smelled of clay and pines, and overhead was a clear clear colorless sky like the eyes of babies. The drying leaves were underfoot that were to make the tired, bombed earth young again. They were just palely yellow, a few red, and the whole damned place smelled of earth.

"It preserves them for years," she said doggedly, and he realized why she felt about the dead as she did, hounded not only as he was by the war, and their own private casualties—but by the memory of Michael, whom he had forgotten. Forgotten! They emerged on the cool autumn *Landstrasse* full of yellow leaves. A policeman in white on a pedestal was behaving like a ballerina.

No, you didn't sell graves, even empty ones. It gave you a curious undertaker-feeling. It was not the kind of commodity one saw one-self as peddling. Yet they did. After a lot of red tape at the bank, some coolness with the Habemeyers (who turned out to be not only chronic borrowers, but overzealous landlords), and a certain amount of hunger, they decided reluctantly to sell the grave.

"After all, she's not in it," Dima pointed out.

"But do you know, to go up and say—"

"Listen!" He had an idea, and though unsettling, as his ideas usually were, it had its lovable motive. "Look, we won't wedge her in. She couldn't stand that."

"No, no," Carmian agreed, wondering how he knew.

"Now, like a true German your grandfather kept the corner place for himself and put her on his left. We'll simply move her over—into *his* grave—and sell the other one. Who cares about it anyway?"

She thought about it. The people next to her grandmother were named something like—they had shuddered in silence—Oppersbop-pel. And there were about six of them. She did not want to leave her to their earth, at least not quite so close. Prolific as they were, they were sure to crowd her from the other side.

"God," she said, "I don't know," and groped as if for a beer. Frau Habemeyer always had about six before lunch, generally at their expense. She shoved her hair back, and he noticed suddenly that it had lost its gray.

It shone. It almost made him cry. Suddenly he loved her grand-mother with the intensity he reserved for his own father. "Like that Englishman, you know, on the corner—"

"1910."

"Yes. Everyone will see her and pay their respects. She won't be so alone. She won't be with a lot of Ottenboppers."

Visitors bending down to wonder, who was that lady? And a

stone with love from across the sea, or something like it, written, to tell them that she was the best of them all. (And she had been.) And not forgotten. "Yes!" she said.

As with everything that happened in Germany, it was fairly disastrous, like the German genius for work and highway accidents; as if they had borrowed the German catastrophe. People who work all the time are bound to run into trouble. To the gravediggers— although it meant money and work, one a necessity, the other sheer delight—these foreigners were crazy, for they lost about half of what they would have gained by the sale of the empty plot. It was a well preserved body, they claimed (on account of the clay) but wartime coffins fell apart like matchboxes. Since they were workmen, however, who all seemed peculiarly to be jolly, red-haired, decent fellows, they promptly set about digging earth, building a platform, and did the rest with sailcloth which must have taken a long time to wash, later.

Dima made her stay home. He supervised everything and came home making jokes about graves and banks and dead bodies, and got sick. She held his head but was reconciled about the grandmother. She *liked* her being in the Corner Place: There was a poet in Dima. But it had done something to him, and so they had lost something. He never talked about sharing the grave with her again. *I shall go into the grave with you*. . . . Never again. The worms had come too close. She knew it, and wished that it could have been undone. But then, she knew, they had always been too much in love with death.

The remaining 105 marks did time in their pockets. Banks had closed for the week end. They spent it sleeping, mostly, quite fragile by now and too proud to confide in the Habemeyers, who were the kind of people who make you remember your pride if you have any. They burst in and out of the closet, saying Good day. Monday morning the sufferers made it, skidding across the polished mosaics of the Deutsche Bank just before it closed for lunch. The teller gave them cash, and they carried home a pound of sausage, a pound of potato salad, a loaf of brown bread, a bottle of Italian vermouth, and locked the door.

"My friend," said Dima—reborn, "you can die in this country!"

"I guess they're used to it," she observed, munching.

He shook his head bleakly over their recent ordeals. "When you leave a pile of manure, you've got to have something solid to step on for a change."

She shrugged, "Do you ever?" and opened the door to admit Herr Habemeyer in a tuxedo, who gave them his Hamlet smile and apologized for wanting a change of clothes. He looked as if he had been either to a funeral, an audition, or at the restaurant where he served as a part-time waiter. They did not bother to ask him which, or to hide the bottle from him, since Frau H. was not along. *His* thirst was unquenchable and divine.

Not hers. Nor her fondness for valuta. She had become a kind of household expense in terms of beer consumption all over town, which Carmian mentally added on to the rent in her unavailing struggle to create a budget. During these treats Frau Habemeyer rewarded them with flattery, one of her finer skills. But she also had some quaint little facets that were less beguiling. One day she complained to Carmian how Dima, strolling about in the kitchen and talking, had picked up an apple and eaten it without any apparent awareness of what he was doing. He ought to have asked.

"Oh," said Carmian laughing, "he's like that, you know. You mustn't mind."

To Dima, Carmian said, "How they've changed!" for her grandparents who had been rich once, and most of the people she had once known down to the very poor and even the subservient, had shown the signs of honor. But she did not tell him about the apple, wanting to save him petty annoyance. He detested their banners still, innocent displays of the new capital, and he had black memories which he controlled very well: Bonn with its peaked and crenellated roofs, its streets named Beethoven, Mozart, and Bach . . . was a gentle town.

The two former trade unionists who lived upstairs were a man and his wife, aged about sixty. And by some chemistry known only to her little ticking cat heart, Mademoiselle preferred their food to others', them to all others. She left the gilded mirror of the Habemeyer room, where once all preened and puffed out she had watched herself by the hour under sneers (she was so cool, so pretty) and disappeared. They found her at suppertime, at table, a bib tied lovingly around her tender velvet throat. She looked at them like an angry child discovered, and they saw immediately that she had found a home in a land where once she might have passed as a rabbit in the soup pot. But she had guts; live guts, the little thing. They stood in the doorway admiring her.

"I am so sorry," the old lady began. Her face was a receptacle for tears.

The old man smiled for his wife.

Imperceptibly Dima bowed.

Carmian said, yes, thank you, they would have a little coffee, and went about graciously giving Mademoiselle away. It took a lot of graciousness to give away something you never wanted in the first place.

"Miss Powder Puff," Dima later said ruefully. "Now Miss *Allemagne*. Adieu, Paris!"

"Ah, she's happy!" cried Carmian.

They looked at each other and laughed, their reckless laughter.

The bank was very stuffy. The difficulty was about some property that had to be unblocked, but finally there was another little lump sum and they paid the Habemeyers who broke into sunny smiles for at least a week, and Carmian bought some clothes for the coming fall weather. Dima, although he was even shabbier than she, refused, saying that Frenchmen preferred to dress their wives rather than themselves. This could not be said of the bourgeois citizenry of Bonn, the men in their well brushed suits and all the pale-lipped women going by in potato sacks; the theory was apparently that they stayed home to scrub and cook and needed to impress no one—they needed clothes no more than they needed a briefcase.

Dima picked out for her a black skirt with a Tyrolean border and a bodice to match. In these, with the black espadrilles from Paris, he thought her devastating. Rather more German-looking then necessary perhaps, but she looked like everywhere she went, acquiring gestures, expressions and the tones of voice as a sort of protective coloring—he was used to it—becoming every White Russian's long-lost girl, every Paris bohemian's little sister. She was even claimed by the alumni of the concentration camps, whose lingua franca was German. They thought that prison spoke out of her eyes.

To celebrate they went out on the town, of which there was dishearteningly little: But what there was they found, and by midnight had collected a little crowd that made Choukin's Easter party seem like a school picnic. Not that there were blows exchanged, noticeably. The charm of this group was its dire, fatal incompatibility, nobly and splendidly surmounted with the help of alcohol through all the better nightclubs in Bonn. There were one American newspaperman, one Rhenish baron whom Carmian had known in the past, a broken-down door-to-door salesman of Beuel, a disbarred lawyer from Frankfurt, and one Soviet commissar. Later on they acquired a young honeymoon couple from East Germany and a Valhalla-minded Nazi dreamer who had worked for Goebbels and known Hitler. He, however, was in a very weak condition and fell by the wayside.

It was one of those lunar nights.

They wound up with the commissar at six in the morning in a restaurant, where he wept while continuing to pay for everything on his expense account. "Everybody is always trying to outdrink us Russians," he said sentimentally, ordering another round. "You see," he sobbed, "they have all left."

Carmian was very sleepy but still there. "I am here," she said.

He gave her a winsome smile and launched into a tragic reminiscence of his wartime love, a German lady whom he had liberated, and who immediately on being free ran off with another man, not a comrade. Dima's shoulder was quite wet. "I am a very powerful functionary," he told them. "Whatever you wish that I can do."

"We wish to go to the East Zone," said Dima.

The commissar promptly showed them his diplomatic credentials and wrote out a paper which was to escort them unmolested into those twilight regions. Apparently his importance was no less magical than his supply of cash. Then he took them home in his black Zis, which he drove very well under the circumstances.

"Listen," Dima said to her in the day, "have you washed well?"

"What do you mean?"

"You shook *everyone's* hand last night."

"Beast! And you?"

"Less sincerely," he said.

"Then wash your own."

"It is a matter of opinion," he conceded.

The newlywed young man had left his wallet behind somewhere, and it turned up in Dima's pocket. So they set about looking for him. He was not hard to find since he worked on a newspaper and possessed only one arm, the other having been left on the Russian front. They climbed some stairs to a dim apartment where his bride was in bed and his mother was cooking. He was still out somewhere but they were very nice. If only one had not noticed, before going, a wooden leg complete with stocking and high-heeled shoe propped up against a corner by the bedside of the bride.

38 Herr Hofstetter, the salesman, came to look them up. He was by his own avowal the first German prisoner of war that his Russian captors had ditched, for they could not put up with him. He talked all the time and did not seem to mind getting the boot and asked them for vodka; besides which he was old and lazy and no good for work. They released him by means of a mimeographed card on which all standard questions had been ignored, but *PYANITZ*—Drunkard—scrawled with an angry red pencil, and left him to seek his native land.

"A triumph over totalitarianism," commented Hofstetter. He was very liberal and called himself a Citizen of the World. One night he defended his friend the baron's inalienable right to visit the railroad station's men's room, closed for painting and repairs: an incident which embroiled him heavily with the Bonn *Bahnhofspolizei*, followed by a court trial making him the darling of the reporters and covering him with quixotic glory.

But Hofstetter suffered bitterly from the grape, his passion and temptress—the Lorelei herself from whom he tried to run. Inevitably the day came when they rambled over the high hills of the Rhineland, lean, hungry, but enraptured, too, for the land lay brown and lovely and smelled of blackberries. They brushed through thorny, thicketed places on to a thoroughfare and to a wood bench, where for a while Hofstetter, their host, left them and returned with apples shaken down from trees and sandwiches begged from housewives. The sandwiches were buttered and very good, the apples wrinkled and sweet. The wind stirred their hair; they breathed well. Still hungry, they agreed to call on a nunnery Hofstetter recommended and paused at the hill's edge watching the river curve below, when abruptly he went down on one bony knee.

"*O Du, mein Rheinland!*" said Hofstetter in this romantic posture, facing the cliffs and castles and smoking factories across the way. "*What have they done to you?*"

At first alarmed, they started to giggle, then choke with uncontrollable mirth, until Carmian—still half solicitous—crept around him and saw tears oozing behind the upraised palms. She withdrew quickly. They waited for him in quiet, and they all descended in quiet for a while.

"I love it," he said, sweeping a hand at the Rhine.

"Of course," they said gravely. "It is beautiful."

"And mine."

"Yes."

"Yes," said Dima, "yours."

Then quite suddenly and softly they found the cloisters of the nuns, and Carmian remembered the clay smell and the rustle of women's habits, all spare and clean—that Gothic allure in its austerity and everlastingness. It was an eternally beautiful building. She took off her shoes in the little arched ante-hall reserved for the paupers and lepers who waited on the bench for soup, for her feet hurt. They had just made it; the nun was very nice about the time. The soup was pretty good. The eating companions—those that were left—seemed odd, most of them. But those were the hazards.

Dima grew unaccountably shy, as if he expected someone to come and wash them all, but was prevailed upon to eat his soup. "Begging . . ." he muttered under his breath.

To an anxious Hofstetter, shattering the hush of a thousand years, Carmian said glowingly and kindly, "It's been a lovely afternoon."

The ringing hammers were rebuilding Bonn and Germany, day and night. It seemed they never stopped working, Dima complained, sick with restlessness. Work was as indispensable to him as food; he itched and bridled at the enforced leisure, unlike Carmian who, having buried and mourned for so much (not the least of which was her old passion for the English language and describing worlds and pictures in it) would have been content with loving him while planning and dreaming of their liberation. Germany with its extremes of life and death was indeed a magic wood worthy of the focused attention of Boris. But it was a deeper, darker forest that had trapped them, and going back to Paris would solve nothing. Here at least there was some kind of hope; some money even if one could not get at it; some air and some elbow room even if emptiness was sadly in evidence. She had grown weary of the incessant French *petit, petit, petit* . . . so many words and much jaw-work for nothing, the well placed mistrust in petty shopkeepers, the shallow sentiment. She would fight off a winter of sitting on radiators, providing there were any. Never again did she want to go to bed for the winter.

They had come here for good or evil and would stay. He deferred to her vein of iron, although bitterly, and she could see the face of his damaged pride. *He must work*, Lala had said. Carmian had never presumed that what an idiot says must always be idiotic. . . . She cudgeled her brains. They must not fail; they must not fail.

Still, it sickened her with a dread of doom. It was lonely and dangerous for them both, and love was sometimes sad. They laughed immoderately about almost everything as usual, and she was his girl of the Western world whom he cradled against its adversities—but she wondered if smelling adorably of soap had not lost its charm, here? And if they won and got out of the forest, would not everything go to pieces? You can't go back. It was his phrase, and the mettle he had once shown about Denise she now brought up from some place she had never dimly imagined.

Then came a letter from an American girl in Frankfurt.

He was bickering with Frau Habemeyer in the kitchen. He had become like an old pensionnaire passing away the hours at home, irritable and cast out from the world of men. Frau Habemeyer now hated him, but perhaps the reason for that was peculiar—she had waited in vain. Her present policy was one of sympathetic blandishment toward Carmian, interspersed with comments on her "husband" (that was the way she pronounced it; she had the shrewdness of that kind of woman, although by now even Dima had forgotten they were not married), his barbarous manners, so *déclassé*, his immaturity, crudity, and taste for hobos, people she would not have in her house. He was a Russian and a gambler, a type she could not stand.

"We are both the type," Carmian had objected, but feeling a clammy fear. The germ of truth was there all right. Why could one not say: Frau H., I would not be you for anything?

When she explained to him about Josie in Frankfurt, hope flared in him and no one ever hoped so fast, so fiercely. It was a matter of an empty apartment and the possibility of finding work.

The next day they departed, scooping up the available cash that had come to its fruition period under Paragraph 52, and leaving some things with the baron (Hofstetter could not be found, and besides he lived in Beuel). Frau Habemeyer was left with three weeks' worth of unpaid rent, but she had made enough money on them already and showed no inclination to go to the rent authorities.

The baron dug absent-mindedly in his pocket and produced an apple which he offered to Carmian. He was dreaming of God knew what, but would be happy to keep their things. On the highway, the trees were gold and auburn.

"Frankfurt," said Dima happily. "*On verra ça!*"

A little DKW picked them up and dropped them in a village across the Rhine from Oberwinter, where her mother had been helped along to her ultimate disaster at a place of learning named *Schule der Englischen Fräulein*. They had a sandwich and a glass of wine. Dima stopped ecstatically to inspect a Roman relic in a churchyard, gazing forgotten at the sky, before they caught another German ride to Andernach. American cars never stopped. Here, where her father had served in the old Occupation, there were enough antiques to keep Dima hopping for days. She watched indifferently as he went from one stone to another. Her grandfather had impressed her long ago with the face of a Roman coin. She liked the whole of it, the steep vineyards and the dark-eyed people. She liked the terrible, extravagant romanticism of the coiling river and its spell, the thing that Heine knew and that had made old Hofstetter fall on his creaking knees. Like him, but negligently and proudly, she knew it as her own.

"This is it!" he exulted, bounding around the corner of a church. "As you go south it comes alive, it grows true here."

"It stops a while farther down," she said dryly.

"If we could stay here a while!"

From Brohl they wandered inland for a few miles to the sound of brooks and rustling silences until she had put flowers on the grave of the grandfather and inquired at the village office about the land she owned there. Coming back they passed their baron's small fifteenth century castle (which he no longer owned), and Dima became further enraptured. He spent a good deal of time looking at it, so that it was dark by the time they had emerged from the Valley and reached the Rhine. Highway traffic was booming.

And so they left the gentler land.

In Rheinprovinz Hessen later in the night it began to rain. A truck dropped them at an intersection and they sloshed through mud, keeping clear of the road, for half a mile or so, while lights flew by flashing, blinding, all of it crashing and rumbling like the end of the world. No one saw them, and the worst of it was one could not lie down in a wet field. Then it began to pour. Curiously, Dima began to cry, but as a man does in rage. She would have plodded on till morning without crying but supposed it was, as he said, that Russians did not consider tears weak. Anyway, she did not have the energy for them. They had stopped hailing American cars long ago, then the German. They had stopped trying altogether when an omnibus affair, a Volkswagen truck, halted dead ahead—and as they rushed up they saw smiling down from his high seat the most beautiful young man. . . .

He was a jazzy driver. They had never seen anything like it. He drove a truck as if he were playing something, talking volubly all the while, gesturing, fooling around with the hard and soft pedals, opening and shutting windows, smoking, caressing the steering wheel for just a moment, keeping time with his head to some inner rhythm. His aim was to pass everybody, and he did, effortlessly, at eighty miles an hour. He had an artist's hands. That young man had been born to drive.

So they thought when he got them to Frankfurt and had waved them a cheery goodbye. Carmian did not know how to get to Josie's house, and they went to a hotel. She was going to be very economical with the unblocked money she had scooped up at the last minute and insisted on an attic room which was the cheapest, the high price of which made Dima grumble and make uncomplimentary remarks ill received by hoteliers who tended to grow pale at the thought of an American-Russian couple, much less give it sanctuary. Especially since the night was so poor. However, a few bills in the restaurant did the trick.

In the forenoon she woke up to find him rigid at the window, gazing earnestly at something across the way. "Come here," he said.

It was, in full view, a cat factory. They saw the girls working on

276

piles of skins. "See how they sort the brown from the gray, the striped . . . ?"

Across the slate roofs they watched.

"What a country!" Dima said. "No sooner have I placed Mademoiselle in a decent home, than I see ten thousand carcasses."

"Pelts," she said. "Perhaps you cannot feel very sentimental about the kind of thing you once ate." She cursed the cat factory and him for having seen it, but then, he saw everything.

"I often wondered," he mused, "why there are no cats in Germany."

"Oh, shut up."

"Can't they just eat them without making fur coats of them?"

"They don't eat them," she said wearily, "any more."

"Well, never mind. In those days Russian prisoners ate the hearts and livers of uncontaminated corpses, newly dead."

"They were fussy about that, eh?"

They glared at each other. A deep and dreadful shadow rose to stand between them. He decided to laugh:

"At least they did not start manufacturing them in tins."

She nodded darkly. "They didn't make fur coats of them."

He grinned, ruffling her hair. "Come, let's go see this Josie of yours.

"Okay."

She was a girl Carmian had known in New York, who had gone abroad to work for the government and given her the Frankfurt address. They did not know each other very well, but sometimes that is a good thing. She was going to Austria and Italy for three weeks and wanted to lend them her apartment and was sure they would both find jobs. She was a fine Irish girl from Oregon, let out of Bryn Mawr, with broad shoulders, a broad grin, and Irish blue eyes under a shaggy mop. She was reckless up to a certain point, and a bit cynical.

"She is funny, your Josie," said Dima, who found all American women excruciatingly humorous, anyway.

Josie gave them the layout, hit him on the back and said he was swell and other banalities, and departed two days later. The place was part of the American beehive, what seemed to them vast and luxurious quarters inside, patrolled by a never ceasing sentinel outside who appeared mainly to be directing traffic when he was not busy providing for his old age by negotiating with a German laundress who carried her black-market wares tucked among the sheets, shirts, and towels.

Dima was horrified, somewhat in the manner of Semyon, at everything: the Occupiers; their vile behavior and their Prussian looks, their caste system and their treatment of the Germans; the fact that she could get neither a job nor American cigarettes. He looked bitterly down at the barbed wire and the patrolling soldier as if to lacerate himself with memories, and she grew fearful.

He found a Russian wherever he went, like a bloodhound. This one was a Soviet ex-tank captain who had skipped (because, he said, he wanted to see the world) and drove a taxi. He took Dima everywhere for nothing, with the result that after the first week Dima had almost a promise of a job at Air France. The young Russian had a sideline in American cigarettes, concealed in his cab, and Dima's melancholy upon spotting them grew intolerable.

"My wife," he said, "is American and has to smoke this filthy German tobacco."

"Why doesn't her government take care of her?"

"Because she is not in the army."

"She is still an American civilian?"

"Yes, they never stop being that."

Their language was not quite the same, but Dima got the gist of his rather stormy feelings. "It could never happen among Russians," said the ex-tank captain.

Thus it happened that one afternoon while Dima was out, the doorbell rang and there he was, pale and stammering and unable to talk in any tongue. At her invitation he advanced into the middle of the room, flung down two cartons of cigarettes, bowed, clicked his heels, and turned to go. She thanked him and offered him a drink of vermouth which was the only thing handy. He drank it standing, bowed deeply once more, set his glass on a table, and left, or ran. She hadn't seen anything like it since *The Student Prince*.

She sat down and patted the cartons absently. The softest brown eyes . . . She was sad. Paris? No, not Paris. He had made her for a moment homesick for a world one had never known.

39

The faces at the streetcar stops were another source of Dima's horror. He thought they were all former concentration-camp guards; or some at least. She started to catch his nervous tic, the click in the throat when breath is cut off. He had lost it. He did that only around Lala.

Perhaps it had been a mistake to come to Germany. But they were living and eating well. He practically had a job. They met a young American named Farrar by simply talking to him on the street —he was neither Army nor Government but was on the G.I. bill and had only thirty pfennigs in all. A German girl musician had given him shelter and loved him pitifully. The four of them went out exploring the neon nightmare of Frankfurt a couple of times, sopping up beer, left only with garish dreams to be spun out and forgotten by daylight.

Meanwhile, Dima waited for his job.

The city was muddy from long rains and on street corners German girls spoke G.I. English to one another, cackling like hens.

Then suddenly the American reporter showed up from Bonn. Dima brought him home.

After that Frankfurt grew, receding and reaching, into the kind of dream Dima had talked of (in the Riff hotel, shaping a spiral in the air). Because one could bear a dream. It was only life one could not bear.

There were many reasons for what happened later, immediate ones—not those dark origins which underlie the most inexplicable and terrifying human behavior. The American was a very attractive man, although Carmian did not think much about it. Dima did: The American also had money. Air France had just turned down Dima, having been in touch with his Paris *flic*, no doubt, and other social institutions of his new-found land. So they betrayed you. He was again an orphan. And mud, mud, mud . . . it rained.

So that, upon coming home on foot through a wood that bordered the highway in autumn, a wood full of leaves wet and shining from the passing automobiles, a lonely wood . . . after a dinner with the American at the Press Club . . . after a few rather casual words of tiredness and irritation, of not knowing where to go . . . she got a blow on the head from her umbrella, a beautiful fashionable green silk umbrella he had bought for her in Bonn. With a carved bird's head on the handle. He was beating her with it.

She started to scream but lacked breath. He beat her about the back and shoulders until she sank into a wet pile of leaves, and rose up again, and flew at him. It was always a mistake. He was much too big. She judged quite coldly that he would kill her, and dashed knee-deep in leaves to the highway, hearing him thrash after her, and wildly hailed cars, shouting and shrieking. Of course no one stopped.

And he had caught up with her again—his brutality and annihilation. Panting, streaming rain or sweat, she turned to face him and to die. He was laughing and handed her the umbrella, bent into a sort of parabola. It was strange how such a strong umbrella could have been beaten like that upon her, and she took it into her arms tenderly, weeping.

"Little girl!" he spat contemptuously. "You will get out of Frankfurt Wood. I'll buy you another umbrella."

She walked strangely, and he was suddenly concerned.

"Are you all right?"

"Yes."

In that monosyllable he knew—he really knew—his death.

"Are you hurt?"

"No."

She was through. The hound fell upon her and slew her, and she would not feel the beneficence again of joy and making poetry, for she was chewed, maimed although not dead. Merely what could happen to you when your heart failed but for the final exact bite at the throat.

Solange, the whore in the rue de l'Ouest had said: Either they love you and are very bad to you, or they don't and are kind.

When she could get up out of bed, she started writing something.

"You have a hard head," said Dima.

"I guess so."

"I am sorry," Dima said.

"That must make you feel better."

He put on his coat and went out the door and left. She saw him from the window. The only thing that disturbed her was his coat. It was too long. And the bend of the shoulders . . . the droop. The long, long overcoat.

There went all the dispossessed of the world.

She ran wildly for two and a half blocks to catch him. The remaining block he stood still and waited for her, his face ashen. Oh, yes, he would have gone. "Come home," she said.

"That cradle does not fit me either, Carmian."

"The M.P. is watching. Come along."

"To hell with the M.P."

"But you are my boy," she said, and took his hand. And he came like someone broken.

"Where would you go?"

"To the D.P. Center."

"God! That was where you started. Don't, don't—ever."

The next morning Josie burst in.

"Look, Josie," Carmian said, "we've got to get back to Bonn. It doesn't work." And she told her about Air France and the necessity of returning to Bonn for money: it was not a transaction to be done by mail since she had to show her passport. Josie, who was a rather tiresome optimist, made them go to see a colonel at a dreadful army post, to which she must wear her gabardine and pearls as soon as her bruises had cleared. In testimony to the bouncy, wide-eyed strangeness of Josie, the wounds failed to impress her. But when Dima almost got arrested as a spy while Carmian flattered the colonel inside, remembering even to call him "sir," they all gave up. Josie gave up. "You're not the type," she concluded. The only problem now was to get back to Bonn. The highway no longer appealed to them.

"Man, I'm flat," Josie said. "But busted!" She drew her brows in heavy thought.

"It's all right, Josie," Carmian said.

But Josie, a woman of public relations and press, snapped her fingers. "I've got it! Let him hitch and you take the train—with the bag, you know—on my I.D. card. You can send it back to me." And she extended the card drawn from her wallet.

"We look so much alike," said Carmian ironically.

"Look, take a chance; it's about one-third the cost and twice as fast. They usually don't ask to see. I'll lend you some American clothes; I've got a bright red coat."

"And if they ask to see and get a look at our faces, where do I go?"

"Well . . ." Josie decided to drop that, but warming to the general plan, she jumped up and walked around the room acting it out. "All right, say you've forgotten it. People often do. If the M.P. asks to see it you dump your purse upside down, clap your hands in front of your face"—she rocked in anguish, showing a rueful eye— "and say: *Jeepers!*" She smote her forehead for good measure. "You're not gonna put me in jail, are you?"

"Josie," Carmian objected coldly. "Josie, nobody says 'Jeepers.' And they would, besides."

"*She* could do it," said Dima critically, squinting through a cloud of smoke.

"Perhaps that's why she doesn't have to."

"Oh, all right, kids." Josie threw up her hands.

"A real American," he marveled. "Now tell her I'll show her how a Russian operates."

Which he did with incredible speed. After several days of driving around town with his taxi driver, he produced enough money for both of them to take the expensive, ancient, dusty German train in the interests of legal travel. It seemed a shame. The taxi driver was fearfully susceptible to the wants of the frailer sex (or perhaps he was sorry for her because she was thin—like those invading Russian soldiers who confused the lady of the house with the cook, since to be prosperous is to be plump). It moved Carmian very much. Waiting for the city bus in a softened mood, with the money in her shoulderbag, she offered a small German girl a cigarette, for the girl who wore Eastern boots and a scarf tied over her head and carried a cracked satchel stuffed to bursting with underwear, had been watching her smoke. Her hand shook accepting it. She reeked of gentle misery and terror. She had been in bad trouble and had crawled across the border between the sentry posts the night before and thought that this side was wonderful, although she knew nobody. But she missed her mother. She was nineteen. And she had no money at all.

"Well," Dima said philosophically when told, "now we have

282

money again for only one on the train. We might as well go out. Come, dushka, I will show you a section of Frankfurt where the Germans still dare not go. They are all post-graduates, there."

They went there and saw what had outlived the concentration camps, Jews, Poles, Russians. . . . The soft consonants flowed around her once more. But their faces, particularly those of the young, were tough, and they carried knives. In that little self-made ghetto they haggled in the streets at night with one another, with trading American soldiers; they drank beer and played cards. But it was true: There were no Germans but for the police, and these were uneasy. It was one of the several worlds of Dima who felt at home there. They taunted him not unkindly about his archaic Russian and called him baby, kidding him softly on the street. In a café a young black-haired woman played cards imperturbably at a table of seamy-faced men, while a drunken sightseer was thrown out and almost into the arms of an alerted policeman. The violence was swift and brief. The girl never blinked or looked up.

It was the black-market district, most desperate and sinister. It was a stronghold of the *bezprizornyes*, a railroad station full of people waiting for a train that might never come. But they found Farrar there, the civilian, to Dima's intense admiration and delight. Farrar was wandering around with his hands in the pockets of some old khaki pants and let them buy him a beer, while he played the jukebox.

"Hell," said Farrar, "there never was a place where I couldn't take care of myself."

The next night, Saturday, not knowing what to do with the money that was left, they invited Josie out and had a lovely time over champagne and a few other things until Josie, who was tired from her vacation, slumped a bit and showed a tendency to slip under the table. When a well dressed Frankfurt citizen approached her and, upon her rebuff, grew abusive toward foreigners with special emphasis on Americans—and Dima hit him—the police were called.

They all signed some rather meaningless papers and moved on to another place, Josie rallying considerably.

"There are too many police around here," Dima said. "Cammie, tomorrow we go to Bonn."

"That's the way it started," Carmian said wearily.

283

"It's no better here. We'll go back to Paris."

She was shocked to the heart, and trapped. Seeing her distress, Josie said: "Oh, listen, now that you have some money, stay. . . . Something will turn up; I know it."

"We don't have it any more," said Dima.

"Well, I'm getting my check the fifteenth . . ."

"Josie," Carmian said, "we have to go to Bonn."

"Why?" Josie asked dimly.

"Well, I've got my typewriter there and . . . you know . . ."

They moved on, to celebrate the departure. The next was a very plushy place with be-plumed and be-jeweled waitresses in gowns of gold. They were utterly beautiful except that, on a closer inspection which was still barely possible, they turned out to be men.

"Jeepers!" said Josie.

The next day they really did start out and got to Bonn by evening, with the help of truck drivers.

("S' long, kids, hang on to each other," was Josie's last word.)

In Bonn there were brisk fall days through the noise of the ringing hammers. Respectable workmen crowded the bars after work, among them here and there the wide-brimmed hats and black corduroy of Hamburg carpenters, like the dress of the Amish. It was a quiet town.

But the most extraordinary things happened there, things irreconcilable with the grandmother in her pelerines; her Old One peering through his pince-nez.

In a bar they were fond of, one week-night, two men best described as ruffian-like entered and passed the hat in the cause of the East German refugees. They had some tokens in exchange, depicting a face pressed against barbed wire. When they had finished collecting, they calmly established themselves at the bar next to Dima and proceeded to drink up the proceeds, although clearly the night had not been without its rewards so far. Dima watched them unabashed, joyous and sly. The fiercest-looking one was a deaf mute; the other spoke, although unintelligibly, just enough to procure Schnapps which they downed without moving a muscle in their throats.

"What are you doing hereabouts?" Dima asked in Russian.

Blank. Wild slant eyes looked at blue slant eyes. Asia at Asia.

"Only a Russian drinks like that."

"*Ya gulyayu*," the deaf-mute said. I walk around.

"He's Kirghiz," said the other one.

"Idiot," said the deaf-mute.

"*He's* Russian."

"His wife is German."

"American," Dima said. "Have a drink?"

They accepted with a startled look at her and fled to a corner, where they spent the rest of the evening sticking pins in a military map.

They were sitting beneath a hideous poster inscribed, "*Frau, komm!*" in which a Mongolian soldier was about to rape a woman with a mouth like an O.

"I'm going mad," said Carmian.

"Germany," he remarked. "A Gothic Tale."

40

As far as she was concerned, Byzantium was no better, nor Gaul. The return to Paris was sadness indescribable. It was not the same place. The old days when they had laughed so much—the old laughter—were gone. And one went about burdened with the longing of what had been and was no longer there.

For a while they lived with a family, half Russian and half French, of which the one and only adored son had been shot as a spy for the Germans: He had been a famous wit and devoted fascist both, oddly enough, and had gone to his death Villon style, calling his handcuffs his jewels. In this one could hardly blame him, since his father had been blinded by the French police—a simple method, poking a needle through the eyes—for refusing to testify. An American from the WAC had turned him in at Brest.

Obviously this homestead could not last, and Dima and Carmian moved on to a place on the rue des Cannettes which resembled the inside of an ashcan or a fireplace. However, it was their own. The grief inside was their own, and the hope that was left. Also, they were now immune to Lala's pleas.

"Why does not Karmianka come to see me?" she demanded piteously of her son.

"Because she's had you up to here," said he.

"I told you you should not go to Germany," Lala said self-righteously, with her usual logic.

He ignored that. Since he no longer lived with her he could afford to.

"Did you take flowers to the grave of Pyotr Alexandrovitch?"

"I would have, Mama."

"Ingrate! When you and your wife were living there! Why didn't you? At least you could have—"

"He was a traitor"—Dima shrugged—"they have an unmarked grave," and went.

"Ai," said Lala in one of those spells of genuine sorrow that she was subject to, for she had known that boy as a small child. Not disdainful and wild like Dima, he had been a merry one full of mischief. She sighed and crossed herself solemnly, although she was not religious.

While Carmian fought the dirt and dust in the rue des Cannettes, drinking Mascara wine to overcome the musty damp—she no longer cared and guzzled whenever it suited her—Dima went through a temporary job at the Théâtre de la Michodière and was quickly swallowed up into the Comédie-Française. The union had long since forgiven him his trespasses and welcomed him home from his barbaric travels as a long-lost brother. He was very happy. He was back in his Paris. Well, they could have each other.

Dizzy with an entirely new sensation, that of wanting to chuck it and go home, Carmian sat on the edge of the bed peering bitterly, longingly, down the dark alleys of the past. What had made them do any of the things that they had done? And she knew that asking reflected an inner change in herself, presaging another death. Leaving Dima would be like death. But the thought was in her, coiled and ready to spring, since he had decided that they must return to Paris. It was unthinkable, another winter of chilblains, of sitting on radiators, of staying huddled in bed, of a cold so damp and penetrating it even froze the mind. She hurled the broom away from her and listened to the noises from the bar downstairs and invented tortures for the landlord.

Dima tried to cheer her up with gossip: Jo-Jo had been compelled to make a transaction involving the sale of Miss Bixby's apartment in the rue de Sèvres whilst leaving the furniture out on the street; there it stood, since Jo-Jo did not know what to do with it and felt, anyway, that he had done his duty after one plaintive letter to Connecticut. "I needed the money, old boy!" Jo-Jo said in his own defense, opening his drooping eyes to their fullest extent, when questioned as to the ethics of this procedure. "I didn't touch the furniture, you know."

She laughed until she heard of the death of Picasso. The little old one had died in one of those places where disasters of the mind and body meet to do the job, and they said it was tuberculosis. Carmian threw up her palms in a gesture she had as if she were being held up at the point of a gun. Knowing his girl, he was silent. Sometimes you just can't take anything, he knew, and this was one of her times.

Christmas Eve passed mercifully without event except that the ceiling of the downstairs bar crumbled, which happened also to be the floor of their room, and they had to be careful not to land quite suddenly among stray revelers. Next day there was some unpleasantness with the landlord into which Choukin stepped, not altogether helpfully, while looking up his old friends in order to buy them a festive drink. He impressed the landlord, but not Dima.

"Lala told me where you were," he explained when the landlord had departed muttering to himself of ruin.

In Dima's slant blue eyes there were lightning appraisal, conviction, and hatred. "You two do what you like," he said; "I have other plans," and left.

She sprawled on the bed like a rag doll. "You see? Now he knows."

"Knows? About what?"

"You and me."

"Poor child, there *is* nothing."

"He knows," she murmured, "he knows, he knows . . . and I never told him."

"All right! Look!" Choukin bellowed, waving his arms and completely losing his temper. "I merely asked you out for a drink. If I love you and think he is a hoodlum, that is nobody's business, not even mine right now."

She got up and put on her coat listlessly. "Take me out somewhere. But I shall return in an hour. Okay?"

"Okay, Cammie."

When she returned five hours later, the door was locked and no one answered her calls and hammering. So she sat on the stone stairs and settled back, prepared to spend the night sunk into her coat collar. The Serbian student from upstairs found her there and let her sleep on his bed, but after some time apparently thought better of it—or worse—and she left him with thanks. It was the kind of unduly moral behavior they expected from Americans anyway, and she felt certain that he would have his recompense in café talk for weeks to come. It was nothing that could start a Third World War.

"All I want to know is . . ." said Dima mildly in German, lying on the bed and smoking *kif*, ". . . what I want to know is did you sleep with him?"

"I couldn't *do* that," she replied just as gravely, standing in the doorway, straight-backed in her coat, and looked at the girl in the chair.

The girl, a Saint-Germain girl in black pants, giggled.

"Send her away, please," Carmian said.

"Madame is showing you the door," he told the girl, who looked her up and down and pranced out breezily, kissing her hand to him: "Bye-bye, Dimá!"

"She is pretty, the little one."

"You chose her for her silliness." Jealousy seized her and choked her. She threw down her coat. It stank of the hall. "What is that mess you're smoking?"

"Hashish. It's very good; you dream and are at peace. Little girls can't seduce you."

"Let me try some." He passed her his butt and she inhaled judiciously for a time. It made her rather sleepy and she stretched out beside him, both of them in all their clothes.

"You'd better stop it," she said in an objective tone.

"Oh, I will. I ran into an Arab. It's too expensive," he added: "eight hundred francs."

"Swine."

"*Kamerad*."

"At least I don't have silly little flirts and turn into a dope fiend overnight and shut you out into the cold."

"I was drunk. If you stop seeing Choukin, I'll stop this. He is a devil. He is my devil, if you like."

288

"I'll not see Choukin. But we must move."

"All right," he said grimly. "We'll move."

The next place was in Saint-Germain-l'Auxerrois across the Pont Neuf. It was clean but cold, with many stairs and a frightful concierge and again close to the Préfecture—but no one knew where they were. Except that in one day shortly thereafter they were visited by Farrar (returned from Frankfurt), Manach, Jean-Philippe, and a French boy who had just got a girl pregnant. They were an odd group with nothing much to say, but made up for it in drinking, at which they were all very gifted.

"Your American Express!" Dima remarked furiously.

"No, no. They don't give out addresses."

"My God, it's a village then."

"Your choice."

Later in the day a quarreling American couple dropped in, and the German girl cellist looking for Farrar.

Going off to work in the morning, Dima was wild. Carmian laughed. She had given up: He saw it in her eyes. Something had left them, and they were almost like the eyes of anybody.

To top matters, Boris had returned from somewhere, her devil. He stayed well away from her, letting his aura be felt. Across the street were gargoyles on the church roof, an admirable evocation of the unseen one, except that they appeared to be screaming in pain, while his hate was cold.

Dima put it in his way: "The jackals are here," he said, looking deeply and bitterly into her eyes. She changed color and looked away in shame and fear. It was upon them, then.

"You will never be a poet until you leave me," he said. "I know that's what's eating you. Always."

"No, no," she said hopelessly. "No."

"Boris says I am a fool."

"I wish he would stick to his scribbling, bad as it is."

"If it is—at least he does it."

"That's true."

He softened, remorseful. "Listen, he never forgave you on account of Denise, that's all. They're close friends."

Carmian's crossed leg began to swing back and forth, a danger sign. "Your Boris! Maybe you are a fool."

He began to laugh. "No, no, Boris is incapable of love."

"Not at all. He is in love with you."

He absorbed this dazedly, rather like a blow on the head, with disbelief in which there swam flashes of specific intelligence. "My God, what a corrupt child you are! Are all Americans that way?"

"Yes," she hissed savagely, "it's the Fall of the Roman Empire, and only the Russians are pure," and went out for a walk.

She walked across the Pont du Carrousel to the quai Voltaire. She liked it because she felt neutral toward it, unlike the Pont Royal and the Pont Neuf. It was just a bridge spanning the moonlit river. . . . Dima had a small but fanatic following of men friends who hated her. One was the quarreling American husband. And the male gypsy. That was strange. In a bistro the man had picked up her hand to read it (a service for which he did not charge, since that was woman's work) after much wheedling on the part of Dima. He studied her palm with a frozen arrogance, repeating the word "fatality" several times. Then it had become positively comic—he casting the offending hand away from him and spitting fiercely on the floor. Dima indulged him and offered him a drink, but he moved away, surly and brooding. It was certainly very curious. And she was rather tired of people acting like that. It made one feel badly.

In a bar here and there, restlessly, she stopped for a drink, and in one there was—like Truth itself suspended in a glass bell—Miss Fairbanks surrounded by three Algerians. She had fallen into circumstances, all right. Miss Fairbanks was quite drunk. Carmian assisted her out, with some difficulty. Miss Fairbanks had aged a great deal and was quite glad to go with someone who spoke to her with the voice of a woman, in English. There was some problem as to where to take Miss Fairbanks, but Carmian finally lugged her into a taxi and directed him to the rue Henri-Barbusse. Thus she left her with a sleepy Manach, whose rage she was prepared to await the next day. They looked rather neat side by side.

She prowled some more and met some Americans she knew and hated, and saw some people she did not know and liked . . . and drank and drank and thought about her ancestral loves.

One can pass a lifetime doing that.

In the early morning everybody was wearing aprons—and a kind of white-and-blue stripe, like her prison-dress days. "My goodness," she said, rousing herself and brushing back her rich hair, "are we in jail?"

Someone took an ashtray from under her chin.

"Must I go?"

"It would be advisable, Madame."

"Of course. *L'addition, s'il vous plaît.*"

"It has been reposing there for some time."

"Don't worry, you won't starve."

The effect of this remark which she thought extremely witty was spoiled by her discovery that she could not pay. Before there was any wrangling, she remembered her German wrist watch and left it, as the butchers and their apprentices piled in for the morning rum and coffee. They were all dressed alike and reminded her of the carpenters of Hamburg. Only she belonged nowhere. A woman of the streets? Yes, in her heart a woman of the streets.

She went home and there was no one there and she went to bed. A bit later in the morning he came in. There was a gasp as he plunged for the foot of the bed, groping for her feet in the half-light, to assure himself that she was truly there. She pretended that she was asleep, letting the pillow get wet. For all was done. All, all was done.

When a week later he beat her up on the quai Voltaire, she knew why, although plainly he had forgotten. The attack came with a rush, blows to the head and face—and she screamed, since this was not Dima in fury, but an animal. And she was Carmian as well as Lala . . . the half-brother who had frightened him behind the henhouse flapping his arms in the dark . . . the lawyers, policemen, and functionaries who never listen . . . the Nazi guards of the concentration camps. He wanted to kill her.

She hurled herself flat on the cobblestones in order to gain time. He picked her up and socked her again, this time putting her tooth through her lip. She fell again, clutching the stone. Unable to dislodge her, he dragged her by her hair, while she waited for his mania to spend itself.

A solitary, elderly Frenchman in a business suit came by. It was late and the quai was deserted. He wept. "Monsieur, I beg of you . . ."

"It's my affair."

"No matter what she has done, Monsieur! One does not treat a woman like that!"

"This is no woman . . . !"

"Thank you, Monsieur," Carmian whispered.

"*Ma pauvre petite,*" said the man.

Dima let her get up. When the man had gone his way forlornly, he hit her twice more and then said that he had done. He took her home to the Auxerrois hotel, and in the morning she was sick and had a face like an overripe squash.

41

It was time to go. She thought about it, sipping the coffee he had ordered, out of the side of her mouth. She needed two days' rest and then . . . "I had an automobile accident," she told the maid.

"Yes, Monsieur said so. I wish you a quick recovery."

"Thank you very much."

Manach came . . . and Farrar . . . and of all people von Kolmau, and she got out the third day wearing sunglasses, while Dima was at work. He had taunted her on her pumpkin-head and her cowardice. Manach shook with passionate hatred of him, though the demon torturer's face was a sickly blue, and his victim no longer seemed to mind anything at all. It was the Breton Manach who came and packed for her, and carried for her, and stayed with her until she could be left alone. With the five thousand francs that von Kolmau had given her they roamed the Ile Saint-Louis looking for a room. Her head had not stopped buzzing since that night and she could not make decisions. She merely shook her head mutely and slowly at everything and asked for more wine. Farrar met them. He had found a good room in the rue du Bac and persuaded her to take it. Farrar was very tough, but there was about him a simian sadness— the animal who is too intelligent—and though he did not feel the quivering hatred of Manach, he was shocked and aggrieved and he would not see Dima again.

When her face had healed, she sought out Saint-Germain at night, moving cautiously on the boulevard and in the streets. She had managed to send a piece to a little magazine and was waiting for their reply; it provided an excuse to stay, or perhaps not to move. To move was unthinkable, but there was no return. She bloomed like a night flower . . . and suddenly fell apart, drained of energy.

She sought the *passages-cloués*, in order not to be run over (since the joke ran, when it did not cost them anything, you were as good as dead).

Manach or Farrer would take her home into her little yellow room where she sat cross-legged on the bed until she could sleep. "You're like a mother to me, Farrar," she told him once, sleep curling the corners of her mouth.

"Son of a bitch," he said.

She would not see Choukin or anyone connected with that former life. Once she saw the red-haired Swede of his Easter party, the Sicilian bandit's girl, in her leopard-skin coat. She looked fierce and oddly scattered. The Swedish loping leopard had gone mad. It was quite plain as she crossed the boulevard Saint-Germain on a spring afternoon.

Once she saw Dima at night, dragging himself into the Royal Saint-Germain. His walk was the way she had seen her father walk the day he heard her mother had died. It was rumored that Dima had taken poison.

"*Keine Arabesken*, Cammie," said von Kolmau.

"No, no arabesques. I see he is still alive."

(But he had fumbled blindly for her feet in the dark, gasping with fear.)

"Self-respect is more important even than love," said Kolmau with his worried hound-dog face.

"But spring!" she cried. "What I cannot stand is the spring!"

He shrugged as if there were no answer to that. "The beloved is always an idea. A delusion."

"I am so ugly. Without him I am so ugly!"

"A month ago," he stated wryly, "you were far less pretty."

"Yes, yes, you're right. It's the spring, the swallows, the air—poisonous. I forget he had black murder in his heart. I remember only . . ." She covered her face with her hands. "Ten thousand things."

"Known as habit." At the door of her hotel he said that he would go now, as she stared down the street of Marie Antoinette. A street of pink and orange lights where they had gone for ices when she'd still had Michael. The Barbac glowed at her solemnly, long having forgotten them and Chedwick.

"The voice of reason. Is it the only voice?"

"Perhaps in this case." He bent and kissed her hand and went away into the heady spring night.

The spring became more and more painful; a trip to the post office a day in hell because she happened to remember how they used to applaud France for having more glue on its postage stamps than anyone else. So unexpected—the Germans had been very stingy with their glue. The magazine took her story, and she pocketed the money dispiritedly; it was a story about a German orphan, once dear to her heart. But the orphan was she. The orphan was he. It gave her no pleasure to remember that. And then when she thought she could bear it no longer—not even Manach's stubborn love of mankind expressed in his measured, muted, yearning way in a language of startling purity, or Farrar's capacity to divert and amuse—along came this glossy American.

She knew him. He was the newspaperman they had met in Bonn. But she had never looked at him from the same interesting aspect. He took her to the races at Enghien-les-Bains for the purpose of bailing her out. They lost. He took her to the Plaza Athénée and around the town and to his hotel room where he lent her his pajamas and they slept, not too unhappily, in resignation. "I'm sorry," she said. "I should have known."

He was a good boy. "It's all right, kid," he said. "But listen, don't go back to . . ."

They exchanged a rather sad look, and he knew that she would. She saw it in the pupils of his eyes, that she would.

She fled to a girl in Saint-Sulpice who was having a baby without benefit of companionship. This was a gallant girl who loved to watch the wheeling of the swallows above the chimneypots. "*Je suis une fille absolue!*" she cried, and Carmian left unsolaced. She could not be absolute.

In the rue de Rennes, Manach had his eye blackened by Dima, who was looking for her, because Manach would not tell him where she lived. "A maniac," people said, infuriated.

And one neon-lighted night she ran to where he would not be . . . nine chances out of ten. The American couple. Vindictively the man swung wide the door, the man who had never liked her, and she knew Dima was there. She stood stock still and dropped her arms and walked in stiff-legged. She had only wanted to look at him one more time. It had been a terrible mistake. It was what she had always done: to put her head in the lion's mouth to prove he would not bite.

The wife gave her a moist, sympathetic glance. And Dima, crying, fell at her feet. She turned to stone and knew she was forever lost, crouching on her cold pedestal, the arrow immovable in her flank, the image graven.

Once you cannot forgive somebody, there is yet another death. But also there is a glow of last things, the saintliness of the invalid, the radiance and sudden well-being of the patient about to die. So they gathered their second wind, and the grief of its impermanence dimly perceived only deepened their passion in the little yellow room of the rue du Bac.

"I am the husband of Madame," he told the concierge, mounting the stairs, and she did not doubt his validity. She was a nice one and had suspected a tragedy of this sort; she smiled at him and let him wait until the next day to register. Everyone smiled at them after this, everywhere, for their parting had come as a shock and even a source of resentment to many of the same people who had used to ask, wearily, "Why do you stay together?" Now they asked, "Why did you leave each other?" As if they had any business doing such a thing, as if through them there were truly no hope for the World. Success at last was theirs, terrifying. One had missed them together, one applauded and loved them. The comptoir of the Royal Saint-Germain had a boom of generosity. In one way or another, society was satisfied.

The delicious love of the rue Masion-Dieu came back when they had been an island, before the onslaught of the jackals . . . and before that love in a succession of dark little hotel rooms, his arms wound about her through their warm nights when she had liked to imagine horrible and desperate things about to happen to her before she went to sleep, it gave her such a feeling of comfort. None of it had been lost; it had multiplied. What had been lost was a fortune in trying to escape him. A small hoard of money and energy, and a whole bank vault of carefully stored rage, disgust, revulsion. Like a miser, she thought, wiped out in one night, one stupid move, and rued her labors.

"I have always been true to you," he murmured. "I have been straight."

"Dima, darling. Like your Aunt Nadya who shot you in the tummy in Nice."

"That was a mistake. She was my favorite aunt because she used to sit with her feet up on the café table drinking *apéritifs*." He laughed gently at this childhood recollection.

"Well, I suppose there is a difference. Perhaps she couldn't shoot straight."

"It was only a scratch. After the doctor's she went out and bought me a kilo of pralines."

"Yes, I imagine she would."

"Are you happy?"

"Yes . . . I'm relieved of misery."

He raised himself on one elbow, set his jaw awry and pursed his mouth, gazing at her in a bitterness of stubborn hope and anger. "You're not happy?"

She laughed, because he seemed to her immensely sweet, and nodded, kissing him.

"You weren't happy before, were you?"

"No, never."

That seemed to content him and he pulled her onto his chest, but his voice grew very deep and bitter. "I knew you were a brave girl, I knew it was there, but I thought your courage was for me. Then I saw you using it for yourself to get away from me."

"I am a coward, Dima."

Half asleep, she thought she understood him better and pondered their grievances. Her own, more than anything, was Boris. Sliding into a dream, it appeared to her that the simultaneous death of Picasso and reappearance of Boris had meant they were doomed; it was over. As though he were a symbol, a terrible sign that had killed the old and benevolent Angel.

She was in the post office of Sèvres-Babylone, and it looked like a tomb. Dima rushed in to get her before the door closed upon her. She pooh-poohed his fears, for she knew it was a dream reminiscent of another dream: the Lawrencian dream of the hospital, although it had no color but merely the same hushed vocal quality: like someone reciting on a far-off stage.

Karmianka . . . Longing goes on forever and is a part of life.

We walk in different cities and separated by an ocean, while the earth goes round counting our years. Is it right?

Perhaps we shall meet. Perhaps not. It does not very much matter.

It was so beautiful together.

Well, we shall see. Beauty has its own intelligence.

I don't understand!

He evaded her, laughing. She awoke to embrace the hospital attendant. But he had not white . . .

"Cammie, wake up!"

"Oh—yes. I thought—"

"Someone is at the door."

Relief and dread made her quick to throw on her robe and admit Manach, who glowered at her in un-policemanlike fashion, carrying food and wine.

"How are you?" she said feebly.

"Just about on all fours. I heard, and came to see if you were all right. I brought you something potable."

There was a growl from the bed. "Why shouldn't she be all right?"

"You are the best judge of that," came Manach's tenor voice, dauntlessly melancholy. One felt that he had sorrowed since the beginning of time.

"Manach is my friend," she declared fiercely, standing between them.

Dima had no intention of getting up, his mind on the provisions. "Rather than see Madame go into an Indian rage, I apologize." He bowed. "I am sorry about the black eye."

"You're a swine, Dima."

There was an intake of breaths. "Yes, he is," said Carmian hastily.

Dima also said: "I am a swine. Forgive me, Manach."

"Let her forgive you if she will."

"I think she has."

"Yes. I have. And I'm going now."

"I thank you, Manach, for taking care of my wife."

"I do not exactly detest her," Manach told him dreamily. "She is not a bad girl." It was his way of phrasing an ironic compliment, the delicate shade of his devotion plus an even more delicate threat seeping through the words and caressing them. Manach's weapon was the rapier, not the coarse anything-goes style of Dima.

"Come," Carmian said, "we'll eat and drink."

Parisians, interminably asked how they are, incline to answer: *Je me défends*, meaning So-so, or, I get along. He was the only human being whose use of that idiom she had ever taken literally, since when the animal nakedness of it had never ceased to startle her. He did defend himself, he had to, and today he left before he could get into a really bad argument with Dima about Ronsard. The buttered croissants and white wine felt very good inside, and the cigarettes Manach had also brought.

"What an ass!" Dima remarked ungratefully.

"That's not true. I would have died without him. One time he took me to the zoo—oh! I don't think I'll ever be able to look at another hippopotamus. He improved my French, have you noticed?"

"I like an American girl who talks Paris slang. It's artistic. When you came to me you talked something left over from the schoolroom. Now you are supposed to talk like something out of his bloody Ronsard. *Il est primaire*, Manach."

"You are a wicked boy."

"The only thing good about me is that I love you. I'm happy to know that it's possible."

"To love me?"

"If one loved a cow that much, one would be good," said Dima.

In the evening he went to work, returning with yellow roses in time for another audience in bed, this time Farrar and the German girl cello-player who had tracked him down—Farrar a little the worse for a session at the Royal. He was in a non-loving mood and would not be refused entrance.

"Don't you ever get out of the feathers?"

"It's exhibitionism," said Carmian.

"No harm in it."

Dima was hospitable, an odd remnant of *noblesse oblige* rather like his constitutional inability to pass up a beggar in the street, but sleepy. He waved them to a drink and shook Farrar's hand. "I never thought I'd do that," Farrar said.

"I don't blame you." He offered the girl some roses.

Carmian hugged him under the covers, pinching him as an afterthought.

Farrar was broke and borrowed some money. He spoke of taking a tramp steamer home while the girl, who was ravishingly pretty, watched him sad-eyed. Farrar had pitcher-handle ears and a look of planning his own brilliant downfall, which just might be difficult enough to carry through. Carmian was solicitous:

"What's the matter, dear?"

"Ah," he said moodily, "these goddam Frenchmen, they don't know how to live."

It was a curious commentary on the fairly Roman scene before him, to say nothing of the generally celebrated *savoir-vivre*. He was homesick, was Farrar.

Leaving, he said solemnly, "I wish you luck, Cammie."

It left her with a dire echo of the young concierge in that first place, rue de la Petite Boucherie.

But in the dark Dima laughed softly. "We've got them all stirred up, the way they talk in the quarter! We'll make it, Cammie. We must this time. We'll make it."

42 The month in the rue Vaugirard was a gawdy, tattered time dimmed with the pathos of the hurdy-gurdy. And spring of course. Such a spring is never forgotten. It enters the nostrils every year, though it is no more and never will be again. In the street every morning was a versatile little man who took the parts of both monkey and organ grinder, doing a little dance all the while. A lady below sold violets and narcissus, and the room, flooded with sunshine, was held together with bits of wire and string like all of Paris. It was a lovely room, and it was only fitting that a month should go so quickly, that kind of month, taking away what it had given.

It had let them postpone some terrible things. Carmian had an offer of a job in New York at a time when the rent loomed insoluble. Dima tore up two application forms for immigration to the United States. When the divorce became final and he came home with the papers, she refused to marry him, laid her head down on her arms and wept.

"I want no illicit love affair," he stormed.

It made her laugh a little bit, then she cried more desperately. What had Jo-Jo said? *L'Impasse des deux anges.*

No jackals now, no devils and angels. They were face to face.

"You won't get another like me," bitterly.

"I know. I know."

"Then go away."

"I love you."

He began to cry too. Because it was all going to pieces and there was nothing he could do, nothing at all.

The month was over, the beautiful time. She rose and picked up her pocketbook. "I'll get my stuff tomorrow."

"No, you stay."

He got up and went to the door. After a pause he turned back and they embraced each other tenderly under the three-pronged brass chandelier. Sickened, she knew she would remember it in every ugly detail . . . on and on . . . when in this particular despair.

"I told you I would never hit you again," he said at the door.

She nodded, speechless. The door slammed.

Waves of nausea poured over her. She drank two tumblers of wine. She walked about, talking and thinking to herself in broken sentences:

"All our sins against each other . . . unfair . . ." she said, wringing her hands. "It's so hard, it's worse now than . . ."

"*Lebewohl . . .*"

"No arabesques . . ."

"You must, you *must*, Carmian . . ."

And so on. "And so on," she repeated, as if listening to a stern other voice.

She went to stare out the dark window. No, he had not hit her again, but perhaps that was worse. The desire was there. It had always been. What did you do with it? He had menaced her again, that was enough. Her forgotten anger had sprung into life full-fledged, as if it had never subsided, a black giant. That was why it would not do—no more *Walpurgisnächte*—although he never seemed to understand how he terrorized her. Perhaps he did not remember. The concentration of his love and hate had killed, burning and blinding but not warming, like a too narrowly directed blaze.

Against that, self-weaning, grudge-building, armor-making was senseless, like building up lawful or unlawful arguments against flood and fire. She had learned that in the rue Vaugirard and admired him for his self-control. No, he was not at all an *Untermensch*, as the camp guards had liked to call him. Not at all.

She went to bed and pretended that he was there. He would let her read a book, her back pressed against him . . . and soon the book would drop. It was the most wondrous moment when the book dropped. He would, with his long arm, put it away for her on the table by the bed or on the floor—and then—and then—her heart always stopped; it was always new. She would fear, and wonder an instant later how she could ever have felt afraid of such a tenderness in her own blood.

We must *love* each other, he would say; we haven't much time. None, Dimitchka.

She saw him on the boulevard Saint-Michel in a gray convertible, with a girl in a bright scarf at the wheel, and made some mental notes on Dima's astuteness and air of idiocy. Unfortunately, he saw her, too, and she started to tremble as though she were falling apart. He jumped out to corner her in a doorway.

"It's nothing; it's a Swiss girl," he said rapidly.

"She looks fine. So do you. So does her car."

"Listen, I want to see you. . . ."

"No, no, no. . . ."

"Tuesday, rue Monsieur-le-Prince. Okay?"

"No."

"Well, I have to get my things, you know."

"Surely not in a café."

"Don't be puritanical. I'll get them later."

Their tone had a slick American finish, European-style. Really, it had been time to go.

The girl honked her horn, waving.

He had started to write a ballet and she was going to help him. Oh, yes, she would help him. Carmian knew the song. Any time, anybody in a convertible with a flying red scarf . . .

He had looked so healthy; that was the worst, rather beefy as a matter of fact. And empty. Almost like anybody.

She did not go to the café rendezvous, but he called for her, waiting downstairs. It was true: Dima sniffing success was a bad sight. Oh, charming, to be sure, in his tweeds with a pipe. But she had loved what he had thrown away. When he had worn blue jeans and his face was sly and dirty, or drawn and transfigured. Not this ox she saw now.

He observed her distaste, and grinned, a cruel little smile showing his sharp, irregular teeth. "All your doing," he remarked, although she had said nothing.

"What do you want me to go there for?"

"There is someone you ought to meet, an editor who admires you."

"Well, I'm not dressed."

"Didn't I tell you an author should always be nonchalant about such things? Come along, Cammie."

"Your things? And there is a book by Gogol and one by Stendhal."

"Burn them up. Do you need any money?"

"No. Thank you."

He gave her a very penetrating look. "It's strange that you always have it when you want to get away from me."

"Otherwise I do not ask people."

"I see."

He steered her down the rue Monsieur-le-Prince. "When are you going to America?"

"Soon, I think."

"I will go to Russia," he told her chattily. "But it will take a longer time. In twenty years it will be all right. My country is a great country."

"Yes," she said sincerely.

In the light from the Tabac his eyes glistened with tears.

The sternness inside her would not let her speak or move. It would not be right, and they drifted quietly to the sidewalk table down the street where wise and worldly, witty people made noise

302

around its marble edge. They joined them, Dima taking a chair next to his Swiss girl. Carmian half-listened to the literary editor, boring him. "I don't understand French very well," she explained, whereupon he leaned back somewhat relieved, shifting his tongue in his mouth. She could see that he did because he left his mouth open.

After about two hours she gathered up her brown leather pocketbook that Dima had given her as a birthday present (which was why they couldn't pay the rent) and said softly that she would go. She shook hands all around, avoiding his eyes. "You don't like my friends?" he asked in German.

"Yes, very much. But I'm tired and I want to go home."

The silence around the table was deadly. "You always were a hypocrite."

"Dima, please—"

The table went over. It crashed with a horrifying and gratifying noise, and he was on his feet. Suddenly no one else was there. "You can stay out all night with your American-loving scum, but when I ask you to accompany me somewhere . . ."

He had the awful, sick look. She went to the curb and vomited quietly and came back to wait with him until the police arrived and took them away through the little crowd.

In the police station she held a handkerchief over her mouth and said, choking: "Dima, don't you know the end when you see it? We got off wrong somewhere back and we cannot return. Don't you know the end?"

"Yes, *dyevutchka*. I had just hoped. I know now."

They asked them bored questions. Since their papers were in order and he could pay damages, they let her go but decided to keep him for the night.

"Cammie!" he said, terror in his eyes.

"Monsieur, it's my fault as much as—"

"Run along, or we'll keep you too."

"Cammie, don't leave me!"

He had begun to sob. Wild with her helplessness she said, "Then keep me, too. Please! I *want* to stay here!"

"Madame," said the *flic* with bottomless scorn after they had all exchanged shrugs, winks, and the rest of it (for foreigners were like that, particularly this sort), "Madame, go home."

"You don't understand, he—"

"Cammie, Cammie!"

"*Allez!*"

"*Tête de con!*" she said, surprising him considerably before she made her way into the street, blinded by tears, still hearing Dima's calling of her name and his mortal fright. Like the cat.

It seemed to happen to her all the time. But perhaps some of the cries had merely come from inside herself.

43 Of course, one feels very bad having just been in jail. Actually Dima survived this one very well, since it was neither German nor Central European and only overnight. And since he had done something wrong for which he was being punished. So he wrote to Carmian, apologizing. He had always connected prison with innocence before.

With the grace of Ronsard he wrote: "If you gave me the sword to cut the souvenir, I should not accept it."

She was shaken, and laughed to herself. At a certain very young age she had possessed the cool efficiency of a French *caissière*.

Behold the trembling adult!

The reborn child taking its first steps.

Yes. A week later she went to meet him, as he had asked, in the Jardin du Luxembourg where it borders on the boulevard Saint-Michel. To say goodbye. To say goodbye.

He was there on a bench, and the air was hazy, smelling of verbena. He rose and bowed in his sometimes courtly fashion. In a pre-summer heat where everything looked like a photograph, he stood looking at her. She might have been Karla Maria Anna . . . her long hand on a slender wrist dangling over the back of a chair. A face looking out from 1890. Or a child in a hat with long ribbons. But he saw an unfortunate girl named Carmian, 1952. She saw a young man of an extraordinary reckless beauty (he had always looked the age Lala had mistakenly given him), and many other young men on this bench waiting for their girls . . . greeting them with that touching mixture of gallantry, mastery, and hope.

304

But they were not a painting.

The willows stirred barely. The pond rippled.

"Are you going to marry me?"

"Dima, no."

"That is the end," he said, and walked away. She did too after a while. It was like walking away from Swan Lake. Or the Garden of Eden.

The last time she saw him was on a wet, charged day in April, and everybody's eyes were blue and the sidewalk shone under a drenched sky, as if the world had been weeping and was now full of smiles. Dima's eyes were the color of turquoise, and he had on a new suit of tweed, very handsome. He crossed the rue de Lille immediately on seeing her, leaving his friends.

"Where are you staying?"

"Hôtel de Londres."

They were in front of it. "Come up," she said.

He looked appalled, as if she had made a social error.

"Come," she said in Russian, smiling, "you are my brother, Dimitchka."

He frowned and said, "You must not go speaking my language all over the place."

"Why not?"

"All right." He entered her room and sat down gingerly in an imitation Louis XV chair.

"Why may I not speak your language?"

"It's mine and you are no longer mine."

"I see."

"I dream. It's all a dream, you know."

She smiled at him with her brown eyes. "Yes, I know. I am the same way."

"I know."

They looked at each other across the room. "I gave you the best years of my life," he said quite seriously.

She laughed. She couldn't help it.

"Why do you laugh?"

"I don't know."

He was busy pouring himself a glass of the wine he had spotted with his usual eagle eye.

She loved him. He was so ridiculous sometimes. "Give me some too. I am going to America, you know. Tomorrow."

"I didn't know."

"I'm sorry about the jail thing."

"It was nothing. Except I can't stand those pigs."

"No, no, of course not."

"Pigs."

"All pigs are terrible."

"I must go, Cammie."

Her back straightened. "Yes."

"Shall you be happy in America?"

"No." She laughed gently.

She followed him to the door, and he looked at her for a last time in the hall, sombrely. "Goodbye," he said in English.

"*Au revoir.* See you."

"Perhaps."

It was cold parting. She went to the bed and lay down, holding her hands over her heart.

There is pain like the slashes of swallows' cries. Hers hung in eternity, preserved, suspended as in a glass bell.

She lay thinking that she must leave his imaginary world of Papa Haydn, happily drunk and distributing sweets to the poor children in Vienna . . . his divine and darling Mozart of the loving heart . . . his Russia where there were no prostitutes, where patriarchs of the steppes, ladling soup, rapped the naughty small child on the head with the wooden spoon (she smelled the hot grass and heard the snuffling of ponies) . . . the Russian tank girl with her guitar singing for her fallen soldier-husband through the smell of gunpowder.

It was as if she had married one of the brothers Grimm—or rather a teller of those Russian fables in which the bear wins. The illustrations are both childlike and Eastern, young and old. The flowers on the skirts of the peasant-girl heroines are without perspective, cut off simply where the line ends, like a piece of material flattened out on the tailor's board. The same flowers frame the whole picture like a wreath, indicating gently and effectively that this is not life but merely a tale.

He was the artist, not she. She was a miserable searcher with no hope, like the scientist's, of ever catching the truth. There is no answer for this disease but death. And then, as the gypsy said, it is too late.

There rose a presentiment of times when, walking in different cities, on different continents, their loneliness and loss would grow unbearable. Of many times in many years ahead when she would think to herself: Dima, Dima, oh where are you now?